Praise for four authors
who put some spice into naughty and nice . . .

Virginia Kantra

"Brilliantly sensual and hauntingly poignant."
—Alyssa Day, *New York Times* bestselling author

"Truly excellent paranormal romance."   —*ParaNormal Romance*

Kimberly Frost

"[An] amazing author!"   —*Romance Junkies*

"An utter delight!"   —Annette Blair, national bestselling author

Eileen Wilks

"Fun [and] very entertaining."   —*The Romance Reader*

"Should appeal to fans of Nora Roberts."   —*Booklist*

Lora Leigh

"Insanely scorching and truly outstanding."   —*Romance Junkies*

"Guaranteed to heat up the cold winter nights."   —*Fresh Fiction*

Tied
with a Bow

VIRGINIA KANTRA

KIMBERLY FROST

EILEEN WILKS

LORA LEIGH

BERKLEY SENSATION, NEW YORK

THE BERKLEY PUBLISHING GROUP
Published by the Penguin Group
Penguin Group (USA) Inc.
375 Hudson Street, New York, New York 10014, USA
Penguin Group (Canada), 90 Eglinton Avenue East, Suite 700, Toronto, Ontario M4P 2Y3, Canada
(a division of Pearson Penguin Canada Inc.)
Penguin Books Ltd., 80 Strand, London WC2R 0RL, England
Penguin Group Ireland, 25 St. Stephen's Green, Dublin 2, Ireland (a division of Penguin Books Ltd.)
Penguin Group (Australia), 250 Camberwell Road, Camberwell, Victoria 3124, Australia
(a division of Pearson Australia Group Pty. Ltd.)
Penguin Books India Pvt. Ltd., 11 Community Centre, Panchsheel Park, New Delhi—110 017, India
Penguin Group (NZ), 67 Apollo Drive, Rosedale, Auckland 0632, New Zealand
(a division of Pearson New Zealand Ltd.)
Penguin Books (South Africa) (Pty.) Ltd., 24 Sturdee Avenue, Rosebank, Johannesburg 2196,
South Africa

Penguin Books Ltd., Registered Offices: 80 Strand, London WC2R 0RL, England

This book is an original publication of The Berkley Publishing Group.

PRINTING HISTORY
Berkley Sensation trade paperback edition / November 2011

Library of Congress Cataloging-in-Publication Data

Tied with a bow / Virginia Kantra . . . [et al.].—Berkley Sensation trade paperback ed.
  p. cm.
  ISBN 978-0-425-24329-9
  1. Love stories, American. 2. Paranormal romance stories, American. I. Kantra, Virginia.
  PS648.L6T54 2012
  813'.08508—dc23

2011033825

PRINTED IN THE UNITED STATES OF AMERICA

10 9 8 7 6 5 4 3 2

Contents

Upon a Midnight Clear

VIRGINIA KANTRA

To Carolyn Martin,
who knows a thing or two about angels.

Chapter One

The angel came down in the long gallery of the Conciergerie prison, the notorious antechamber to the guillotine.

Stone walls could not keep him out. Stench and darkness offered no deterrent. He was a child of the air, elemental, immortal, one of the First Creation. As long as he did not materialize completely, he could go anywhere.

Cold seeped through the blocked grates and up from the flagstones along with the miasma of human misery. The corridor was alive with sighs and sobs and vermin. In the bloody wake of revolution, the prisons of Paris were filled to bursting with the *ci-devant* aristocracy and their suspected sympathizers. Few had the money or influence to secure the comforts of a private incarceration, a bed, food, firewood, perhaps a chamber pot. Cells intended for one or two prisoners held four, six, a dozen men, women, and children, packed together on the filthy straw like so many bottles of wine.

In the stone blocks adjoining the exercise yard, some poor soul had scratched BIENVENUE EN ENFER. Welcome to Hell.

But this was not Hell. There were still those here who called on God in their distress. So the angel had come, drawn by a dying mother's prayer to provide . . .

Not escape, the angel acknowledged. He felt the brush of some unusual emotion, threatening his angelic detachment. Frustration, perhaps.

The children of air were forbidden from interfering directly in worldly affairs. With rare exceptions, humans must work out their own fate, their own salvation. But the angel could offer comfort to ease the woman's soul from this life to the next.

His frustration—if that's what it was—deepened. Tonight, solace did not seem enough.

He flexed his shoulders at the admission, feeling a prickle between his shoulder blades. He was an angel of God. Comfort was his stock in trade. It must suffice.

A woman's hoarse Latin slipped through the bars to hang like frost in the air. "*Sancta Maria, Mater Domini nostri, ora pro nobis peccatoribus.*" Holy Mary, Mother of our Lord, pray for us sinners. "*Nunc et in hora . . .*" A cough. "*Et in hora . . .*"

More coughing, deep, wracking.

"Lie quiet, Maman." A girl's voice, sweet and clear and welcome as water in this dirty hole, speaking the King's French. "You must save your breath."

The angel followed the voice through the square iron grate into the cell. Two women—a woman and a girl, rather—huddled on the straw inside. The girl knelt on the brutally cold floor, supporting her mother's shoulders, trying to ease her breathing.

The child was very pretty, the angel observed dispassionately, with a delicate nose, a heart-shaped faced blunted by a firm, rounded chin, and eyes as blue as an October sky. But it was the mother who had called him here. Citoyenne Solange Blanchard, former Comtesse de Brissac, convent bred and barely thirty.

"*Nunc et in hora mortis nostrae,*" the *comtesse* whispered. *Now and at the hour of our death.*

"Maman, you must rest," the girl scolded gently. "You need your strength."

The angel could have told the girl that no amount of rest would make any difference. The infection in the *comtesse*'s lungs had attacked her already weakened system.

But the girl's tenderness moved him anyway.

He spread his power over the dying woman like wings, extending over her the peace of the presence of God.

Solange opened her eyes in the darkness, focusing on his face. "An angel," she whispered. "Come to save us."

He was hardly surprised that she could see him. She was very near death. "I cannot," he told her gently.

Must not.

"Save her," the woman insisted. Her daughter, thirteen-year-old Aimée. "When I am gone, she will be alone."

The girl chafed her mother's hands. "Maman, you must not upset yourself." Doubtless the child believed the *comtesse* was talking to herself, out of her mind with fever and grief.

The whole country was mad. After centuries of privilege, the Old Regime was paying for its sins of pride and abuse of power. In three short years, the *comtesse* had been stripped of everything: lands, tithes, and titles. The life of her husband. Their son.

These humans went too far in redressing old wrongs. They had no concept of Heavenly justice, no understanding of divine mercy.

Comfort, the angel reminded himself.

"Your family will be reunited soon," he assured Solange.

She would be dead by morning. And her daughter would follow, executed within the week, sacrificed to nationalist fervor and bloodlust.

Underneath the familiar flowering of compassion, anger stirred, like a worm at the heart of a rose.

Solange wet her dry lips. "One day. Not yet. You must . . ." Another cough rattled the *comtesse*'s frail frame. She met the angel's gaze, the light of faith or determination in her eyes. "You *will* save her."

Such faith should be rewarded.

Shouldn't it?

"I will." The words falling from his lips caught him by surprise.

He was an angel, bound to discern the will of God, to protect, and to obey. He regarded the dark sweep of the child's lashes, the sheltering curve of her shoulders.

What if the charge to protect, the call to obey, pulled him in different directions?

He would be punished for his disobedience, of course. Not for the first time. Michael, leader of the Heavenly host, took a dim view of insubordination. But perhaps Gabriel would intercede for him. It was almost Christmas, after all. The season of miracles. There was some precedent for his intervention in human affairs.

"You promise," Solange insisted.

Recklessness seized him. "I swear."

The girl glanced up, almost as if she heard him. Those clear blue eyes narrowed. "Who are you?"

The angel jolted. She saw him? Was she that pure? That innocent? Or was she like her mother, close enough to death to feel the brush of his wings?

"The answer to our prayers," Solange said.

"Can he get us out of here?" Aimée asked, direct as a child, pragmatic as any of her countrywomen.

"Of a surety he can save you," Solange said. "You must go with him."

The girl raised her head. He had no idea what she could make out in the dark. She should not have been able to see him at all.

"You will have to help my mother. She cannot stand."

The angel held Solange's gaze for a long moment.

"I do not go with you, *mignonne*," the *comtesse* said softly.

Aimée stuck out her rounded chin. "Then we will not go."

"My dear . . ." The *comtesse* coughed. "You have no choice."

"I won't leave you." The girl's voice rose, provoking glances and whispers from her fellow prisoners.

But the cell's other inhabitants were too respectful of her grief, too fearful of fever or sunk in their own despair to intervene.

"I cannot remove her against her will," the angel said.

"You promised to save her," Solange said.

Irritation flickered through him, crackled like ozone in the air. Frustration with her, with himself, with the sins of men and the limitations of angels. "She does not wish to be rescued."

Intervention was one thing. He might be forgiven for granting a dying mother's prayer. But violating a human being's free will was another, far more serious offense.

He looked at the girl, her springy dark curls, her clear, wide eyes, the jut of that childlike chin. She was old enough to make her own decisions.

His chest tightened. And far too young to die. Her goodness shone in this mortal Hell like a star.

Solange continued as if he had not spoken. "I have family in England. A cousin." Her voice, her strength, flared and faded like a sullen fire. "Héloïse married an Englishman. Basing. Sir Walter Basing. You will . . . take my Aimée to them?"

"No," the girl said fiercely. Her cheeks were flushed, her shoulders rigid. "It is my life. My choice."

Stubborn. He would need to silence her to get her past the prison guards.

He did not look forward to taking solid form, to descending into the flesh and the stink and the pain of human existence to lug her through the barricades. He dare not save them all.

But the girl would live. She would be safe in England. He would be damned before he'd let this child's light be extinguished.

His lip curled. He might be damned, anyway.

He breathed on the girl, catching her slight body as she slumped. They didn't have much time.

The straw rustled and prickled. *Pailleux*, the guards called the poorest prisoners, after the *paille*, hay, they slept on.

Aimée squeezed her eyes shut, burrowing back to sleep, reluctant to exchange the comfort of her dreams for vermin-infested straw. Soft, dark, velvet dreams of being carried in hard, strong arms while the stars wheeled and pulsed overhead. Dreams of being safe, protected, warm.

Hay tickled her arms, poked through the shabby protection of her shawl. She sighed. It was no use. She lay still, waiting for the stench of the prison to assail her nostrils, but she smelled only sweet cut grass and the richness of cows. Earthy smells, homey smells, like the stables of Brissac.

She frowned and opened her eyes.

A man stood in the window of the hayloft. Her heart bumped. A very large man, his broad shoulders made broader by a cape, silhouetted against the starry sky. His profile was silver, outlined by the moon.

Except . . . Her gaze slid past him to the spangled sky. There was no moon.

Fear skittered inside her like a rat. "Where am I?"

He turned at once at the sound of her voice. She could not see his expression, only the bulk of him against the sky, but she remembered his face, beautifully severe in the darkness of the dungeon. "Do not be afraid. You are safe now."

Which was no answer at all.

Her head felt stuffed with rags, her chest hollow. She raised herself cautiously on the straw.

"Maman?" Her voice cracked shamefully on the word.

Silence.

"Your mother entrusted you to my care," he said at last.

Which meant . . .

Which could only mean . . .

Her mind splintered, and her heart, shattering like a thin sheet of ice over a puddle, the bright shards of her former life melting into nothingness. Her body was cold, cold. Her throat burned. She swallowed, pulling her shawl tighter around her.

"I will see you reach your family," he said.

Her family was dead. Maman was . . .

A scream built and built inside her head, a wild, discordant squawk of rage and grief like a peacock's cry. She felt it swell her lungs, climb in her throat, press against her teeth. But all that emerged was a whisper. "*No*. Take me back."

He shook his head. "Too late for that. For both of us."

Her lips were numb. "I do not understand."

"The tide turns in a few hours. Our boat goes with it."

"A boat," she repeated. Her hands were shaking. She hid them in her shawl.

He nodded. "To England."

Impossible. She was no student of geography, but Paris was many miles from the coast. She had not slept long enough to make such a journey.

Her dream rushed in on her, the swirling stars, the cool night flowing and parting around them like a river, the road a silver ribbon unspooling between the hills below. The texture of his shirt againt her cheek. The strength of his arms.

She shoved the memory aside.

And *England* . . .

Loss blanketed her, heavy, wet, cold. Her head was a roaring snowstorm, her stomach a lump of ice.

"You tear me away from everything I know." *Everything loved and familiar.* "You will rip me apart."

"I saved you." His voice was deep. Implacable.

"You are killing me," she said passionately.

She wanted to die.

"I offer you life," he said at last, softly. "In accordance with your mother's last prayer. What you make of it is up to you."

Almost, she was ashamed.

A door creaked in the silence. Her breath stopped. Sounds drifted from the stable below that were not made by cows or mice. The scrape of a boot. A jingle of harness.

Cold sweat snaked down her spine. Had they been followed? Maman was gone, Papa and little Philippe, dead. In her guilt and grief, she longed to join them. But the will to live was not so easily extinguished.

She did not want, after all, to be discovered.

"Stay," her rescuer commanded.

He flowed past her and climbed—jumped—*floated* down the

ladder. His cape billowed from his shoulders as he dropped silently to the floor.

Aimée sat frozen in her nest of hay, her heart beating like a rabbit's. Snatches of conversation rose through the trapdoor.

". . . into Portsmouth . . ."

". . . look the other way . . ."

". . . pay for passage . . ." In her rescuer's deep voice.

"We don't need your money." She could barely make out the langue d'oil of northern France, spoken with a distinctly British accent. "These little trips pay for themselves."

"If you sell her," her rescuer said, clear and cold, "I will destroy you."

"We don't traffic in children." Equal disdain in the speaker's voice.

She crept closer to the trapdoor, trying to get a glimpse of the men below. They were barely more than shapes in the dark: her tall rescuer in his broad-shouldered cloak; a burly fellow in an oversized coat and battered hat; a younger man, slim as a steel blade.

"Your girl isn't the first aristocrat we've smuggled across the Channel," the burly man continued.

"You're one of us," the younger man said. "You should know that."

One of what? Aimée wondered. *Smugglers? English?*

A light flickered. Not a flare like a match, not the honest yellow glow of lamplight, but a slow growing silver light, cupped like a ball in her rescuer's hand. The eerie light illuminated his face, cold, pale, and perfect as the statue of Apollo in the chateau gardens. Wide, clear brow. Long, straight nose. Firm, unsmiling mouth. His fair hair fell, unpowdered and untamed, to his shoulders.

She quivered deep inside with fear and an instinct she did not recognize.

"But I am not like you," he said softly.

"Not yet, maybe," the younger man said. He, too, was beautiful, with a lean, clever face and a handkerchief knotted around his throat.

"Just a matter of time now," the older man agreed. "Lucky for you we found you."

"You came for the girl."

"We were looking for you both." The burly fellow swept off his hat to scratch under it. "Lord Amherst's orders. You're under his protection now."

"I do not serve your earthly lord. Or require his protection."

The boy shot him a look from thick-lashed eyes. "You won't feel so high-and-mighty after they toss you out of Heaven."

The large man cleared his throat. "Amherst will take you in. Assuming you make it to England."

Aimée frowned. But he was taking her to England. He had said so.

"Damon Carleton, Earl of Amherst," the burly man repeated. He replaced his hat carefully on his head. "Try not to forget."

"I believe my hearing and my memory extend that far," her rescuer said dryly.

"You'd better hope so. When you lose your powers, your memory goes, too. You come down to earth as a child. A little older, if you're lucky."

"So I will be . . . human." His voice was flat, strained of emotion.

Aimée blinked. Of course he was *human*. What else could he be? *An angel come to save us,* Maman had said.

Ah, no. Aimée's mind whirled. Phrases floated up in the dark, muffled and indistinct, like voices in a blizzard.

". . . gone before morning."

". . . find her relatives. Basing, you say?"

". . . I can feel . . . not much time."

"It's all right, lad. We'll get her where she needs to go."

They were talking about her, she realized dully. It was *her* future they were deciding, these strange men with their shabby clothes and English accents.

Her pride stung. Her throat burned. She was young and dazed with grief but not spiritless or stupid.

She erupted from her nest in a flurry of skirts and resolution. Bits of hay scattered on the men below.

"I do not go with anyone until I know who you are," she announced. *What you are,* she thought, and shivered.

They looked up, startled.

She had a brief glimpse of their faces, the young one, lean and sardonic, the older man's, broad and shrewd, before the light winked out.

But her rescuer . . .

Aimée forced air into her lungs. Her tall, handsome rescuer was already gone.

Chapter Two

Damon Carleton, the Earl of Amherst, pinned Lucien with a look like a rapier blade, glinting, gray, and cold. "You need an occupation."

Despite the autumn chill of the library, sweat pricked under Lucien's high, starched collar. He resisted the urge to tug at his neckcloth. "I had an occupation," he reminded the earl. "I was an angel. Now I am nothing. A cipher. A human."

"You have had eight years to accustom yourself to that condition," Amherst said evenly. "During which time you have been sheltered, educated, and well provided for."

Lucien stiffened. He was well aware that he owed everything to Amherst. Still, the reminder stung. "Because the world believes me your bastard."

Amherst raised his eyebrows. Even if one disregarded the earl's earthly rank and powers, he was a formidable man, with a brawler's build and an aesthete's face. "When the old earl took me into his nursery to replace his dead heir, only the boy's mother knew of the substitution. But you arrived on my doorstep as a youth of seventeen. I could hardly claim you as my legitimate son."

"Especially as you never married," Lucien said.

Amherst shrugged. "I have brought eleven bastard children to live at Fair Hill. Fallen, every one, of course. No wife could be expected to tolerate such flagrant reminders of her husband's excesses."

Lucien inclined his head. "Indeed, sir, we are all grateful for your single state. As well as your ongoing liberality."

"Ongoing," Amherst said, "but not without limit."

Lucien eyed him warily. It had been years since he was last summoned to the earl's study for discipline, but he recognized that tone. "Sir?"

"It is time you demonstrated some initiative. Made something of yourself. Made a difference in the world."

Lucien swallowed the bitterness in his mouth. "My last attempt at initiative could hardly be termed a success."

And that, of course, was the source of his discontent.

Amherst, he was sure, was aware of the resentment simmering under his small rebellions. But even the earl, the head of the Nephilim, the Fallen ones, in England, did not guess at Lucien's loss of faith.

His heart burned.

He had been punished—cast out of Heaven, demoted to the mortal world—for trying to make a difference. For trying to do some good. For answering a dying woman's selfless prayer.

In recent years he had concluded it was better not to try. Only with Fanny . . .

"You did well enough during the Terror." Amherst interrupted his thought. "Gerard tells me you saved his life or Tripp's on more than one occasion. The three of you rescued hundreds of innocents from the guillotine. You were only a boy then, but you cannot have changed so much."

He remembered. He had made the moonlit channel crossing too many times to count, nearly puking with seasickness and excitement. At least when he'd been dodging French gendarmes and secret police, he had not questioned the value of his existence or the rightness of his decisions. *Hundreds of innocents saved.* The memory kindled a flicker of satisfaction.

But then . . .

"The Terror ended six years ago," he said flatly. "Napoleon is in power now."

And Lucien had been bundled off to Oxford for a gentleman's education. To equip him, Amherst had said, for what was to be the rest of his life on earth. Older than most of his classmates, lacking any of the shared boyhood experiences that might have helped him fit in, Lucien had been stamped as Amherst's acknowledged bastard. Neither man nor angel, neither noble nor of humble birth.

Outcast in a completely different way.

"Napoleon's ambition threatens all Europe," Amherst said. "If it's action you crave, I will purchase you a commission."

"I have no wish to kill for England." Lucien stared out the library windows; the dying sun stained the winter brown hills the color of blood. "I have seen too much of men in war to believe one side is any better than another."

"Ah." The earl studied him with those too-perceptive gray eyes. "It will have to be the church, then. There are not many angels among the clergy, but if you are prepared to study and be patient—"

Lucien shook his head. He was disillusioned, even angry. But not yet so cynical he would lead others into unbelief for the price of a vicar's living.

"You must do something. I will not stand by while you waste your life along with my capital. I have here"—the earl tapped a sheaf of papers on his otherwise ordered desk—"a report of your expenses in London. Boots, wine, candles, horses . . ."

"I am not a schoolboy, sir, who has exceeded his allowance. Living in Town necessitates some expenditures," Lucien said.

"Doubtless that explains the residence on Maiden Lane occupied by a Fanny . . ." Amherst lifted a single sheet in one elegant hand and pretended to peruse it. "Grinton."

Lucien stiffened. How the devil did he know about Fanny?

"Miss Grinton is not your concern."

"Everything that affects the well-being of the Nephilim concerns me. It is my duty to watch out for you. For all of you. I would not object to your supporting a mistress. But apparently there are several other, ah, women residing in the house with her."

Lucien stared at him in disbelief. "You've been spying on me."

"You are not the only man seen entering the premises. Callers have been observed coming and going at all hours."

Lucien gritted his teeth. "Are you accusing me of frequenting a brothel? Or of running one?"

"Whichever it is, it stops now."

Fury tightened his throat. "You have no idea . . . You have no *right*—"

Amherst raised a hand, palm out. "Spare me your explanations. I have tolerated a certain wildness from you, Lucien, but I'll not fund meaningless extravagance."

A hot band settled around Lucien's head and squeezed like a vise. "I haven't asked for your assistance. I can support myself with the income from Leyburn."

Barely. The realization settled coldly in his stomach. He would have to economize somewhere. Fanny would balk. She complained she could hardly manage now. But there was no choice for either of them.

Amherst regarded him with frustration. "And that is all your interest in Leyburn? The income you derive from the estate. You've never even visited the property."

"You wish me to visit Leyburn?" Lucien asked slowly.

He was not averse to the idea.

Fair Hill was home. Or as close to a home as his earthly existence allowed. Unlike Gerard, the oldest of the Fallen, or Tripp, who had been raised by the earl since early childhood, Lucien had never accompanied Amherst on a tour of his other estates.

But Leyburn had provided him with a living since leaving Oxford. Amherst had made similar arrangements to support his other Fallen fosterlings. There was even an unspoken understanding that the earl would divvy his various unentailed properties, Leyburn included, among them when he died.

Lucien trusted—indeed, he hoped—the earl wouldn't pop off

anytime soon. The Nephilim could live almost twice the normal span of human years, and Amherst was a vigorous man.

Still, it could do no harm to take a look at the place.

"I expect you to do more than visit," Amherst said. "You need to take some responsibility for the property. For your life." He leaned back in his chair, regarding Lucien with cool gray eyes, obviously determined to force his compliance. "I will give you three months. If you can learn to manage the estate in that time, you'll continue to receive its income."

Lucien's muscles were rigid. "And if I refuse?"

The earl's face tightened in resolution. "I will cut you off without a penny. You'll do as you are told."

It was a punch in the stomach. A slap in the face. Lucien's ears rang with it.

In his mind, he understood Amherst's offer as fair and reasonable, even generous. But his soul rebelled at the ultimatum, the choice between abject obedience and penury.

Knuckle under or be cut off. Cast out. Again.

Insurrection flared in Lucien's blood. Pride hardened his voice. He would not plead with the earl for understanding. "I'll be damned first."

"Not damned. But condemned, nevertheless, to a significant decline in your standard of living." Amherst tilted his head. "Possibly even to debtors' prison."

"Unless I marry," Lucien threw at him.

Amherst stared as if a second head had sprouted suddenly from his shoulders. "Marry?"

Lucien clamped his teeth together. It was a stupid idea.

Or was it?

He needed money. He wanted his freedom. There was no way he was giving up the little house on Maiden Lane even for a hundred estates.

"If I must woo for favors, I would rather court a woman." Lucien forced his lips to curve in a mocking smile. "Unlike you, I do not doubt my ability to convince a wife to tolerate my flagrant excesses."

The library was very silent.

Bowing deeply, he left without another word.

And without looking back.

Miss Julia Basing leaned across Aimée's battered dressing table to tweak at a butter-colored curl in the mirror. She was a pretty girl, a true English beauty despite her half-French mama, but this afternoon she did not appear at all pleased with the image in the glass.

"This mirror is too small," she complained. "And very spotty. How ever do you see what Finch has done with your hair?"

Her cousin, Aimée Blanchard, sat on the bed, darning. The small chamber's only chair was presently occupied by Julia, who had gone to the unprecedented effort of climbing three flights of stairs to find her. Aimée doubted Julia had ever even seen the servants' quarters before. She thought of pointing out that Finch hardly had time to dress Aimée's hair in addition to all her other duties. But since she did not wish to criticize the lady's maid, she merely shrugged. "One accustoms oneself."

Julia left off fussing with her curls to glance over her shoulder. "You truly do not mind, Amy? Giving up your room for the holidays?"

Aimée summoned a smile. It wasn't Julia's fault that she had been banished to the attics to make room for Lady Basing's other guests. Aimée had learned upon her arrival eight years ago that as a poor female relation she existed to serve the whims and convenience of others, to earn her place in her cousin's house—if not her cousin's affections—by acting as an unpaid, invisible drudge. "Indeed, I do not. And it is only for a little while," she said reassuringly.

Though which of them she was attempting to cheer she could not say.

"That's true." Julia brightened. "Anyway, it's quiet up here. Mama says you will be more comfortable away from the noise."

Aimée's hand tightened on the darning needle. Her new quarters *were* quiet. No one of consequence would hear her if she screamed. The maids at least shared a bed, which offered them some protection. Aimée had taken to sleeping with the chair propped against the door and her sewing shears tucked under her pillow.

"But I told Mama you must come down to dinner sometimes and not hide yourself away as you usually do," Julia continued, blithely unaware of the realities of survival on the fourth floor. "I want you to meet him."

Aimée pricked her finger. "Him?"

Julia dimpled. "Mr. Hartfell."

Aimée blinked, unable to contain her surprise. She had heard the name, of course. Hartfell's sire, the Earl of Amherst, lived half a day's journey away—not near enough to be counted a neighbor but certainly close enough to be topic of gossip. As for Mr. Hartfell himself, Julia could talk of little else since the family's return from the Naesmyths' house party a few weeks ago. Mr. Hartfell was tall—much taller than Lord Echlin, who had *almost* offered for Julia in London this Season. And handsome, more handsome even than Sir Andrew Waugh, who had danced two sets with Julia at her come out and had such a delightfully wicked reputation. And charming, far more charming than Tom Whitmore from the neighboring estate, who treated Julia with the blunt familiarity of friends who had grown up together.

Used to tales of her cousin's conquests, Aimée had received her confidences with a grain of salt. But . . .

"Hartfell? He is a bastard."

"Amy!"

"I do not criticize his character, you understand. But he is Amherst's natural son."

Many noblemen had children out of wedlock. But eleven seemed excessive, even for an earl as wealthy as Amherst.

Personally, Aimée did not care what Mr. Hartfell's birth was. But she worried her cousin might be courting heartbreak. Lady Basing did not in any way espouse the Revolutionary principles of liberty, equality, and sovereignty of the people. Surely she would not approve of such a connection.

Julia tossed her curls, moving away from the mirror. "Lucien's father is an earl. Papa is only a baronet."

"But Hartfell has no fortune," Aimée said.

"I believe the earl has settled some unentailed property on him. Anyway"—Julia lifted her chin—"what is the point of having a large dowry if I can't buy the husband I want?"

"Your parents will never consent," Aimée warned.

"Mama has already invited him. She'll do what I want," Julia asserted with all the confidence of a girl whose wishes had been indulged for the past eighteen years. "And Papa will do what she tells him."

Aimée raised her eyebrows. "The perfect model for marriage, in fact."

Her memories of her parents' marriage were colored by the golden haze of childhood, when she had been safe and secure. But she liked to think they had loved one another. Certainly they had loved her.

Julia met her gaze, her eyes alight with mischief. "Precisely. A purchased husband will be so much easier to manage, don't you think?"

Aimée laughed and shook her head. "I will tell you after I have met the gentleman. He may be less tractable once he has control of your fortune."

"Unless he falls wildly and madly in love with me." Julia did a little twirl of glee, almost knocking into the bed. "Oh, Amy, it's going to be the most delightful Christmas ever."

Aimée raised her eyebrows. She had always enjoyed the church service on Christmas morning, but the holiday was marked primarily by presents to the servants and children. She found it difficult to understand her cousin's enthusiasm. "You expect Mr. Hartfell to present himself tied with a bow?"

Julia giggled. "No, silly. Mama's promised to hold a ball on Christmas Day. A masked ball, just like at Vauxhall. Isn't that exciting?"

A masked ball. At Moulton. On Christmas Day.

Just for a moment, Aimée's heart lifted as if she were quite as young and pretty and privileged as her cousin. Her head swirled with visions of candles, dresses, and dancing.

"I shall be Venus, goddess of love and beauty," Julia said dreamily. Aimée smiled wryly, recalled to reality. "Naked on a clamshell?"

"I won't be naked, silly. Mama has hired Mrs. Pockley from the village to make my costume."

Aimée smothered a sigh of relief. At least she would not have to add costume sewing to her other duties. "I don't remember Venus wearing many clothes."

"Diana, then. The virgin huntress, fair and unattainable as the moon. With lots of silver drapery and diamonds like stars in my hair. And you must dress up, too."

Aimée wondered what Lady Basing would say about that. Certainly, there would be no diamonds for *her* hair.

Her throat tightened. She had a sudden, poignant memory of Maman, her hair dressed high and a jeweled locket—a gift from Papa—at her throat, swooping down to envelope Aimée in a warm embrace and a cloud of perfume.

Gone now. All gone.

But such thinking was foolishness.

Aimée straightened her spine.

She would *not* give in to self-pity. She was grateful to her mother's cousin for the roof over her head and the food she ate and . . . Well, she was grateful. With the servants already run off their feet with preparations for the house party, it would be her duty to make all of Lady Basing's arrangements go as smoothly as possible, to keep track of the guest list and write the invitations, to assist with the menu and the decorations and the hundred and one other details that must accompany a ball, even in the country.

This was her life now. Aimée stabbed her needle at a large darn, ignoring the jab at her heart.

What she made of it was up to her.

Chapter Three

Lucien had always scorned the London marriage mart, the annual parade of well-bred chits trotted out like fillies at auction by their fond mamas and ambitious papas in hopes of attracting a buyer.

But now he himself was on the block.

As the Basing house party assembled in the drawing room before dinner, he was aware of his supposed bloodlines being dissected, his grooming inspected, his likely performance assessed.

He made his bows, his collar chafing. His evening jacket squeezed his shoulders in a too-tight embrace. Miss Basing clung to his arm, hanging upon his every word.

Julia Basing was everything Lucien should want—pretty, young, rich, and compliant. A month ago, when he was still hot with fury over Amherst's interference, he had pursued her with single-minded skill and determination.

His blood had cooled before two weeks had passed. But his circumstances had not changed. His time was running out.

So here he was, committed to Lady Basing's house party for the holidays. Not simply as her guest but as a prospective son-in-law.

A chill traced down his spine like the brush of a feather. Almost, he wished he had not come.

Julia took his arm with a proprietary air to present him to the local squire and his two unmarried sisters.

The squire, Tom Whitmore, was a young man with thick dark whiskers that did nothing to disguise his very square jaw or his frown.

Possibly he disapproved of bastards, however well connected. Or perhaps he would look askance on any rival for Miss Basing's affections.

He stuck out his jaw belligerently. "What brings you to Moulton, Hartfell?"

He needed to marry money. Soon. Or crawl back to Amherst at Fair Hill. The rent on the Maiden Lane house was only paid through the end of the month.

"I am here at Lady Basing's invitation," Lucien said.

The squire's square jaw became even squarer. "You have no family who require your attendance over the holiday?"

It was a challenge, by thunder. A reference to his bastard status.

Whitmore's sisters looked anxious. Julia Basing caught her breath.

"I am fortunate to be free to follow my personal inclinations," Lucien said.

Whitmore glared. "And those are?"

Lucien smiled thinly. "Personal."

The sticky silence was broken by a rush at the door as a late arrival caught herself on the threshold. Lucien had an impression of bouncing dark curls and a wide, heart-shaped face before the woman lowered her head, slipping quietly into the room. Her unobtrusive demeanor was so at odds with her animated expression that his attention was caught. He narrowed his eyes, taking in her lace-trimmed cap and shapeless, faded gown. There were no rings on her fingers, no jewels around her neck.

Not a guest, then. Nor quite a servant. Most likely a poor relation, one of the army of drab, dependent, unmarried females clinging to shabby gentility in the corners of England's drawing rooms, indispensable and invisible to their wealthier relatives.

Normally he would not even have noticed her. But the energy of her entrance lingered a moment, charging the stale air like a blowing storm.

Lady Basing reclaimed his attention, leading the way into the dining room.

Despite his lack of title, he found himself paired with Miss Basing at dinner. Amherst's lineage, of course, was impeccable. And Lucien was connected, however irregularly, with Amherst. If Leyburn were truly his, if he were the man of property he pretended to be, he would be considered an acceptable match for a baronet's daughter.

He wondered how much time he had before Sir Walter demanded an accounting of his prospects.

He forced himself to listen to Miss Basing chatter about the Season just past—her first—about whom she had met and what she had worn and which gentlemen she had danced with. He sipped his wine, bored almost out of his mind. Fortunately, as long as he inserted compliments at appropriate intervals, Miss Basing did not appear to find his attention lacking.

Across the table, her brother, Howard Basing, made sly observations to the Misses Whitmore on either side. Lucien knew Julia's brother only by sight, brown-haired, handsome, with sharp white collar points and teeth.

A few places farther down, the poor relation divided her conversation between a country gentleman old enough to be her grandfather and a spotty boy barely out of the schoolroom. Lucien was not close enough to overhear a word of their conversation. But something about her compelled his notice.

Beneath her cap, she had strongly arched brows and thick black lashes, a wide, curved mouth and a charmingly blunted chin. She tilted her head—the better to hear her elderly dinner partner?—when suddenly, for no reason at all, she raised her gaze across the table.

Eyes as blue as the October sky stared into his.

The charge this time sizzled clear to his toes. Like the shock of recognition, a bolt of lightning, a jolt of longing.

She was almost familiar to him. Not Nephilim, despite her angel's face. She was . . . He didn't know what she was. His hand curled around his wineglass.

She did not immediately drop her gaze as any well-bred lady ought, as any meek companion must. She stared back at him, her lips parted, her eyes wide and dark. He watched her take one swift, deep breath, giving shape to her shapeless dress, and his own breathing stopped.

Her lashes swept down. With a visible effort, she collected herself, turning to address a remark to the spotty youth at her side. The boy flushed and launched into speech.

Lucien released his grip on the glass. His hand shook slightly.

"Amy does not often join us for dinner when we have company," Miss Basing confided beside him. "I am so pleased Mama invited her to make up the numbers after Freddy threw the table off. But he is home from school so seldom, poor boy, it would have been a shame to exclude him."

Lucien dragged his memory. Freddy would be young Keasdon, the son of local gentry. And . . .

"Amy?" he repeated.

"Cousin Amy. Weren't you looking at her just now? Oh." Miss Basing bit her lip. "But you were not presented, were you?"

"I have not had that pleasure," he said curtly. "She was not in the drawing room before dinner."

"I expect she was still in the nursery settling my sister's children— my sister Susan, Mrs. Netherby," Miss Basing explained. "They were overexcited after the long carriage ride here."

"She is their governess?"

Miss Basing looked surprised. "Oh, no. My sister let the governess go to her family for the holiday. Why should Mr. Netherby be put to the expense of paying the creature a Christmas bonus when Amy is willing to watch the children?"

Lucien hid his distaste. "Very obliging of her."

"Amy is always obliging. Of course, she must be conscious of what she owes Mama. We took her in, you know, after her parents were killed. In the Terror. It was a great tragedy," Julia said comfortably.

She was French, then. An émigré. A refugee.

Perhaps that explained his jolt of recognition, his feeling of déjà vu.

Perhaps he had seen her, even rescued her on one of his forays across the Channel.

He frowned at the ruby reflection of his wine on the snow white tablecloth. He and Gerard and Tripp had snatched hundreds from the shadow of the guillotine, men, women, and children. He could not remember them all.

"How long ago?" he asked tightly.

"Oh, ages. I was just a child when she came to live with us. Ten? Eleven. Amy was older, of course."

Before his time on earth, he thought. Before he'd found Amherst. His mouth dried. *Holy God.*

He remembered very little from before his Fall. The Nephilim were not born as human infants. That distinction was reserved for the Most High. They Fell as children or adolescents, losing their knowledge of Heaven along with their angelic powers, thrust into human existence in the land and year of their offense.

But the circumstances of that night were seared into his brain, the filthy prison, the dying mother, the defiant child in her nest of straw.

You are killing me, she had cried passionately.

He stared unseeing at the table, recalling her wide blue eyes, her rounded, jutting jaw. He had violated her free will, tearing her from both the life she knew and the death she had chosen.

And so he had been condemned to lose his own life, his very identity as a child of air.

His stomach knotted. *Was it possible . . . ?*

He reached for his glass, risking another glance down the table at Julia Basing's French cousin.

Amy. *Aimée.*

She was not very old. Early twenties, at a guess. The cap aged her. She could be . . . Ah, he hoped she was not. He hated to think he had saved her from one prison only to thrust her into another. Both of them sentenced by his choice to live out their lives in the shadows, condemned to a life of servitude. Her bright light, dimmed.

He set down his wine untasted.

It made no difference, he told himself. His course was set. Even if she were the same woman, she was not his responsibility now.

He glanced again down the table. But he had to *know*.

He was staring at her. Mr. Hartfell. He had beautiful eyes, bright and green as emeralds, gleaming in the light of the candles.

Aimée's heart beat faster. For a moment, when she first looked up and caught him staring, she had been drawn. Dazzled. Like a moth to a flame, like Icarus flying into the heat of the sun, completely insensitive to danger.

She clasped her hands together in her lap, focusing with determined concentration on sixteen-year-old Freddy Keasdon, who had launched into a description of his last cricket match at school.

". . . off the wicket on the on side," he said, his Adam's apple working earnestly. "So I went out at it on my left leg—no, wait, it was my right—and . . ."

She had no idea what he was talking about. But as long as their conversation revolved around him, he was quite willing to give her his full attention. Like any other man, she supposed.

Living in her cousin's house, she had learned to be wary of masculine attention. But Freddy—"caught it square a couple feet from the ground," he told her—was charming in his enthusiasm. And quite harmless.

She felt very sure the same could not be said of Lucien Hartfell.

Really, he had no business staring at her at all. He was here to court Julia.

Her cousin was sitting right there beside him, looking as fresh and lovely as spring in a gown the soft pink of apple blossoms. The deep neckline and short, puffed sleeves revealed a great deal of her rounded bosom and arms.

Aimée had taken care that her own dress revealed nothing at all. Its original sour green color still showed faintly at the seams where she had picked them apart, letting out the bodice until her shape resembled nothing so much as a sack of flour tied with ribbon. She would not be accused of luring Cousin Howard's attention again.

At least Mr. Hartfell had been staring at her face and not her breasts.

It was a relief when Lady Basing signaled that dinner was over. The ladies withdrew, leaving the men to their port.

In the drawing room, the other young ladies engaged in polite competition to entertain the company. Aimée began to calculate how soon she could excuse herself. But then Julia required her sheet music and Lady Basing demanded her shawl. Aimée had just finished passing the cakes from the tea tray when the gentlemen trooped in.

A throat cleared behind her. "Er, Miss Blanchard."

No escape. Her back stiffened. She turned to smile at young Freddy Keasdon.

And Mr. Hartfell. She caught her breath as her gaze tangled with his.

Close up, he appeared even more handsome and very large, his broad shoulders made wider by his tight-fitting evening clothes. His thick gold hair, worn slightly longer than was fashionable, created a halo around his severely beautiful face.

Something wavered in the corners of her memory, but she could not bring it quite into focus.

Freddy ducked his head bashfully. "May I present Mr. Hartfell?" he asked, indicating the man beside him. "You didn't meet him before dinner, did you?"

She had not been presented to any of the Basings' guests, a slight that did not trouble her in the least. She would have preferred to say in the nursery, out of sight. Out of mind.

Out of trouble.

Mr. Hartfell bowed. "Miss Blanchard," he said, a faint emphasis on the first word.

As if he had the slightest interest whether she were married or not, Aimée thought wryly. *She* was not an heiress like Julia.

She bobbed a curtsey. "Mr. Hartfell."

"Your name is an old and noble one in France," he said politely. "You are not by chance related to the Comte de Brissac?"

For a bastard, he was very interested in her antecedents. Perhaps his own birth made him sensitive to such things? "My father," she admitted.

His eyebrows arched. "Then—forgive me—are you not the *Lady* Aimée?"

"A distinction without a difference," Aimée said. "Titles have been abolished in France, Mr. Hartfell. The king himself signed the decree a decade ago."

Even if her rank had survived the Revolution, it could not have survived life with her mother's relatives. It would be untenable, intolerable, for the impoverished Lady Aimée to take precedence over Miss Julia Basing and Lady Basing in their own home.

She glanced toward the pianoforte where Julia was settling herself to play. Her cousin was bright-eyed and pink-cheeked with anticipation. Or annoyance. Tom Whitmore hovered stiffly beside her, ready to turn the pages of her music. Julia, however, turned her gaze hopefully toward their corner of the room, rustling the sheets of music together.

Hiding her amusement, Aimée addressed Mr. Hartfell. "I believe my cousin requires your assistance, sir."

He raised his brows, in no apparent hurry to heed Julia's summons. "You do not play, Miss Blanchard?"

Why did he not *go*? "I do not play in company."

His green eyes filled with lazy amusement. "You are too modest."

Something in her rose to meet the challenge of those eyes. "Not at all. But since I am not in the running for a husband, I see no point in showing off my paces."

He laughed, a short, surprised bark that transformed his rather cool, disdainful expression to wry humor. "And if I were not forced into the running for a wife, I would keep you company in your corner."

She grinned foolishly back.

Very foolishly, she realized a moment later as heads turned. She should not be seen amusing herself.

She must not be seen amusing *him*.

Too late.

"Ah, Cousin Amy." Her stomach dropped into her thin-soled

evening slippers as Howard Basing approached from the direction of the tea tray. "Teasing *another* gentleman?"

"Basing." Hartfell nodded shortly. "You must not blame Miss Blanchard. She is guilty only of bearing with my company. I am at fault for monopolizing her attention."

She lifted her chin. "I was telling Mr. Hartfell I do not play."

Howard leered. "As I know, to my sorrow. You are cruel to deprive your admirers of enjoying your . . . hidden talents."

She was growing very tired of Cousin Howard, his wandering eyes and speaking pauses. But she must not make a scene in Lady Basing's drawing room. "You must content yourself listening to the other ladies," she said.

"Must I? But they are tame entertainment." Howard's gaze flitted over her face and fastened on her bosom. "I prefer more vigorous, ah, pursuits."

Aimée's cheeks burned.

Freddy Keasdon had just enough wit to look embarrassed.

Lucien Hartfell took a half step forward, looming very large indeed. "Your comments are offensive, sir," he said, his voice chilled and soft.

Aimée's heart beat faster. She might have appreciated his gallantry—*One rake defending her from another?*—but it would not do at all for Julia's chosen suitor and her brother to come to blows over a perceived insult to a poor relation. Julia would be mortified. Aimée would be disgraced.

"I am sure Mr. Basing meant only that he would prefer dancing to singing," she said.

Hartfell narrowed his eyes. "Indeed."

She looked at Howard. "I believe your mother plans a ball on Christmas Day. That should be sufficient outlet for your energies."

"Then you must save me a set, Cousin." Howard smirked. "I can only be satisfied in your arms."

Hartfell inhaled sharply. But as long as she did not protest, there was nothing further he could say.

And nothing she could do, Aimée thought. Her skin crawled as if she had touched a slug. But her mother's cousin refused to hear any criticism of her son. In Lady Basing's eyes, any improper behavior must be Aimée's imagination.

Or her fault.

She held her tongue.

The silence stretched.

Howard's smile broadened. "You will dance with me? I have your promise?"

The unfairness of her situation burned her throat. But she must be practical.

She swallowed. "Yes."

"If the music is not your liking, Basing, I suggest you visit the card table," Hartfell said, still in that calm, cold voice. "I see Lady Basing has set up a game. Perhaps Keasdon here will partner you."

Prompted, Freddy blushed and stammered his willingness to play.

Hartfell waited while the two men made their way to the opposite side of the room. He bowed curtly to Aimée, his face impassive. "I will leave you to your amusements, Miss Blanchard."

Dismay washed through her. He could not believe she *encouraged* Howard's improper attentions.

But of course he could, she thought as he walked away. He had just heard her excuse Howard and then agree to dance with him. What else could he think?

Howard probably thought the same.

She felt faintly ill. And unreasonably disappointed. Why she cared for Hartfell's good opinion she did not know.

Except for that moment when their eyes first met and she had felt a quiver of . . . What? Recognition? Yearning?

Foolishness.

She watched him cross to Julia's side, his broad, black back, his gleaming golden hair, and her vision blurred suddenly.

She took a deep breath. She would not indulge in regret or self-pity.

It was stupid, *stupid*, to sigh and dream over a man simply because he had sought an introduction and shown her a little courtesy. Women like her—dependent females at the mercy of their relations—had little chance of attracting a suitor or changing their situations.

Besides . . . Her gaze skittered to Howard, taking his seat at the card table. Hartfell's politeness, innocent as it was, had had the unwelcome result of provoking Howard. Her cousin was like a dog snarling over a bone, anxious lest it be snatched away.

She sighed. She had no desire to be slavered over. Or mauled. Better for her, safer for her, to avoid them both.

Chapter Four

Lucien stared out the long French windows at the snow covered lawn and frozen pond. The winter clouds were cold and gray as steel, the ground as hard as iron.

In his mind he saw *her* eyes, blue as the October sky, heard her voice, warm and fierce as sunlight. *You tear me away from everything I know. You will rip me apart.*

His hands clenched behind his back. He knew who she was now. Amy Blanchard. Lady Aimée, daughter of the Comte de Brissac.

What he didn't know was what the devil he should do about her.

His head pounded. Maybe nothing.

He was no angel, after all. His responsibility for her had ended eight years ago when he delivered her from prison and the guillotine. Damn it all, he'd saved her life.

You are killing me.

His jaw set. Bollocks.

A burst of laughter recalled his attention to the room behind him, where pretty Julia Basing was holding court by the fire.

He felt no desire to join them. For the past several days, he had been confined to the house and his role as Julia's suitor. The hard frost, followed by an inch or two of snow, had discouraged even the most avid sportsmen from going out. There had been one foray to the local taproom to take tea, where the very young ladies in his party had declared the private dining room dirty, the cakes dry, and the whole trip scarcely worth the trouble. In desperation yesterday, Lucien had proposed an expedition to the tiny Norman church in the village to admire the twelfth-century frieze. A shivering Julia Basing had refused even to descend from the carriage, demanding to be taken home.

Aimée Blanchard had not joined either outing.

"Is Miss Blanchard indisposed?" Lucien had asked Julia that morning.

Julia had blinked at him, obviously bewildered by his interest in her cousin. "Amy? No, why?"

"I did not see her at breakfast."

Nor had she been at dinner the past two nights nor in the drawing room to play cards or charades.

Julia's pretty face had pleated. "I think Amy is taking her meals in the nursery. She is a great favorite with the children, you know."

He could imagine.

He could also guess that Aimée's popularity with the children made life a great deal easier for the other adults in the household.

Irritation rose in him.

It was none of his business if Aimée was taken advantage of by her English relatives, he reminded himself. She was not his charge. But he found himself watching for her all the same, driven by emotions he did not understand and could not name.

Attraction? Guilt? Concern?

Behind him, the conversation had turned to the Christmas ball and whether the guests would come in costume or wear dominos.

"Costumes, definitely," Howard Basing said. "At least for the young ladies. Why cover their charms? I quite fancy myself a satyr disporting with nymphs and goddesses."

Several of the young ladies in question tittered.

Lucian clenched his hand on the windowsill. He did not like Howard Basing. The only satisfaction he had was that Basing had spent the past few days with the rest of the house party. Whatever Aimée was doing, at least she wasn't with him.

Movement disturbed the gray and white landscape outside. Figures lugging a basket down the gentle slope that led to the frozen lily pond.

A woman, he guessed by her clothes and her size, and two—no, three—children. She carried the smallest in her arms.

Lucien's pulse quickened. *Aimée.*

He watched from the window as she set the child down and grinned at the boy with the basket. Lucien had imagined her confined to the nursery, pressed into reluctant service while the house party went on without her. But there was nothing false in the smile she flashed the boy, nothing forced in the way she took the little girl's hand, nothing grudging in her manner or apparent affection.

"Mrs. Pockley is making my costume. She says I have the prettiest figure she has ever measured," Julia confided. "Of course, she is only the village seamstress, but she has some very interesting ideas for matching costumes."

One of the girls clapped her hands together in excitement. "Romeo and Juliet."

"Mars and Venus." A giggle.

"Anthony and Cleopatra."

"Punch and Judy," muttered Tom Whitmore.

Lucien ignored them all, his attention on the scene outside.

Aimée Blanchard was . . . By thunder, she was actually lying down with the children on the snowy bank, all of them waving their arms and swooshing their legs as if they had been struck by illness or madness. He could not hear them, but the two little girls were clearly giggling. Aimée's face was bright with laughter, her bonnet knocked sideways in the snow, her dark hair and pink cheeks glowing against the stark white backdrop.

He did not think her existence as an unpaid servant in her cousin's house could bring her much joy. And yet frolicking with the children, she looked genuinely happy, young, exuberant, and vividly alive.

Perhaps she made her own happiness.

She slid on her bottom and rose carefully to her feet, leaving a crude outline behind her on the snowy ground.

An angel.

Inside him, something stirred and yearned like a hawk stretching its wings, straining to be free.

"Mr. Hartfell," Julia called. "What is your opinion of matching costumes?"

He forced his attention from the window to focus on her pretty, expectant face. "My opinion must depend on the preferences of my partner."

"And on her identity?" Julia suggested, with a sideways look at poor Whitmore.

Lucien was already tired of her game, but he had come to Moulton to play. Because he needed a rich wife. "Certainly on her identity."

Julia dimpled, satisfied. "Then perhaps you should apply to Mrs. Pockley for suggestions on your own costume."

The chit was telling him in no uncertain terms that she expected him to dress to match her own disguise.

He bowed. "I will be guided by Mrs. Pockley's expert knowledge."

The conversation around the fire turned to what feathers and trimmings the dressmaker might have in stock, what ribbons and laces might be purchased locally, what treasures might be found in the guests' own wardrobes or in the attics. A reconnaissance trip to the village was proposed.

Outside, Aimée and the children had abandoned snow angels to troop to the open summerhouse. She lined them on the bench while she dug through the basket. Lucien caught the glint of metal, a tangle of straps. Skates.

A smile tugged at his mouth. His first winter at Fair Hill, Tripp had taught him to skate on the mill pond.

"And I must have silver ribbons," Julia declared. "Perhaps we will go this afternoon to look for silver ribbons at the shop. What do you think, Mr. Hartfell?"

Aimée kneeled before the smaller girl to strap on her skates. They were not her children. But she cared for them as if they were.

Did she have so much love to give, then, that she would lavish it on anyone?

He watched her hold the little girls' hands as she coaxed them to stand.

"I think," Lucien said slowly, "I would rather go skating."

. . .

"Stay near the shore!" Aimée called as ten-year-old Peter Netherby struck out for the center of the pond.

After three days confined to the house, she understood the boy's restlessness. Fortunately, the harsh weather that had kept them all in the nursery had also frozen the pond across. Aimée was almost as happy as the children to be outside again. But she was not taking any chances with their safety.

Near the bank, Harriet, two years younger than Peter, waved her arms and fought for balance.

Five-year-old Lottie Netherby clung to both Aimée's hands, her short, double-bladed skates scratching back and forth on the ice. "Look at me! I'm skating!"

Aimée smiled down at her, towing her gently along. "You certainly are."

Lottie's cheeks were red with exertion and excitement, her lips almost blue with cold. Despite their thick stockings, pantalettes, and petticoats, the girls' pelisses and play dresses simply did not provide the protection of Peter's breeches and overcoat.

It had been a mistake to make snow angels before skating, Aimée admitted. The back of her hair and her skirts were damp, and ice had melted under her collar. She would have to herd the children back inside soon before they all caught cold.

A burst of women's laughter floated like snow on the air, followed by the rumble of men's voices. Aimée glanced toward the house. A line of bonnets and top hats bobbed along the balustrade—the house party, coming to invade her snowy sanctuary.

Howard. A chill trickled down her spine.

And Mr. Hartfell.

Her heart beat faster. She knew him at once, his powerful body and chiseled profile making him stand out from the other gentlemen.

But it was more than his golden good looks that drew her. Something about him teased at her memory or imagination like the refrain of a familiar song, like a scent from childhood, beloved and familiar. As if her body recognized him, as if her soul responded to his.

Lucien Hartfell.

Julia's suitor.

Who believed she was encouraging Howard's attentions.

She gave herself a mental shake.

"Peter! Harriet! It's time to go in."

Predictably, the children protested and delayed. Aimée managed to cajole them toward shore as the adults ambled toward the frozen pond. Hoisting Lottie onto the bank, Aimée turned to give a hand to Peter.

"There's Mama," Lottie observed, keeping hold of Aimée's skirts.

"And Papa." Peter dropped Aimée's hand and lurched unaided up the slope.

"Mama! Look at me!" Harriet called, wobbling on her skates.

But the adults milling in the open summerhouse either could not or chose not to hear.

Harriet's face drooped. "Why don't they come see us?"

Aimée's heart squeezed. She understood—too well—the little girl's disappointment. After her own arrival at Moulton, Aimée had quickly learned that Lady Basing had little time or attention for her own children, let alone the demands of a penniless orphaned relation. Lady Basing's daughter Susan was obviously cut from the same maternal cloth.

"Come," Aimée said quietly. "I will ask your *maman* to visit the nursery before dinner."

Peter sneered with an older brother's superiority. "She won't come see us."

Aimée feared he was right. The one time Susan had sent for the children, she had returned them to the nursery a half hour later, complaining their noise made her head ache.

Harriet scowled. "Why not?"

"Because you're ugly," Peter said cheerfully. "Your nose is all red."

"It is not!"

"Peter . . ." Aimée warned.

He was old enough to have accepted his parents' neglect. Lottie, perhaps, was too young to have noticed. But Harriet . . .

"Look at me, Mama!" she cried. "I'm skating!"

She took two bold strides out onto the ice.

Aimée started down the bank, only to be stopped by Lottie's grip on her pelisse. "Harriet!"

Several heads turned.

Buoyed by her success in attracting the adults' attention, Harriet skated faster, flailing her arms, headed for the smoother ice in the center of the pond. "I can skate! You can't stop me!"

"Take your sister," Aimée ordered, thrusting Lottie at Peter.

The five-year-old wailed as Aimée stumbled onto the ice.

Too late.

The ice cracked with a sound like a falling branch. Aimée watched in horror as Harriet flung up her hands and collapsed in a billow of blue skirts through the fractured surface of the pond.

Aimée's heart froze in fear.

A woman screamed.

A man leaped the low bench in front of the summerhouse and rushed down the hill. A tall, blond man in a long black coat that he tore off as he ran.

Once again that sense of almost-recognition brushed through Aimée's mind like wings. *Lucien.*

He launched himself onto the ice.

Her stomach jumped into her throat. "Careful!" she cried. "The ice won't hold you."

"The air will," he said, she thought he said, or maybe that was the roaring in her ears.

Three longs strides and then he stretched out on the ice, reaching for the girl in the water.

Aimée scanned desperately for something to help him, a fence rail or a fallen branch, but the manicured landscape was bare.

She spotted Freddy Keasdon, running with the other guests down the slope, and shouted, "The house! Get help!"

He stared at her, mouth ajar in his white face, a boy not much older than Peter.

"Run!" she yelled.

He bolted for the steps.

She turned back to Lucien. Somehow he'd managed to grab hold of Harriet's arm and the back of her coat. With his arms fully extended over his head, he *lifted* the child straight from the water—an amazing feat of strength—and hauled her onto the ice.

Susan Netherby was sobbing. "My baby! Oh, my baby!"

Lucien inched backward, dragging Harriet, dripping, slipping, and crying, with him.

Aimée held her breath, afraid to venture nearer. Surely the ice would break under their combined weights.

But it did not.

Another inch. Another yard. In a long, smooth motion, Lucien pulled Harriet level with his shoulders and then pushed her down toward his feet.

Aimée skated forward and snatched her up. Clutching the wet, shivering child to her chest, she stumbled to the bank.

Hands grabbed and supported her up the slope.

"You stupid girl! I thought you were watching her!" Susan's face was pinched and pale. "How could you be so careless?"

George Netherby, Harriet's father, pushed through the crowd.

"Your coat," Aimée said through chattering teeth. "She needs . . ."

"Yes, yes," he said impatiently and peeled the little girl from Aimée. "You've done quite enough."

The front of Aimée's pelisse was soaked with icy, rank pond water. Her arms felt empty and cold. She wrapped them around her waist as a flock of servants led by Freddy Keasdon swooped from the house.

The servants enveloped the children and their parents in a cloud of blankets and concern, sweeping them up and carrying them off toward baths and fires and safety. George Netherby carried Harriet up the stone steps of balustrade. Peter trudged in his father's wake. Lottie sniveled in her mother's arms. Most of the house party trooped after them, leaving Aimée standing on the bank.

Forcing her weighted limbs to move, she dropped onto the bench. Fumbled with her straps.

"Let me help you." Howard Basing crouched at her feet, brushing aside her frozen fingers.

She glanced over her shoulder, shaken and more hurt than she would admit by the Netherbys' recriminations. "I have to go. They will need me in the nursery."

Howard tugged on her skate buckles. "We have servants. Let them deal with the brats. It's even possible that my sister, now that she's been reminded of her offspring's existence, will care for them herself."

Aimée barely heard him. On the frozen lily pond, Lucien was getting slowly to his feet, brushing ice from the front of his waistcoat. His right hand dripped blood.

She sucked in her breath. Harriet must have kicked him with her skates when he pulled her across the ice.

She felt a touch on her ankle and then on her calf. Startled, she looked down.

Howard smirked and squeezed her knee, his hand under her skirt. "We must get you back to the house and out of these wet things."

She froze a moment in numb disbelief.

And then hot anger flowed through her veins, flushed her cheeks, burned in her heart. She lashed out, kicking at him, his hands, shoulder, stomach.

With a grunt, he slipped and tumbled backward.

"*Connard! Cochon!* Pig!" Rage, kindled by fear and fueled by disgust, thickened her voice. "Don't you touch me! Don't ever touch me again!"

Howard scrambled up, an ugly look in his eyes. "You little bitch, I'll—"

"You heard her." Lucien stood at the bottom of the bank, tall and solid as a church, his eyes hard and cold. "Back off."

Howard glanced over his shoulder. Growled. "This is none of your concern."

Aimée jumped to her feet, prepared to throw herself between them.

Lucien narrowed his eyes. "I have bloodied my knuckles once already rescuing your niece. It would cost me nothing to bloody them again."

Howard sneered. "Except my family's goodwill."

"Miss Blanchard is also family, is she not?" Lucien asked in a deadly soft voice. "You are cousins."

Howard's face reddened. "Once removed."

"And now removed again." Lucien shook out the coat draped over his arm and dropped it around Aimée's shoulders, overlapping its edges in front. The collar reached up around her ears.

His coat was wonderfully warm and smelled like him, like man and sandalwood. She clutched its heavy folds gratefully, shielding herself from the cold and Howard's eyes.

A dizzying memory swept over her, an impression of hard, strong arms and wheeling stars and a road far below unspooling like a silver ribbon in the dark. She almost staggered.

Lucien offered her his arm. "Permit me to escort you to the house."

She blinked at him, disoriented, trying to force her mind to function.

If she went with him, Howard would be furious.

But if she refused his escort, she would be leaving the two men behind to fight.

Slipping a hand from the shelter of his coat, she gripped Lucien's arm.

He did not speak as they climbed the hill. She was aware of Howard staring after them, his face an ugly red, as she squelched and slipped up the icy slope. She shuddered with cold and reaction, hard, deep tremors that shook her chest and radiated outward through all her limbs.

"Thank you," she said as they reached the shallow stone steps of the walk. "I don't know what I would have done if you had not come along when you did."

"You must tell me if he bothers you again."

He thought she was talking about *Howard*, Aimée realized with a jolt. "I refer to Harriet. It was very brave, the way you ran out on the ice. You saved her."

He looked at her sideways, his face inscrutable. "She is not the only one I have saved."

Another spark, another contact, another flutter in her heart or memory. She swallowed. "Naturally, I am grateful. But I can look out for myself."

"You were quite fierce. Formidable, in fact." He lifted her hand where it rested on his arm and unexpectedly kissed her knuckles. Shock held her still. The pressure of his lips, the warmth of his breath, seared through the wet fabric of her glove. "But you are a woman."

Aimée reclaimed her hand, conscious of the staring windows of the house. Of Howard, somewhere behind them. "And because I am a woman, I must be weak."

"Not weak. But smaller than a man. In any physical encounter, you are outmatched."

She licked her upper lip, made suddenly aware of his size, his strength, his overwhelming masculinity. *In any physical encounter . . .*

She slid her gaze from his. "I hope your interference will not spoil your chances with Julia."

Lucien frowned. "Your cousin cannot excuse her brother's behavior."

"Oh no," Aimée assured him. "But if Howard were to complain to Lady Basing . . ."

"She would defend his abuse?"

"It is not as bad as you are thinking," Aimée said, leading him around the side of the house, out of Howard's sight. "It is only that she does not wish to think poorly of her son."

"You give them too much credit."

"They are my family."

"They do not deserve your loyalty."

His concern was seductive, more seductive even than his austerely handsome face or the warmth of his hand or the strength of his arm.

She had never had a champion before. Or a confidant. There was no one at Moulton who understood, no one she could talk to.

"It was better when I first came here," she said. "Howard was away at school then. Even now, he spends most of his time in Town."

"He is Sir Walter's heir. He must visit."

"Not as often as his parents would wish. There is little here to hold his attention."

Another assessing, sideways look. "Except you."

She shrugged, uncomfortable with his admiration. If that's what it was. "I can keep out of the way. Until he leaves again."

"Or you could leave," Lucien suggested.

Ah. He did not truly understand. He was a man, after all.

"And go where?" she asked. "I have no money, no family, no other acquaintance in England."

"You have skills. You speak French. You play the piano—even if you will not play in company," he added with a glint of humor. "You could seek employment."

"As a governess."

He nodded.

"I have no references."

"You have experience."

"Not enough to impress an employer." She winced. "Particularly after today. You heard the Netherbys."

"The Netherbys are fools."

His support warmed her. But she said, "Susan was upset. Any mother would be."

"Any other mother would not blame you for her own neglect. I know a woman in London who could find you a position if you wish it."

Aimée snorted inelegantly. She could not let his interest blind her to reality. "I have heard of such women. They meet the stagecoaches, looking for poor dumb girls from the country. Me, I am not so stupid."

"Not stupid at all. But Miss Grinton is completely legitimate, I assure you."

"Maybe." He meant well, she told herself. "Even if your Miss Grinton could help me—and I do not believe it is as easy as you think to find a position without references—I would only be exchanging one situation for another. I might find it harder to escape the attentions of an employer."

She led him to a small side entrance. "You do not know what it is like to be without resources or defenses. At least here I have a family." She turned her head to look up at him. "If I left, I would have nothing."

Lucien regarded her upturned face in the shadow of the doorway. Conviction lent passion to her voice, passion and the faintest hint of accent, like the scent of wine or sun-warmed grapes. Her eyes were as blue as the vault of Heaven.

Her words stabbed him. *You do not know what it is like to be without resources or defenses.*

Lucien opened the door for her to get her out of the cold. To give himself time to think.

He had quarreled with Amherst about his lack of freedom and independence.

But Aimée had even fewer options.

"You could marry," he said when they were both inside. The hallway was dark and cramped. A servants' entrance, he thought with another stab.

Her look was pure French, pragmatic and a little amused between long dark lashes. It stirred his blood. "I have no dowry."

He took a deep breath of stale air, imposing control on his unruly thoughts. "There must be some gentleman in the neighborhood who would value your other qualities."

"But of course," she responded promptly. "There is Mr. Willford, one of Sir Walter's tenant farmers, who needs a wife to help raise his seven children. And old Mr. Cutherford, who requires a nurse. Perhaps one day I will choose to exchange one form of servitude for another. But not yet."

"Not every marriage is based on convenience."

She gave him another direct look from those blue, blue eyes. Despite the cold, her lips were pink and ripe. "Indeed. Why are you courting Julia, Mr. Hartfell?"

He was beginning to wonder that himself. But he said stiffly, "My situation is different. I need a wealthy wife."

"Because the earl's estate is entailed?"

"Because he's bloody threatened to cut me off."

"Ah." She regarded him thoughtfully. "Then you should understand my fear of being cast out."

His mouth tightened. Aimée's defense of her own wretched family made him realize that Amherst deserved, if not Lucien's loyalty, then at least his honesty.

"Amherst would take me back if I asked," Lucien admitted. The acknowledgment tasted bitter in his mouth. "If I dance to his tune."

She tilted her head. "And you would rather dance attendance on Julia."

They were almost the exact words he had used with Amherst. *If I must woo for favors, I would rather court a woman.* But coming from her, they made him sound like a sulky schoolboy.

He glared at her, annoyed. "I have responsibilities," he said curtly. "People who depend on me."

"We must both be grateful, then," she said in a polite tone, "that I am not one of them. Good-bye, Mr. Hartfell."

She slipped out of his coat. Her wet pelisse molded to her small breasts.

"Keep it," he rasped. "You are half soaked and shivering. I'll send a maid up to your room to get it."

"The servants will all be busy in the nursery."

"I will send a maid," he repeated stubbornly, fixing his gaze on her face. "You need one, anyway, to help you out of those wet things and into a bath."

A short, charged pause while he thought she might argue with him. He was torn between amusement and exasperation. Damn the wench, must she question everything?

And then she smiled, a wide, genuine smile that curled warmly around his heart and dazzled his eyes. "Then . . . Thank you. For everything."

Turning, she ran up the steps, the sodden hem of his coat dragging behind her.

He watched her slender figure retreat up the dim passageway and out of sight, feeling as if all the light and warmth of the day went with her.

Chapter Five

Only fools and children wasted time wishing for what they could not have.

Aimée regarded her bright eyes in the spotted tin mirror and sighed. It was entirely possible she was a fool.

Because despite all her practical words to Lucien Hartfell, when she was with him she could not help wishing that she were Lady Aimée again, with wealthy and indulgent parents and a dowry sufficient to secure the attentions of a tall, blond, and angelically handsome fortune hunter.

She pulled off his coat and dropped it on her bed with a little shiver of loss and longing.

It would not do.

She fumbled with the fastenings of her wet pelisse. She did not think she had misinterpreted the gleam in Lucien's eyes or the kiss on her knuckles. Quite possibly he desired her. Most certainly he felt sorry for her.

But he was not for her. Not only was he her cousin's suitor, but he had openly admitted he intended to marry for money.

All of which made him more dangerous to her peace of mind than Howard Basing could ever be.

Standing in her damp chemise, she pulled her second-best gown from the wardrobe. The door to her room opened. She had forgotten to prop the chair under the knob.

Aimée whirled, her heart in her throat.

But it was only Finch carrying towels and a pitcher.

"Sorry, Miss Amy," the lady's maid said. "I didn't mean to scare you."

Aimée swallowed her rapidly beating heart. "You surprised me, that is all."

Stupid, *stupid* to let her guard down with Howard in the house. Had he rejoined the other guests? Or was he upstairs, changing?

Finch set the towels on the bed. She was a personable young woman, with coal black hair and a round, usually cheerful face. "I couldn't manage a hot bath, like Mr. Hartfell asked for you. But I brought up some warm water."

"That was kind of him. And you." No one lugged hot water up four flights of stairs to the servants' quarters. Aimée had grown accustomed to breaking through a film of ice in her pitcher every morning.

"It's no problem, miss." Finch poured water into the basin, holding the pitcher at an awkward angle, as if its weight was too much for her.

"They don't require you downstairs?"

Finch shook her head. "Miss Julia and them's all still in the drawing room. Taking tea."

"Are the children all right? Harriet?"

"Seem to be. I hear Mrs. Netherby visited the nursery, which is more than she's done since they got here."

So poor little Harriet had gotten her wish.

"And Mr. Basing?"

Water splashed. The heavy ironstone cracked against the floorboards. Aimée jumped backward as the pitcher rolled under the bed.

"Oh, miss, I'm sorry." The maid looked close to tears.

"It's all right, Finch." Aimée stooped to retrieve the pitcher. "See, it's not really broken. Just a chip."

Finch reached out a shaky hand to take the pitcher.

Aimée sucked in her breath. "Why, you have hurt your wrist."

A mottled bruise circled the maid's arm like a bracelet.

Finch colored and tugged on her sleeve. "It's nothing, miss."

Aimée drew in a slow breath, taking in the maid's red eyes and nervous manner. Something wasn't right. "You can tell me." she said gently.

"I can't tell anyone. He said."

"Who said?"

"I'll lose my place," Finch burst out.

Ah. Comprehension slithered down Aimée's spine. She met the maid's gaze in perfect, horrified understanding.

I might find it harder to escape the attentions of an employer. She had said it herself, to Lucien, less than an hour ago.

"Howard?"

Finch looked away.

Outrage kindled under Aimée's breastbone. Determination squared her shoulders. "We have to tell Sir Walter."

Finch trembled. "Please, I can't risk her ladyship finding out. I've only got another couple of months to save up, and then where will I go? Nobody's going to hire a lady's maid with a full belly and no character."

Aimée's gaze dropped instinctively to Finch's waistline. Did she mean . . . ? "You are with child? His child?"

"He says it isn't his."

Of course he did. *Connard.*

"And you?" Aimée asked. "What do you say?"

The maid's mouth twisted. "It doesn't matter, does it? Who's going to believe me?"

"I do."

Finch looked at her sadly. "Begging your pardon, miss, but your word doesn't carry much more weight around here than mine. You can't help me."

Aimée flushed at this bitter reminder of her own powerlessness.

But this wasn't about her. If the Basings cast out Finch, the maid would be pregnant, vagrant, and destitute. How long before she ended in prison or a pauper's grave?

You can't help me.

"No," Aimée admitted slowly. "But I know someone who can."

• • •

Lucien rested his head back against the high, curved edge of the mahogany tub, his long arms stretched along the sides, his knees poking out of the water. Warm water lapped his chest and thighs. A red fire snapped in the grate.

His body was heavy. Relaxed. His injured hand throbbed. His thoughts drifted to Aimée, shooting him a look of amused challenge through thick, dark lashes.

Why are you courting Julia, Mr. Hartfell?

The question bobbed around his brain, slippery and hard to handle as the soap in his bath.

He wasn't ready to grapple with the answer yet, so he pictured Aimée instead. Her bright face vivid with laughter or anger. The subtle arch of her spine, made for his hand. The sweet shape of her breasts under the wet pelisse. Blue eyes a man could drown in.

Under the water, his body stirred. She stirred him. Aimée.

Sinking lower, he reached his uninjured hand into the water.

A tap on the door roused him.

Irritated, he opened his eyes. "Come in."

She was there, wavering on the threshold, stepping out of his dreams, a mirage fashioned of lust and steam, summoned by the force of his longing.

Aimée, small-breasted and slender, her eyes dark and startled in her pink face.

He narrowed his gaze.

Instead of vanishing, she stepped into his room and closed the door.

Aimée moistened her lips. He was so very large. And naked. A big, golden, naked male, lapped in water and firelight.

She didn't know where to look, at his broad, bare, muscled chest or his narrowed, heavy-lidded eyes.

Her heart thumped.

"Forgive me if I don't get up," he drawled.

Wild heat stormed her cheeks and flooded her insides. Resolutely, she focused her gaze on the top of his head. His damp hair had the sheen and color of honeycomb, carelessly blended strands of amber and gold.

"I beg your pardon. I thought . . . While the other guests are downstairs . . ." She sounded like a stammering imbecile. She drew a deep breath and tried again. "I needed to see you."

"Well." A corner of his mouth turned up. "You can certainly see me now."

She bit her lip on an inappropriate spurt of laughter. "Indeed. I did not realize you would be . . ." She waved her hand, as if a single gesture could encompass all those muscles, that bare expanse of flesh. There was gold hair on his chest, too, she noted, fascinated. Fine, crisp hair glinting in the firelight. His large, square knees rose like mountains from the surface of the water.

"Bathing," she finished weakly.

"You should not be here," he said softly.

Her gaze collided with his. The air crackled with the warmth of the fire and the tension building between them. Flames licked along her veins and the insides of her thighs.

She took a deep gulp of warm, soap-scented air. "You would never hurt me."

She spoke with absolute conviction borne in her heart, in her soul, in a place deeper than memory. This man was not Howard. He was nothing like Howard.

Lucien shook his head. "Doesn't matter, sweet. If you're caught in my room, we'll both be compromised."

Even to be seen alone with him was risky. That's why she had sought him out here. But to be discovered alone with him naked in his bedchamber would be disaster. She would be hopelessly ruined.

For the first time, it occurred to her that Lucien would be . . . Not ruined, precisely. Society forgave a man's transgressions more readily than a woman's. But even if Lucien did not feel honor bound to offer for Aimée, the scandal would destroy his chances with Julia.

The thought of her cousin sent a trickle of cold down Aimée's spine. She glanced around the empty room. "Where is your servant?"

His brows rose. "He went to fetch a bandage. From the housekeeper, I imagine."

They did not have much time, then.

She clasped her hands together. "You said you knew a woman in London who could help me find a position."

"Yes." Lucien gripped the sides of the tub. "Turn around."

Distracted, she watched his muscles flex and bunch under his smooth, wet skin. "Why?"

Foolish question.

He pulled himself up, bath water streaming down the hard planes and ridges of his chest, his abdomen, his . . .

Aimée whisked herself around, her face on fire, heat pooling low in her belly. Water sloshed and dripped.

"Tell me what happened," he said. "To make you change your mind. Did Basing bother you again?"

"No, I . . . He . . ." She could hear him moving behind her with a rustle like bedclothes.

Like clothes, she informed her imagination sternly. Obviously, he must dress.

She had not known a man would look so, not like a statue at all, but large, dark, eager. She might never have known. She felt like a starving beggar standing at the kitchen door, glimpsing the meal inside. She was hungry for more than scraps. She would have liked to feast her eyes on him.

"It's all right." Lucien's voice was low and soothing and much closer.

She made herself remember Finch. "It is not all right, he . . ."

"I meant you can turn around now."

Oh. She swallowed and faced him.

Not dressed. Not entirely.

He wore a robe of dark silk, belted at the waist, exposing a broad golden V of chest. The damp fabric clung to his belly, the muscles and bones of his thighs, before falling in folds to his calves. His feet were bare. Big, masculine feet, almost as much a revelation as the rest of him. Strong arches. Hairy toes. So different from hers.

She felt another pang like hunger and jerked her gaze back up to his face.

He watched her, his green eyes hot, amused, aware.

"Aimée," he murmured. A whisper of amusement, of frustration, of desire. "What are you doing here?"

She barely remembered. She felt damp. Feverish. The heat of his body, the warmth of his breath, reached out to her. "I needed to speak with you. Alone."

She knew very well that she should move away.

She was equally certain he would do nothing to stop her.

But she might never have another opportunity to indulge her curiosity. Her desire. She stood her ground, motionless as a rabbit when the dogs were in sight, her heart beating, beating, beating.

"Then you must tell me," he said, a hint of laughter in his voice and in his eyes, "how I can be of service to you."

Despite herself, she felt her lips curve. She wanted this, to revel in this moment without fear or shame. She wanted him.

She closed her eyes to the extreme foolishness of what she was doing and simply breathed him in, the scent of his soap, the flavor of his skin, as if she could store up enough sensations to last her for a lifetime.

His fingers stroked the hair by her temple, a tiny, tugging pleasure. His hand cupped her cheek. With his thumb, he traced the shape of her smile, rubbing lightly on her lower lip. Languor invaded her limbs, weighted her eyelids.

She was playing with fire. Inside, she was melting.

She would stop him. In a minute. Not yet.

She opened her mouth, tasting the rough, salty pad of his thumb. He inhaled sharply.

The door at her back opened with a flood of cool air.

"Cobs. I knew I should have knocked," a male voice proclaimed in disgust.

Aimée froze.

Lucien stepped back unhurriedly, adjusting the front of his robe. "It's all right, Martin. You can come back later," he said over her head.

He was sending his servant away.

For a moment she was glad.

She wanted Lucien to herself, wanted privacy and freedom to savor and explore. To slide her fingers under the silk of his robe. To touch his warm, hair-roughened chest. To gather up memories she could take out and treasure in the nights and years to come, like flowers pressed in the pages of a book.

Only for a moment, before her brain, which had turned to mush as a result of all the lovely melty things going on inside her, reasserted itself and the reality of their situation rushed in.

Finch. She had to think of Finch.

Howard.

Julia.

Aimée's throat tightened. She really could not bear it if Lucien married Julia now.

She swallowed painfully and took a step back, away from temptation. "No. I will go."

He raised one eyebrow. "You wanted to talk."

"I need to speak with you alone, yes. But . . ."

"Martin was just leaving," Lucien said, without taking his eyes from her. "Weren't you, Martin?"

"If you say so, sir."

Aimée glanced at Lucien's valet, a slim, handsome youth with an expressionless face and dark, knowing eyes. She had no doubt the servant would make himself scarce if ordered to do so. And then what? Would he report in the kitchen on the goings-on upstairs?

What would happen then? Aimée's reputation would be ruined. The chance to help Finch would be lost.

"No," she said again, proud of the firmness of her voice. "I find I have miscalculated entirely the danger of being alone with a man in his bedchamber."

Lucien frowned. "Then you can both stay."

He truly did not understand. She shook her head.

"You can trust Martin," he said. "Trust me."

Did he realize how persuasive she found him? Almost she would agree to anything he suggested. It was very humiliating.

"Perhaps it is myself I do not trust," she admitted.

Something shifted in his face, flared in his eyes. He took a step toward her. "Aimée."

She felt a flutter of panic, a quiver of desire. She forced herself to gather her scattered thoughts and emotions, to form a plan. "Lady Basing has asked me to supervise the decorations for the house and ballroom."

Lucien watched her carefully. "So?"

"So"—she exhaled—"tomorrow after breakfast I will go into the woods to collect what I need."

It was considered bad luck to bring greenery into the house before Christmas Eve. But there were few flowers available in England in wintertime. She would need to store the boughs in the potting shed and bring them in to decorate the day before.

"You want me to find you in the woods." Disbelief edged his voice.

In the cold, in the snow, where they could be private. Safe. Fully dressed.

She nodded. "There are a number of fine holly trees in the oak-wood beyond the orchard. Near the gamekeeper's cottage," she added, in case he needed further direction.

His gaze searched hers before he bowed curtly. "Until tomorrow, then."

She moistened her lips. "Tomorrow."

The word hung between them like a promise. She felt committed to far more than a mere meeting.

Which was pure spinster foolishness, concocted of nothing more than loneliness and imagination. Surely by tomorrow she would be herself again. She had too much sense—didn't she?—to lose her head or her heart or her virtue to a man who was courting her cousin.

She met Lucien's heavy-lidded gaze and flushed.

However much she might want to.

. . .

The door clicked shut behind her.

"It's not like you to have a woman in your room," Martin observed.

"I did not *have* her," Lucien said.

Damn it all. He didn't know whether to curse his luck or bless his escape. He must have lost his mind. He knew better than to take advantage of a gently bred virgin in his bedchamber, no matter how lovely or willing.

Aimée's blue eyes, shining with trust and desire, seared his memory. *You would never hurt me.*

God.

If Martin had interrupted them only a few minutes later . . . Lucien broke into a cold sweat just thinking about what he had almost done.

What he'd lost the chance to do.

Martin snorted as he laid out scissors and gauze on the dressing table. "And I suppose you didn't arrange to meet her for a little romp and tumble in the woods tomorrow, either. Let me see that hand."

Lucien scowled. The skate blade had cut from the fleshy side of his palm to the knuckle of his little finger. Not deep, but painful. "A proper servant would pretend not to have heard that."

Martin pressed a pad to the wound. "Likely so," he agreed. "But a proper servant would be nagging for proper wages."

Guilt and frustration roiled inside Lucien. He gritted his teeth. "You know I cannot afford to pay you now. If you prefer to return to Maiden Lane—"

"I'm not going back to that henhouse." Martin wrapped the pad with gauze. "Anyways, you ain't never abandoned us, and I'm not abandoning you. A gentleman needs a valet."

"I'm not a real gentleman," Lucien reminded him. As far as this world was concerned, he was the Earl of Amherst's bastard.

"You're as much a gentleman as I am a valet," Martin retorted. "Pretend to be something long enough, and it comes true."

Lucien had never been any good at pretending. Perhaps that was why he had so much trouble feeling truly human.

There was no pretense in Aimée at all. Circumstances may have forced her to play the drudge, yet her essential spirit was not dimmed by her role in her cousin's house.

Could he say the same about his life with Amherst?

Lucien shut the thought away. "You could do better for yourself elsewhere."

Martin shrugged. "Maybe. But I got a bed and three squares a day now, which is more than I had before you pulled me out of that gutter."

Less than a year ago, Lucien had stumbled over Martin's body in an alley behind Covent Garden, where he had been beaten half to death by a client who had used him thoroughly and then claimed outrage at being tricked into paying for a boy. After Fanny had nursed the boy back to health, Martin had attached himself to Lucien as his manservant.

"But we're running short of the ready," Martin continued, tying the bandage into a neat knot. "Here and at Fanny's place. This girl, she's not the one we came for, is she? The rich one."

"No," Lucien admitted.

No money, no family, no other acquaintance in England, she had said.

It didn't matter. She was in his head and in his blood, a distraction he did not need, a temptation he could not avoid.

"What do you want with her, then?" Martin asked.

"I don't know yet," Lucien admitted. He had Fallen for her once. He was prepared to sacrifice for her again. But how much this time? "She wants my help."

Martin clipped the bandage ends. "Seems to me you got enough strays counting on you already."

"Then one more should make no difference."

But Aimée was different. She always had been.

"Tell that to Fanny next time you give her the housekeeping money."

Lucien's jaw tightened. "She asked for my help," he repeated stubbornly.

"Coming to your room with you starkers in the bath, she's asking for something else. And you looked ready to give it to her."

Lucien chafed. But there was no point in being offended by the truth. No point in denying it, either, to Martin or himself. More than his own fate depended on his decisions now. He would not risk his future or theirs again.

"I have nothing to offer Miss Blanchard," Lucien said stiffly. "Except my assistance."

The manservant met his gaze, his own eyes dark with sympathy and understanding. "Best you remember that, then, sir. Next time you see the lady."

Chapter Six

In his dream, Lucien struggled up and up a long, twisting stairwell, his pulse thudding, his face wet with perspiration. Cold seeped from the ancient stone. A draft rose from the depths of the tower.

Aimée climbed ahead of him, around and around, her light flickering like a candle in the dark. She turned, her smile beckoning, her face glowing in the shadows. "This way. Follow me."

Reckless little fool, she wasn't looking, she might slip, she might trip, she could fall and break her neck. His mouth dried as her slipper scraped stone. He lunged to save her.

And missed. His reaching hands grasped at air, at nothing.

For a moment he hung suspended, her cry echoing in his ears, before he fell.

And woke in a tangle of sheets, his heart pounding and a headache pulsing behind his eyeballs.

Gray sunlight slanted across the carpet of his room. Lucien swore and stumbled from his bed. It was late.

By the time he made his way downstairs to breakfast, the room was full of far too many fellow guests, flapping and jabbering like crows in a winter landscape.

No Aimée.

Lucien blinked his bleary eyes, stupid with lack of sleep. Was she still in the house? Had he missed her?

He struggled against the remnants of his dream, sticky and persistent as cobwebs. Outside the windows, the snow lay thin and hard across the lawn. A line of footprints and the icy tracks of a cart led past the orchard and into the wood.

Aimée.

This way. Follow me.

His head throbbed. His stomach growled.

Julia lifted the teapot invitingly. "Will you have some tea, Mr. Hartfell? Or do you drink chocolate in the mornings?"

He wanted coffee desperately.

He glanced once at the sideboard set with pound cake, plum cake, breads, and rolls and then again out the window. Imagined facing Julia's pert prettiness across the breakfast table every morning for the rest of his life and said, "Thank you, no. I have just remembered an errand that requires my attention."

"I haven't had my tea yet," Tom Whitmore announced beside her.

Julia set the pot down with a little thump. "You might have taken breakfast at your own house rather than call on us so early in the morning."

"I can't get what I want at home," Whitmore said.

Julia looked at him through her lashes. "And what is that, pray?"

Whitmore grinned. "Plum cake," he said, and reached for a slice.

Lucien was heartily sick of Julia Basing and her games and her suitor. It was a relief to escape outside into the cold air and the quiet.

He crunched across the frozen ground under the dark, straggling cover of the trees, trying to ignore his pounding head and empty stomach. Small outbuildings huddled under a thin blanket of snow. The cart had dug shallow ruts in the ice. He thought he could hear the squeak and rumble of its wheels through the trees.

Lucien frowned. Of course Aimée would have servants with her to bring back decorations for the ballroom. He would have to find some way to speak with her alone. Last night she had refused to confide in him in front of Martin.

His jaw set. Or perhaps she had simply used his manservant's presence as an excuse to run away.

Perhaps it is myself I do not trust.

He expelled his breath in a cloud of frustration.

Movement flashed through the trees, a bright spot in the barren landscape.

Aimée, standing on tiptoe against a backdrop of dark holly to cut a cluster of red berries from a bough.

He felt, absurdly, as if the sun had come out.

Every detail emerged, etched bright and clear on his senses. The scent of the wet wood, the rush of blood to his groin, the tingle of cold in his fingertips. Aimée's glossy dark curls and deep blue eyes. Her skin, gleaming and smooth as the snow but warm and pink with life.

You, he thought, and shuddered with longing.

You that I wanted. You I've been searching for all of my life.

Aimée inhaled deeply, breathing in the peace of the snowy wood, holding it inside her. Away from the house, she could exist purely in the moment, absorb the naked beauty of the trees and the little mist hanging over the snow; the song of a blackbird hanging on the cool raw air; the prickly green leaves and glowing red berries clustered just beyond her grasp. Tempting. Taunting. Out of reach.

Like Lucien.

The holly leaves pressed against her breast, a hundred tiny pin-pricks to counter the sting at her heart. The berries blurred.

She blinked fiercely. She would not mope like a child crying for the moon. Perhaps she would never have the things that she'd once accepted as her birthright, beaux and châteaux and freedom to follow her heart and inclinations. There would still be opportunities for satisfaction. There could still be moments of joy.

All she had to do was find the courage and determination to reach for them.

Gripping her little pruning knife, she stood on tiptoe to slice through the holly branch.

Snow crunched behind her. Someone walking over the ice.

She teetered. Turned. Her heart leaped in recognition and delight.

C'est toi.

"Oh," she said softly, foolishly. "It's you."

You that I wanted. You I've been waiting for all of my life.

Lucien left the cover of the trees and strolled forward, his thick gold hair drawing all the brightness of the day. "Allow me."

He reached over her head, his warmth pressing her back into the bushes, his chest brushing her breasts. He smelled of wool and sweat and sandalwood, earthy and exotic. His arms were hard and long.

She shivered as he stretched above her, a subtle pressure, a shift of muscles. She heard the rustle of leaves, felt their tiny barbs against her back and him, solid and male against her front.

The branch cracked and broke off in his hand.

Lucien eased away. "For you." His voice was husky.

He was still close, so close, his hair a disordered halo around his face, his emerald green eyes intent. Something quivered in her belly like a plucked harp string, vibrating like music all along her bones. Her throat ached with longing.

She swallowed.

So did he. She watched the movement of his throat against his starched white collar.

"Where are the servants to help you?" he asked.

Her brain scrambled for words. "I sent them away. Ahead. To cut the log for the Christmas fire."

In case he came for her.

Her answer trembled between them. They would not be inter-rupted this time.

She looked up, her mouth dry.

"There you are!" Julia's voice shattered the bright crystal air. She bustled through the trees, bouncing and breathless, pink-cheeked with cold. Her glance darted from Lucien to Aimée. "I couldn't imag-ine what could drag you from the house so early."

"Some of us were out earlier," Tom Whitmore remarked beside her.

Julia tossed her head. "Country hours," she said with scorn.

"You're a country girl," he pointed out. "Or you were before Town spoiled you."

"Your mama asked me to collect decorations for the ballroom,"

Aimée said before Julia could snap at him again. She held out the bunch of holly berries. "Aren't they pretty?"

"I am not spoiled," Julia declared. "Take it back."

"Spoiled." Tom nodded. "And bossy."

Lucien narrowed his eyes.

"They grew up together," Aimée explained in an undertone. "Tom and his sisters and Julia."

He raised his brows. "Not you?"

"At first. When I first came." The memory made her smile.

Despite being the only boy—or perhaps because of it—Tom had always been dragged into his sisters' games to play the prince or highwayman. In return, he'd taught the girls to spit and to skip stones and to swim.

"And then?" Lucien inquired.

Lady Basing had caught the girls sneaking into the house one summer afternoon, hair wet, shifts bundled under their arms.

Aimée's smile faded. She had been whipped and confined to her room for her bad influence on her younger cousin. And Julia and Tom's childhood friendship had been quashed by chaperoned visits and calculated courtships and the success of Julia's London season.

"And then . . ." Aimée shrugged. "We could not play together as children anymore."

Julia stooped suddenly for a handful of snow and smashed it against Tom's waistcoat.

"They seem to have no trouble taking up where they left off," Lucien observed dryly.

She snuck a look at his face. He did not sound jealous.

"It is the woods," she offered, to appease any pang he might be feeling. They had all strayed away from their customary roles and paths this morning, into the woods, into a dream, into a fairy tale. "We played here."

Tom lobbed a snowball, spattering the bright blue of Julia's pelisse with white. She shrieked and returned fire.

"Shall we leave them to make up for lost time?" Lucien inquired.

He looked at her, an indefinable glint in his green eyes, an expectant curve to his mouth.

Anticipation quickened Aimée's heartbeat. She observed the snow battle now raging between Tom and Julia. Would her cousin even notice if they slipped away? Would she care?

That was the risk of the woods. Once you had left the accustomed paths behind, could you ever go back?

"You wanted to speak with me," Lucien reminded her. "Alone."

She flushed deeply. "Yes, of course."

But once they were strolling among the trees, she was at a loss how to begin. Lucien adjusted his long stride to hers, apparently in no hurry to break the silence between them. Mist wreathed the trunks. Above the bare black branches, the sky was cloudless, hazy, tinged with blue. The only sounds were their footsteps and Julia's fading laughter. The hush, the solitude, the stark beauty of the snowy forest wrapped them in intimacy.

Aimée cleared her throat. "Did you play in the woods when you were a child?"

"No." His tone did not invite further questions.

He was the illegitimate son of an English nobleman, she reminded herself. She had no notion who his mother might have been. Perhaps his memories of childhood were not happy ones. "How old were you when you went to live with . . ." *Your father.* "The Earl of Amherst?"

"Seventeen." A pause. "I think."

He did not even know his age? Poor boy.

"And before that?" she persisted.

He turned his head, his eyes hooded. "I don't remember."

Or else, she thought, his memories were too painful to recall.

She squeezed his arm. They both had been forced to start over. And at almost the same time, it seemed. "I was thirteen when I came to Moulton."

"Yes, I know."

She blinked. How could he know? But of course he had been talking with Julia. "I did not want to be here," she confessed. "For a long time, I resented the . . . the circumstances that brought me. I missed my life in France. My home. My family."

For weeks and months, the gray wet English weather had seemed to overshadow her very soul. She had succumbed to clouds of grief, storms of tears, and homesickness.

"You escaped the Terror," Lucien said, his voice flat. "If you hadn't, you would have died."

"*Bien sûr.*" The French slipped out, as it did sometimes when she talked about her childhood. She smiled up at him in apology. "At thirteen I did not always think very clearly, you understand. Now I am wiser. And grateful."

"Grateful." His face was unreadable, as it often was, with the marble austerity of a disillusioned saint.

She wished she could make him smile.

"To be alive," she explained. She gestured around them at the winter wood, the dormant trees, the wisps of frost, the forest floor sleeping under a blanket of bracken, leaves and snow. "All this—life— is a gift. What you make of it is up to you."

His words.

Lucien stared down at Aimée's bright face.

His words, wrested from the dark prison of memory on what must have been the worst night of her life, offered to comfort and encourage him. The irony cut him like a knife.

He had saved her life and ruined it, and she was bloody *grateful*.

She smiled at him, her eyes shining with sympathy, her fingers light and warm upon his arm. Their gazes locked.

He felt it. The snap of connection, like a key in a lock, like a piece in a puzzle, like two halves sliding together to make one whole. *It's you.*

Behind her blue, translucent eyes, recognition wavered. Doubt bloomed.

Tension thrummed along his nerves.

If she knew the role he had played in her life, would she still feel grateful? Or would she hate him?

It didn't matter. She could never know. The threat of demons, the unpredictability of humankind, compelled the Nephilim to live secretly.

She could never know him.

He drew a ragged breath, torn between relief and regret. Though why he should feel regret he was not sure.

"Is that why you want to go to London?" he asked. "To make a new life?"

She blinked those long, lovely lashes like a dreamer waking from sleep. "What?"

He helped her over a log fallen in the snow. "You wanted to talk with me about a position in London."

"Not for myself. For Miss Finch. Julia's lady's maid."

Lucien raised his brows. "If the girl thinks to improve her lot in London, why doesn't she apply to your housekeeper for a reference? Or Lady Basing."

"Her lot is not so easily remedied," Aimée said. "She is with child."

Ah.

Lucien considered. "Can the father be brought to marry her?"

Aimée pressed her lips together. "No."

Suspicion stirred in his gut. "Basing?" he asked grimly.

She lifted one shoulder in a little shrug. "He denies it. He will not take any financial responsibility for her or the child."

Swiving son of a bitch. "So you came to me."

"I am not asking you for money," Aimée said hastily. "I know you are . . . That is, this is none of your affair. But . . ."

She knew he was short on funds. She had applied to him for help anyway. He was oddly moved by her trust.

"You did the right thing," he said. "Martin can take her to Fanny."

"Fanny?"

"Fanny Grinton on Maiden Lane. She can give your maid shelter until permanent placement can be found."

Aimée bit her lower lip. "How much will it cost? I can contribute a little to Finch's keep, but . . ."

He shook his head. "It isn't necessary."

She shot him a skeptical look, very French. "Your Miss Grinton takes in boarders out of the goodness of her heart?"

"Yes," he said shortly.

She looked unconvinced.

"Fanny was in service herself once," he explained reluctantly. "Until she was debauched by the master of the house. When his wife threw her into the street, Fanny prostituted herself to survive. Now she rescues others who have suffered a similar fate."

"This is an inspiring story. But inspiration does not pay the bills."

"The residents of the house take in sewing and laundry. They contribute what they can," he said.

"And you provide the rest," Aimée guessed with an approving nod. "Which is altogether noble and generous of you."

He was shaken by her faith in him. Unlike Amherst, she believed the best of him without hesitation. Without question.

He did not deserve her good opinion.

"I am no hero. No angel. I am not even a very good man."

"Most gentlemen in your circumstances would not spend their resources on those less fortunate."

"I have to." His hands curled into fists at his sides. He forced himself to relax them, forced himself to say, "I hired her."

Aimée's brow puckered. "This house on Maiden Lane . . . It was your idea? You hired Miss Grinton to run it?"

"Yes." His head throbbed. He was tempted to let her go on believing that. To let her think well of him. But he had never been good at pretense. "No. I was her last client."

Aimée continued to regard him, her face calm.

Didn't she understand?

"I hired her as a whore," he said harshly.

He didn't know why he told her. To shock her, to drive her away? Or was he hoping, against hope and all reason, for her absolution?

He held himself stiffly, prepared for her blushes, braced for her condemnation.

She did blush, a rosy flush that swept from her jawline to the brim of her bonnet. "If you set up every lady of intimate acquaintance in a house with a budget and instructions to rescue other unfortunates, it is no wonder you are short of funds."

He wanted to laugh. He wanted to kiss her. He wanted to do any number of inappropriate things.

Because he could not, he glowered at her instead. "I am not intimately acquainted with any other woman."

She tilted her head. "Only the one? Miss Grinton."

What was she getting at?

"Yes," he snapped.

"Did you . . . Do you love her?"

The wistfulness of the question caught him off guard.

"No. It was a *transaction*," he said curtly. "It meant nothing."

Something that Aimée, in her goodness and innocence, could never understand.

"And yet you felt guilty enough afterward not only to rescue Miss Grinton from her situation but to save others as well."

He was furious. Found out. He had never put it in those words, even to himself. Perhaps Aimée understood more than he thought.

"Amherst thinks I am running a brothel." *Now why the devil had he told her that?*

"The situation is unusual," Aimée acknowledged. "But surely he should understand that you are only trying to help these poor women."

"I didn't tell him," Lucien admitted.

He had resented being forced to justify himself. At the time his reticence had been a point of pride. Now, however . . .

"Amherst has other concerns," Lucien said. "He would say Fanny and the others are not our kind."

Not Nephilim.

"You do him an injustice," Aimée said. "He obviously cares about you more than he does for the world's opinion. Why else would he have brought eleven out-of-wedlock children to be raised at Fair Hill? You should not let your pride come between you."

"I'm not currying favor with the old man for money."

Aimée widened those blue eyes at him. "It is not his wealth you should worry about losing. It is his regard. He is your father. Your family. It would be a great sorrow for you to lose him."

As she had lost her family.

Remorse seized Lucien. "I'm sorry, I'm a brute. I didn't think . . . I didn't realize . . ."

Aimée shook her head. "No brute. Perhaps no angel, either. But I think you are a very good man." Standing on tiptoe, she brushed her lips against his cheek. "Thank you for helping Finch."

He was not good.

But he felt, at that moment, very much a man. God help them both.

He stopped in the snow and placed his hands on her shoulders, turning her to face him. She stared gravely up at him, her eyes clear and unafraid.

With a groan of longing and surrender, he covered her mouth with his.

Lucien's kiss was warm and firm and seeking, his lips parted. Aimée could feel the heat and moisture of his mouth, and an answering heat and moisture rose in her, in her stomach and breasts and between her thighs. He pressed against the seam of her lips and then he . . . Yes, he did, he put his tongue right in her mouth, shocking and delicious.

Her toes curled in pleasure.

She ought to stop him. She knew the dangers of indulging in desire. She had too much sense to throw away her heart on an inappropriate liaison.

But what had her good sense ever gotten her but alone? For years, she had been starved of affection, of connection, of simple human touch. She was hungry for life.

For Lucien.

The branch she was holding slithered to the ground. He licked into her mouth, coaxing, exploring, and she grabbed the lapels of his coat and sucked eagerly at his tongue.

Heaven.

His tongue stroked, dabbled, thrust. Against her stomach she could feel that part of him, the part she had glimpsed when he rose from his bath. A picture of him formed in her mind, large, dark, exciting. She squirmed against him, trying to get a better fit between their two bodies. His hands slid from her shoulders to her upper arms, lifting her, aiding her.

There. She shivered in delight.

He raised his head, his eyes dark and penetrating. A flush stained his cheekbones. "You are cold."

She was tingling. Melting. "No."

Don't stop.

His hands tightened again on her upper arms before he put her gently from him. "We have been gone too long already."

Disappointment speared her. Disappointment and desire. "There is a gamekeeper's cottage close by." Her heart beat faster at her own daring. Her knees trembled. "We could shelter there."

His muscles were rigid. He did not move. Indeed, she almost fancied he did not breathe.

He exhaled. "I will not risk your reputation more than I have already."

She honored him for his concern. How could she not? But she also saw her opportunity to know passion, to feel close and loved and alive, slipping away. She had no illusions. Lucien had made her no promises. But she was terribly afraid that if she did not grasp at life now, she would regret it all the long and empty years to come.

"It is my reputation," she said. "My risk. My choice."

Lucien stared down at her, an arrested expression on his face.

For a moment her words seemed to echo between them. *My life. My choice.*

For no reason at all, her heart stood still.

"Sometimes our choices have consquences beyond what we can imagine," he said at last. His face was flat, unreadable. "Let me take you back."

He was rejecting her.

Aimée recoiled as if she'd been slapped. She supposed she should be grateful to be rescued from a fate like poor Finch's. Perhaps by tomorrow she would even appreciate Lucien's restraint.

Right now, though, she was mortified. Her face, her chest, her whole body burned with humiliation and frustrated desire.

She bent to hide her face, retrieving the branch from the ground, ignoring the barbs that pricked through her gloves. "You go back if you want to," she said coolly. "I have work to do."

Clutching her bouquet of holly, she left him there alone under the trees, leaving behind her a trail of berries like heart's blood on the snow.

Chapter Seven

The following afternoon was Christmas Eve. Julia sat in front of her mirror as Aimée coaxed another blond ringlet around the brush handle.

Julia turned her head one way and another, critically regarding her reflection. "Mama offered to send her own maid to me. But she always leaves a frizz in the front."

Aimée pinned the curl on top of Julia's head. "I don't mind helping."

"As long as you have time," Julia said.

Aimée popped a hairpin in her mouth before she said something hasty in response. She had been kept running all day. Now that the greenery could be brought indoors, she needed to direct the decoration of the house and the arrangements for the ballroom. She had barely gotten started on the kissing bough when Julia's summons came.

"It's very inconsiderate of Finch to disappear like this," Julia continued. "Ouch, you're poking. I wonder where she's gone."

Aimée had a very good idea where Finch had gone. And with whom. Last night, long after the houseguests were in bed, Finch had come to Aimée's attic room to ask if Mr. Hartfell's manservant could be trusted. Aimée had assured the maid she would be in good hands, pressing money on Finch for the journey to London.

Now Aimée wondered how Lucien was faring without his valet. Her throat tightened. Not that it was any of her business.

She secured another curl, pleased that her hand did not tremble.

"I don't know how I am to get ready for the ball tomorrow without assistance," Julia fretted. "Those blasted *wings*. I don't know what Mrs. Pockley was thinking."

They both looked at the dressmaker's form in the corner. Julia's gown shimmered, high-waisted and graceful, with a low, square neckline and diaphanous skirt. But it was the wings that raised the costume to ethereal fantasy, extravagant wings of stiffened taffeta with silver ribbons that tied under and across the bodice, exquisite and ephemeral as the promise of youth or a dream of young love.

It made Aimée want to spit. Or cry.

"She was thinking how beautiful you will look." Aimée forced enthusiasm into her voice. "Like a butterfly."

Assuming butterflies' wings were sewn with hundreds of glittering crystals.

"Psyche," Julia said glumly.

Aimée pinned the final curl. "What?"

"Not a butterfly." Julia frowned into the mirror. "I'm supposed to be Psyche. Mr. Hartfell is dressing as Eros."

Aimée swallowed the lump in her throat. They were still a couple, then. Psyche, the personification of the human soul, and Eros, god of love. Not the chubby cherub that infested ceiling corners, but the sculpted young god of the Greeks, naked, winged.

Her heart stumbled. She found it shockingly easy to picture Lucien with a gleaming sweep of powerful wings. But . . .

"Surely Mr. Hartfell is too"—*masculine, hairy, large*—"old to play Eros?"

Julia shrugged, oddly indifferent. But then, Aimée reminded herself, Julia had never seen Lucien rising naked from his bath, water streaming from his chest and down his thighs. Her face grew hot.

"Tom says costumes are silly, anyway," Julia said.

Aimée regarded her cousin's drooping mouth in concern. Yesterday she'd thought Julia and Tom had made up their differences. But perhaps their understanding had not survived the return from the woods.

"You shouldn't let what Tom says ruin your pleasure," Aimée said gently. Swallowing her own pain, she added, "It is Mr. Hartfell's opinion you should care about."

Julia twisted the bracelets on her arm. "I suppose."

Aimée tried again. "What matters most is what *you* want."

Their eyes met in the mirror.

"You're right, of course." Julia's smile broke like dawn. "Thank you, Amy."

Aimée smiled back uncertainly, a pang at her heart.

What if what you wanted most was something you couldn't have?

The pots of rosemary and bay, decorated with silver ribbon and gold paper, had been moved to the ballroom. The buckets of holly branches and ivy vines stood almost empty. But the scent of green, growing things lingered in the potting shed, a promise of life and rebirth in the midst of winter.

Aimée twined ivy around the kissing bough, already heavy with waxy white berries of mistletoe. Each time a man claimed a kiss beneath the bough, he would pluck a berry until they all were gone.

She stared sightlessly at the glossy foliage, remembering Lucien's kiss, the warmth of his breath, the taste of his mouth, the feeling of homecoming in his arms. Her lips tingled. She pressed them together.

Why had he stopped?

She was an innocent, but she recognized a man's desire. She had felt him, felt *it*, hard against her stomach. Her body pulsed, remembering.

She would not have stopped him.

The realization lashed heat into her face. She barely understood her own reactions. She did not understand his at all. Was Lucien truly concerned about the risk to her reputation, as he claimed? Or had he worried that lying with her would jeopardize his courtship of Julia?

Did it matter? Either way, he had demonstrated more honor and restraint than she had.

Either way, she had to live with the knowledge of his rejection.

"Very pretty," Howard observed behind her.

A chill slithered down her spine.

Her fingers stretched for the pruning shears before she turned. "I thank you for the compliment. I think it will look well in the ballroom."

"I was not speaking of your arrangement." Howard's smile flashed, displaying all his teeth. "Though I like it. A kissing bough, is it not?"

Her heart banged. With Finch on her way to London, Howard had already been deprived of one victim, whether he knew it yet or not. She was not eager to be his next quarry. "Yes."

"Perhaps we should test its efficacy," he suggested.

Aimée swallowed. She wasn't afraid. Not truly afraid, not yet. But he was blocking the door. "I think not. There are only a limited number of berries. Once they are gone, the bough no longer serves any purpose."

"Then we should make the most of this opportunity."

She tightened her grip on the shears, reluctant to meet his gaze, afraid he would see the knowledge and disgust in her eyes. "Your absence will be noticed in the drawing room."

"Not at all. The tea tray is gone. Our guests are all in their rooms dressing for dinner with their servants in attendance. No one will miss either of us for some time." He strolled forward, running a fingertip down her arm to her elbow, displacing her shawl. She restrained her shudder.

"You deserve the chance to enjoy yourself," he murmured, watching her face. "You must feel very confined here. Lonely. No one truly appreciates your talents, do they? I could make your duties much more pleasant."

She twitched up her shawl, jerking her arm away. "If you are offering your assistance, Cousin, there are still some pots to be carried into the ballroom."

He pressed closer, trapping her against the potting bench. "I had other duties in mind. Personal duties."

Bile and rage rose in her throat. "I would rather scrub floors."

He laughed softly, making her skin crawl. "I quite like the thought of you on your knees."

"Enough," she said firmly. "Let me go. Or I will tell your mother."

"She will not believe you."

Aimée raised her chin. "Perhaps her guests will. I am still a lady, Howard. You cannot assault me with impunity."

Society would look the other way as long as Howard confined his attentions to the servant class. But Sir Walter and Lady Basing could not let it be known that they tolerated his abuse of their own young relative in their home.

Howard's eyes shifted. His expression hardened. "Then I will have to make sure you don't tell anyone."

He reached for her.

She flung out her hand to stop him, to push him away, and the shears in her hand slashed his chin, drawing blood.

His face twisted. "Bitch."

He grabbed her hand, wrenching cruelly, wresting the clippers from her grasp. She opened her mouth to scream, and his meaty hand clamped on her jaw, stifling her cry. *Ah, no.* She fought as hard as she could, kicking him with her thin slippers, rolling and scratching to get away, but she was hampered by her skirts, her shawl, her tight sleeves. His weight, his strength, overpowered hers. The edge of the table ground into her back. His fingers dug painfully into her cheeks as his other hand scrabbled at her skirts.

She struggled, panting and twisting. Inciting him. She could feel his erection pushing at her, and her gorge rose.

Dear God. She could not scream. She could not breathe. Her mind grayed with terror. He was going to ravish her, and she could not stop him.

She bit his hand.

He swore, his breath hot and harsh against the side of her face.

And then his weight was gone, plucked, ripped from her. She staggered, catching herself against the table, as he catapulted across the shed and crashed into a wall. Buckets overturned. Water sloshed onto the floor.

Lucien stood over him with a face like thunder, flexing his knuckles. To her fevered imagination, he almost seemed to glow, lit from within by righteous anger.

An angel come to save us.

The answer to her prayers.

"Get up," he ordered, his voice low and deadly.

Howard shook his head, sprawling in a puddle of water and branches. "She's not worth it."

Lucien hauled him to his feet by his neckcloth and smashed a fist into his stomach. Howard doubled over, wheezing.

She should stop them, Aimée thought numbly. But she could not find her voice, could not make her shaking limbs move. She clung to the table for support.

"She is a lady," Lucien said through his teeth. "Worthy of protection and regard."

Howard wiped blood from his chin. Licked his lips. "You don't know her. Or maybe you do. She's a hot little piece. I only gave her what she was panting for."

Aimée cringed.

Lucien slammed Howard up against the wall. A pot fell from a shelf and shattered.

Howard clawed at Lucien's arms.

Lucien shook him like a mastiff shakes a rat. "You don't touch her." More blows, hard and punishing, to Howard's ribs and gut. "You don't look at her. You don't bother her ever again."

"This is my parents' house," Howard said thickly. "You have no authority here. I'll have you thrown out."

"Not before I tell Sir Walter and everyone else the reason why."

Howard's face was greenish white. "They won't believe you. It will be your word against mine. The word of a bastard."

"An acknowledged bastard," Lucien shot back. "The Earl of Amherst never abandoned *his* by-blows. My word will be accepted. And once the story of your villainy gets out, your family's reputation will be ruined."

He released Howard, dropping him to the floor. "I cannot deal with you here as you deserve. But if I hear you have troubled Miss Blanchard again in any way, you will be lucky to escape with your life. Now take yourself out of my sight."

Howard stumbled to his feet, blood dripping from his chin, one eye swollen nearly shut. The other shot a hate-filled glance at Aimée. She shivered, pulling her shawl around her.

"I will inform the company that you are indisposed," Lucien said still in that deadly soft voice. "Doubtless you will wish to remain in your rooms until your return to London."

Howard lurched from the potting shed without answering. The door banged shut behind him.

Lucien turned to Aimée. "Are you all right?"

Her hands trembled. She made an effort to pull herself together. "Yes. Thank you."

Lucien's brow creased. "I cannot prevent him from coming back in the future. But bullies prey on the defenseless. I believe he is sufficiently cowed now to leave you alone."

"I did not arrange to meet him here," she said, twisting her hands together. "I did not invite his attentions."

"I know," Lucien said.

"How can you know?" she demanded. "I certainly threw myself at you. How can you not think I am ripe for any man's attentions?"

"I know because I know you," Lucien said. "You are passionate, not promiscuous. And far too wise, too fine, for the likes of Basing. The man is an ass."

Startled, she met his gaze. Slowly, her lips curved. "He is an ass," she admitted.

Lucien made a move toward her, quickly checked. Understanding flooded her. He was afraid to touch her, to remind her of Howard's attack.

So she went to him. Slipping her arms around his waist, she laid her head on his hard chest.

His arms came around her. His hands moved down her back,

stroking, comforting. With a little sigh, she squeezed her eyes shut. He was warm and solid, wrapped around her, and she nestled against his big body, absorbing his comfort. His strength.

"Do not be afraid," he murmured. "You are safe now."

A memory tickled, soft, dark, velvet. She opened her eyes in wonder, recognition unfurling inside her like a flower.

"I know you."

His arms tensed. His breathing stilled.

"I recognize you." She lifted her head to study his features. Wide, clear brow. Long, straight nose. Firm, unsmiling mouth. His fair hair, long and untamed, an aureole of gold around his angel face.

"You are overwrought," he said carefully. "Under the circumstances, it is natural for you to imagine . . ."

Her breath exploded, a puff of impatience with him, with herself. "I am upset. I am not stupid. I do not ignore the evidence of my senses." Or the prompting of her heart. "It was you. In the prison."

It was you all along.

He hesitated. "Yes."

"How?"

"Aimée." Just her name, like the whisper of leaves. His green eyes were full of shadows and secrets like a forest. She could get lost in those eyes.

"Tell me," she said fiercely.

He sighed. "During the Terror, Amherst organized a secret ring to smuggle victims fleeing France across the channel. When I went to live with him, I . . . joined them."

When he was seventeen, he'd told her yesterday. Before that, he remembered nothing.

Her blood drummed in her ears. Her mind boggled, teetered on the edge of comprehension. A great void opened at her feet.

It was not possible. The man who had spirited her to safety seven years ago had been no youth of seventeen. He had appeared out of the darkness like the answer to a prayer, tearing her from her old life, setting her on a new course. The same man. This man, Lucien Hartfell. Her brain could not conceive it.

She could not hear, she could not think, over the pounding in her head. She could not remember every word overheard eight years ago in the barn, in the dark. So she listened to her heart instead.

"When you came to Moulton to court Julia, did you know you would find me here?" she asked.

Lucien held himself as stiffly as a prisoner before the Tribunal, condemned before he opened his mouth. "No. I lost . . . track of things for a while."

An unexpected tenderness unfolded inside her, an aching pity, a sorrow for something she did not understand.

When you lose your powers, your memory goes, too.

Had she recalled those words? Or imagined them? It did not signify. What mattered was that Lucien was not invulnerable after all. In his own way, he was as lost, as confused, as she.

"Then I must be grateful," she said, "to God or the Fates, who brought you to me again when I was in need."

His gaze met hers, stunned.

She smiled and stood on tiptoe to press her lips lightly to his. "I *am* grateful. For both times."

His marble face flushed. He made her a bow, oddly formal. "I am always here," he said. "If you need me."

Chapter Eight

Everyone—from Sir Walter and Lady Basing in their separate rooms on the second floor to the hall boy on his pallet by the kitchen fire— was settled for the night.

Aimée tossed on her narrow bed, unable to get comfortable. Her feet were too cold. Her sheets were too rough. An unfamiliar restlessness invaded her veins. She thanked God and Lucien that for the first time in weeks she could sleep without a chair jammed under her door, alone without fear.

Except she no longer wanted to sleep alone.

Aimée flopped onto her back and stared at the ceiling. She was a Frenchwoman. She must be practical. Lucien had rejected her once for what she was certain were very good reasons. She was not at all sure she had the courage to gamble her heart and risk her reputation only to be rejected a second time. She needed to think of her future.

A future without love? Without passion? Without Lucien.

She threw back the covers and reached for her dressing gown.

Foolishness.

Or very great wisdom.

She found she did not care.

She crept down the attic stairs. In the past, she had been grateful for each small telltale creak that might warn her of Howard climbing up the stairs. Now every betraying sound made her teeth clench and her hand squeeze the bannister tighter. She breathed easier when she reached the carpeted hallway on the second floor. Bedchamber doors stretched along either side of the corridor. Downstairs, a clock chimed. *Bing bong, bing bong.*

Christmas Eve. A night for miracles.

Aimée stopped outside Lucien's door, her bare toes curling into the carpet. Her heart thumped. Stay or go? Knock or open the door? A rap might bring Lucien. Or it could attract the attention of another guest.

She took a deep breath for courage and opened the door.

Shutting it behind her, she stood a moment on the threshold to get her bearings. A faint light filtered through the open draperies. Of course. Martin was in London. Lucien had no manservant to draw the curtains, to turn down the bed.

She peered into the shadowed recesses of the room. She could barely make out the dark bulk of Lucien's body on the bed, the pale curve of one bare shoulder rising above the covers.

Her mouth went dry with daring and desire. She wet her lips and whispered. "Lucien?"

A flare of silver light, quickly doused.

Lucien spoke out of the dark. "What is it, *mignonne?*"

The endearment—her mother's endearment, spoken in that deep, masculine voice—made her tremble. She straightened her spine. "I couldn't sleep. You said before . . . If I ever needed you . . ."

I need you. Now and again and forever, you.

She gleamed like a candle in the darkness, slim and pale and utterly desirable.

Lucien almost groaned. Her dark hair tumbled around her shoulders. Beneath her thin nightgown, her dainty feet were bare. He wanted her with a ferocity that would make her recoil, in ways that would shock her, if only she knew.

But she could never know. She had come to him for comfort, not lust. Because she could not sleep.

God help them both.

His body throbbed. Under the covers, he was naked. His dressing gown was across the room. He could not rise to get it without her seeing exactly how she affected him.

Imposing a rigid control on his muscles and his voice, he lifted the duvet, silently inviting her into his bed. They would still be separated by a sheet. He prayed it would be enough.

She drifted toward the bed. Her groping hands slid over the mattress before she slipped in beside him. The stuffing gave under their combined weight, tipping her against him. With a little sigh, she pillowed her cheek on his shoulder. Her warm breast pressed against his side. Her cool, naked feet touched his.

She was under the sheet with him.

He thought he would explode. He forced himself to lie on his back, trying to ignore the scent of her hair and the blood pooling hot at his groin.

She nestled closer, a small, confiding shift, and before he could stop himself he pressed his lips to her hair, her brow, her temple. For comfort, he told himself, and knew he lied.

She raised on one elbow and kissed him, almost missing his mouth in the dark, and he cupped the back of her head and drew her head down.

You. Her mouth was honey and home to him, sweet and welcome.

She opened to him eagerly, feeding his hunger and his soul. He rolled her onto her back, and instead of pushing him away, her arms came around his neck. Her legs parted to receive him. He was cradled against her hips, between her thighs. He rocked against her, finding his place through the fabric of her nightgown, the place that was warm and wet and waiting for him.

Madness. They had to stop. He had to stop them.

He kissed her jaw, her throat, the tender curve between neck and shoulder, and she arched under him, a taut bow. Her nipples thrust against her nightgown. It was easy, so easy, to nuzzle aside the neckline, to discover her small, firm breasts, the delicious hardness of her nipples. Her breathing quickened. Her fingers threaded through his hair as he opened his mouth and tasted. Suckled.

He lifted his head to watch her face. Her lashes drifted open. Her eyes were dark and drowsy. Trusting.

His heart lurched. "Stop me," he ordered, his voice ragged.

Her brows twitched together. "I don't want to stop you."

"You don't want this," he said, although it was harder and harder to remember why.

"I want you. I need you." She gave an impatient wriggle under him. "Lucien, *please*."

Only an angel could have resisted her. And he was no longer an angel.

Thank God.

Lucien bent his head, returning her attention to his other breast.

Thank God.

Aimée stretched and sighed as his hands and mouth moved over her, setting off showers of sparks under her skin. She was burning, melting, as he pushed up her nightgown, stroking between her thighs. She caught her breath in embarrassment—*so wet*—but he only murmured encouragement, his long fingers playing over her sensitive, secret flesh until she arched like a cat under his touch.

"All right?" he asked.

She made a sound he must have taken as assent. One finger slid inside her, then two. She rocked her hips and felt him hard against her, against her hip, between her thighs. He was hard and smooth and very large, and for a moment apprehension tightened her stomach.

"Lucien . . ."

He nudged her legs apart, pushing deeper. The pressure became pain, became sweetness and fire.

Aimée squirmed. Was it supposed to be like this? She felt stretched. Invaded.

Lucien exhaled against her hair. "Relax," he murmured. "You're ready. I'll go slow."

She moistened her lips as the burning intensified. "Wouldn't it be better to do it quickly? And get it over with?"

His laughter shook his chest, vibrating against her belly. Her own lips curved in involuntary response. And then he surged forward, his weight pinning her to the mattress as he thrust fully, finally inside her.

Oh. Her fingers dug into his shoulders as she struggled to adjust to the fact of his possession, to the feel of him hot and hard and thick inside her. It felt curious and not altogether comfortable.

One flesh, she thought, and relaxed slightly. At least it didn't hurt anymore.

He held himself still, almost as if he were waiting for something. She wriggled, trying to relieve the pressure, trying to make him move. He inhaled sharply. And then he did move, slowly, out—she felt a definite relief, mingled with disappointment—and in again.

Ah. She swallowed in sudden comprehension. They fit. It was very odd. And altogether wonderful.

Out . . . Her internal muscles clenched around him, protesting his withdrawal.

And in. She gasped.

Their eyes met. His face was hard, intent as he covered her, as he worked her, out and in. He caught a strand of her hair between his fingers, pulling it away from her lips, and she wanted to weep at the tenderness of the gesture. Slide and thrust, out and in, so deeply connected, in touch, in tune.

Out. And in. There was a rhythm to it, she realized, like riding or dancing, both awkward and fluid. He caressed her everywhere, inside and out, until she was surrounded in pleasure, encompassed in warmth. She savored the flex of his arms, his back, his buttocks, the lovely sliding sensations, out and . . .

She hitched her hips, trying to match his pace, desperate to recapture his rhythm, and he pressed deeper, reaching under her to grasp her buttocks, to tilt her for his possession. *In. There.* She jolted as he struck a different place inside her, setting off chords, sparks, cascading fountains of stars. Her heart flew, her senses soared as they moved together, beat for beat, stroke for stroke. She was panting, trembling, reaching for . . . what? Pushing her legs wide, he thrust inside her, pounded inside her, hard and fast, slick and hot. She shuddered and gripped him tight, the night pulsing and whirling around them, until at last he turned his face into her hair and jerked, convulsed, emptying himself at her center, giving her everything he was.

You, in me. Inevitable. Right.

Poignancy pierced her like a dagger. She closed her eyes at the sweetness of the pain and gave him everything she had, whispering the words against his throat. "I love you."

Silence settled over them.

Perhaps she slept then. She thought he did. She listened to his deep, even breathing as she drifted, floating on clouds of pleasure, tethered to earth and the bed by the weight of his body and the relaxed heaviness of all her limbs. The mingled scents of sweat and sex hung heavy in the room. In the quiet, in the dark, she allowed herself the indulgence of touching him the way he had touched her, intimate, exploring touches. Her muscles went lax, remembering. She would not regret this, she thought fiercely, whatever happened in the morning. She had him now, tonight.

Her fingers wandered, learning him by feel, rough and smooth, heavy and warm. She imagined him over her, inside her, and her nipples tightened and everything inside her softened and loosened in remembered delight. Her skin flushed. Until her stealthy pleasure roused him, and he woke and rolled with her, and memory and imagination gave way to need and joy.

Lucien woke alone.

The morning dawned clear and cold, the sky heavenly blue, the sun on the horizon glorious gold. Lucien swung open his window, admitting a draft that flowed over the sill and stirred the curtains of his empty bed. The dripping ice and glazed snow captured the light and threw it back in shards of rainbow brilliance.

Christmas Day, when Love was made flesh and the world made new. He had never understood until now. Until Aimée.

Because she loved him.

He could not wrap his mind around it.

Last night she had not asked him for promises or assurances. She had only given, freely, generously, out of love and with joy.

She was merely mortal, fully human. Yet she embraced love and happiness as her birthright.

How would his life be different if he learned to do the same?

He stood naked in the light of day, his skin pebbling with cold, his blood on fire. He couldn't. Not without her to show him the way. He needed Aimée, all of her, her delicate body and bold heart, her practical mind and generous spirit.

But what did he have to offer in return?

His hand clenched on the windowsill.

In the gray, cold hours before dawn, he had stirred, his body protesting the loss of her warmth as Aimée had slipped from his bed. He lay enthralled, entranced by the curve of her naked buttocks as she stooped to retrieve her nightgown from the floor.

"Where are you going?"

She had turned to smile at him, her eyes liquid. His heart had clenched painfully in his chest. "I must return to my room before the servants are up."

"Let me go with you."

She shook her head, one dark lock falling forward to curl around her perfect breast. "It is not necessary. Or wise."

"I must do something for you."

Mischief lit her face. "But you have. And I am grateful. For both times."

She'd said the same thing once before, he remembered. *I must be grateful to God or the Fates, who brought you to me again when I was in need.*

Lucien expelled his breath in a frosty cloud. If he had not Fallen, would he have found her again? Could he have loved her as a man loves a woman?

And what did it mean, now that he did?

The sun edged over the trees, making the snow sparkle. The rest of the house party would sleep late today in preparation for the ball tonight. But in the village, the church bells pealed and tolled, their bright notes shaking the air, calling the faithful to service.

Lucien stared out at the bright morning, considering the future. Facing facts. Aimée was of noble birth. He had taken her virginity. He could see only one course of action open to him now.

He had to go.

Aimée did not encounter Lucien at all the following morning. She walked alone to church before plunging into the hundred and one last-minute preparations for Christmas dinner and the ball that would follow, approving the pudding and the table setting, supervising the placement of the musicians and card tables, settling the servants' disputes.

But through it all, she carried Lucien with her, a secret joy hugged to her heart, a trembling anticipation.

Tonight was the ball. She would see him. Dance with him. And then . . .

But she refused to think of then. Now must be enough. Now, and the memory of last night.

Her cheeks were flushed as she tapped on the door of Julia's room to help her cousin dress for dinner.

The door popped open. Julia grabbed both Aimée's hands and whisked her into the room.

"What do you think?" Julia demanded with a little twirl.

Aimée's mouth dropped open. "I think . . ." She didn't know what to think.

Julia shook her golden curls, only partially confined by an enormous mobcap topped by an absurd green bow. Her skirts were bright green satin with the wide side panniers that had gone out of fashion ten years ago, her small waist bound by a white apron she must have borrowed from one of the house maids.

"I'm Judy." Julia picked up one of little Lottie's dolls and waved it about by the neck. "From Punch and Judy."

Aimée felt her mouth forming a smile. "I can see that. But . . ."

Her cousin's eyes were bright, her face tinged with color. "Tom is going as Punch."

"Oh." Aimée drew in her breath. "*Oh.*"

Her knees felt weak. She sank on the edge of the bed.

Julia met her gaze. "I know. This Christmas has not turned out at all the way I imagined. First Harriet falling in the pond—not that I blame you for that, whatever Susan says—and then Susan spending all her time in the nursery, which is most unlike her, and then Howard taking to his room so suddenly. Not that I mind about Howard so much. And then the Misses Whitmore came to call with Tom, and I was saying how I wished that Tom could be my brother, because he's always sort of *there*, you know, and he said in this gruff voice that it was a very good thing he was *not.* My brother, I mean. And then . . ." Her blush deepened. "And then . . . Well, I am dancing the opening set with Tom. And the supper dance, too."

Inside Aimée, something unfurled and expanded like wings. "But what about . . ."

"My costume? You can have it."

"Mr. Hartfell," Aimée said gently.

"You can have him, too. Oh . . ." Julia frowned. "Except he's not here anymore."

Aimée's heart tripped. She was glad she was sitting down. "Not here?"

"He departed for Fair Hill before breakfast this morning. In a very great hurry, Mama said, leaving all his things behind. I expect his servant will return to pack them."

Aimée barely heard. Her brain was numb. Her face felt frozen. "This morning."

After she had gone to his room. After she had told him she loved him.

"Are you disappointed? I wondered if perhaps you fancied him. Tom said Hartfell fancied you." Julia's pretty face creased. "But I suppose he couldn't have, could he, if he's gone."

"No." Aimée forced the word through stiff lips. "I suppose he couldn't."

He had not said he loved her, she reminded herself. The omission had barely registered at the time. She had *felt* his love in every touch, with every breath, flooding her soul, imprinted on her flesh.

The room blurred with rainbow colors. She blinked fiercely. She had been very foolish, it seemed.

"Never mind," Julia said kindly. "If Hartfell doesn't like you, you'll find another man who will. There will be plenty to choose from at the ball tonight."

"I'm not going to the ball," Aimée said.

How could she dance when her heart was breaking?

"Oh, but you must." Julia swooped and enveloped her in a scented hug. "I'm so happy, Amy," she whispered. "I want you to be happy, too."

Aimée closed her eyes and leaned her head against Julia's shoulder, overwhelmed by the genuine affection in her cousin's embrace.

She was loved, after all.

Not by the man she longed for. Not in the way she'd believed.

But just because her heart was broken didn't mean her life was over. Life, after all, was a gift. Lucien had taught her that. What she made of it was up to her.

Her throat ached. Her eyes burned.

If only it didn't hurt so much.

Aimée teetered on the stairs of the great hall, off balance in her jewel trimmed heels and glittering wings.

It had required the better part of two hours and the best efforts of the second housemaid to lace her into Julia's discarded costume. Aimée had sent her regrets for dinner, aware that Lady Basing would be upset at having her table arrangements disturbed. But Aimée had needed time to compose her face and her feelings.

Anyway, she had no appetite.

She shivered as she edged down the staircase. Outside the windows, snow was falling, white on black. Tonight the house would be filled to the rafters with stranded guests.

The weather did not seem to have dampened anyone's spirits. Strains of music drifted into the hall along with the hum of conversation and occasional bursts of laughter.

Carriage wheels crunched on the gravel outside. Sir Walter and Lady Basing had already joined their guests in the ballroom. But it appeared Aimée was not the last arrival, after all.

She hovered like a butterfly on the stairs, uncertain whether to retreat or step forward to welcome the last guest.

The footmen hurried forward to fling open the door. Cold air swirled. Candles flickered. The butler bowed low.

Two guests. Two men, one a distinguished looking stranger in a many-caped coat that made him look exceptionally broad and tall.

And the other . . .

Her heart froze. Her hand tightened on the bannister.

The other man removed his hat to knock snow from the brim. His thick gold hair gleamed in the glow of many candles. His eyes were as green as hope, as spring.

Perhaps she made some sound. She did not know.

He looked up and saw her, and her poor, ice-encrusted heart began to beat again.

The other man was Lucien.

To Lucien, she looked like an angel, a miracle spun of air and light.

He wanted to snatch her up and run up with the stairs with her, to carry her to his room and tumble her onto his bed. He wanted to untie every silver ribbon, loosen every lace, uncover every delicious bit of flesh, every hint of pink, every inch of white.

But of course if he did those things, it would defeat the purpose of his journey.

Besides, Aimée might object. It had occurred to him on the long carriage ride back, as his trip met with delay after delay, that he might have explained to her why he was going. But he'd had no guarantee of success then. He'd wanted to come to her without conditions or reservations.

He bounded up the steps and took her hand. She wore no gloves—part of her costume, he assumed. Her fingers were cool and slight and trembled in his grasp.

Holding her gaze, he lifted her hand to his lips.

Her eyes widened as he kissed her knuckles. "You are late," she observed.

Her admonition made him smile. "Yes. I'm sorry."

Still holding her hand, he walked with her down the stairs and led her to his companion. "My lord," Lucien said proudly, "I have the honor of presenting Lady Aimée Blanchard. My love, this is the Earl of Amherst."

Aimée shivered in confusion and joy and the draft from the door. Lucien had brought the earl here? What did it mean?

Amherst bowed. "I trust Lady Basing will pardon my instrusion."

Aimee pulled herself together enough to manage a curtsy. "My cousin will be honored, my lord."

An understatement. Lady Basing would be beside herself at snagging the Earl of Amherst's attendance at her Christmas ball.

"The honor is mine," Amherst said politely. His eyes gleamed. "Hartfell is not the only one who struggles with impatience, it seems. I could not wait to meet the lady who has reconciled him to himself. And to me."

Aimée's eyes widened. Her head whirled.

Lucien squeezed her hand, his grip almost painful. "Speaking of impatience, my lord . . ."

"Yes, yes." The earl waved them away. "Go dance with the girl while I make my apologies to our hostess."

Aimée danced as if her feet, not her dress, had wings. Because it was Christmas, and the ballroom was alight with candles, and her heart was burning with love and happiness. Because Lucien had called her his love. Because tonight, when all the guests were gone or settled in borrowed beds, she would find her way back down the stairs to his room and . . .

"You were right," Lucien said as the movement of the dance brought them back together.

She dragged her attention from his mouth, struggling to focus on what he was saying.

"About Amherst," he provided helpfully, a glint in his eyes that suggested he knew exactly what she was thinking. "Once I informed him I was actually funding another sort of rescue operation, all was forgiven." His smile turned wry. "Of course, first he tore a strip off me for being too damn stiff-necked to tell him the truth to begin with. I told him he had you to thank for bringing me to my senses."

She didn't know where to look or what to say. "I am glad you have made your peace with him."

Family was important.

"So am I." Their eyes met. "I could not speak to you until I had settled matters with him," Lucien said quietly.

Her heart stumbled and then soared. "I thought you had left me," she whispered.

Lucien clasped her hands in the figures of the dance. His lips quirked ruefully. "You have so little faith in me, then?"

"Perhaps it was my own judgment I did not trust." Her hands held his a little tighter. "I am glad you are back."

"I must go away again soon. Amherst has given me management of his estate at Leyburn," he explained in response to her inquiring look. "I want you to go with me. As my wife."

Joy spread through her. The musicians had stopped playing, but inside her soul was singing.

"But . . . You could have any woman. Especially now that you no longer need to marry for money," she added pointedly.

He grinned. "But I don't want any other woman. Only you, *mignonne*." His face turned suddenly serious. "It's always been you."

Ignoring the couples around them leaving the dance floor, he knelt and took both her hands in his.

Aimée held her breath. With part of her mind, she was conscious of the whispers flying around the ballroom, of Lady Basing's frown and Julia's delighted grin, of the Earl of Amherst's sardonic gaze.

But with all of her heart, she was aware of Lucien kneeling before her, his hands shaking and his eyes steady on hers.

"I need you, Aimée. I love you. I thank God for every choice or chance or circumstance that brought you to me." He kissed her hands and then her wrists and then the centers of her palms. She curled her fingers, holding happiness in her hands, as he looked up again. "You said once I had saved you. But in truth, I need you to save me. Will you marry me?"

She smiled down at him through a rainbow of tears, her heart overflowing with love and certainty. "But of course I will, *mon ange*." *My angel*. "We will save each other."

And she stooped and kissed him.

First Light

KIMBERLY FROST

Acknowledgments

Many thanks to my friend David Mohan, for always finding the time to read and provide feedback on my stories. I'm grateful also to my agent, Elizabeth Winick Rubinstein, for all that she does in support of my writing career. And special thanks to my editor, Leis Pederson, who invited me to write a novella to introduce readers to my Etherlin series and who provided extremely valuable suggestions during the conception and revision of this story.

Chapter One

Snow fell through rising steam. Laughter and music from the New Year's Eve celebration drifted from the house to the deck where Kate Devane, submerged to the shoulders in her hot tub, drank a Brandy Alexander and watched a shooting star skid across the Colorado sky.

The thunk of a rock hitting the deck drew her gaze. She glanced at the smooth undisturbed mounds of snow and then up at the roof. Had it rolled from there? The night's stillness seemed otherwise undisturbed. She rose and climbed from the water. She walked to the fallen object and crouched close. *Not a rock.* There were red drops splattered like a sunburst around an antique ring that was battered and crudely made. An ancient coin formed the ring's top.

She peered into the dark sky, finding only stars and a sliver of moon. She lifted the ring, examining the dark brown metal dotted with crimson blood. This ring had a story, and she wanted to know it, just as she wanted to unravel all the world's mysteries. She held the ring between her palms for a moment before trying it on. Sized for a man, it fit loosely on her left thumb, which tingled within its cool embrace.

Wind—because what else could it have been?—rustled the evergreens, and snow that had rested on the branches fell heavily to the ground. She followed the line of the deck rail, trying to see around the trees.

She walked to the steps. Muzzy-headed from too many New Year's toasts, it took a few extra moments to don her ski boots and jacket. Steadying herself with the rail, she descended and wove through the trees. The snow shimmered like powdered sugar. With the house noise muted, she heard breathing. If she'd been thinking clearly, she would've slowed, but the night contained a secret and she wanted to share in it.

She thought him a boy at first. Panting, he rested on one knee like a knight about to be christened. When he looked up, she realized her mistake. The pale-as-moonlight hair made him look young, but his eyes were knowing. His face was so beautiful it reminded her briefly of Alissa the famous ice blond muse with whom Kate worked for inspiration. For a confused moment, Kate wondered where her camera was. She wanted to capture him the way he looked in the snow. Then she wondered what party he'd wandered away from and where he'd left his shirt.

Dazedly, her gaze traveled lower, and she saw that blood flowed lavishly over his marble white skin from a gash in his side. Her eyes widened, her heart kicking into a pounding rhythm.

"My God. You're bleeding," she said. "Come on. Come to my house, and I'll call an ambulance." Her eyes darted side to side, looking for signs of trouble that might want to put a large gash in her, too.

When she glanced back at the man, his smile was almost coy. His right hand caught her left one and raised it toward him, eyeing her thumb.

"Is it your ring? What happened to you?" she asked. When he didn't answer, she added, "Were you at the Andersons' party?" She gazed in the direction of her nearest neighbor's house.

He moved with stunning speed, rising and spinning her so she faced away from him. From behind her, his right arm held her waist, his left pressed across her collarbone. She felt something prick her skin and realized that his left hand held a knife, the blade lying against the column of her throat. Her coat gaped open, exposing her skin. Ears buzzing, she tried to move.

From between the trees, a second man appeared in front of her. He was stunning in a different way from the first. His face lacked any traces of feminine beauty but was no less compelling. The moonlight shone like a spotlight on his bronze skin and on the damp golden brown waves skimming his shoulders. He, too, was bare-chested and bloody, with a dagger in hand, but he was taller and broader than the man at her back.

The lighter one pressed his hips against her bottom. Through the thin material of her swimsuit, his erection probed her. Startled, she jerked forward.

Ugh! What the hell?

"Let go of me," she snapped, trying to squirm free as he whispered foreign words in her ear. "I *said* let go of me, you creep!"

The bronze one narrowed gold-flecked brown eyes and gave a sharp jerk of his head at the one behind her. The wrist over her collarbone slid down slowly toward her chest, the tip of the dagger snagging and cutting her bikini strap. The blade peeled the material away from her breast.

She cursed, struggling to escape, and the knife nicked her skin. The slice stung, then burned. She froze and sucked in a breath.

The bronze one scowled and clenched his jaw, his liquid brown eyes capturing her gaze. "He thinks to taunt me with your naked beauty, but no distraction will prevent me from avenging every injury he visits upon you and on those who came before."

Her jaw dropped. "What? I don't know what's going on, but I don't want to be part of it," she said.

The bronze one moved too fast for her eyes to follow, but suddenly they were fighting and she was caught between them, pinned in place by their battling bodies. She could do nothing, not even breathe.

"Stop!" she screamed and sat bolt upright. Panting and shaken, her mind raced.

A damn dream, she realized. Just a nightmare!

Her eyes darted around the room, finding the familiar . . . her Christmas tree strung with white lights and covered with plump bulbs, the wrapped gifts beneath it, the scent of gingerbread and vanilla icing.

Harry Connick Jr. crooned carols, and an empty wineglass sat next to the stack of photographs she'd been reviewing for inclusion in the article she'd been working on. The door to the deck was closed, bolted. She wore a navy nightshirt and thick socks, not a wet bikini.

Her galloping heart faltered, and she pushed back her sweat-dampened hair.

"More dreams of him and that ring," she murmured, trying to shake off a sense of foreboding as her heart churned.

The dreams are getting closer together. She rubbed her arms.

In college, she'd found an antique ring while walking through a deserted section of campus. She'd felt compelled to slide the crude ring on, and it had circled her thumb possessively as she studied it. The ring's raised feature had been a coin capturing the image of a long-dead Roman emperor, and there'd been a deep scratch scoring the coin's face, as if someone had tried to X the emperor out.

Only after she'd stared for a long time did the realization dawn that the grit on the ring wasn't dirt. It was dried blood. She'd taken the ring off, but she couldn't bring herself to simply turn it in to campus security's Lost and Found collection.

Being a journalism major, she'd investigated, trying to determine how the ring had been lost and by whom. There had been no recent fights or assaults, no missing persons, and no inquiries or postings about a lost ring.

"It's like this ring fell from the sky," she'd told a friend, and the image stuck. Kate pictured it falling and landing with a thunk. She saw the fresh blood on its surface explode outward into tiny flecks as it struck the ground. The vision was so vivid that at moments she could almost believe she'd seen the ring fall rather than having found it on the ground while walking.

Then, three days after she'd discovered the ring, it disappeared from her dorm room and she'd begun dreaming about the bronze-skinned man. Often she dreamed of him standing on rooftops or swooping through the air. He either wore the ring or dropped it.

Sometimes in her dreams, he wasn't alone; she was in his arms. They kissed in places she'd never been. And in one deeply erotic dream, he made love to her on a mountain ridge under an amber sky.

That dream left her twisted in her sheets, aching for him, and she woke breathless.

Recently, the dreams had taken a darker turn. There were scenes of him fighting with another man, the one with white-blond hair and alabaster skin. She was often caught in the middle. *What the hell does it all mean?* she wondered.

The memories of her dreams of the bronze man haunted her by day and chased her by night. Over the years, she'd tried to put a name to his face. She'd looked through thousands of student photos and had asked questions on message boards and alumni loops. No leads ever panned out. The man was a ghost. A ghost who lived in her subconscious and tantalized her. A mystery that could not be solved, but would not fade. For someone like Kate, it was torture.

She'd begun to imagine that the ring had some sort of supernatural power, which initially had seemed ridiculous, but then she'd wondered, *Why not?* Magic existed. Muses and vampires proved that—although the vampires were all gone now, and the magic wielded by the muses was subtle and led to great things like Pulitzer Prizes rather than to unsettling recurring dreams that always left her wanting more. More information. And more of him.

Determined to photograph the sunrise from a new vantage, Kate washed down a breakfast taco with milk and pulled on her ski jacket. She adjusted her camera strap and hung it from her neck, then clicked her boots closed. She took a deep breath as she stepped out onto the deck, bracing herself. The cold clean air startled her lungs in the best possible way.

Once on her skis, she set out at a brisk pace, thinking about the upcoming night. As an aspirant—a human chosen to receive muse attention and magic—she would attend the muses' exclusive holiday party. It was an invitation coveted by most of the world, and she'd been excited about it for months. This was her chance to celebrate her and Alissa's accomplishments. With Alissa's help, Kate had won awards and climbed to the top of her profession in seven short years.

Dawn's first light emerged, and Kate slowed to a stop. She raised her camera and trained the lens in different directions. So often, she chose the mountains for a backdrop, but this morning she wanted the endless expanse of snow stretched over what in summer was a field of yellow wildflowers.

She popped out of her skis and lowered herself to rest her knee on the trail. The contours of the drifted snow were even more breathtaking from the new angle. Finding her shot, she waited for stronger light and saw a beam of it. She chased it with her camera, centering it within the frame. As her finger depressed the button, she paused. Something disturbed the snow's perfect lines. She zoomed in, and her breath caught when she realized it was a hand, pale and unmoving.

She shuddered, lowering her camera. Shocked, a part of her wanted to return home and call the police, but the investigative reporter within her moved of its own accord. She dropped the camera against her chest, not even bothering to cover the lens. She snapped her boots back into her skis and pointed them off the trail.

Her legs glided back and forth in a steady rhythm; she was determined to learn who was dead and half buried in the snow.

When she was only a few feet away, she noticed that there were no tracks around the body. She came to a stop next to the wintry crater that held him. The folds of snow cradled him like billowing fabric.

"Oh my God," she said, forgetting to breathe when she realized who it was.

No!

Frosted strands of brown hair clung to his neck and shoulders. Her body trembled.

It can't be.

No, this is wrong—he can't be dead, she thought frantically, staring at his handsome lifeless face. Her heart squeezed tight in her chest. *All those dreams . . . all those moments . . . I was supposed to meet him, not find his body.*

Her eyes misted. *I was supposed to have . . . What?* A violent passion that consumed her? Something that would rival her love for her work? *Yes.* She had wanted something epic with this man.

Wait! This—this is a dream. It's a nightmare! she thought desperately. With trembling fingers she touched his outstretched hand, finding it cool as frost.

His hand twitched.

She gasped, recoiling in shock, then dropped to her knees next to him. He opened his eyes, the dark hazel reflecting the light. They sharpened, focusing on her. As he began to move, his skin seemed to visibly warm, color emerging.

Wait. What? she thought, her initial anxiety easing to relief but also confusion. What was happening?

"It's freezing out here," she mumbled. "Are you . . . Can you stand?"

He moved with precision and strength, coming to his feet without any evidence of stiffness or pain. He cleared his throat.

"What happened to you?" She studied his odd clothes. Thin boots, a loose linen shirt, and pants that laced in the front as if he were considering a life of piracy on the high seas. Had he been in some Christmas pageant before stopping in the field?

He put a hand to the back of his head and rubbed it. His fingers came away wet with melted snow. He looked around.

"What's your name?" she asked.

He seemed perplexed. Could he be foreign?

"Do you speak English?"

"Yes, I understand you," he said, squinting at the horizon.

"Tell me your name."

He paused, then said, "I would if I knew it."

Her brows rose. "What do you mean?"

"I don't remember . . . anything."

Amnesia? Truly? The number of people with complete amnesia was infinitesimally small. She looked at the snow where he'd been lying. There was no blood. He didn't look bruised or battered. It made no sense.

It has to be a dream. But I never realize I'm dreaming in the midst of one. And during a dream, I never remember the other dreams I've had of him.

She looked around, confused and unsettled.

I feel awake.

She pinched herself, wincing at the pain. *That hurt. So I must be awake, right? But just how reliable is a pinch at distinguishing reality from dreams? Has anyone really studied pinch-pain accuracy with regard to consciousness?*

"I don't understand this," she murmured. He stepped close, and a rush of heat coursed through her. She sucked in a breath, clenching her fists to steady herself.

"Are you unwell?" he asked.

I'm warm. In the dreams, I never notice the temperature. Not the frigid air and snow. Not the heat from the hot tub. She'd realized that fact once upon waking. Walking through snow or wrapped in his muscled arms, she never felt the temperature.

This . . . is real.

"I'm not sure," she mumbled in response to his question about whether she was all right. No matter how intimate they'd been in dreams, he was still a stranger, but standing so close to him triggered thoughts of the way he'd been in some of those dreams, the way he'd made her body tighten and bow under his touch.

She hesitated, exhaling a sigh, then took a step back. And another.

He didn't pursue her. He remained still as a statue. Preternaturally still, it seemed to her.

She glanced back to where he'd lain. There were no tracks besides her own leading to that spot. It was as if he'd been there for a long time, and the snow had drifted around him. Or as if he'd fallen into the snow from the sky. She glanced up reflexively, then shook her head. There was nothing around for him to have fallen from. If he'd dropped from a helicopter or small plane, he would've been injured. Instead he looked . . . perfect.

And how had he recovered from being unconscious in the snow? He'd looked frozen—had been frozen—skin cold, body stiff. One possible explanation dawned.

Oh, God! She stiffened. *He can't be one of them.*

Surviving the fall from an aircraft and an icy sleep could make him a ventala. The ventala, human-vampire half-breeds, were violent, unpredictable, and difficult to kill, but often incredibly attractive. It might also explain the way he invaded her dreams.

"I'd like to remove these wet clothes and dry myself," he said.

Drawn in by the idea of him stripping, she shivered. If he was ventala, she needed to get away from him, but she couldn't make herself so much as take another step back.

"Which direction to the nearest dwellings?" he asked.

Dwellings? What's up with the way he talks?

"The closest houses are that way," she said.

He glanced where she'd pointed, then back at her face. "It's not safe here. Why are you traveling alone, girl?"

That stopped her. "Girl?" she echoed skeptically. "I'm a Pulitzer Prize–winning journalist."

His expression was puzzled and innocent, which made her frown. Surely he'd heard of the Pulitzer Prize.

He stretched his back. "Come," he said, walking on her tracks toward the trail.

What the hell? He's got amnesia. Shouldn't he be the one following me?

Bronze didn't hesitate, however. He struck out with strides that ate the ground. She skied after him until she was a few feet behind and tried not to notice the way the light gilded his hair.

He glanced over his shoulder. "You asked my name. That means we haven't met before, but you seem familiar. Are we from the same village? Perhaps we've seen each other, but haven't been introduced?"

"Not exactly," she said, not prepared to explain about the dreams. As they followed the curve where the trail meandered through the woods, a flash of light glinted off his hand.

"Hang on a minute."

He stopped and turned. "Yes?"

She reached for his right hand where he wore a ring on his fourth finger. His skin blazed with heat now, the warmth as sensual as a touch caressing her. She shivered and gripped his hand tighter, battling the urge to step forward and press her entire body against his.

There is no way he's just human.

She shook her head, fighting to clear the fog of attraction. He watched her reaction to him with deep interest, making her blush self-consciously.

Get a grip, Kate! He could be a bloodthirsty monster. Are you going to be a simpering little victim who plays right into his fangs? You have a goddamned Pulitzer for investigative reporting. Act like it!

She cleared her throat, then took a deep breath, her muscles locking with resolve. She looked over the antique ring—the exact one that had been taken from her dorm room.

"How do you have this?" she mumbled.

Pulling his hand from her grip, he raised it to examine the ring. "As I've already said, I can't remember."

The ring had to have some larger significance.

"I had this ring years ago, and it went missing."

He tipped his head up as though he'd consult the sky on the matter, but instead of arguing or explaining, he cocked his head like an animal listening for predators—or prey.

"Journalist," he said, grabbing her arms and turning her toward the trail. "Hurry home."

"What? What's going on?" she asked, giving him points for not calling her *girl.*

"Go," he yelled.

Then she saw a trio of figures threading their way through the trees. They were dressed in black and carried sickle-shaped blades like modern-day grim reapers. They moved fast, and she wasn't sure she'd be able to get past them quickly enough. Her heart pounded when she saw their faces, which were pulled into rictus smiles, exposing fangs. *They* were definitely ventala.

She pumped her legs back and forth, skiing as fast as she could. Would she reach her house before the ventala caught them? It didn't seem likely, but she had to try, and if she could just get out of the woods, the ventala would be disadvantaged by the morning light.

A shout of pain made her slow and look back. Bronze had not fled with her. From where he stood now, he must have rushed into the trees to face them.

One of the ventala was down. She was relieved to see that Bronze looked unhurt—so far. They swung their blades, and all of them moved in a blur of speed. He knocked another down and grabbed his dagger. Slicing in stunning arcs, Bronze tested the blade on them with devastating results. Then, with a few swift downward thrusts behind their left collarbones, he killed them one by one.

Bronze lowered himself to a knee, shoved the dagger into the snowy ground, and hung his head, whispering. Perched on her skis, she remained frozen, staring at him while he rose, reclaimed the dagger, and returned to the trail. Blood and melted snow dripped from the dagger tip like a deadly faucet.

"You waited," he said.

It took her a moment to find her voice. All she managed was, "I did."

He shook his head, walking briskly. "You should not have stopped when I told you to go on."

She shrugged. "I'm one of those people who always has to know how things turn out."

He quirked a brow but didn't pursue the discussion, which left her feeling vaguely dissatisfied. She wanted him to be interested in her life and her work. In some of the dreams, there'd been a profound connection between them. At the moment, he didn't even seem attracted to her, which was irritating because the mountain-ridge dream had always been so vivid and . . . satisfying. Her nipples tingled, and she glanced away to hide her flush.

His current indifference was more like his attitude in the nightmares. She bit the inside of her cheek, trying to focus her concentration away from anything erotic.

"So," he said, wiping the blade on his pant leg. "I don't know who I am, but I think I know what I am. I must be a soldier."

"I think you're more than a soldier. Pull your lips back. Show me your teeth."

"Why?"

"I want to see if you're a ventala."

"Ventala," he said. "What's that?"

She blinked. "Ventala. Part human. Part vampire." When he didn't respond, she added, "You know, vampires bred with humans to try to save themselves from extermination."

He stared at her blankly.

"After the mutation. The bat plague? The Vampire Rising?"

"Before my time, I suppose," he said.

"It's before a lot of people's times. It happened in the 1950s. But everyone knows about it. Everyone. All over the world. Surely, you must remember something! Even people with amnesia know some basic things about the planet."

He shrugged. "Apparently, not always."

Who the hell was he that he didn't know about the vampire extermination? "What were you doing after you killed those ventala? You knelt and lowered your head like you were—"

"I was offering thanks."

"To God?"

"Of course, who else? I was grateful for my victory. It seemed right to say so."

"That definitely doesn't seem ventala-like, but just to be sure, show me your teeth."

He retracted his lips. All his teeth were perfectly normal, not a fang among them. Relief flooded through her with confusion on its heels.

"Then what are you?" she murmured. "Human beings don't move the way you do. And why were those ventala lying in wait for you? There's so much to figure out, and I'm not sure we have a lot of time. Ventala usually sleep during the day, but they came for you despite the sunrise." She paused. "Come nightfall, they may come out in force."

"Journalist, what's your name?"

She smiled. "Kate."

"Kate," he repeated as if tasting the word. He nodded. "It's kind of you to offer me aid. It speaks well of your character, but you're a young woman. I wouldn't enlist your help."

Was he seriously going to discount her ability to help him because she was female? All the times she'd had to fight the condescension of her older male colleagues came roaring back.

"Perhaps your father or brothers would—"

"My father and brother live in Vermont, which is about two thousand miles away, and when it comes to investigating something and connecting the dots, there's no one better than me."

"No one?" he asked. "I suspect you're overconfident."

"You know what?" she said. "You're right. Why don't you knock on some doors and find some random men to help you? See how that works out." She skied past him, and as she emerged from the forest, the houses popped into view.

"Ah, good. Shelter," he said, keeping pace with her.

"Yes, my shelter. My house that I own *alone*. A concept that may be too much for you to get your caveman head around. Who raised you? The Taliban?"

His brows rose. "I'm not sure who that is, but you're obviously angry. I meant no offense, Kate, but for a young woman to be so sure of herself is surprising."

"You're unbelievable." She popped her skis off and snatched them up.

He frowned. "Could you have fought those men and survived?"

"Nope."

"Then what is offensive about me suggesting that I'm a dangerous person for you to be around? I have a feeling that—"

"Save it," she said, stomping up the deck steps. She propped her skis and poles against the house and took off her boots.

Walking inside, she slammed the door behind her. By the time she got to the kitchen counter, her heart was pounding. She'd finally met the bronze guy from her dreams, and he turned out to be a clueless sexist. Well, she wasn't going to try to prove her worth to anyone. She'd already done that many painful times before.

What a disappointment he was. She'd expected him to be . . .

what? *More.* Definitely more. Maybe even her soul mate. Admitting that to herself made her feel worse.

She shook her head. How could her subconscious have wasted hundreds of nights on him? Those recurring dreams had made her invest tons of waking hours on the search for his identity.

Whatever, she thought, yanking off her jacket and throwing it on the couch. She couldn't change the past, but she could control the present. She just wouldn't waste any more time on him.

Chapter Two

Despite her intention to stop thinking about him, Kate's mind ran circles around the mystery of the bronze man. While showering, she considered where he might have come from. Many of her theories, though, were pretty unlikely unless her life had become a comic book.

Dressed in a turtleneck, jeans, and warm socks, she returned to the ground floor, expecting him to be gone. He should have wandered to one of her neighbors' houses to knock on the door for help. Instead, he was huddled in a deck chair.

You were supposed to leave, so I wouldn't be tempted to talk to you again.

Staring out the window, she couldn't prevent the surge of compassion that rose up, nor the small spike of pleasure that came from finding him still within reach.

Don't even think about it! Just because that mouth was made for kissing doesn't mean you want the rest of the package that goes with it.

She went to the guest room, grabbed a towel and blanket, and strode to the door. Pulling it open, she said, "What are you doing?"

"I expect that's fairly obvious."

She scowled, thrusting the bundle toward him. "Here."

He rose and took it. "This is all the hospitality you offer after I saved your life?" he asked. "When I said you were of good character, Kate, I believe I judged you prematurely."

"I doubt you saved my life. They were coming for you, not me," she said, feigning confidence. Actually, those ventala might have been after her, too. They were a vengeful breed, and if they were nostalgic for their vampire sires, they might feel they had reason to want her dead, considering that the biggest story of her career had uncovered a nest of vampires who were later executed.

He rubbed the towel over his head and wrapped the blanket around his shoulders.

"I'll call an ambulance. The hospital can treat you for your amnesia, and they can call the police who will check the missing persons database and help you figure out who you are. Until then, they'll make sure you're taken to a public shelter. One with central heating and other important features."

"No," he said, sitting back down in the chair.

"What do you mean *no*? You can't stay outside. You'll freeze to death."

He wrapped the blanket tighter, tipping his chin down so all of his neck was covered.

"Did you hear me?"

"I will remain here," he said stubbornly.

"Why?"

"Because I'm not ready to leave yet." He clenched his jaws and then glanced at her. "And before you ask, I don't know why."

She threw her arms up in exasperation, stepped back into the house, and closed the door, but she didn't walk away. She rested her palms on the doorframe, leaning against it.

"What are you going to do?" she murmured. "Leave him out there until he turns into a Popsicle?"

She sighed and swung the door open. "Come inside," she said.

As he passed the threshold, he blinked and said, "Your home is palatial."

"Not really," she said, but tried to see it with fresh eyes. The open floor plan stretched from back door to front, encompassing the living room, dining room, and kitchen. The ceilings soared two and a half stories. It was a lot of space for a solitary resident, but plenty of career women lived alone and invested in real estate.

He rolled his shoulders and twisted his back.

"I've noticed you keep stretching. Are you stiff?"

"My back aches. I may have injured it."

"I can drive you to the hospital."

"I don't think the damage is serious. Could I wash and hang my clothes to dry?"

Her eyes widened. "I'd love to know what cave you've been living in," she said, grabbing his forearm and leading him to the guest bathroom.

Just inside the door, he stared at the shower. "I thought of a basin of warm water, but this is familiar, too. I stand inside and hot water rains down," he said, shrugging his brows at her, clearly pleased with himself for remembering something.

"Right," she said, putting her hands on her hips. "Congratulations. You remember how to take a shower."

He hauled his shirt over his head, and she should have turned but didn't. He was incredibly well built. His smooth lines conjured a feeling that he should've been on a pedestal, like a statue or a sports car at an auto show. Though sleek and perfectly designed, he had one imperfection. A round quarter-sized scar on the left side of his chest. The puckered skin was lighter than the rest that surrounded it. She stepped forward to examine the mark, but he cleared his throat, making her look up.

"Kate," he said in a tone of voice that was both amused and stern. "I'm a strange man and clearly dangerous. Should you be this close to me while I undress?"

"You kill ventala. There's not a single door in the house that you couldn't come through if you wanted to. Actually, you probably could have kicked open the back door, too."

He smiled, which turned his handsome face glorious. Things low in her belly tightened, and she fought not to reach for him. Her fingers wanted to touch. Her mouth wanted to taste. Was his overwhelming appeal magical? If not ventala, could he be a male descendant of the muses?

"I assume that smile means you realized you could've broken the door open," she said.

"I did."

"Were you tempted to force your way in?"

"A little," he admitted. "It's very cold out there."

"And yet you restrained yourself. Well done."

He raised his brows. "You suspect it was a struggle for me?"

"I honestly don't know." In her nightmares, despite the blade against her throat, he didn't try to reason with his enemy, didn't try to get her out from between them. He lunged into battle, oblivious to whether she would be injured. That thought sobered her. She turned, holding her hand out to the side. "Give me your clothes. I'll take care of them for you."

A moment later, she had them, such as they were. She exited without looking back and heard the water jets as she closed the door.

At the washing machine, she glanced over his clothes. No underwear? And what was with the uneven stitching? Were they hand-sewn? There were no care tags inside, and the fabric was rough. She pictured him buying them at a bazaar in a third-world country. Maybe he had been a soldier. Perhaps stationed in the Middle East? But that didn't explain why he wasn't dressed for Colorado weather now.

In the kitchen, she warmed corn chowder and toasted thick slices of buttered French bread in the oven. In between preparing lunch, she checked the Boulder Police Department's online blotter. The only local missing person report was of an elderly woman who'd wandered away from a nursing home.

After she fed him, Kate would drive her mystery guest to the police department to start the formal process of finding out who he was.

"Kate," he said, rushing into the room with a towel barely fastened around his hips. Muscles deep inside her contracted. Wet and nearly naked, he looked . . . edible.

Then he flashed a smile, and his sudden exuberance was like champagne and strawberries, intoxicating her, curving her lips into a smile.

"Kate," he repeated, tapping the counter with his palm.

"Yes?"

"What part of the Roman Empire is this?"

She raised her brows and set her spatula on the stove. "No part. There is no Roman Empire anymore."

"Defeated? How long ago?"

"Around fifteen hundred years ago."

"That long," he mused, taking a step back. "Apparently I'm very good at what I do."

"And what is that?"

Triumphant as a conquering hero, he grinned. "I'm a time traveler."

Chapter Three

"There's nothing as satisfying as breaking the law," Tamberi said, smirking.

Her brother, Cato, laughed in agreement.

Dark as a womb, the deep, damp cave sheltered bats, rats, and a delicious secret. It was about to become a vortex of forbidden magic.

"Don't go outside the lines," Tamberi said crossly.

"What are we? Five?" Cato asked, rolling his eyes.

"You paint like you're five," she said, dipping her brush into the small bowl of blood. She pressed the black bristles against the side of the bowl, allowing the excess to run down into the crimson pool.

"I get to lick both bowls when we're done," Cato said. A few drops fell from his brush onto his arm.

"Speaking of which, for fuck's sake, don't waste it," Tamberi snapped. She bent her head and snaked her tongue over his arm, licking away the savory spots. He grinned and leaned forward, nipping her bare neck with his fangs. Tamberi's black hair was buzzed to about an inch long, which should've made her look as repulsive as an army recruit, but Cato found her sexy as hell.

"There," she said, dabbing in a last spot on the inverted pentagram. She smirked and caressed the head of one of the shackled virgins. She backed away to get the full effect. A small mat on the floor had been covered with purple velvet. The human sacrifices were arranged in a V formation with the pentagram forming the third side of a triangle into which they would welcome the demon Gadreel. Tamberi couldn't wait to see him in the flesh. She'd done a ritual to commune with a demon and had been communicating with Gadreel through her dreams ever since. He was an incredibly powerful presence in her unconscious world, but she was sure that her dreams of him would pale in comparison to what he was like when alive.

Large tears rolled down the bound girl's round cheeks.

"What?" Tamberi demanded. "You see where all that 'saving yourself' got you? You couldn't have been a virgin sacrifice if you hadn't been a virgin."

Cato snorted with laughter. "Did the demon really specify virgin sacrifices? Or did you want to use virgins because they piss you off?"

Tamberi ran a hand over the bound boy's hairless chest. "Gadreel likes them innocent."

"Speaking of what he likes, you sure he won't mind me being here for the raising ritual?"

"Why should he care? Two sacrifices means twice the power. And I want you here." She stretched and cracked her neck. "All those muses getting ready for their Christmas party, they have no idea what they're in for. This year I'm not raising some pathetic minor demon that Merrick could slay without breaking a sweat. This year, if the beautiful enforcer decides to crash the party, Gadreel will dine on his heart and pick his teeth afterward with Merrick's finger bones."

Cato sighed. He hadn't known that Tamberi had been the one who'd raised the demon in 2007. Before the ventala syndicate had sent Merrick to deal with it, that monster had killed four people in the Varden, including Cato's friend Davy Roma.

"And Gadreel's smart," she added. "He's not going to cause trouble in the Varden, so Dad won't even call Merrick. What happened in '07 is what I get for trying to avoid using a human sacrifice. Minor demons are like rabid dogs. Can't control them once they're raised."

"Fuck, Beri, Davy used to be part of my Friday night game. You know Lou can't play Texas Hold 'Em for shit."

"Yeah, sorry. I cracked a few eggs making that omelet, but this time is going to rock. After Gadreel gets his ring of power, those prissy pricks from Etherlin Security are going to have a slaughter shoved down their throat."

Kate's startled laughter echoed off the walls. "Time traveler. That would be the story of a lifetime," she said. Faced with his warm, magnetic presence and the smell of soap and male skin, her body registered its strong inclination to do more than photograph him for a story. "I guess your DeLorean is buried under a snow drift. Why don't you sit and tell me why you think you've been traveling through time?"

He sat on a barstool at the counter, and she set soup and toast in front of him.

"I remember living in Rome. This," he said, holding up his fist and pointing to the ring, "is Nero. Claudius adopted him and made him his heir. Claudius built things. Nero burned them down." He chewed slowly. "This tastes extremely good, Kate. Do you have any figs?"

"Figs?" she said with a smile. "It's the middle of winter in Colorado. Sorry, no figs."

"I remember that I like them." He swallowed several spoonfuls of soup. "In Rome, I had a family. I can't remember many details, but something terrible happened to them. It was Nero's fault, but not his fault alone. I don't know why it's important to me after all these years, but I need to remember those details. I want the name of the man who hurt my family."

"I would, too." Her pulse thrummed excitedly; evidence of time travel had never been documented. If this were real . . . No, it was just as likely—probably more likely—that he'd read books or seen movies that his mind was trying to incorporate as his own memories. But he did seem foreign, his clothes were old and crudely made, and he'd appeared from out of nowhere. Not to mention his antiquated ideas about gender roles. If he did really turn out to be from the past, she would have to make more allowances for him.

He finished his lunch and licked the excess butter from his thumb. "Thank you, Kate, for your hospitality."

"Sure." *Figs*, Kate thought, suddenly recalling the chocolate-covered figs she'd ordered from a chocolatier in Seattle. It had been a whim that she hadn't understood at the time. Now it made her shiver. How exactly was she connected to this bronze Adonis?

She walked to the cupboard and took down the dark brown box and tugged away the gold ribbon. She set the confection on a dish and brought it to him.

He licked the dark chocolate coating and swallowed thoughtfully. "There's a fig inside," she said.

He picked it up and popped the entire thing in his mouth. He chewed while she admired his square jaw. When he swallowed, he nodded. "I think I prefer them fresh, but that tasted good as well. Thank you."

"Your clothes will be dry soon, but you really need a coat. My brother forgot a sweatshirt when he was here last, but I don't have any other men's clothing."

"It's no problem," he said, then grimaced, bowing forward.

"What's wrong?"

He let out a hiss of pain. "My back hurts."

She moved behind him and found streaks of fiery red crisscrossing his back. *What the hell?* Anger surged as she wondered if the marks were from an assault. She hated the idea of anyone hurting him . . . or even touching him. Then she paused and shook her head. *You just met this man*, she reminded herself, but she couldn't seem to keep that in focus. The intensity of their closeness in some of her dreams kept surfacing. She felt like she already had a long history with him. *So surreal.*

"Your back looks really inflamed. How hot did you have the water during your shower?"

He twisted from side to side. "Not very hot, but my back burns like someone touched a flame to it. And underneath the skin, my muscles feel as though they're being twisted around a sword hilt, sometimes nicking the blade itself."

"I can't tell if these are burns or a rash or contused skin from an injury. We should go to a hospital, so they can run some tests."

"No."

"Yes. Pain means there's a problem. We have no idea how you ended up in the snow. Maybe you were assaulted. There could be internal damage and bleeding."

He twisted and stretched. She watched his muscles bunch and contract. No bones jutted out of place or gave an indication of serious injury.

"I'm not badly hurt," he said. "I feel certain of that."

"Okay," she said, but continued to scrutinize him.

He does look all right. Better than all right actually.

She admired his broad shoulders and the slope of his muscles as they tapered to his waist. From her dreams she knew the feel of him; his body was like stone wrapped in velvet.

Her fingers reached out, unable to resist any longer. Before her fingertips could stroke his skin, he turned as if sensing she was about to touch him. Their eyes locked, the air suddenly charged.

"What are you doing, Kate?" he asked, his voice low and sexy.

She looked at her outstretched hand and licked her lips. His full attention centered on her, making her heart pound. She basked in the heat that radiated from him, and, after a moment's hesitation, she swallowed. "You said you aren't badly hurt. I wanted to check for myself." The moment stretched as they watched each other.

"How would you . . . check?" he murmured, his lids lowering as he focused on her lips. She could only see alluring glimpses of hazel through his dark lashes. Mesmerized, a slow burn warmed her deep inside.

"I'd just . . ." She trailed off as she walked around him. The smooth skin invited her touch. She laid a palm against him, the satin heat enticing her. His muscles tightened, and he looked over his shoulder at her, his breath slightly ragged. She recognized the raw hunger in his gaze.

I know that look.

Her lids drifted closed, and she spiraled down into the mountain-ridge dream.

The fading light curved around him as an amber halo. Her body was stretched naked over a mattress covered in soft cotton sheets.

She arched up as he bent his head and captured her nipple. Under his mouth and teasing teeth, the torture was exquisite. She writhed, restless for more.

He pushed her legs apart. She lay open for him, her need tight as a bowstring fully stretched. When he raised his head, his smile was purely male, a warrior laying claim to the spoils of war, instincts as old as time driving them both. He stroked her, stoking an internal fire. She couldn't catch her breath, and her legs spread wider, inviting a deeper touch.

Powerful fingers thrust inside her, her body clenching, throbbing, seeking.

Please, she moaned. And then she gripped his shoulders as he moved above her, his voice a low rumble in her ear as he slid inside her moist heat, stretching and filling her. She sank her nails into his flesh.

"Yes, Kate, hold on tight while I take you. You're mine," he said in a ruthless rasp, deep with lust. "Your flesh will know the full measure of my love even if you're sore for days."

She screamed in orgasm in the dream and shuddered in orgasm in real life.

Wracked with sensations more incredible than any she'd felt with a real lover, she trembled. Her eyes fluttered open and she stared at him, breathlessly. His cheeks were flushed, his pupils dilated. The front of his towel tented forward.

He felt that, too. Whatever is between us, it's mutual.

She sucked in air, her hands shaky, her skin tingling, her womb throbbing. At the moment, he looked so beautiful to her. The overhead light fractured around him in an echo of the sunset gilding him on the dream mountain.

You do something to me. Just by existing.

Her hand drifted toward his chest. "I—"

He stepped back stiffly, clearing his throat. "I think I'll stand under the cool water awhile longer, Kate. It would make my back feel better."

"Right," she whispered. "A cold shower for your . . . back."

His smile was rueful and shy and sweet enough to make her heart creak.

"Something like that," he murmured. His hand touched her cheek so briefly it was only the ghost of a caress, but it was still powerful enough to implore her to step toward him. He closed his eyes and clenched his jaw as if the struggle within him was intense.

"I'd better go," he said, then turned and with that long and powerful stride, escaped into the bathroom.

Body still thrumming with unsatisfied cravings, she thought, *His willpower is stronger than mine.*

She pictured him standing naked in the shower and knew it would take all her will just to keep herself from joining him there.

The doorbell startled Kate. She wasn't expecting company. *It's probably a holiday package*, she thought, but when she opened the door, she found a group of uniformed men. A sheriff and three deputies armed with shotguns.

"Hello, ma'am. May we come in?"

A trickle of unease dripped down her spine. Why had they come to the door with their weapons in hand?

"What's this about?"

"We're tracking a fugitive. The trail led here."

"A fugitive, you say? What's he wanted for?" Her heart thumped more quickly, her eyes studying their faces. Their eager expressions didn't put her at ease.

"He? I didn't mention it was a he," the sheriff said, looking past her. They pressed forward.

"Most fugitives are men," she said.

"Is he inside?" the sheriff demanded.

"Sure, he's inside," one of the deputies said with an angry sneer, and she spotted the tips of his fangs.

"Oh!" she said, backpedaling into the house. She swung the door, but one of them grabbed it and shoved it open. They pushed forward, spinning her and cuffing her hands behind her back.

Her outrage spilled out as curses, but they didn't break their stride. They shoved her onto the couch and told her to stay there.

"The disguises don't fool me. I know you're ventala."

"The show wasn't for you. It was for your neighbors," one said as he hurried to the back of the house and opened the deck door. More men spilled in, and she gasped.

"Get out of my house!" she yelled as they started checking rooms and some rushed upstairs. They kicked in the guest room door where her visitor had just been showering.

"Katherine Devane," the fake sheriff said, looking inside her wallet. "I know who you are. You're an aspirant. You wrote the story about the vampire nest in South Dakota and got them all killed."

She ignored the sheriff and held her breath, listening for sounds from the guest room. Had they found Bronze? Overpowered him?

A group of ventala pounded down the stairs. "Upstairs is clear."

"There was an open window in the downstairs bedroom. He must have climbed out."

"Outside then. Fast!" The sheriff turned to her. "Did he have his memory, Kate?"

She pursed her lips and glared at the fake sheriff. He grabbed her arms and squeezed them. "Where did he go? Tell me right now."

"I'm not telling you anything."

He backhanded her across the face. Her head snapped back from the blow, and she fell against the cushions.

"Here's the thing. You will tell me what I want to know eventually. You can do it after being beaten bloody or before. It's your choice."

Her cheek flamed, and she didn't doubt the sincerity of his threat.

"You tell me where he is."

Even with a watering eye, her vision wasn't completely blurred, and she saw Bronze. He stood naked in the doorway, his wet hair dripping water. He looked like a Viking berserker, the dagger in his right hand slick with blood.

It felt as though she stared at him forever, but it must have only been seconds. She dragged her eyes away to look around and realized there were only two ventala left in the house with her. The fake sheriff bared his fangs and grabbed her. Teeth scraped her neck. Her mouth opened in a silent scream.

She saw Bronze's eyes, dark with fury, as he sailed through the air.

The sheriff was yanked away from her by the hair, his head snapping back. Her visitor slit the ventala's throat in a smooth motion while still airborne. He landed nearly silently, turned and drove the dagger down behind the sheriff's left collarbone. The ventala's eyes widened as he slammed to his knees, then fell facedown.

Bronze fought the other ventala, dispatching him with equal efficiency, but Bronze didn't escape unwounded. She gasped at the half-buried knife in his flank. He grimaced and slid the blade out on a river of blood.

"Oh no!" she said, struggling to her feet.

When she reached him, she saw other wounds. A slice through his left shoulder that gaped open when he moved, a hole in his left thigh, a slice along his hip. He rested the dagger on the couch and sank to his knees holding the gushing flank wound.

She fumbled for the keys on the sheriff's belt, her hands damp with sweat. She brought Bronze the keys with shaking hands.

"Can you uncuff me? Then I can help you."

He groaned. "My back isn't the only thing that hurts now."

"I know. I'm sorry. Oh God," she said, wincing. *Please let the bleeding stop!*

He took the keys. "Small shackles," he murmured. "Delicate like your wrists."

The cuffs popped open, and she turned back to him. He forced himself to a standing position, panting for breath. He bent forward so that the front of his body rested on top of the couch, then he rolled over it so he lay lengthwise.

"Come here, Kate."

"Where the hell's my phone? I have to call an ambulance," she said, searching frantically.

"No, stay close," he said, grabbing her hand. "I want—"

"Yes?" she asked, leaning over him.

"Stay with me."

"I'm not going anywhere," she said softly, squeezing his hand. He looked so vulnerable. Waves of tenderness crashed over her. *Don't let me lose him.* "I just need to call for help. Lie still."

He shook his head. She tried to pry her hand free of his grip, but couldn't. He drew her arm to him, tugging the rest of her with it. "I want you close."

"I promise I'll come right back."

"I won't hurt you. I swear."

What? Is he confused from losing so much blood? God, I need to hurry. "I'm not worried about that! You're bleeding to death! Can't you feel it? There's no time to waste."

He tugged her closer, shifting so he lay sideways. She tried to yank herself free, but he was still ridiculously strong. He positioned her against him, and at least he didn't feel cold.

"This is crazy. You're going to die."

"Not today," he said, and his breathing, which had been shallow and short, slowed to an even rhythm. His arm pressed against her back, and through her clothes, she felt his groin, which apparently wasn't dead yet.

"You have got to be kidding me," she said dryly, but it was a relief that he had enough blood left for that or anything else.

He wrapped his other arm around her, holding her tight to his body and buried his face in her neck. She felt him inhale.

She didn't struggle because there was no point; his grip was obscenely strong. She waited, expecting it to loosen as his blood drained away, but instead he pressed his lips to the side of her throat. Moments stretched like a bowstring. When he began to reposition them, she forced her fists between their chests.

"Hold on," she said.

"I think you're mine," he whispered. He kissed her jaw and a moment later, her body was beneath his.

"Stop," she said.

He stilled. "Are you certain? My instincts tell me—"

"That's not your instincts talking!"

He hesitated, and for a moment she didn't know if he would let her go, but he did. Then he rose. He was still magnificently naked and clearly unconcerned about it. She shouldn't have noticed, but God he was beautiful.

"Don't be afraid of me. I won't hurt you," he said.

"I'm not afraid. I think you're a lunatic," she said, keeping her eyes on his shoulders and above. "You have to let me take you to the hospital."

"No."

"Why not?" she demanded.

He flashed a heartbreaking smile and shrugged. "Because I don't need to go there. And because . . . I want to stay with you."

She watched his muscles flex as he walked away. It was only after he'd disappeared from view that she realized his wounds no longer bled.

So whoever he is, he's immortal.

Kate quickly retrieved his clothes from the dryer while he rid the living room of ventala bodies. He tossed them unceremoniously into the snow, ate two roast beef sandwiches, and showered again, though she told him they should just leave. The ventala he'd fought might not be fully dead. Unless their heads were cut off, the strongest ventala could heal what should have been fatal wounds. Bronze shrugged indifference at the possible threat, and who could blame him when all his wounds had closed and disappeared within three-quarters of an hour?

When he was dressed and the house locked, he followed her to her jeep, helping to load her bags into the car.

"I've had dreams with you in them," she confessed.

"Oh? What kind of dreams?"

"Usually you're falling off buildings or fighting with a really pretty blond guy." She paused, wanting to raise the subject of the other dreams but unsure of how to phrase things to cause the least embarrassment for them both.

"I have no memory of anything like that yet." He climbed into the passenger's seat and eased it back to accommodate his long legs.

Eyeing him, she started the car. She'd hoped he might ask her more questions about the dreams, but he didn't seem inclined to. She drew in a deep breath and exhaled audibly. Maybe it was a topic better left alone.

"So the ventala knew you were at my house," she said, talking more to herself than him. "I wish I knew how. Maybe one of the ones you fought in the woods had time to call and tell the others."

"That's possible. I didn't see what they did before they attacked us."

"I'm going to take you to the Etherlin. It's a private community that the ventala can't enter."

"The Etherlin," he said, trying out the word.

"It's the home of a group of women who descended from the ancient muses."

"Muses? From the Greek myths?"

"Yes, the modern muses inherited magic from their ancestors. They inspire people to create art and music, to excel athletically, to invent things—basically to imagine better and greater things for themselves and the world. The people the muses inspire are called aspirants. I'm one of them."

He nodded but didn't comment.

"While I'm in the Etherlin, I'll talk to Alissa, the muse I work with. Talking to her always revs my mind. It'll help me come up with new theories and ideas about why the ventala are after you."

"How do the muses help human beings have ideas?"

"They're part magical. Scientists have studied them and noticed that the muses have special proteins circulating in their blood and that the timbre and quality of their voice changes when they speak to someone they're trying to influence. Their voices contain a vibratory note that activates more parts of the brain than normal human speech, particularly the areas used for creativity."

"The muses have a divine gift."

"Yeah. Pretty great of them to share it, huh? They're very altruistic. Unlike the ventala, who are totally self-serving. If you really are from the past, maybe they're worried you know something dangerous. Maybe there's something you came here to do that will hurt them . . . so they want to stop you before you get the chance," she murmured.

"What do the ventala fear in general?"

"They're afraid that people will decide that the ventala are too violent to live among us. Of course, attacking people only makes us more likely to think that, so they must want you dead very badly to risk the consequences of attacking in daylight in a human neighborhood."

"Were the ventala slaves?"

"No."

"But they don't have full citizenship? They're treated like foreigners?"

"Kind of. Vampires were predators and were killed for that reason. The ventala are part vampire, so they're treated differently from people who are fully human. The laws put special restrictions on them. It pisses them off. They'd like more freedom, but it's tough to trust them with it."

"Since they're stronger and more violent than human beings?"

"Exactly. They're impulsive, and they sometimes fly into a rage without warning. In this case, though, their pursuit of you is obviously premeditated. You know what's strange? They knew you'd lost your memory. Maybe they attacked you and gave you a head injury? But how did you escape if you were badly injured? And if you can heal wounds so fast, why wouldn't you have healed a head injury just as quickly?" She paused, shaking her head. "So many questions. Not enough answers."

"Nathaniel."

She blinked.

"My name is Nathaniel," he said triumphantly.

"That's great! Do you remember your last name?"

He shook his head.

"ES—Etherlin Security—should be able to help us. They have sophisticated equipment to identify nonhuman creatures and people with superhuman abilities. If anyone can figure out what you are, it's ES, so don't worry."

"I wasn't worried, Kate. I have faith that my memory will return in its own time. Now tell me about your dreams of us. How did we meet? And what's the nature of our relationship? Are we in love?"

Her gaze slid to him. "Well," she said, and then smiled self-consciously. "Sometimes we are really . . . close. Other times you're very focused on fighting and barely register that I'm there."

"Is that so?" he said, clearly skeptical. "I don't think your presence is something that would easily escape my attention." He clasped his hands, tapping his thumbs against each other. "They're only dreams. They don't tell the entire story."

"You're sure of that, are you?" She smiled. "And what do your instincts tell you is supposed to be between us? A great love affair?" she teased, wanting him to say yes.

"No," he said, and her smile faded. "Not an affair. That would ruin your reputation. You'd be a fallen woman."

Oh my. There's some more of that two-thousand-year-old morality, she thought, her spine stiffening.

"If there was love between us, I'd make you my wife, Kate. And you'd belong to me for life."

Belong to him. For life. Wow.

The idea sent an odd thrill through her, but was also kind of terrifying. What would it be like to be married to someone as stubborn, archaic, and uncompromising as Nathaniel? What would that mean for her career? Would passion totally consume her and leave room for nothing else? Emotions certainly seemed to swallow her whole in those dreams. She shivered. Yes, thrilling. And also terrifying.

Chapter Four

The white stone walls around the Etherlin had been sanded smooth and covered with a gloss that made them opalescent. They were topped with glittering silver barbed mesh that matched the silver and white gates.

Kate pulled over and killed the engine. If she had been alone, she wouldn't have needed to get out of the car, but since she had a visitor unknown to ES, she walked to the guard post. The blazer-wearing guard looked like he should have been rowing crew in the Ivy League. His mop of curly hair had been aggressively tamed with gel, but it still made him look slightly boyish.

Kate explained that she'd brought someone whose nature was, as yet, unclear and that she hoped they could help. She waited while the guard, whose badge identified him as J. Pinter, called for a more senior officer. Nathaniel emerged from the jeep and stood silently beside her as she chatted with Pinter.

Kate smiled when she saw Grant Easton, the ES director. Grant lived up to the blue-blood cut of his nose and jaw. He strode forward like he owned the world—or soon would.

"Well, if it's not our vampire-hunting aspirant," Grant said with a broad smile. "How are you, Kate?"

She smiled, too. "I'm well. Thank you."

"Vampire hunting?" Pinter asked.

"Sure. Kate's an investigative reporter, and she uncovered a hot spot for missing persons. A human Bermuda triangle for travelers on road trips that turned out to be the hunting ground for a huge nest of cave-dwelling vampires who escaped the extermination."

"That was you?" Pinter asked.

She nodded.

"I saw those photographs. You were as close to them as I am to you." He clucked his tongue. "You could've been killed."

"No guts, no glory," she said.

"Spoken like a champion of the gods. Next up, recovering the Golden Fleece," Grant joked, giving her shoulder squeeze.

"There's one God," Nathaniel said, putting a hand on Kate's arm and drawing her away from Grant. "And when waging war for him, the weapon carried is not a camera."

"Muses are real. The gods of Olympus may have been real as well," Grant countered.

"Many groups of superhuman creatures have resided on the earth or presided over it, but they were all created by a single source. And if they exploit their powers and toy with men for sport, their existence is reduced to myth."

They all stared at Nathaniel.

How could he know that unless he's—? No, Kate thought. *I saw his back. No wings. No scars. He can't be an angel. But what about his back pain? And the red marks?*

"No one knows for sure what happened to the Olympians, but that's an interesting theory. Where did you hear it?" Grant asked.

Nathaniel shrugged. "It's an echo through my soul."

Grant raised his brows. "That's an interesting way of evading the question."

Nathaniel walked to the jeep. "Come, Kate."

"No," Grant said. "Kate's an aspirant, which means she's under our protection. She's not going anywhere with you until we've established who and what you are."

Nathaniel tried the door, but it had locked automatically.

Grant rounded the jeep. "Come this way."

"I decline your invitation," Nathaniel said.

"Why? What are you hiding?" Grant demanded.

"Hold on," Kate said, horrified by the rising confrontation.

Pinter drew his gun.

Nathaniel stiffened. "No!" Nathaniel said, stretching a hand toward Pinter. "You must not attack me with intent. I am bound to defend myself by a higher law than my own will. And if we fight, you will not survive."

"What?" Grant said. "What are you claiming?"

"Rest easy, boy," Nathaniel said as Pinter's hand trembled.

"Pinter, do not lower that weapon."

Nathaniel looked at Grant then, the gold flecks in his eyes blazing. "Do not push him to make a mistake."

Grant grabbed Nathaniel's arm. "That's—"

Nathaniel's palm slammed into Grant's chest, and Grant flew backward, landing hard on the ground. Nathaniel said, "Free will comes with consequences."

"Nathaniel, don't!" she said.

"You would take sides against me?" he demanded.

"I'm not taking sides."

Grant regained his feet with effort and held out a hand to Pinter, who had his weapon trained on Nathaniel.

"Demons sometimes disguise themselves as men and other creatures," Grant said. "They spout prophecies and try to trick us with claims that they're God's messengers or soldiers, so we don't kill them. You'll come with us, so we can discover your true nature."

"Killing demons is not the responsibility of men. Resisting temptation is work enough for mankind."

"And we should let the demons kill us whenever they want?"

"Kate," Nathaniel said, resting his hand on the roof. "I don't belong here. Open the door."

"Kate, you should stay with us," Grant said. "I'll take you into the Etherlin where you'll be safe."

She felt like a wishbone about to be broken between them. The Etherlin represented all the world's promise for her dazzling future, but Nathaniel might become the love of her life. She wanted both.

She couldn't allow them to be at odds with each other. She had to smooth things over.

She glanced at the gates and then walked around the car to Nathaniel. "You remember what you are?" she whispered.

"I have an idea, yes."

"So you don't need my help anymore?" she murmured.

"I never needed your help."

She flinched.

"Let's go, Kate."

He still wanted her to go with him. That was something. "Hold on. This isn't just about you," she whispered fiercely. "I have a relationship with this community. This amazing community. You can't ask me to jeopardize that. I need for you to come inside and to submit to a few tests so that they'll be satisfied that you're not dangerous."

"I am dangerous, and I won't submit to anything." His tone was so hard and even. So final. As if what she needed didn't matter to him at all. Her body became rigid, her emotions brittle as glass.

"You owe me an explanation," she said.

"I'm leaving this place right now. You can accompany me or not."

She glared at him. She was not going to be steamrolled. "We need to talk this out."

He scowled and pulled her forward, his fingers digging into her pocket to retrieve the car keys.

She shoved him and backed away. "Don't manhandle me."

"You accuse me of such a thing? Perhaps you should stay here, Kate, until you decide with whom you belong."

She frowned, her back stiffening. The thought of him leaving rattled her more than she wanted to admit, which only made her struggle harder not to cave.

He opened the back of jeep and took out her bags.

"What are you doing?" she asked.

"You," Nathaniel said, pointing at Grant. "You want her to stay, so be it. I leave her in your safekeeping. Let harm come to her, and you'll answer for it."

"Nathaniel," she snapped. "I'm still here."

"Obviously," he agreed.

"I meant don't talk about me as if I were property or some weak little female that the big strong men need to protect."

"You do need protection sometimes. You're foolish to claim otherwise," he said. He clasped her hand and she felt his ring cool and hard in her palm. He closed her fingers around it, clenching her fist within his.

"Wear my ring until I return."

"What, are we in high school? I'm not—"

He caught her face in his hands and kissed her, hard and tender at the same time. At first she resisted but then couldn't.

Delicious, she thought as her body tightened in anticipation of what she wanted . . . *more.*

She kissed him back, until normal consciousness melted, and an image burned her mind. She lay in her dorm room asleep. Nathaniel stood over her, his chiseled features rain-soaked as he opened her hand. Water dripped onto the ring transforming the flecks of dried blood into pink droplets in her palm. His harsh breath quickened, and his thumb rubbed the moisture along her hand creases. "We're bound by blood," he whispered, shaking his head. "You shouldn't have touched the ring. Should never even have spotted it." She stirred, her lips parting. "Who are you?" he asked, staring down at her face, and then he leaned forward and brushed his lips over her mouth. When he straightened, he licked his lips. "Bound," he whispered, taking the ring. Then, with a rush of air, he escaped through the open window.

The image blurred as Nathaniel stepped back.

"What the hell was that?" she gasped, trying to catch her breath.

"A good-bye kiss," Nathaniel said, climbing into the driver's seat. He shoved it all the way back to accommodate his height.

"I saw you in my dorm room. I was asleep . . . It wasn't my memory . . ." she stammered. "Did you see that just now?"

He shook his head, starting the car.

"Where are you going? The next four blocks are the Sliver, which is neutral territory, but the entire city beyond that is the Varden, which is controlled by the ventala."

"Maybe a visit there will help me figure out what they want from me."

"So you're just going to do what? Drive around? See if something seems familiar while half the ventala in the Varden may be hunting you?"

"If you wish to know, come with me."

She still felt slightly disoriented from the kiss and the dorm room vision. Had it been a memory? One of his? Or just a dream that felt real? "No, Nathaniel. Driving around randomly makes no sense. Come inside the Etherlin with me and tell me what you remember, so we can figure things out together."

"I don't know where I belong, but it's not inside those walls."

She glared at him.

"I'll return for you, Kate."

"Don't you dare leave."

"I'm not yours to command," Nathaniel said, scowling as he swung the wheel. He drove away. Feeling crestfallen, she stared after him until the jeep disappeared.

Finally, she turned to Grant. "What do you think?" she asked, saying what they were all wondering. "Is he a fallen angel?"

"He may be. According to legend, the angels who rose against God were cast out. Those who embraced the rebellion were damned to hell. Those who regretted their choice were doomed to walk the earth, always seeking God's forgiveness, which would be withheld forever. They're tortured souls without a seat at the table of the afterlife."

"A lonely existence."

"Exactly. I'm sure he'd enjoy having someone to ease that loneliness, but what would that mean for you?"

"Heaven's gates would be barred against me, too," she said, shivering.

"Very likely, which is why you should come inside and never see him again."

"I have a connection to him. It's palpable."

"I'm sure it is. Remember that if he's trying to trick you, he's more than fallen. He's damned. Don't forget that higher demons are experts in subterfuge and temptation."

Yes, he could be trying to trick me, she thought, *but he's not. A part of me already belongs to him, whether I want it to or not.*

"It's time," Tamberi said, glancing at the clock and tapping her foot nervously. She opened the grimoire.

"All right, don't get your panties in a bunch," Cato said.

"No. At least not yet," she said with a sly smile as she started reading from the book. The floor cracked open, and orange light spilled from the center. Flames danced up, singeing the curtains and the dangling hair of the sacrifices who screamed behind their gags.

When the ritual was finished, seconds ticked by and orange and white flames exploded in the circle. Smoke writhed and took shape. Bones clattered and creaked, covering themselves in flesh as pale as milk.

Gadreel rose from his crouched position. White-blond hair hung around his exquisite face, and eyes of the brightest blue stared at them. The corner of his mouth curved into a smile.

"Hello, world of men, so nice to see you again." His left hand slid lazily down his flat belly to stroke himself. "What have we here, Tamberi? You had a helper?"

She nodded. "My brother, Cato."

Gadreel laughed and stepped out of the circle. With his free hand, he cupped her face. "Blood, black magic, and virgins—three of my favorite things. And now incest? Is it my birthday? Why, yes it is. Of sorts." He licked his lips and kissed her mouth. "Thank you for my presents. There's a reason you're my favorite."

"You say that to everyone."

"Yes, but in your case, I mean it." He glanced at Cato. "So what do you think, Beri? Should we start with him in the middle?"

"What?" Cato choked.

Tamberi nodded and laughed.

"Don't worry. I won't ride you too long, Cato. There's a lot to be done before sunrise. My angel enemy's distracted by a girl, and I've risen before he's got his bearings in that new body." Gadreel stretched with lazy sensuality. "Did you follow all my instructions, Tamberi?"

"Yes, everything's ready and in motion."

"Beautiful. By morning, I'll retrieve my ring, defile his girl, and cut out his wings." Gadreel's smile flashed wicked and bright. "Happy birthday."

Nathaniel rubbed his chest as the piercing pain faded. For an instant, an inky blackness had fallen over his vision. Then, with a blink, it cleared, leaving a powerful urgency in its wake. Nathaniel pressed the gas pedal down and struggled to make sense of what he'd felt.

Hurry. The word beat in his mind like a drum. "Hurry where? To do what?" Nathaniel demanded.

He hadn't recovered his memory yet. At least not fully. He was a soldier of Heaven. That had been a sharp realization that came without memory. He didn't know how he'd come to be, but when he'd been confronted by the men from Etherlin Security, a knowledge of himself had emerged. In the same way that he knew his right hand from his left and how to wield a weapon, he knew he was an archangel, an instrument of God's wrath, and that he was not meant to be examined or interrogated by men. Nathaniel had felt that if he'd stayed, the men would've become more insistent and the situation would have escalated to violence. Also, he'd felt a rising tide of jealousy and desire. When Kate had been friendly and familiar with the other men, a part of him had wanted to lay claim to her in the basest, most primal way.

He tightened his grip on the wheel. His passion for her had become volatile. He'd wanted to conquer her resistance, and that battle would have made the exchange between him and the men impossible to control. So when Kate refused to leave with him, he'd left her there, though even now he wanted to turn back.

What are she and I meant to be to each other?

No answer presented itself, but he realized that thoughts of her cooled the urgency that had overtaken him when he'd felt the pain in his chest. It was as though duty and desire pulled at different parts of his soul, each conquering the other in his mind from moment to moment. He shook his head, and then ran a hand through his hair to push it back from his face.

Duty, first. Surely that's how things must be. But even as he had the thought, a part of him rebelled against it. *Go back for Kate,* a calm voice seemed to whisper. Nathaniel clenched his jaw. *No. Not now. Not yet.*

Instinct made him drive southwest from the Etherlin gates until he was among glossy black-and-white high rises that looked familiar. A building with a red awning over the front entrance caused a flash of memory wherein a crowd of people dressed for a night out stood in line. In his memory, he passed them on his way inside.

Do I live in this building?

Nathaniel twisted his spine by moving each shoulder forward and back. The muscle cramps worsened, but now that he understood why, he didn't mind. *Wings.* He would have wings, and when he did he would fly and hunt.

Hunt what?

Demons, he thought. *Archangels hunt demons. It's what I'm on this earth to do.*

He waited for more detail to emerge, but none came.

Instead, recent memories scattered across his mind. The way Kate had laughed when he'd mentioned time travel, the sound as bright and self-assured as the midday sun, her head tipping back so her hair swung like a curtain inlaid with bronze and gold. And the way she kissed, which was so uninhibited that it shocked him . . . and made him ache. He could've kissed her deep into the night. He'd wanted to steal her away, to stake his claim on her body by burying the swollen organ between his legs inside her. He knew with certainty that making love to Kate would feel like a slice of Heaven. Need throbbed heavily through his flesh.

I should have taken her. She belongs to me.

He inhaled sharply and clenched his teeth against instincts so raw they threatened to overwhelm him. *No, her consent is compulsory.*

Strength is not a license to take by force what must be freely given. Strength of character must match strength of body, or I am no better than my enemies.

Even as thoughts of Kate swamped him, something else fought for his attention, too.

Hurry.

Again, the rush of adrenaline, the urgency to move without an exact direction.

He rubbed his temple and pulled into a parking spot, looking up at the building's lacquer accents and Art Deco lines. He had a knowledge of architecture, he realized. He'd lived through thousands of years of history, had seen buildings and monuments erected. Fragments filtered through like light through a veil.

Nathaniel climbed from Kate's jeep and walked to the smoked glass doors under the maroon canopy with white lettering that announced CRIMSON. He remembered the thump of loud music.

Crimson's a nightclub.

He wondered if Kate liked to dance. His body tightened at the thought of holding her in his arms again. All that softness that smelled sweet as spring rain, her lips the texture of flower petals pressed . . . He shook his head to clear it.

In the lobby, the security officer looked down from his perch and raised his eyebrows.

"And who are you supposed to be? One of the wise men after he's been mugged?"

Nathaniel glanced at his clothes. Kate had mocked them as well. He'd assumed that he'd traveled through time in them, but that was apparently not true. He ran his hand over the rough cloth. It felt comfortable and familiar, but he clearly needed to change if he didn't want to invite derision.

He doesn't know me; this is not where I live.

"I'm Nathaniel. You don't recognize me?"

"No," the man said with a laugh. "You'd never get into Crimson in that get-up."

"I probably wasn't dressed this way, and I may not have been at the club. I could've been here to visit someone who lives in the building."

"You must really have tied one on if you can't remember what you were doing here last time. Why don't you go home and come back when you know who you want to see."

Nathaniel glanced past the desk to the bank of elevators. The ones in the foreground had numbers, but the back one was separate and had the word *penthouse* above it.

Nathaniel pictured a rooftop garden. Statues. Orange trees. He'd been on the building's roof.

"I'd like to see the person who lives in the penthouse."

The man laughed again. "Buddy, except for a few beautiful babes and the guys who work for him, nobody tries to see the boss. And you'd better hope he doesn't want to see you either because that would mean your number's up." The man continued to look amused.

"He's an assassin?" *Another archangel?*

"He used to be an enforcer. Now he owns this building and about five blocks in every direction. His name is Merrick, and he doesn't see anyone before five."

Merrick.

Nathaniel knew of Merrick. He was a member of the ventala. Nathaniel pictured a man in a dark suit who moved with precision and killed without remorse. He'd been trained like no other ventala. *Lysander.* The name reverberated through Nathaniel's mind. Merrick had been trained by Lysander—one of the fiercest archangels of all time. A fallen archangel.

"I've heard of Merrick," Nathaniel said.

"Most people have."

Nathaniel stepped forward and rested a hand on the counter. He studied the man, who shifted his considerable bulk. There was no malice behind the man's eyes. No instinct dictated that Nathaniel challenge him.

"I understand that you are bound by your duty, but I would like you to call Merrick and tell him a member of Lysander's former brotherhood asks to see him."

The man's jaw dropped. "You're saying—" The man leaned forward and lowered his voice. "None of us has ever seen him, but everybody who works for the boss has heard rumors about Lysander." The man narrowed his eyes and looked Nathaniel over. "You better not drop that name unless you are what you claim."

Nathaniel smiled. "As with your employer, you would not like to witness me prove what I am."

The man lifted the phone and conveyed Nathaniel's message to the person on the other end. Setting the phone back in its cradle, he said, "They'll check with him and call me back."

Nathaniel nodded as the man looked him over again.

"So you're allowed to tell people what you are?"

"If I revealed myself to you, then I must not be barred from it," Nathaniel said, though he wasn't sure that was true. He only knew that his instincts had not railed against his making the revelation.

"So what's it like? Heaven?" the man asked eagerly.

"It defies description." *At least at the moment.* "You need to see for yourself."

The man shrugged. "Not sure that's going to work out. This patch of concrete's been pretty godforsaken. We do what we have to do to survive. Not sure how that's gonna go over come Judgment Day."

"It's not too late to live as you were meant to."

The phone rang, and the man picked it up. He listened for a moment. "Sure." He replaced the receiver. "The penthouse elevator will take you all the way up. The code is 198724."

"Thank you. And good luck on your journey."

"I'm gonna take a journey?"

Nathaniel smiled. "The journey of your life."

Nathaniel crossed the black marble tile to reach the elevator. He keyed in the code and the door slid open. Inside there were sleek steel walls. A pewter-framed painting of a white orchid dotted with crimson hung at the back, managing to be both sensual and ominous.

Nathaniel stepped inside and ascended.

Chapter Five

Nathaniel walked down the wide hall with its alternating lengths of indigo carpet and white marble. A black-and-white photograph of a French horn seemed to float above the ground, held in place by thread-thin wires. The walls were papered in a silver geometric pattern as though the corridor had been gift-wrapped by a mathematician with a taste for jazz.

Merrick answered the door in a white bathrobe and dark sunglasses. Nathaniel didn't understand the sunglasses since the penthouse apartment was as dark as a cave. Nathaniel had the urge to throw the heavy drapes open and let in the light.

"Hello," Merrick said, going into his kitchen. He emerged with a bowl of dates, dried figs, and spiced almonds. "What else would you like? Bread and cheese? Some spiced meat?" Merrick asked.

"This is plenty. Thank you." From the first bite, a flood of warm emotion coursed through Nathaniel. These were flavors from a time now lost.

"A drink?"

"Is there wine?"

"There's everything," Merrick said, going to his bar. He uncorked a bottle and poured dark red wine into a goblet. Then into a heavy asymmetric highball glass he poured amber spirits and dropped a lime wedge.

Nathaniel watched Merrick. The ventala who had attacked

Nathaniel were strong, quick, and agile, but they hadn't been trained to fight by archangels. Merrick's movements betrayed his superior training. No wasted motion. Nathaniel admired that.

"So you and I are well acquainted?" Nathaniel asked, taking the offered wine.

"No," Merrick said, sitting across from him. "We spoke once when you and Lysander had a disagreement on my roof."

"I fought with Lysander? Over what?"

"You didn't want Lysander killing demons you're meant to kill."

"Ah. Well, Lysander's fallen. He's nearly one of them."

"Say that to him, and I'll have more broken marble statues to replace."

Nathaniel saw a flash of himself and Lysander falling from the sky and crashing into solid stone. After which Nathaniel's left forearm bones poked through his skin like a button through a button hole, and Lysander's golden skin was mottled purple from a dozen cracked ribs that made his chest look like a canvas splattered with paint. It had been a brutal exchange, and Merrick had silently watched with a grim expression until they finished. After, Nathaniel had flown away. Lysander had stayed.

"Is Lysander the reason the ventala are hunting me?"

Merrick shook his head. "Lysander does his own hunting. What makes you think there are ventala after you?"

Nathaniel explained.

Merrick nodded, returning to the bar to make himself another drink. Nathaniel waited, but Merrick said nothing.

"I'm having a problem with my memory."

"I noticed. New body?"

"New body?" Nathaniel echoed, leaning forward.

Merrick drained his glass.

"What did you mean by that question?" Nathaniel asked.

"Nathaniel, we're not friends."

"You allowed me into your home."

"You asked to meet; I was curious. Also, refusing hospitality to an angel courts the kind of trouble that's best avoided." Merrick looked him over. "I don't know what you're doing in the Varden if you haven't recovered your memory."

"Where am I supposed to be?"

Merrick shrugged. "The Italian Alps? On some untouched, unreachable mountaintop in the country where you first lived."

"So why would I wake up in the snow near Kate's house?" Nathaniel wondered.

Merrick smirked. "There's a woman?"

Nathaniel frowned, not sure how much he wanted to reveal about Kate. "There are many women," Nathaniel said absently. "They make up half the world's population."

"They do. The more beautiful half," Merrick said, setting his glass on the table.

Nathaniel appraised the ventala. Merrick seemed to have an appreciation, and perhaps an understanding, of women. His insight might be valuable. "Could an attachment to a woman have pulled me so far off course?"

"I don't know, but on the list of things that make mortal men cross oceans, women are at the top."

"So the trouble I find myself in may be Kate's fault," he mused.

"That's one way of putting it—a way that will ensure she doesn't talk to you until you get your next body. But, hey, it's your dead end."

"You're right; fault isn't a good choice of words. She'd be insulted. Kate's got great spirit, but she takes offense easily."

The corners of Merrick's mouth curved up. "Yeah, you're going to do really well with her." Merrick walked to the door and opened it. "Good luck."

"This is an end to your hospitality?"

"It is," Merrick said.

Nathaniel sighed. Being asked to leave was a suboptimal turn of events. "May I ask for a piece of advice?"

"You can ask."

Merrick's hard edges were showing. A ventala who'd been befriended by a fierce fallen angel was likely more wild and dangerous than the lions of the Coliseum. But what choice did Nathaniel have but to seek counsel when he recalled so little about the modern world?

"Kate is in the Etherlin visiting her friend, but I don't want to join her there. In my place, where would you go while awaiting your memory's return?"

Merrick narrowed his eyes, suddenly attentive. "What's Kate's last name?"

"I don't know. Why would that be of consequence?"

"Is her friend a muse?"

"Yes."

"Which one?" Merrick asked, becoming very still.

"She called her Alissa."

After a moment's silence, Merrick said, "Kate's an aspirant. Her last name is Devane." Merrick rested his hand against the doorframe. "Nathaniel, how would you like my help for the night? With me providing information and advice . . . and clothes from this millennium?"

"I would appreciate that very much," Nathaniel said, suddenly wary. "In exchange for what?"

"For delivering a package."

"As long as the package isn't an instrument of malice or harm, I foresee no difficulty."

Merrick swung the door closed.

Kate approached the Dome, which was headquarters for the Etherlin Council. A reimagined version of the iconic blue and white Greek buildings, the white stone had a slight shimmer from crystalline paint and the blue dome was rimmed with silver swirls around the base.

Kate had visited the Dome's reference library once before with Alissa as a chaperone. When they'd left, Kate had turned in her electronic parking key card rather than the identical-looking key card to the library archives. The investigative reporter in her always resisted giving up access to any amazing source of information. Now having the card would allow Kate to do some reading without relying on Alissa, which was good because that might have been awkward since Grant and Alissa were involved and Grant likely wouldn't approve of Kate's research into Nathaniel's history.

Nathaniel. His name roused memories of the kiss. Well, of both kisses. The one born of heat and frustration that had demanded her attention at the Etherlin gates. And the cooler, wistful one in the dorm room that she'd witnessed in the memory or whatever it was. *A bond that ties us together,* she reflected. How to feel about that? She wasn't sure. Apparently the connection to him had been thrust upon her by chance when she'd found his ring, and that didn't sit well. She didn't want to be at fate's mercy, just a plaything with which to be toyed. She pursed her lips. She'd never consented to a lifelong connection, but clearly one did exist. She would have to figure out a way to break it or learn to live with it. With the feel of Nathaniel's body still fresh, it didn't seem like such a hardship, but in terms of having him around, it was early days.

Down wide hallways of mosaic tile, she kept her head up and nodded at the security officers she passed within the Dome. In the hushed corridor that led to the locked collections, she showed her identification and held her breath.

The ES officer facing her was older. He had light hair and wolf's eyes.

"This is an unusual time to be doing research. Aren't you going to the holiday party?"

"Of course." *Which is why I'm in a hurry! I've got to go back to the guard post for my bags and find a ride to the Clarity Hotel since an alleged angel took off with my car. Then I need to check in and make myself presentable for what may be one of the most important networking opportunities of my life. Jeez, what the hell am I doing here trying to sneak in to look at thousand-year-old books? I'm a complete head case.*

"Which books are of interest, and what's the urgency?"

Damn. He wasn't supposed to ask that.

"Actually," she said, leaning slightly forward and lowering her voice. "A council member has asked for help with his speech, and I've agreed to help—very discreetly. It's got a historical theme, and he suggested"—she rolled her eyes—"that maybe I should look in the original archives for some inspiration. He suggested documents by Tacitus," she said, grasping for material that would cover Nero's reign. Actually, what interested Kate most were the writings of whatever muse had lived in or near Rome at that time. Muses were keen observers and attuned to supernatural phenomena. If Nathaniel's life on earth had begun during Nero's time as emperor, a muse may have noted it. "And before you ask anything else, let me just say that that's all I can tell you. If you'd like to turn me away, go ahead. Honestly, I'm really pressed for time, and I'd love to tell him that I couldn't get past ES."

The corner of the ES officer's mouth curved toward Heaven. He tipped his head forward and said in a low voice, "Since no one called ahead to let me know you were coming down, I don't think speechwriting is the reason you need to look at those books."

Her heart thumped in her chest. If he called Grant or a member of the council and caused trouble, Alissa would not be pleased with Kate. She cringed inwardly at the thought. Alissa had been extremely good to her. Kate didn't want anything to damage their rapport.

"You do some brilliant work, Ms. Devane, so I'm going to trust that if you're here on the night of the holiday party, you've got a good reason."

Thank God! She pressed her lips closed and nodded.

"Don't disrespect my trust. You remember how to handle the materials?"

She nodded again.

"Then go in."

She didn't exhale until she was inside the climate-controlled, moisture-controlled safe-deposit box of a room.

Nathaniel ate spiced lamb with peppered figs in an apricot glaze. It might have been the most delicious food he'd ever consumed, but given the current state of his memory it was hard to tell.

Merrick's knowledge of archangels was secondhand but useful. Apparently the fallen archangels kept their bodies for eternity, but those who had not fallen were given new and better bodies on occasion. It took about a day for the soul to bond with its new shell and for the angel's memories to organize themselves within a new brain. It was fascinating.

"If this body is new, how did you recognize me?" Nathaniel asked.

"You get upgraded DNA with each body, but you look the same."

Nathaniel nodded. "That explains how Kate recognized me from her dreams." Nathaniel paused as warmth flowed through him at the thought of her. He had woken near her house, so it stood to reason that Heaven had wanted him to find her, but to what end? Was his association with her meant to provide him with information he needed? Or was there something else—something more emotional— that he was to gain from his relationship with her? He hoped for the latter, recalling the feel of her soft lips against his.

Nathaniel asked, "Do you consider yourself skilled with women?"

Merrick quirked a brow. At moments like this, the dark-haired ventala seemed to regret the bargain they'd forged. *Talkative* wasn't an adjective ever associated with Merrick, and at present, Merrick had apparently far exceeded his conversation quota for the day.

For him to do this, that muse must be very important to him, Nathaniel thought.

"You're an angel, Nathaniel. Once you bond with that body, very few women will be able to resist you. Give it a day, and you won't need my help. Or anyone else's."

"I'm not certain it will be that easy with Kate."

Merrick steepled his fingers. "Then find out what she wants and what she needs, and give her those things."

"How can I find out what she wants and needs? By asking her?"

Merrick laughed. "No. She may not even know, and if she did, she wouldn't tell you. It's your job to figure it out. Spend time with her and pay attention."

"The problem is that I want her now. Without delay."

Merrick smiled. "Welcome to the plight of being male."

Nathaniel tipped his head back and stared at the ceiling. "I wish there was a demon she needed me to kill. I could accomplish that with pleasure and efficiency."

"That would be convenient."

"It seems to me that it was easier in the time of my birth. Women needed men for many things. Less so now. Kate lives alone and earns her own living. And though she was quick to offer me aid, she doesn't want to admit that at times she needs help in return. It puts us at odds." Nathaniel glanced at Merrick, whose expression revealed less than the Sphinx's. "She was angry when I left. I was gruff because I was jealous that she chose to enter the Etherlin with another man, rather than come with me. She was so friendly with them. It infuriated me. I want her for myself alone."

"Be careful of jealousy."

Nathaniel nodded. "I recognize the danger, but her appeal is distracting. I find it challenging to organize my thoughts when I'm near her."

"The muses' holiday party will be a good opportunity. Humans like celebrating, and they're sentimental during the holidays. Kate will probably be in a good mood and a little better for wine; she'll be more likely to forgive you if you make a mistake."

"Good. Kate's important to me," Nathaniel said. "At moments, it's hard to think of anything besides her. That seems significant. Perhaps she was chosen for me. If so, I have to comply with what's ordained, and so must she."

"Don't tell Kate, or even imply, that you're pursuing her because you're under orders to."

Nathaniel frowned. "You suggest subterfuge and dishonesty? Demons deal in those, not angels."

"I'm not suggesting that you trick her. I'm telling you that you have to be selective about what you share. And when. And how."

Nathaniel's scowl deepened. "I don't know. Being direct and pushing for a quick resolution appeals to me."

Merrick shrugged. "Then don't take my advice. Follow your instincts."

Nathaniel narrowed his eyes. "But you don't think I'll succeed if I do?"

"I didn't say that. If Heaven's your matchmaker, I'm sure the girl doesn't stand a chance. But you probably won't win her over as fast as you'd like."

"You have something more to say on this subject. I wish to know what that is."

Merrick smiled. "Vampires and demons have seduced their way through entire continents. Both the angels I know could fit what they know about women in a shot glass."

Nathaniel frowned. "I don't believe that learning about women has been my priority. This body was made for fighting."

"Yeah, but you'd like to use it for something else, right?"

Nathaniel took a deep breath in and exhaled slowly, trying to overcome the urge to send his fist smashing into Merrick's amused face. "Yes, I want her the way men want their wives. The desire runs deep," Nathaniel said, pausing as thoughts of making love to Kate diverted blood to the lower part of his body and made him ache. "But I won't compromise my nature during the negotiation."

"The negotiation," Merrick said, and from his dubious expression, Nathaniel knew that wasn't a word to which women would respond favorably.

"The courtship?" Nathaniel said.

"Sure, if we were in Regency England. Listen, archangels have the gift of tongues. You probably speak a dozen dead languages. When in doubt, lapse into one of those. Something like Etruscan, so she'll have no idea what you're saying."

"Merrick?"

"Yeah?"

"Fuck off."

Merrick laughed.

"How was that for use of the modern vernacular?" Nathaniel asked.

"Not bad."

• • •

Kate's initial excitement at gaining access to the archives had given way to impatience and fatigue. The pages were so stiff and fragile that she couldn't quickly thumb through them. And Nathaniel's heavy ring had caused a cramp in her hand.

She returned to the metal table with the two last resources on the period when Nathaniel had supposedly lived. Sitting on the uncushioned metal chair that was modern, sterile, and incredibly uncomfortable, she carefully examined page after page of the original texts and the corresponding translations. She pictured the modern muses in monks' robes slaving over the ancient documents. The work must have been so tedious.

The joint at the base of her thumb ached and she slid the ring forward, rubbing her skin. Then she turned a page and sucked in a startled breath. Pictured in a gilded full-color illustration was Nathaniel, bloody and restrained by men who forced him to kneel; standing over him was the very blond, eerily pretty man who'd held the knife to her throat in her dreams.

The text seemed to leap out at her, and she had to stare and concentrate to read the words. The white-blond man was identified as Gaius Gadreel Seneca, the brother of Nero's tutor and advisor. The muse wrote, "His external beauty disguises the darkest of souls. I believe Gadreel to be a demon in human form, for it's hard to accept that anyone human who was capable of such depravity and malice could be so embraced by reasonable men, no matter what services he's performed or aid he's rendered them. His hold is supernaturally strong. I have heard Gadreel boast of using both the young emperor and his mother Agrippina as whores. Nero's advisors are clearly afraid and in awe of Gaius Gadreel. How can anyone wield such power over the most powerful people in the whole of the Roman Empire? It is unnatural. He is a vortex of evil, and my influence has been no match for his. Murder is rampant, and not only for political gain. For Gadreel, humiliating and destroying good Roman citizens is a ripe plum. Impotent and unable to watch any longer, I am bound for the coast tomorrow. I hope never to lay eyes on his terrible face again. I hope also that my prayers for justice are answered."

Staring down at the page, Kate slid the ring back on her thumb. The world seemed to tilt and blur and waves of pain crashed over her. She was on her knees, bloody and battered, swallowing dust. Everything hurt. Bones broken. Flesh torn. She saw her swollen hands in the dirt, but they were a man's hands. Bruised, calloused, and tan. Memories of a hundred hours of torture roared through her mind as she looked up through tear-blurred eyes. Pain screamed and screeched within the body—Nathaniel's body. This again was his memory, but she felt everything, the hurt so pervasive, so profound that she wanted to wail, but Nathaniel only groaned, his hoarse voice nearly gone.

"I warned you, Nathaniel, that God would not protect you, didn't I?" Gadreel said. "I promised you that Nero would not help you. And he did not. That his advisors would not listen. And they did not. No one can stop me. Now your family is dead. Where is your precious God? Not with you, that much is certain, because he cares not for the suffering of men. He allows me to do what I will."

A knee slammed into Nathaniel's chin, jarring his body and causing a fresh wave of sharp pain that made him crumple into a heap. Blood gushed from his split lip. Kate shrieked in frustration. She wanted to cover Nathaniel's body with hers, to protect him from any more abuse. She wanted to tear Gadreel to pieces.

"Denounce him," Gadreel hissed. "Kiss my ring and call me master. I will end your pain."

She felt Nathaniel's soul recoil. There was no defiance left, only exhaustion and an unspoken prayer that he'd be strong enough to remain silent. She wanted to scream. She wanted to shove Gadreel away, but she had no body other than Nathaniel's, which was too weak.

Shards of light broke over the room. Gadreel went on talking, unaware. His men pulled Nathaniel's body so that he knelt upright. Gadreel placed the ring, the one with the coin image of Nero against Nathaniel's broken lip.

"Kiss my ring and pledge your allegiance," Gadreel screamed.

Tears streamed over a shattered cheekbone and swollen skin. One eye bled and watered from having been poked with a dagger.

Gadreel bent his head low. "Not ready yet?" he whispered, the malice in his voice so evil it sent an icy wave of fear through Nathaniel. "Well, men, this boy is anxious for more. Strip him, dip him in the pool to rinse away the filth, then bring him to me. Naked."

Their harsh laughter was more than Kate could bare. She wanted to kill them. She tried to shoot up and smash her fist into Gadreel's face, but Nathaniel's broken leg crumpled beneath her. She fell, striking her head, and darkness fell.

"Kate," a gorgeous voice said.

Kate opened her eyes to the soft light of burning candles. Pine and vanilla scented the air, a warm comfort, and Alissa North leaned over her with concerned pale blue eyes.

Kate put a hand to her aching head, finding a small knot on the back of her scalp. She grimaced, but then remembered the horrific pain that she'd endured in Nathaniel's memory and the mild headache seemed insignificant.

"Where am I?" Kate rasped.

"My house. The ES duty guard at the Dome said you fainted. He said you'd mentioned that you'd missed lunch and down you went. He couldn't get around his desk quick enough to catch you."

Kind lies. "How long was I out?"

"Twenty-five minutes. A neurologist is on the way over."

A house call from a specialist. *The muses do indeed have magical powers*, Kate thought wryly.

Kate sat up and took the glass of water Alissa offered. "I'm fine now, but I am having a very strange day."

"So I've heard," Alissa said. "Grant called and said that the man who dropped you off was probably a fallen angel."

"He's not fallen!" Kate blinked. "Sorry, I didn't mean to yell. I'm just not sure he's fallen. I don't want to paint him with that brush yet."

"Not fallen, but you do think he's an archangel?"

Kate nodded, then shrugged. "I'm not sure."

"Kate," Alissa said gently.

"What?" Kate said. She'd felt the soothing, persuasive vibration in Alissa's voice that pushed Kate to suspect the worst of Nathaniel. "Why does he have to be fallen?" Kate demanded, resisting.

"The archangels of Heaven don't mix with people. Legend allows that they might save a human being in the course of killing a demon, but they don't join the community of man. Heaven's real ranks are a thing apart."

"Well then, Nathaniel's not an archangel because he lived and had a family."

"Why do you think he didn't want to come into the Etherlin?"

Kate shrugged.

"Do you think he worried that his true nature would be revealed?"

Kate thought about the overwhelming pain she'd felt for that brief time in Nathaniel's terrible memory. What else had happened to him that she hadn't seen? Had it been horrible enough for him to renounce God? Had he fallen or become damned? She shuddered. His intention had been so pure. If his will had been broken, it hadn't been his fault. God could have shown him a little fucking mercy. She lurched from the sofa, feeling ill. She swallowed hard. "I'm gonna be sick. Bathroom?" She slapped a hand over her mouth.

Alissa guided her to the bathroom, and then in a surreal turn of events, the most beautiful woman in the world who never had so much as a speck of dirt on her clothes held Kate's hair back while she retched so violently it tore sobs from her.

Alissa's fingers soothed the back of Kate's neck. "It'll be all right. After the doctor sees you, you can take a hot shower and lie down."

Kate shook her head and banged Nathaniel's—no, Gadreel's—ring on the cold tile, hard enough to bruise her finger. She took a deep breath and said, "Absolutely not." She exhaled, wincing at the rough condition of her throat. "I've been looking forward to this holiday party all year. I'm not going to sleep through the damn thing." *Besides, if Nathaniel wants to see me later, he may not be willing to enter the*

Etherlin, but he could come to the Clarity Hotel in the Sliver. She'd mentioned the name of the hotel to him on the drive to the Etherlin.

Alissa's crystalline blue eyes seemed to peer into her soul. "You hardly seem ready for a party."

Kate narrowed her eyes. "Pulitzer Prize–winners don't let little things like concussions put them off their schedules."

Alissa smiled. "You don't need to prove how tough you are, Kate."

"I don't need to, but I like to."

Alissa's smile widened. "And your determination to go to the party has nothing to do with the fact that Nathaniel expects to find you there?"

"Of course not," Kate said, but the corners of her mouth curved up guiltily. "You didn't meet him. He's somewhat—I don't know. Sublime."

"Some men have impossibly strong charisma," Alissa said wistfully.

Kate inclined her head. "Speaking from experience?"

Alissa blinked and shuttered her expression. "No, but I'm a great observer of human behavior, you know. It helps me be a better muse."

"Well, you're certainly an amazing muse," Kate said, fighting her investigative reporter's instinct to dig. As friendly as Alissa was, she was also an enigma. She'd dated Grant for years, but theirs didn't seem to be a particularly passionate relationship. That they'd never gotten married, or even engaged, caused some speculation, but Alissa had never been caught in an affair with anyone else or even seemed interested in anyone. It was odd, given how often men pursued her.

"How are things between you and Grant?"

Again, Alissa's expression became carefully neutral. "Grant's a wonderful man. I'm lucky to have him in my life."

Kate burned with curiosity. Was Alissa's relationship a sham?

"Are you sure you're up to going tonight?" Alissa asked.

"Yes, I feel all right now." *The aftereffects of that brutal memory have passed.* Another stab of compassion rocked her body. Nathaniel had been through so much. And now Kate felt like she'd been through some of it with him. Deep wounds. The trauma, both physical and emotional, had been almost unbearable. She shuddered. Where was

Nathaniel now? She regretted not going with him. The raw emotional connection they had was something she'd never experienced with anyone else. She shivered, missing his warmth. She needed to see him, to be sure he was all right.

"Did you bring your dress with you? The party people will be here soon."

"Party people?"

"The people who get me ready for important events." Alissa rolled her eyes. "I think I could be trusted to manage on my own, but the Etherlin Council likes us to be picture perfect at our own parties. And at everyone else's," Alissa added with a wink. "If you don't feel like doing your own hair and makeup, you can just sit next to me. They style everything in their paths, like a swarm of compact-carrying locusts."

"Since I don't get the spa treatment every day, I don't think I'd mind. Do you think they would be annoyed at having another woman to make up?"

Alissa shook her head. "They're artists, and nothing tempts an artist like a fresh canvas."

Nathaniel's memories flooded his mind in torrents of bright visions that were hard to sort. He stood straight as Merrick's tailor popped platinum cuff links into the shirt he wore, but Nathaniel was only half paying attention. His mind was full of the first time he'd seen Kate. He'd been looking for his ring, and he'd found it on the hand of a pretty girl. She'd been lying on a bench, the sunlight streaming over her as she highlighted the book she read. She'd muttered something and laughed, putting a yellow X over a passage. In that moment, he felt something tug his soul. A memory of himself using a dagger to cut a slash across Nero's face on the coin. *Defiance.* Yes, he understood that. The girl's animated expression, the life shining on her face—they drew him to her. He'd wanted to approach her, to hear her voice, to whisper to her soul. But he hadn't spoken to her. Not that day or any other that he could remember. Why hadn't he? He could feel how much he'd wanted to. Unleashed now, the desire roared through him. More than anything, he wanted Kate.

This drive to be with her is significant. By instinct, I'm more drawn to her than to anything else. There must be a reason.

"You like it?" the tailor asked, nodding at Nathaniel's reflection in the mirror.

"It's formal. I don't believe I normally dress this way."

"If you don't want to get bounced, you need the right camouflage," Merrick said, slipping money to the tailor who nodded and left.

"It's generous of you to help with this," Nathaniel said.

"One hand washing the other. Here's your invitation."

"It's forged?"

"It is, but it's a very good forgery, right down to the bar code and the invisible stamp."

"If you can create an invitation of this quality, why can't you deliver your gift in person?"

Merrick grinned. "I'm infamous. If there's an ES officer who doesn't recognize me on sight, he needs to be fired."

"Ah."

Merrick handed him a wrapped package.

"If there's no note, and I'm not allowed to tell anyone—even her—who sent this, how will she know it's from you?"

Instead of answering, Merrick handed Nathaniel the card key for the hotel suite they currently occupied. "I'll be here until eleven. After that, the room's yours."

Nathaniel nodded, understanding that by their arrangement Merrick was willing to answer questions that had to do with Nathaniel but not about himself.

"I still can't remember how I was called to become an archangel," Nathaniel said. "Shouldn't that have come back by now?"

"Seems like it," Merrick said.

"It's like seeing a picture where part of the image has been blacked out. And it's right in the center of the frame. I can't ignore what's missing, but no matter how long I stare at that spot, I can't restore what's gone. The image is stubbornly marred."

"And you don't remember the demons you've killed?"

"I remember some battles but not all of them."

"How do you know?"

"I feel it. I have an enemy. I don't know his name or his face, but there's an anger that burns through me." Nathaniel clamped his fist closed. "Rage isn't born of nothing."

"No," Merrick agreed.

Nathaniel let his fist relax, staring at his hand where the ring should have been. He needed to retrieve it.

A warning slithered through him, a feeling that duty and desire were converging. From the stillness, he felt the kiss of darkness. Of pain.

Danger has risen. He comes to destroy.

Nathaniel stiffened.

Kate wears your ring, and you left her unprotected.

Adrenaline poured into his veins. "I have to leave now," he said, striding to the door. He yanked it open as his instincts suddenly drove him in a single direction. Toward the party. Toward Kate.

Chapter Six

The city blocks that hugged the Etherlin's outer wall were called the Sliver, and the area courted Etherlin society. The Sliver couldn't legally ban ventala from driving down its streets, but it did its best to make them unwelcome.

In honor of the muses holding their holiday party within, the Sliver's opulent boutique hotel, Clarity, was strung with lavender and white lights and huge silver bows and wreaths. A deep purple carpet stretched from the front doors to the curb where white limousines delivered tuxedo-clad men escorting women adorned with jewels to rival a queen's.

Waiters in white gloves served onlookers coffee, hot chocolate, and eggnog, courtesy of the muses who wanted their fans and admirers to feel like part of the celebration. Each time a famous Etherlin resident emerged from a car, they were greeted by cheers and applause.

Kate glanced at Alissa, who looked like royalty in her white velvet cloak. Tiny crystals clung to Alissa's eyelashes like sparkling dewdrops, emphasizing her otherworldly beauty. Alissa's stylists had worked their magic on Kate, too. She barely recognized herself in the gown of gold and bronze taffeta that she'd chosen because its colors reminded her of Nathaniel.

Nathaniel. Again. Her preoccupation with him filled every corner of her mind.

"You're lovely in that dress, Kate," Alissa said.

"It's quite a departure from the camos and khakis I wear on field assignment. And there's no layer of salt and dirt on my skin; my editor will be shocked," Kate said, smirking. "I hope someone gets a picture."

"I don't think you have to worry about that." As the door opened and hundreds of flashbulbs popped, Alissa gave the crowd a picture perfect view of her wide blue eyes and slightly parted lips.

Kate slid from the car and glanced at the onlookers. ES bodyguards flanked Alissa who paused, smiled, and waved. The muse moved very slowly toward the door, allowing people to capture her with their cameras as well as their eyes.

"I'll meet you inside," Kate said with a smile.

Alissa nodded and smiled apologetically. "They've waited in the cold for hours."

"Of course, take your time. You know me, the intrepid reporter. I can take care of myself." Kate edged toward the door, her gaze following a bright spotlight that wasn't trained on the carpet. It highlighted an enormous seven-and-a-half-foot-tall angel ice sculpture standing near the door. The arches of frosty white wings rose above the crest of broad shoulders. He wore an armored breastplate, and the edges of his sword's blade glinted like the facets of a jewel. She couldn't take her eyes off him as she approached, and then he moved. Her breath caught, and she slowed. The clustered people had left space for him but didn't register his presence. Could they see him?

She stared up when she reached him. He didn't step over the velvet rope, standing sentry instead, face impassive.

His breath was wind rustling her bangs, chilling her skin.

"It does not belong to you," he said with a slight incline of his head. She looked at the ring circling her thumb.

"He asked me to keep the ring for him," she said. People glanced at her curiously, bestowing polite smiles since she was an aspirant.

"Do not hold what does not belong to you."

The urge to tell him to mind his own business spiked through her, but she held her tongue. As she passed, a phantom wing beat the air directly in front of her and she strode through an icy mist that dampened her skin. She gasped for breath and pushed her way inside.

The ES security officer blinked. "Is it raining?" he asked.

She shook her head, handing him her invitation before she hurried to the bathroom to dab the moisture off her skin. Fortunately, her makeup wasn't terribly smeared and the damp evaporated quickly as she stood beneath the vents blowing heat.

Who—and what—the hell was that?

She looked at the ring, bending her thumb against her palm, pressing the ring tight to her skin. She wondered if the ice angel had meant something other than the ring when he'd told her to let go of what didn't belong to her. She scowled. It wasn't as if she'd tried to sink claws into Nathaniel. On the other hand, she didn't intend to just pass him his ring and walk away. She wanted to help him, and if she was being honest, she wanted to be near him again. At moments, the way she craved him overwhelmed her.

Kate took a deep breath, pulled her shoulders back, and exited the bathroom, wishing she had a way to reach Nathaniel. What if he didn't return for days? Nothing drove her crazier than waiting.

Crossing the prism-patterned sapphire and periwinkle carpet, she'd nearly reached the ballroom doors when she heard birds chirping. She turned, and a pair of lime-colored lovebirds with salmon pink faces flew into the stairwell just before its door whooshed closed. Impossibly, she still heard tweeting.

Frosted angels at the door and chirping lovebirds in the lobby that no one seems to see except me? Surreptitiously, she pinched her arm. The sharp pain sobered her. *Okay then, Alice, go down the rabbit hole. Or up, as the case may be.*

Kate strode to the stairs, dragged the heavy door open, and ascended.

On the roof, snow-dusted wire topiary skeletons of mythical creatures stood next to planters filled with rock crystal and alabaster. A *winter garden*, she mused. She pulled her wrap tighter, her breath smoky on the cold air.

"One of these things doesn't belong. Which one?" she whispered the childhood singsong, spotting another enormous angel. Formed from golden light that shone outward, he wore a buff-colored loin-cloth and a gold ring around his neck. Skill had apparently not been spared when forming the angels, but despite the aggressive muscula-ture, he carried no armor or weapons and his tousled hair flowed carelessly.

"Hello, Kate," he said as the lovebirds flew past and landed on the head of a bear topiary.

She approached him. "If you're about to bark out some orders or recriminations, you can save your breath."

He smiled. "Not recriminations. Advice."

She raised her brows.

"Destroy the ring now, and when you see him, don't allow yourself to hesitate. Let instinct guide you."

"Who are you?" she asked, unable to move away from his glowing warmth.

"Don't waste time on things that are of no consequence to you, Kate. Ask important questions as your education and experience would dictate."

"Why should I destroy Nathaniel's ring?"

"That ring was forged in the flesh of a future angel. Gadreel flamed the ring and burned Nathaniel with it, leaving a scar that never fades. Hatred bound them together, demon and angel, in an epic battle. When the angel's wings are fully formed, he will take up the dagger and hunt, the urge irresistible. They track each other through the ring, drawn to the symbol of their malice. Destroy the reminder, and you'll spare him the memories for that much longer."

"He doesn't remember what happened?"

"Not yet. I was given permission to alter the course of his memory's return."

"Why? By whom?"

He smiled. "Nathaniel was not born an angel. He was human, and after nineteen hundred years his heart needs more than ven-geance. It seeks what it lost. Love. In you, I saw a spirit that suited his. So I showed you to him. When the ring was torn from his finger during their battle and fell to earth, I cast it into your path and let you see it. You took it up and kept it of your own accord. The angel chief of war thinks Nathaniel carelessly let the rain hydrate the blood and soak your skin, that you were bound by an angel's blood by accident. I say there was nothing accidental about Nathaniel's distraction. He did not dry the water from his skin before taking the ring and you had it clutched in your hand while you slept for a reason. In anticipation of each other."

"But he never talked to me. Never introduced himself. It's been years since that night. If we're so fated, why did he ignore me all this time?"

"Ignore you?" The angel's laughter warmed her skin like sunshine. Her muscles loosened and relaxed. She felt that she could have lain on the nearby bench and slept for an age.

She shook herself, trying to steel herself against the effect his presence had. "Cut it out," she growled.

"So you think he's ignored you? Lovely Kate, I want you to remember something. The investigation for which you won your great award—do you recall the details of that day?"

"Of course. The discovery of that nest of vampires changed my life."

"In the cave, when your flash woke the oldest, the most powerful, you ran toward the cave's yawning mouth, toward the sunlight, but you knew you wouldn't make it. You'd gotten too close. You felt the brush of cold fingers, and sharp nails grazed your skin when you were still eight feet from freedom. What happened?"

Adrenaline spiked her blood at the memory of that terrifying moment. If that vampire had gotten a firm hold, her bones would've joined the pile of human remains in that cave. "I got lucky. The vamp tripped."

"Are ancient vampires clumsy? And even if one stumbled, could you outrun it once it regained its balance?"

"What are you saying?"

"I'm saying something watches over you. I'm saying a warrior angel waded into the shadow and when that vampire reached out and would have grabbed you and dragged you back, a deadlier creature struck him down. You travel to the most dangerous places on earth and live in solitary safety because you claim the attention and the protection of an archangel."

Her jaw dipped open as her mind reeled. Had Nathaniel been there? It shocked and pleased her to think so. She wished she'd realized . . . had been able to thank him . . . to touch him. "He never spoke to me or made himself known."

"He fears it."

Why? I'd never have rejected him. I wanted to find him so badly!

"Fears it because he's shy?" she mumbled, confused.

"No, because he sensed if he got so close, he would not be able to pull back. Angels belong to Heaven. They may not consort with humans."

"Never?"

He shook his head.

"Then why show us to each other?" she cried, sharp pain piercing her heart. She couldn't have Nathaniel. "That's cruel! Why let us meet now when nothing can come of it?"

He frowned, casting a thousand shadows that chilled her skin. "If you believe it's a hopeless cause, it will be. I don't offer a solution. Only a choice. For him and for you."

"Why? When there isn't time enough for us to commit? I'm sure his wings will be finished forming soon. When? How long?"

"Hours."

"Hours?" she snapped. "But we've just met. We barely know each other."

"I've shown you what you needed to see. You've felt his pain and know his character. Take action or do not. I only offer a chance. The rest must be chosen."

As Nathaniel used his invitation to enter the hotel, he heard music emanating from the ballroom. B. B. King sang "I'll Be Home for

Christmas." Nathaniel smiled. He'd been to a King concert in Philadelphia sometime in the 1970s. He'd listened from the stadium rafters.

Nathaniel wasn't sure if he'd loved music when he'd been human, but once he'd become an angel, he couldn't resist it. The original angels had invented dancing, and a passion for music had been passed to every generation since.

When Nathaniel spotted Kate, she was laughing, and he thought there might be something he could love as much as music.

On his way across the ballroom, he encountered Alissa whom he recognized from a picture that Merrick had shown him. Nathaniel wanted to ignore his promise to Merrick because he hated for anything to delay him reaching Kate, but an archangel's promise had to be honored.

"Hello," he said.

"Hello." Alissa smiled, and Nathaniel noted that she smelled nice, of fresh and powerful magic and pretty perfume. Still, it didn't move him the way the scent of Kate's skin did when they were close.

Nathaniel removed Merrick's gift from inside his jacket and passed it to Alissa.

"A present. How kind of you, but unnecessary, Mr.—?"

"I'm Nathaniel, and that's not from me."

"Kate's friend Nathaniel?" she asked, her gaze darting around. "I thought you had a run-in with Director Easton at the gate. How did you get into the party?"

"I was able to acquire an invitation."

"That's not possible," she said. "Grant's here, you know? Why don't you wait in the lobby, and I'll send Kate?"

Nathaniel shook his head. "You have a different appointment. You're supposed to open that on the balcony of the second floor bar at ten thirty."

"According to whom?"

He leaned forward and whispered, "According to the man who sent it. He couldn't deliver it himself because he's infamous."

Her cheeks turned the color of pink roses. In a cool voice that didn't betray the flush, she said, "It was very kind of you to bring me a gift. Come with me." She took his arm and turned him. "Director Easton is headed this way," she said. "If you want to talk to Kate, you'd better hurry before he spots you and ES throws you out."

Nathaniel smiled. "Forcing me to leave before I'm ready isn't as easy as it might seem."

Alissa tilted her head, causing the jewels dangling from her ears to sway. "You want to make her happy, not cause trouble, don't you?"

He felt the persuasive magic in her voice. Magic didn't affect him, but he understood why humans would be influenced by it. "I don't want trouble. I just want Kate."

"Glad to hear it," she said, gliding gracefully away.

Nathaniel glanced at the clock. Ten twenty-five. He hoped she found the balcony in time.

Merrick stood at the open window of the suite he'd rented for Nathaniel. Two stories down and across the street, the second-floor balcony door opened. Merrick raised his binoculars and waited, his muscles tight with anticipation.

In all the years that he'd been sending Alissa North gifts, he'd never seen her open one. Just as she'd never seen him open one of her letters. A law, a wall, and hundreds of security officers separated them and probably always would. And yet the exchange of letters and gifts didn't stop.

Alissa stepped out and stood just under the lamp.

"Exactly there," he murmured.

She glanced around, but even if she looked up she wouldn't see him. There were no lights on in the suite. He stood, as he lived, absorbed in darkness. The single spot of white light in his world wore a silvery blue dress and carefully removed the indigo tissue paper from her present.

Alissa claimed that she couldn't keep the gifts he sent, which goaded Merrick to find something she wouldn't be able to part with. Alissa came from the line of muses who inspired authors, and he'd read that she collected rare books. In an interview, she'd once talked about how the world becomes what a person perceives it to be, quoting a line from John Milton's epic poem, *Paradise Lost.* "The mind in its own place, and in itself can make a Heaven of Hell, a Hell of Heaven."

Merrick had liked the line, too, and so a search was begun that took two years.

When Alissa finished unwrapping the 1669 edition of *Paradise Lost,* her hand fluttered to her mouth in surprise.

Merrick grinned. "I defy you to give that away."

She stared at the book for several long moments and shook her head.

"Yes, that was extremely hard to acquire," he said, imagining what she was thinking. "And worth every penny to see your face when you opened it."

She glanced up, and it was as though she looked right at him. Those eyes, so pale and blue, trapped him in her gaze. A second later, she looked around again. Then she touched her lips and extended her fingers, blowing a kiss into the night.

He didn't move, didn't breathe. She stood still as a statue, too. It was like being frozen in time together. Snow began to fall, casting her as an angel in a snow globe.

Her lips moved silently. "Merry Christmas, Merrick."

He exhaled slowly, every inch of him alive for a girl he'd never even kissed. Whispering, he said, "Merry Christmas, Alissa."

"Hello, Kate."

She glanced over her shoulder and found Nathaniel, tuxedo clad and as beautifully bronze as ever. Her heart sped to a pounding rhythm on a rush of heady adrenaline. Normally, she would have hesitated, but nothing was normal anymore. She was elated to see him unhurt and looking for her. If she'd been through all he had, she would've gone into the revenge business, too, and never looked back, never noticed a girl. But here he was, and it felt like a missing part of her had been returned.

Her heart thudded, her throat burned, and her eyes stung as she stepped forward. She slid her arms around his neck and hugged him, shocked by how amazing it felt to touch him.

"Hi," she whispered.

His arms folded around her. "Kate, you're trembling."

"Yeah, I've been through a lot today. So have you, of course." She started to step back, but his grip tightened.

"Don't go yet. Doesn't this feel right?" he asked, his voice deep and earnest. "When I was wounded, you were my comfort. Now you're shaking; I'll be your strength. I'd like to give you what you need. Or want. I won't ask you what that is . . . though it could make things more—but perhaps not—" The corner of his mouth turned down, and he shook his head, then added something in a foreign language.

She chuckled. "What was that last part?"

"Etruscan. You don't speak Etruscan, do you?"

"No."

"Good," he said.

She tipped her head back, looking him in the eye. "And neither does anyone else, other than you." She smiled at him. "You should let me go. People are starting to stare."

"If we danced, I wouldn't have to let you go, right?"

"I don't really dance."

"Why not?" he asked, sounding as surprised as if she'd said "I don't really eat."

"That's not important right now, is it?" Her palms slid off his shoulders, and she drew her hands back, leaning away. "I still have your ring. Do you remember how you got it?"

He shook his head.

"Nathaniel, there are things we need to talk about."

"Of course, Kate. We can do whatever you'd like."

Wow. That created a riot of pleasure in every part of her.

She slid the ring from her thumb, but hesitated. Could she put it on him and risk that the memories would come flooding back to him in so public a place? She closed her fist around the ring and dropped her hand to her side. She stared at his untroubled eyes. She always wanted to know every secret, but his past . . . those memories were so destructive; anyone sane would be happy to forget them. "But maybe that can wait a little longer. What do you want to talk about?"

"I'd like to hear about your work."

"Wow," she said. "You really are five shades of irresistible."

He smiled. "That may be because I'm an angel."

"No, it's more than that," she said, then she saw Grant Easton approaching, and her smile faded. "And here comes trouble. We cannot catch a break."

Nathaniel looked over his shoulder, then back at her. He inclined his head to speak in her ear, his warm breath tickling her skin. "I still want to dance with you." He released her and turned.

"This is a private party," Grant said coolly.

"I came to see Kate."

"You've seen her."

Nathaniel looked Grant up and down. "I have no wish to interfere with the performance of your duties, but I will not leave her."

"Then we have a problem," Grant said, sliding a hand inside his tuxedo and unsnapping a shoulder holster.

Kate sucked in a breath, catching Nathaniel's arm. "It's too crowded to dance here. Let's leave."

"Yes," Nathaniel said to Kate. To Grant, he added, "No need to die tonight, Mr. Easton."

Grant bristled and shook his head at Kate in disapproval.

Looking at Grant she said, "I'm sorry, but you don't know him."

"Neither do you," Grant said, frowning.

Yes, I do.

She threaded her fingers through Nathaniel's, tightening her grip on his hand. When they reached the lobby, she realized she hadn't needed to worry about a scene erupting. Nathaniel hadn't given Grant a second glance, and Grant hadn't interfered with her decision to leave. Kate was grateful for reasonable men.

"I have a room here," she said.

"Does your room have a balcony that looks over the city?"

"No," she said with a smile. "I may work with a muse, but I don't have her bankroll. Because of tonight's event, this hotel is booked solid with people who can afford to pay a lot for a great view."

"Well, I have a balcony to my room. At the hotel across the street."

"You have a room at the Grand?"

"A suite, yes. For the night," he said, nodding. "Will you come?"

With a slow smile, she said, "Yes." Her gown whispered over the lobby carpet as they crossed to the front doors. "But aren't you worried about ruining my reputation by taking me there?"

"No," he said, holding the door for her.

"You remember that the world has changed?"

"Yes." He paused. "Also, I plan to convince you to marry me." Her brows rose, and he flashed a smile, stepping outside. "A handfasting ceremony is easily accomplished."

"What kind of—?" Kate didn't complete the question on the tip of her tongue because the words evaporated when she spotted a killer.

Chapter Seven

"Shit. It's Merrick," Kate said.

"You know him?"

"Of him. The ventala have sent their biggest gun after you. And he's not alone," she said. "That pair next to the black sedan are the son and daughter of the syndicate boss. And the guys getting out of the car are more ventala. A hit squad," she said, yanking his arm, trying to pull him back toward the Clarity.

"No, Kate," Nathaniel said, standing firm. "Archangels don't run. If Merrick has betrayed me, I will deal with him. And anyone else who confronts me."

She blinked at the set of Nathaniel's jaw. One moment he was all romantic innocence. The next he was harder than bronze and battle ready.

Nathaniel caught her face in his hands and kissed her forehead. "Please wait for me inside, Kate. I'll try not to be very long."

An incredulous sound rose from her throat.

"Go ahead."

"Like hell," she said, yanking open her purse and clutching the antique dagger she'd taken from a wall display in Alissa's house. Kate would've preferred something with firepower, but the muses collected things for their historical significance and beauty, not for actual use.

"You're carrying a weapon?" Nathaniel asked. "Don't you trust me to protect you?"

"I know you're very capable, but we're often pretty outnumbered."

"*I'm* outnumbered. That need not be a risk to you, Kate. Go inside where you'll be safe."

"No."

"Why not?"

"Because you're very outnumbered, and Merrick's extremely deadly."

Nathaniel blinked and then grinned. "You want to stay to help me? To protect me?"

She glared at him.

Nathaniel fought to banish his smile. "That you feel the need to assist me in a fight is both insulting and endearing, but you are out of your depth and are smart enough to know it."

She pursed her lips, still holding the dagger's hilt. "How about a compromise? I'll go inside and watch from the window. If you don't get wounded, I'll stay in the lobby. But if it looks like you're losing, I'm coming out."

He glanced at her as they crossed the street.

"Got that?" she asked. "Don't lose."

"I have plans for us tonight, Kate. I won't lose."

As Kate and Nathaniel reached the front of the sedan, Tamberi Jacobi stared at Nathaniel and said to her brother, "That's him."

"You don't have a line big enough to hook that fish," Merrick said to the ventala who seemed to be in charge of the hit squad.

"Why the hell not?" the ventala asked. "I've never even heard of this guy, and there are six of us and one of him."

Merrick shrugged. "Your funeral."

"What's with you, Merrick?" Tamberi snapped. "You don't butt into things that have nothing to do with you. Walk away."

"A gun battle in the street outside the muse's holiday party will be trouble for everyone. Marco, who gave the order for you guys to come?"

"It came from the top," Marco said.

"By way of what messenger?" Merrick asked, glancing at Tamberi and Cato.

"Piss off, Merrick," Tamberi snarled. "This is none of your business."

"It's not syndicate business, either. I'd stake my patch of the Varden on that," Merrick said coolly. Merrick's dark eyes bored into the others. The stare was pure vampire. *Challenge me,* it said, *and I'll drown you in your own blood.* Kate shuddered, even as she wondered, *Why is he helping us?*

The ventala assassins looked around at each other. Marco cleared his throat. "Let me check this with the boss."

"*I* am telling you!" Tamberi said. "That bastard has been killing ventala. Haven't you?" she demanded of Nathaniel.

Merrick leaned casually against the wall.

"Ventala are not my natural enemy . . . but I'm flexible. There need not be a battle for me here, but attack me and I will answer in kind," Nathaniel said, pressing Kate toward the doors of the Grand. She took the steps slowly, unable to tear herself away.

"Go in," Merrick said to Nathaniel. "You're burning midnight. If the syndicate wants you dead, the fight will come to you soon enough."

Nathaniel spoke, but not in English. Then he strode up the steps to Kate.

"And in they fucking go," Tamberi snapped.

"You bunch of gutless pussies," Cato yelled. "Get out of my way," he said, shoving the other ventala away from the car. "And, Merrick, you cross me again, you better grow eyes in the back of your fucking head."

"Sure, and I'll buy a pair of boots so I can quake in them," Merrick said flatly.

Kate stifled a smile as the door closed, cutting off whatever Cato and Merrick said next.

"You're friends with Merrick?" she asked.

"No, but we're not enemies," Nathaniel said, leading her into a glass elevator with shiny brass rods between the panes.

"What did you say to him before we came inside?"

"I was glad he suggested that I not waste the night waiting for a fight. I told him that his advice is worth more than it costs."

"There's more to this story, isn't there?"

"I knew you would want more information. You always do," he said, idly tapping the tips of his fingers together. "I don't need advice on fighting, but my experience with the other parts of life is limited. Merrick's experience extends beyond killing. He knows about . . ." Nathaniel extended a hand in a vague gesture.

She raised her brows when he hesitated.

"Women," he said.

She fought not to smile at the heightened color in his cheeks. "I'm sure he does," she said dryly, finding it almost inconceivable that Merrick, black-hearted ventala enforcer, would offer advice to anyone about anything. "So what words of wisdom did he share?"

"You're not my wife yet, Kate."

"Meaning the advice was too graphic to tell me about?"

"No!" Nathaniel said, his flush deepening. His jaw tightened. "I meant, you're not my wife yet, so I don't have to tell you everything. And I don't intend to," he said stubbornly.

"If you plan to marry me, Nathaniel, I suspect whatever experience you lack, I'll find out about it pretty quickly."

He shrugged broad shoulders and said coolly, "I suspect when that time comes, I'll be too preoccupied to worry about it."

The smile won out. "I bet you're right." Kate, who prided herself on having been worldly from a young age, found it a huge surprise that she was charmed by the fact that Nathaniel was not.

"The view from here is great," Nathaniel said, pushing open the door to reveal another rooftop garden. Apparently, they were quite popular, and Kate could see why. The Grand's was just as beautiful as the Clarity's and had an accompanying tent creating a covered bar and dining area.

Clearly delighted, Nathaniel beckoned her. She guessed that it wasn't surprising that angels liked heights. With their wings, they were used to having a bird's-eye view of the world.

Flecks of snow dotted the ground, and when they rounded the

fabric wall of the large tent, she slowed. Steam rose from a hot tub, and snowflakes disappeared as they fell through the smoky condensation. An echo of her dream reverberated through her, and she went still, looking around sharply.

"This way," Nathaniel said, tugging her hand to lead her to the roof's edge. "The Etherlin lights are—what's wrong?"

"I'm cold," she said, shivering as thoughts rushed through her mind. The first two ventala attacks were unsuccessful. High-ranking syndicate members like Cato and Tamberi Jacobi would've known that, so if they'd realized that the third team to attack Nathaniel might fail and end up dead, why had they come along? And why had they been looking for him in the first place? Did they perhaps serve a demon named Gadreel?

Nathaniel slipped his warm tuxedo jacket around her shoulders. "Just have a look, and we'll go in and light a fire."

The ring's dead weight dragged on her thumb. She hadn't wanted to destroy the ring without talking to Nathaniel about it first, but now she wished she had.

The night's stillness hovered, and she walked uneasily to the roof's edge. The Etherlin holiday lights made the night sky blossom with color. Another time, she would have stared and been compelled to take photographs, but now Kate only wanted to escape the roof.

She backed away from the rail, holding tight to Nathaniel's hand to keep him with her.

His eyes narrowed. "It's not the cold. What's wrong, Kate?" he asked.

She glanced around. No swooping demon in sight. "I really need to talk to you about something. Let's go to the room."

"All right," he said.

It wasn't possible to drag an archangel anywhere, but as she rushed across the roof, she pulled hard on his arm. Her heels clattered on the stairs as she descended to their floor. Shoving the door open, she checked the hall. Satisfied of its emptiness, she strode out and thrust a hand into her purse, clutching the dagger. Nathaniel used a key card to open the door and she stalked into the room, sweeping through it to be sure that no demon lay in wait for them, checking even under the bed.

When she turned back to Nathaniel, his eyebrows rose in question.

She set her purse on the desk facing the balcony and made sure the balcony doors were secure and locked. She tossed the suit coat on the back of the chair and asked, "Will you light the fire please? There's something I think we should burn."

He removed his cuff links and rolled his sleeves up, then started and tended the fire until it crackled. Kate felt its reassuring heat from the middle of the room. Striding to the fireplace, she pulled the ring from her thumb and set it on the granite mantelpiece.

Nathaniel reached for the ring, but she stayed his hand.

"Don't touch it yet. How's your back?"

Nathaniel stretched and nodded. "Good. There's no aching now, only twitching of the muscles. My shoulder blades and ribs feel like they're rattling at times, which startles me, but it doesn't hurt. Well, it doesn't hurt much," he amended with a sheepish smile.

Honest and true. Just what one would expect from an angel, she thought. "In a little while, you're going to remember why you became an archangel and those memories are going to be awful. They should have come back first, but someone wanted to give us a chance to . . . a chance to fall in love, I guess," she said, hesitating. Her finely honed skepticism made having faith in anything, especially a whirlwind romance, difficult to embrace.

"I am in love," Nathaniel said.

Honest and true. Always, Kate thought.

"But I don't know that these few hours caused it. I think I always loved you. Everything I remember from my life before seems to revolve around trying to be near you."

"My supernatural stalker," she said with a small smile.

"What about you, Kate? What of your feelings for me?" The light around him glowed, reaching out to her, soaking into her skin, the warmth curling deep.

"Oh, I'm definitely in danger of falling in love with you." She stared at him. "It may already be too late."

"Is that such a terrible thing?" he asked, stepping close and inclining his head so their breath mingled. "Must you try to resist it?"

She closed her eyes, so she wouldn't have to look at him. That was too hard. "I have to be cautious, yes."

"Why?"

"Because you might not choose me."

"Of course I will. There's no one else."

"Not what I meant." Drawing in a breath as if it were courage, she paused, then exhaled audibly. "According to the chief angels, you can be an archangel or you can be a married man. You can't be both."

She felt the warmth fade, and when she opened her eyes, she found he'd taken a step back.

"Is that a law of Heaven?"

"Apparently so."

He nodded thoughtfully, then lowered himself to one knee, taking her hand. "Kate, would you do me the honor of becoming my wife?"

Her throat tightened, and she swallowed. "Don't you think you should wait until your memory is fully restored to make this choice? It's a big decision."

"I'm accustomed to taking things on faith, Kate. If Heaven didn't want me to act upon this love, it wouldn't have laid me in your backyard for you to find. It wouldn't have shown me memories of you, while suppressing memories that could have drawn me away from you. If a choice must be made, I choose a mortal life with you." His low voice was smooth and without hesitation. "Will you choose me as well?"

A matched set of tears rolled down her cheeks, and she swallowed hard. "I never make big decisions on a whim or take things on faith. Investigating, gathering information, making long lists of the pros and cons is really more my style," she murmured, feeling as though she stood at the edge of a cliff.

Don't hesitate, the golden angel from the Clarity roof had warned.

She brushed the moisture from her cheeks. "But sometimes, when I've had to make spur-of-the-moment decisions, I've followed hunches that changed my life. This feels like one of those moments." She swallowed against the emotion burning her throat. "Yes, Nathaniel," she whispered. "I will marry you."

He exhaled and smiled, devastating her with that unbelievable beauty. Rising, he gathered her to him and kissed her. Long moments passed during the kiss, and his grip became so tight, she couldn't catch her breath.

She pulled back, laughing and gasping. "You are so strong."

"Did I hurt you?"

She shook her head, sucking in a breath. "I'm just . . ." She laughed. "A little giddy, I guess."

He nodded, the corner of his mouth curving up. "Excitement seems natural under the circumstances." He studied her, his gaze moving over her body. Then he looked at her face through his long lashes. "If we were handfasted, we could have our wedding night tonight." He took a slow breath. "Unless you would prefer to wait."

Wait? Not freaking likely. She'd taken a terrifying leap of faith. She wanted to enjoy her reward . . . him.

She stepped close and ran her thumb over his lower lip. "Are you anxious to get started?" she teased.

He flushed, and his smile widened. "I am. A bit."

"Me, too." She licked his lips with the tip of her tongue. He pulled her against him so hard, she could've counted his muscles. His mouth hadn't exactly been tentative before, but now his kisses scorched her. His body knew it would be satisfied, so passion was given free reign.

When she was almost blind with wanting him, she dragged herself back, panting. They were on the floor, and she didn't remember lying down.

He resisted her attempt to pull away and breathlessly asked, "What is it? What's wrong?"

"Nothing. It's all very right, and that's how I want it to stay."

"I don't understand," he said, sliding his hand along her arm, not allowing her to escape his grasp.

"On Judgment Day, I'm not going to be accused of corrupting an angel." She pushed his hand away from her half-unzipped dress. "Handfasting? What is that? And how do we do it?"

"Oh. Right," he mumbled, putting a palm to his head. "I—I can't think."

She laughed.

"Give me a minute." His unbuttoned shirt gaped open, showing smooth strong muscles and the small scar below his collarbone.

"Oh damn," she said, rising.

He caught her ankle. "Where are you going?" he asked.

"Nowhere," she said, but his grip stayed firm. "Really, Nathaniel, nowhere. Just to the fireplace. If you don't need that ring as a reminder anymore, I want it destroyed."

"Destroyed? Why?"

She explained about meeting the angel on the Clarity roof and paraphrased what she'd been told. "He said the ring ties you to your enemy, and the only person I want you tied to anymore is me."

Nathaniel let go of her ankle. "That's my wish as well. Go ahead and destroy it."

She walked to the mantel and stared at the ring. "I can't believe you're not even curious. We are so different."

"I'm actually very curious about a great many things. For instance, is all of your skin as soft as your cheek? And what places that I touch will make your breath catch the way it does when I—"

"Got it," she said, holding out her hand with a grin. "You're a lover, not a fighter now, and with sex in your immediate future, you couldn't care less about anything else."

"More proof that you're as perceptive as you always claim."

She laughed. "You know a good way to not end up in bed with your wife? Tell her she brags too much."

"Sorry," he said, glancing at the ceiling. "Well . . ." And then he lapsed into a language she couldn't identify.

"What was that?"

"That was me following advice that will hopefully help me end up in bed with my wife." His hand lay on his washboard abs, the ones she was tempted to explore with her teeth, and she silently reflected that there was absolutely no risk of him not getting her into bed.

"For a handfasting ceremony we exchange vows. And we need a length of ribbon," he said.

She picked up the ring, pinching it between thumb and forefinger and cast it into the fireplace. "Good riddance, Gadreel. May all your good-byes end in flames."

Fire roared outward, singeing her dress. She leaped back and watched to be sure that none of the embers caught the carpet on fire. Then she leaned forward and pulled the screen closed.

"Does it have to be a ribbon?" she asked, turning.

Nathaniel stood with a palm over his left collarbone, pressing the scar. Pleasure and flirtation had fled his features. Now he only looked furious.

"You remember," she whispered.

Staring into the flames, he said grimly, "I remember."

"We would've put some holes in him, so he'd be weakened for your fight, but things didn't go as planned," Tamberi said, scowling.

Gadreel bit the knuckles on her left hand in a makeshift punishment, but he was grinning and gleeful. "Beri, the angel took the girl to a *hotel room*. This is monumental. You don't know how single-minded these pricks can be when a demon rises. Especially him when the demon is me." Gadreel jabbed a wire into the block of C-4 explosive. "I knew this crush would be his downfall. He's part human and all that watching the girl and denying himself a taste? All that pining? It's how I always play people. Show them something, make them want it, and then deny them. They will sell you their soul to get it."

Gadreel took a puff off his hand-rolled cigarette and blew a smoke ring. "Now he's totally lost his focus. He should have just fucked her and gotten it over with. Instead, he's the one who's fucked." He took another deep drag, then bent to snort a line of cocaine.

"I can get you a rock. You know that smoking crack is a more intense high, right?" Tamberi asked.

Gadreel's withering look turned her blood to ice. She clenched her jaw.

"Sorry. Of course, you know. You invented the more intense high."

"True that. With coke, I like it old school. Recalling the eighties. No one thinks demons are sentimental, but we miss certain things. Like when people thought greed was good. Now yoga's spread over the entire fucking planet and half the best-seller list is for people seeking enlightenment. Again with that crap? It is fucking tiresome. Here, hang this bomb from that light. And play me *Devil's Haircut* again," he said, before lapsing into song.

"You've got a great voice," Tamberi said, stepping onto a chair so she could hook the bomb to the light fixture.

"Yeah, when we were cast out, they didn't take it all. In the heat of the battle, we got away with murder and so much more." Sucking on his cigarette, he grinned, and added, "Good times."

Kate watched as Nathaniel flipped the ring out of the fire using a poker. It landed on the marble, soot-covered but not melted. He set the poker in its stand, waiting a moment for the ring to cool before retrieving it and sliding it onto his finger. He closed his eyes for a moment, lost in thought and frowning.

"So the warrior wins out," she murmured, trying to keep her voice even. A part of her had known this would come. She'd seen those memories. A history like that would not stay buried. Still, she felt cold and empty. She'd promised to marry him and had for a while felt the promise of that future . . . to be in love, to be loved. She bit the inside of her cheek.

She understood. If her editor had called and offered her a story like Watergate or the Afghan "kill squad," how hard would it have been for her to walk away from it for a guy? To give up what she'd built? The thing that had defined her? She would have done it for Nathaniel, but a part of her would've died in the process. So how could she blame Nathaniel for reverting to archangel status instead of clinging to a life with her?

Still, it hurt. A cut-to-the-bone kind of hurt.

"Kate—"

"No," she said, holding out a hand to stop him. "No need to explain. I understand."

"Someone raised Gadreel. He's loose in the world right now."

"Like I said, I get it," she said in a rush. She stalked to the desk and dropped in the chair. She grabbed her iPhone from her purse and opened her e-mail. He rounded the desk and stood in front of her. When she didn't look up, his hand gripped the phone. She held tight, trying to keep him from pulling it away.

"Let go," he said.

Just leave me alone. Please.

She pulled the phone, but it didn't come free. With a small tug, Nathaniel took it from her grip.

"Give it back," she said, pushing the heel of her hand against his hip.

He moved the phone out of reach and kept his palm over it, pinning the phone to the desk.

She glared at his chest.

"Kate."

"What? What do you want from me?"

His voice was soft. Insistent. Devastating. "Kate."

She looked up, still glaring, despite the tears that burned her eyes. "I said I get it. You're an archangel, and you've got work to do. Go ahead."

"I love you."

Her gurgled laugh was bitter. "But you hate him more. Sure. Of course. I would, too." The tears scalded her cheeks. Nathaniel clenched his teeth, and tears shone in his own eyes.

"I love you."

"I heard you the first time! Will you just shut up and leave?"

He swallowed, strong throat muscles working. "Left alone, he would burn down the world. There are nuclear weapons now."

"Don't get melodramatic. He would never destroy the world. Then there would be no people for him to torture. And we both know that's what he likes."

"He tortures people to torture Heaven, but he'd like it even better if the world was no more."

"Why?"

"God used to love mankind and all the angels. God still loves mankind. He still loves the angels of Heaven, but he does not love Gadreel. Jealousy, bitterness, and hatred are very bright emotions. If Gadreel were left to it, he would destroy your world. To take away what God cherishes, I promise you, that's what Gadreel wants most."

"Well, we can't have that. If he blows up the world, what would I write about?" she said, her voice hollow.

Nathaniel rubbed his eyes. "I don't hate him more than I love you, Kate." He shook his head, continuing to cover his eyes. His voice, heavy with emotion, caught, making her own throat clench. "You're what I cherish. My every happiness. That I can't be with you . . . it's a thousand knives slicing my heart. It's wounds that will never heal."

The tears poured from her eyes, dropping like rain onto the blotter.

"I know someone has to stop Gadreel, but does it have to be you?" she demanded, choking on her tears.

He looked at her then. "When he's flesh, only an angel of flesh can engage him. I'm the only one here."

"Huh." She wiped her face, a useless effort as tears continued to spill over her lower lashes. "You guys need a better recruitment plan."

He swallowed. "I made you a promise," he whispered. "I need you to release me from it."

Her brows rose, and she licked her lips. "You mean I could keep you if I wanted to? I could just say you made me a promise and that you have to honor it, and you'd have to stay?"

He nodded.

"You know," she said, choking out a laugh. "I told them it wasn't fair that they showed you to me if I couldn't have you. It would serve them right if I just kept you for myself and said to hell with the world. Do you have any idea how freaking beautiful you are? You're dawn's early light that I chase every daybreak. Do you know that I've never loved anyone else? And that I probably never will? I've had one dream for the past decade, and it's been you," she whispered breathlessly. "Always . . . every night . . . you."

The sobs took her.

Nathaniel reached over the desk and lifted her from the chair, cradling her against him. She felt him shaking, too.

"It's not fair. Not fucking fair," she gasped.

Moments stretched by, and she cried out her pain and frustration, the final tears struggling to reach her jaw. "I love you," she said in a hoarse whisper. "And I release you from your promise."

He held her for an age. She wondered if he'd heard what she said, but she'd be damned before she repeated it. *Damned.*

As if she'd thought the word loud enough for him to hear, Nathaniel's grip loosened, then fell away. She took his hand and led him to the bathroom. She wet a cloth, wiped her face and handed it to him. He scrubbed it over his lids and cheeks. His lips were pale, she noticed, and his eyes bloodshot.

"Okay," she said softly as he dropped the cloth in the sink. "Kiss me good-bye, and I'll see you in my dreams." She closed her eyes and waited for a kiss that never came. When she opened her eyes, he'd gone.

For a long time, she couldn't think what to do. She filled the tub with water and turned on the jets, pouring in half a bottle of bath gel. Then she climbed in and sat numbly in suds to her shoulders until the world exploded.

Chapter Eight

Smoke, fire, and churning water. Alarms rang in the distance, but Kate's ears felt full of water. Kate climbed from the tub, choking on smoke, and slipped. Something sliced her calf and she shrieked in pain, but her voice sounded muffled. She crawled through shards of broken glass, feeling her way toward the door. She needed to get to the stairs. Water sprayed from the walls where the sprinkler pipes had busted, but fire still burned. She felt the heat.

As she pulled at the door, a hotel bathrobe fell onto her, and she slid her arms into it. Smoke clogged the air. She kept her eyes tightly closed as she moved. The door to the suite had to be nearby.

Something slimy slithered across her cheek. She jerked back, but something caught her arm and yanked her up. She dangled blindly, thrashing her limbs, and felt the world tilt and herself being dragged upward.

The smoke thinned, and then she breathed clean, frigid air.

"So here you are, but where is he? He was supposed to be with you."

She struggled to open her eyes because her lashes were crusted with soot and dried soap and tears. When her vision was clear enough to see, Gadreel's face came into focus. Stretched behind him were oily black bat wings. She stood facing him. They were on the roof.

"Hey there," she said, and then slammed her fist into his perfect nose. The crunch was satisfying. His arm was a blur as it struck her.

She flew back, landing on the concrete, every bit of air knocked free of her lungs. She wheezed out a single word. "Asshole."

A moment later, he dragged her up by the front of her robe, the way a toddler would snatch up a fallen doll. She worked to get her feet under her, but her toes barely touched the ground.

She watched the brackish blood stream from his nose over his lips.

"What happened? Did he get tired of you already?" Gadreel asked.

"There's a divot in the bridge of your nose. I guess that means I broke it," she said.

"You did. It'll take about thirty minutes to heal. When I break yours, though, about four weeks."

"Gadreel."

The demon spun, skinning her toes over the concrete. He whipped her in front of him and thrust the tip of a dagger against her throat. Familiar dread washed over her.

Nathaniel closed the distance between the three of them until Gadreel pricked her skin.

"Close enough, or I'll open a window from her windpipe to her spine."

Kate grimaced, but she clenched her teeth. "I've had this dream so many times before," she said.

Gadreel said, "Too bad for you, this time isn't a dream."

"Too bad for you, too. The part coming up is where he kills you."

Gadreel levered his forearm across her throat, choking off her air.

"Does this one belong to you, Nathaniel? Or can I have her?"

Nathaniel's eyes were deadly cold. "If you kill her, you have nothing with which to bargain."

The pressure on her throat eased. "There's only one bargain that interests me. You give me back my ring, I go free, and you hunt me no more."

"You can have the ring and a day's head start, but you're damned, Gadreel. Whenever you're on earth, an archangel will hunt you."

"Then Kate is very unlucky. If she'd never met you, I'm sure she would have lived a nice long life." Gadreel ripped the robe down, exposing her chest. She tried to free herself, but Gadreel nicked her shoulder in warning.

"Everything you do, I will visit back on you tenfold," Nathaniel said.

Gadreel laughed, and he bent his head and bit her shoulder hard enough to break the skin. She screamed, the pain like fire burning through her flesh.

A dagger flew through the air and stabbed into Gadreel's arm. Gadreel shouted and yanked it out, dropping it without ever giving her enough room to break free.

"Nice throw, but see how you grimace, Nathaniel?" Gadreel licked Kate's blood from his lips. "You don't have a taste for torture. In two thousand years, each time we fight, it's been a clean kill every time. And I rise again. And again. And again. I have an easy way into the world now. We'll go on and on, you and I. But Kate will be gone. And you'll have nothing to do all year but wait for me and visit her grave."

Nathaniel eyes didn't meet hers.

"Or I could let her go, and we could keep this just between us."

"I'm listening," Nathaniel said.

"Her life for your pain."

"Go on," Nathaniel said.

"You submit to me for twenty-four hours. I can do anything I want, short of taking your wings. After, they'll take your soul out of your broken body and put it in a new one. When you get back, the battle resumes. No matter if you kill me later, Kate is free to live her life. No demon will ever touch her or even try to entice a human to kill her. Hell will forget she exists."

The memories of Nathaniel being tortured flooded her mind. If Gadreel killed her now, her own death would be quick. The thought of Gadreel being able to do anything he wanted to Nathaniel curdled her stomach.

"No," Kate said.

"Quiet," Gadreel sneered, twisting her finger.

She screamed, then fought past the pain. "Nathaniel, no. If he kills me, the angels will come for me. It's nice in Heaven, isn't it?" she asked, trembling all over.

"Are you going to let her sacrifice her life for you?" Gadreel crooned. "I got to kill both of your sisters. Your brother. Your mother and father. Are you going to let me cut short the life of your girlfriend, too? I must admit it would be nice to have the whole set. I eventually hope to add you to it. What do you say? Her life for your pain? Or shall I slit her throat?"

"Let her go."

"No!" she screamed.

"Your promise that you'll submit for one day?"

"Yes," Nathaniel said.

Her head spun, and she fought to free herself, to pummel Gadreel. The demon pushed her away without a glance.

Gadreel laughed at Nathaniel. "Beautiful angel boy, I promise to make you regret your choice. Let's go."

"I can't fly. My wings aren't ready," Nathaniel said.

Gadreel grinned. "Well then, we'll start the fun here until the firefighters make their way up and interrupt us. I want you naked and on your knees." Gadreel's eyes shone blood red in the moonlight. He was in the throes of dark pleasure.

Nathaniel discarded his shirt and unzipped his pants.

Rage and fury and frustration wailed through her.

This will not happen! I won't let that monster touch him! Not for my sake. Not for anything or anyone. Never. Never. Never!

With a hand massaging his crotch, Gadreel strode toward Nathaniel.

Kate snatched up Nathaniel's dagger that lay at her feet. She felt as though she'd left her body and watched from above as she rushed forward and drove the dagger into Gadreel's wing, slicing down like it was fabric and then plunging the dagger into his back with a banshee cry. She gouged him and wrenched the blade sideways, coring a huge chunk of flesh as she dragged it out and then stabbed him again.

He wailed and spun, striking her so she flew backward. Her back slammed into the concrete, knocking her breath and the dagger free as Gadreel leaped forward, his own blade raised. He would kill her. She didn't care. She would've died a thousand times for the chance to stab him again.

Gadreel's blade arced down, but Nathaniel jerked him back. She watched, frozen, as Nathaniel tore Gadreel's injured wing from his back.

Gadreel's screams pierced the night. Nathaniel pinned the flailing Gadreel to the ground and sliced open his back, ripping out the other wing.

The wings burst into flame and burned to ash. Then Nathaniel cut Gadreel's throat and climbed off him. The pale body, smudged with black blood, was consumed by blue flames. The smell of sulfur filled the air and then there was nothing but ash.

For several moments, she couldn't speak, couldn't move, couldn't breathe.

Nathaniel bent over her. "Are you all right, Kate? Are you badly hurt?"

"No," she stammered, then looked to the black ash that had been Gadreel. "But you . . . you promised to submit," she said through chattering teeth.

"I did promise," Nathaniel said, pulling on his pants and zipping them.

"And then you killed him."

"Yes, I did," Nathaniel said with a smile. "Not only that. I managed to take his wings first. Whenever he enters the world again, no wings."

"He'll never regrow them?"

"Never."

"But you broke your promise."

"No. I traded my submission for your life. He said no demon would touch you. Then he struck you, so our agreement was void."

"And what if he hadn't touched me?" she asked.

"Then you would've hacked him apart piece by piece while I enjoyed the show."

"What if he'd tossed your knife off the roof?"

"You would've cut him with something else."

She looked around, gaze stopping at the pool bar. "I would've used a broken bottle." Eyes darting, she spotted several other possible weapons. A poker for the fire pit, a mirror she could've shattered.

"He should've expected me to attack," she said. "The very first thing I did when I met him was break his nose."

"He's never been afraid of human beings, and he was too blinded by his greed to think clearly."

"His greed?"

"For power over me. To have me at his mercy again. When we fight, I always win. He really wanted to make me pay for that with my blood."

"I was very afraid that he was going to get his wish." She shivered. She was cold but wildly exhilarated, too. "Helping you kill him was so . . . satisfying."

"Yes, ridding the world of Gadreel always is. Until he returns," he said, sliding his dagger away and walking toward the stairs.

She followed. "How does he keep coming back?"

"Someone must have an ancient grimoire that they use to raise him." Nathaniel held the door and said, "Probably the brother and sister ventala," at the same time Kate said, "Cato and Tamberi Jacobi." They smiled at each other.

"So you'll deal with that?"

"I will."

"And maybe Gadreel will stay gone for a very long time?"

"Perhaps."

"But maybe not. And there may be others," she said slowly, her mood crashing. "And you're still the only flesh-and-blood archangel here to fight them?"

"Yes."

Vanquishing Gadreel didn't change anything. We still can't be together. A world of pain swallowed her.

"For now," he added gently.

There were emergency lights flashing in the stairwell. The fires were all out, but the water and smoke had badly damaged several floors. It was a long descent, her heart growing heavier with each passing step.

Please, God, don't let me break down again. It'll hurt him to see it.

They descended the dark stairwell. Down and down and down. She fought the tears that threatened, biting hard on her lip until she tasted blood.

Please, let me be strong enough. He's been through a lot. Help me pretend that I'm okay.

When they reached the ground floor, her throat was so tight, she couldn't swallow the pain. Her feet moved numbly as he led her across the street to the Clarity, her resolve draining away as the moment of letting go got closer.

I know I can't have him for good, Lord, but would one night be too much to ask for?

Please, just let me keep him for a few hours more.

"Do you need a place to stay for the night? I have a room with an extra bed. We could just talk—just be together for a little while."

"The temptation of that," he said, shaking his head. "I'm not strong enough."

Tears welled in her eyes, and he clenched his fists helplessly.

"Kate, please don't cry," he whispered.

"Sorry!" She jerked her head to the side as the drops spilled over her lashes. "Good-bye for now," she choked out, then rushed into the lobby before the sobs took her.

Kate didn't dream, but she still woke breathless and sweating. Two angels stood at the foot of her bed. The ice angel and the golden angel watched her.

"What? What the hell do you want?"

"The reason archangels aren't allowed human friends and lovers is that demons can use them for leverage," the ice angel said. "Word will spread by morning that the archangel Nathaniel has a weakness. He loves a human woman."

"That is not my fault," Kate snapped.

"I will take the credit," the golden angel said.

"You mean the blame," Kate said.

"You attacked a demon and defended one of my angels," Ice said.

"Yes."

"We will give you a body better equipped to defend itself from harm, if you're willing to train."

"What are you saying? You want me to become an archangel, too?"

"No, not an archangel, but if you should come across a demon and feel inclined to kill it, we will not object. Mostly we want to be sure that if a demon comes across you, you will not be inclined to die."

"How long is the training?"

"Until an archangel deems you ready."

"Which archangel?"

"The one who put you in harm's way by binding you to him with angel blood."

She barely managed to keep herself from shouting for joy.

"If I'm already a target for demons and they already think they can use me as leverage, then whether I marry Nathaniel or not doesn't change anything."

"Correct," Ice said.

"So he could marry me without having to give up being an archangel?"

"Correct," Gold said, smiling.

"Did you tell him?" Kate blurted.

"Do you agree to a new body and the training?" Ice asked.

"Yes! Did you tell him?"

"We did," Gold said as Ice disappeared. "He's waiting on the roof."

She sprang from the bed, grabbing a pair of jeans. "I can't believe this."

"You must always have faith, Kate."

She paused after pulling a sweater over her head. "Thank you."

He nodded. "Well done with the demon. The warriors were impressed by the couple you and Nathaniel make."

She smiled. "And you can accept the blame for that."

"Yes, I do accept the credit," Gold said and disappeared.

Kate raced into the hall and bounded up the stairs. She shoved the roof door open and rushed out. Bathed in moonlight, Nathaniel waited with silvery wings spread behind him.

She didn't hesitate. She ran and launched herself at him. He caught her, folding his arms and then his wings around her. Silky feathers brushed against her.

"Wow," she said, sliding her cheek over them. "Feathers feel really amazing against bare skin."

He kissed her hard on the mouth, crushing her body to his. After a moment, he lifted her and set her away from him.

"Hey," she said, reaching toward his bare chest.

"Wait," he said, taking a step backward. "Don't distract me, Kate."

"Distract you from what?" she demanded, very much wanting to touch him.

"From our handfasting ceremony."

"Oh," she said, smiling. She clasped her hands together behind her back and nodded. "Then go ahead and marry me, Nathaniel, so you can finally take your wife to bed."

He smiled, sliding a length of ribbon from his pocket. "I have a marriage bed ready for us. It's high on the ridge of a mountain among the clouds. There's a light dusting of snow, but so long as you stay close, my body will keep yours warm," he promised.

"A mountain ridge," she murmured. "Where better for an angel to make love than among the clouds? It sounds perfect, Nathaniel," she whispered. "Just like a dream."

Human Error

EILEEN WILKS

Chapter One

There were worse ways to spend the holidays. Even leaving out nuclear winter, Benedict could think of several. Like in a hospital. On a battlefield. At a Humans First rally—no, that was the same thing as a battlefield. At least it had been in October, when he'd lost six men himself and too many others had died, including . . .

"Good grief. Don't look so grim."

"I'm not grim," he said automatically. He had the sense to shut his mouth without explaining that he'd been cheering himself up by comparing visiting Arjenie's family to spending time with tubes in his veins and other places. Never mind that the visit came out ahead. It wouldn't sound right.

She didn't say a word. This was unusual enough to get his attention. He stole a glance away from the unfamiliar road.

The woman in the passenger's seat was slightly above average height, definitely below average weight, with black-framed glasses, a narrow face, and long red hair so extravagantly curly it seemed to have a life of its own. She was shining with happiness. And his. She was his, and beautiful beyond words, and he'd cross the country on foot if that's what it took to give her such joy.

Everything in him softened. He reached for her hand. "Grim, huh?" It was foolish to drive one-handed, even for someone with his reflexes, when he didn't have to. But missing a chance to touch her was surely a greater folly.

"Not so much now." She squeezed his hand. "They aren't going to eat you, you know. They're good people."

He smiled because he knew that was true, and it made him happy that she had good people standing behind her. People who'd stepped in, opening their home and their arms to her when her mother was killed. But good people wouldn't be happy about her relationship with him. Perhaps, as she claimed, they wouldn't have a problem with him being lupus. Most human families would, but Arjenie was sure her people weren't like that.

Maybe not. And maybe they wouldn't be upset that he and Arjenie had no plans to marry, even though she couldn't explain why that legal binding was unimportant compared to what truly held them together.

Humans weren't told about the mate bond. Ever.

But because of that bond, Arjenie had to live far from her family now. Because of Benedict, she'd been exposed to danger, violence, and death. And probably would be again.

How could they accept that? Why should they?

Benedict thought, however, that they'd be courteous. People who raised someone as generous and openhearted as Arjenie would be courteous to him for her sake and their own. Clearly he had nothing to worry about. "I may be a little nervous."

Her bright grin flashed across her face. "You think? Oh, look—that's the oak! Turn there—just beyond that magnificent oak—the gravel road, do you see it?"

Obediently he slowed. She was vibrating with excitement. It had been nearly four months since she'd see her aunt and uncle and cousins. Other aunts and uncles and cousins would be there, too. The gravel road he turned onto would take them to an old farmhouse that had been the home and heart of the Delacroix family for nearly two hundred years. It was like a small clanhome. Everyone who could, came there for Christmas.

Not Christmas, he corrected himself. Yule. They were Wiccan. The center of their celebration was the solstice, which they called Yule, and which fell on the twenty-second this year. Then, on the morning of December 25th, they joined the rest of the country in what Arjenie called a grand explosion of culturally sanctioned greed. Presents, presents, presents.

They turned onto a tree-crowded lane. Branches arched overhead—bare now, but it must be pretty in summer. Moonsong hummed in his veins rather the way the car's engine sounded to his ears. Her song was constant, having nothing to do with whether the moon was visible, but this close to the full moon it grew ever stronger.

He checked the rearview mirror. The car behind them was identical to the one he drove. Both rented, of course. He hadn't actually been called on to cross the country on foot. They'd flown to D.C., stopping there for a couple days to pack up Arjenie's apartment.

She'd cried. When they boxed up the last of the things in her bedroom, she'd cried, and he almost did, too, looking at her wet eyes. She called it "getting all teary, which is not the same thing," but tears were tears. He'd told her she didn't have to let her apartment go. She could keep it as long as she wanted—for the rest of her life, if she wished. They'd come to D.C. as often as possible . . . which probably wouldn't be all that often. Not when they were at war.

Maybe the present he would give her on Christmas morning would help a little. He hoped so.

Arjenie's phone pinged with her text alert. She checked it and exclaimed, "Oh, Uncle Nate and Aunt Sheila got in last night with their crew! That's Jacob, Noah, and Emily. Emily's the one I used to babysit."

"You thought they were spending the holiday with Sheila's family this year."

"Yes, it's her turn. They alternate between his family and hers, you know, but . . ." She scanned her phone. "Oh my. There was an argument. Aunt Robin doesn't give any details, but I'll bet Sheila's mother got in one of her huffs. She does that. Anyway, the woman decided all of a sudden to go on a cruise. Can you imagine?" She shook her head. "A cruise instead of family at Yule."

Benedict checked his memory, trying to place people he'd never met. "Nate is the physician. Family practice. He and your uncle Ambrose are twins. Nate's wife, Sheila, is . . ." He frowned. He'd studied the family pictures Arjenie had on her phone, and he remembered a smiling woman with honey-blond hair. But he was drawing a blank on the details. "A landscape architect?"

"No, that's Gary, Uncle Hershey's partner. Sheila's a stay-at-home mom, though she's been talking about dusting off her lit degree now that two out of three of the kids are in high school." Arjenie's thumbs flew over the screen as she replied to her aunt. She had no problem carrying on multiple conversations. "And Uncle Ambrose and Aunt Carmen are here already with their brood. Oh, and she brought her brother. Good."

"Her brother."

"Uh-huh. Ben Avelar. He's divorced and has joint custody, but his ex has the kids for the holiday and his own family's in Portugal, so Aunt Robin must've told Carmen to bring him along."

Benedict stopped trying to add up all the people he was about to meet. "The twins are already there, too."

"Oh, yes. Both their colleges let out a week ago. I just wish Tony could have made it. You'd like him, and he'd be glad of someone to talk to who gets him."

Tony was the oldest of Clay and Robin Delacroix's three children and, like the twins, was more of a sibling than a cousin to Arjenie. A younger sibling. Tony had been born the same year Arjenie's mother died and Arjenie went to live with her aunt and uncle. "He couldn't get leave."

"The Air Force does not seem to understand how important it is for him to be home for the holidays." She shook her head. "Poor Tony. It's not like Wicca is inherently antiwar, but my family does seem to breed more pacifists than warriors. He's sort of the odd man out sometimes."

Benedict wished Tony could have made it, too. As it was, he'd be very much the odd man out. He was nothing but a warrior.

Fortunately, there was a lull in the war at the moment. In October the enemy had launched simultaneous battles at four Humans First rallies, the opening salvo in an intricate yet elegant strategy for destroying the lupi and toppling the U.S. government. It had nearly worked. If Lily hadn't figured out what was going on . . .

But she had, and even the Great Enemy would need a little time to regroup after such a defeat. *She* had to work through human agents, after all, who required mundane resources—money, followers, fake IDs, weapons . . . and an ignorant and frightened public she and her people could deceive.

After October, the enemy was ahead on the fear front, but the public was slightly less ignorant. Benedict had no idea how that would play out, but figuring it out wasn't his job. He was in charge of security at Nokolai Clanhome, not PR and politics. Guessing which way humans would jump—and trying to manipulate that direction—was Rule's job, not his.

Thank God for his brother. Who was helpful in other ways, too. Benedict had gone to Rule for advice about what clothes to pack. At first Rule had suggested he ask Arjenie, but Benedict had explained that he didn't need to know what was appropriate. He needed to know what cultural messages his clothes were sending. Rule understood things like that.

It seemed strange that he ended up wearing pretty much what he would have on any other day, except for the jacket. Somehow adding a leather sports jacket changed the message of his jeans and dark blue T-shirt from "I didn't bother to dress up" to "I'm a casual person but want to honor our meeting."

". . . not that you've heard a word I said. Which is okay, because I'm babbling to an insane degree, but you're supposed to nod or say 'uh-huh' now and then, anyway."

Promptly Benedict nodded. "Uh-huh."

She laughed.

"You wish your nana and papa could be here," he added. "It seems strange for them to be gone at Yule, but they're having such a good time backpacking in Europe and it seems to be helping them heal after Samuel's death."

"Oh." She squeezed his hand. "Oh, I do love you. A lot."

He glanced at her, pleased but baffled. He hadn't done anything special.

Just then the road finished curling around a low hill and the tree tunnel vanished. Ahead the Delacroix home place snuggled into a sunny meadow backed by woods. The house was tall and white and sturdy and wore its black roof like a British gentleman's bowler. A veranda ran the length of the front. There were two outbuildings visible from the road, both set well away from the house. The barn was relatively new construction and currently housed four horses. The Delacroix family had long been horse lovers; Robin Delacroix was a large-animal vet who'd met her husband when she came to treat one of his family's horses. The other building was local stone, at least as old as the house, and held Clay Delacroix's forge and workshop. On the far side of the barn, five vehicles were parked in a recently mown field.

There was a detached garage, too, though Benedict couldn't see it from this angle. That's where his guards should have been bunking. He'd been overruled on that, however. Robin Delacroix did not want guests sleeping in an unheated garage.

They were his guards, not her guests, and would be exterior guards at that. Having them bunk in the garage offered an extra layer of security. Even a sleeping lupus was hard to sneak up on. But Arjenie said that her aunt would not budge about this, so Benedict had been forced to agree to her terms.

The gravel road split well back from the house, with one track veering for the field while the other looped in front of the house. Benedict put down his window and signaled Josh, who would park and wait until Benedict summoned him and Adam. It was not exactly normal to bring bodyguards along on a holiday visit; Benedict wanted to keep them as inconspicuous as possible. He kept going. Arjenie had said he was supposed to pull up in front of the porch and unload their bags before moving the car out of the way.

"Oh, look—there's Uncle Hershey coming around the side of the house!" She waved, then twisted around to grab the green wool coat he hadn't seen until she dug it out of her closet at her old apartment. She hadn't needed it in San Diego.

The man she was waving to waved back and broke into a jog. He was under fifty and powerfully built, with a silver streak in his dark hair and a big grin. "They're here!" he hollered, presumably to those in the house.

Before Benedict got the car stopped, people boiled out the front door—three kids, two dogs, two men, and one woman. Everyone but the dogs wore jackets. The woman was nearly a foot shorter than Arjenie, a couple decades older, and had Arjenie's hair. She'd knotted it on top of her head at some point that day, but like her niece's hair, it sneered at attempts at restraint. Escaped strands frothed and fluttered as she skipped down the veranda steps as lightly as a girl.

One of the men was well over six feet and lean, with wavy brown hair and glasses. The other was shorter, broad and strong, with a close-cropped salt-and-pepper beard. That would be Clay Delacroix, blacksmith and sculptor and everything Arjenie knew about fathers.

The dogs barked excitedly. The smallest child—three or four with freckles and a missing front tooth, too young to be the Emily Arjenie once tended—tripped and fell. The brown-haired man scooped her up and parked her on one hip while the other two youngsters slammed into the passenger's side of the car like guided missiles. The taller boy—he looked Pakistani or Indian—yanked it open. "Arjenie! Arjenie! Is it true your new guy turns into a wolf at the full moon? It's full moon tomorrow! Can we watch?"

"Malik!" Robin said, rebuke in her voice, adding quickly, "Danny, grab Havoc."

The shorter boy with chipmunk cheeks snatched up the terrier before it could duck under the car.

And Benedict breathed a sigh of relief. All of the Delacroix, even Aunt Robin, were wearing jeans. Just like him. So far, so good.

Arjenie explained that Benedict only Changed when he chose to, but full moon was a time when he really wanted to Change, and no, they couldn't watch, and if they didn't *move* so she could get out of the car, their aunt Robin was going to turn them into hoppy toads.

That made them laugh—but they backed up. Arjenie bounced out and grabbed her aunt in a hug. Benedict got out on his side. The moment his feet were on the ground, earth tried to surge up through him to join with the moonsong. Automatically he repressed it and reached back into the car for the new leather jacket. He didn't need it, not with the temperature at least ten degrees above freezing, but he was supposed to wear it.

Questions were spilling from Arjenie as she was scooped into hugs—where's Uncle Nate and Aunt Sheila and Uncle Stephen and Uncle Ambrose and Aunt Carmen and the twins and the rest of the kids? Everyone answered at once. Benedict picked up something about holly and horses as he slipped on the jacket and eyed the dogs.

He wasn't worried about the Lab mix, but the other one was a recent adoption, Arjenie had said, a scruffy little Jack Russell terrier. Most dogs either ran or submitted quickly when they met him, but a few just had to challenge. Especially terriers. Terriers were genetically convinced of the dictum that size doesn't matter—it's what you do with what you've got.

Robin Delacroix told the boys that they had apparently forgotten everything they'd ever learned about manners, and did they want a refresher course from her or from their fathers? The Lab mix rounded the hood of the car and stopped dead, staring at Benedict in utter astonishment.

He chuckled. "You don't know what the hell you're smelling, do you?" He snapped his fingers. "Here, boy."

The dog flattened his ears, lowered his tail, and wagged it once, uncertain. Benedict averted his gaze slightly—*I'm not challenging, either*—and snapped his fingers again. The dog trotted up to him. Benedict rubbed his ears. "Good boy."

"Did you see that?" a young voice piped up. "Did you see? He told Harley to come, and he *did!* Just like that!"

"Hold on to Havoc," Clay Delacroix reminded the boy in a voice deep enough to rival that of Benedict's father. He nodded at Benedict in a friendly way. "Harley there is an expert at selective deafness. He knows all the usual commands. He only hears them when food is involved."

Arjenie turned in the circle of her uncle's arm to beam at Benedict. "Benedict, this is Clay Delacroix and my aunt, Robin Delacroix, and the man holding little Amy is Uncle Gary—Gary Brown—and this is Uncle Hershey," she said as the man they'd first spotted reached them, "and the two hellions with all the nosy questions are—"

"Oh, no!" cried the boy who'd been holding the terrier—past tense, since the dog had squirmed free. "Havoc! Come here, Havoc!"

The dog ignored such poor advice to race around the car, barking madly. Both boys raced after her. Which, of course, just increased her excitement. Being chased was almost as much fun as chasing, and maybe the boys would help her get rid of this weird-smelling intruder.

You never know what will work with a terrier, and Jack Russells could be fearless bordering on suicidal. But they were smart and curious, so sometimes . . . Benedict dropped down on his heels and stared at the little dog charging him.

Havoc skidded to a stop, startled into silence, then darted to the right, trying to flank him. Even a Jack Russell hesitates to charge straight at a predator twenty times her size, but she knew she was fast, and for all that he smelled like the scariest canid she'd ever run across, he was shaped like a big, slow human. She figured she could outmaneuver him.

She was wrong. Crouching on his heels was more awkward than some positions, but Benedict taught a version of the *troika*, or Cossack dance, as part of his training program. He kept up with Havoc's movements easily as she circled him, looking for an opening that didn't appear, and he kept his gaze pinned to her. *I see you, little warrior. I respect you, but I can take you. You know this. Will you make me prove it?*

"What's he doing?" one of the boys asked. "He's not afraid of Havoc, is he? Mr. Benedict, why are you—"

"Shh." That was Arjenie. She'd come around to his side of the car—as had the others. "He's talking to Havoc."

"He's not talking," the boy objected.

Robin Delacroix answered. "Yes, he is. It's a language we don't speak."

It occurred to Benedict that this was not the way to blend in with humans.

Havoc stopped. Cocked her head. Gave a single wag of her tail.

Benedict smiled. He held out one hand down low—*Come greet me, see, I understand how to do this*—

And a wall of power slammed into him like a mountain's belch or the laughter of gods.

Benedict had no chance to fight. His control was superb, but control governed only whether or not he entered the Change. All the will in the world couldn't stop the Change once it began—and that giant hand had swatted him into it as easily as a child's foot can send a beetle tumbling. He could only submit and speed it along.

Between one breath and the next, the man was gone, his clothing fallen to the ground in the instant of transformation, when he was neither truly here nor not-here. An enormous black wolf stood in the Delacroix front yard, snarling with rage at what had been done to him.

Chapter Two

"Stay back! No, he's safe, he's perfectly safe, only he isn't supposed to—that shouldn't have happened!"

Unlike many lupi, Benedict had never thought of his wolf form as something separate or distinct from the rest of him. He thought differently as a wolf, perceived the world differently, and some instincts were heightened. But he had no sense of the man needing to control the wolf, as many did. Man or wolf, he remained himself. Man or wolf, control was necessary.

Benedict heard his Chosen, heard the fear in her voice, and mastered his anger. "Benedict?" she said, and stepped toward him—and the man beside her, who smelled like charcoal and iron and smoke, seized her arm. "You'll stay back, too."

The smoke-and-iron man was not an enemy. Names were uninteresting to him at the moment, but he knew the man was dear to Arjenie, so he forgave him for restraining her. She would rebuke him for it herself, he was sure. Arjenie did not like to be restrained.

He wanted to go to her, but he had no idea what had happened, where the threat lay. So he gave her a quick, reassuring nod and leaped onto the hood of the car, then the roof.

This startled the humans. He was sorry for that, but he had to see and smell out what was going on. His men—had they been Changed, too?

The breeze came from the south, so he allowed his nose to advise him on what lay in that direction while he used his eyes to check north, east, and west. Nothing looked threatening or obviously out of place, but he didn't know this place.

His men had not been forced into Change; they stood two-legged beside their car, aware something was wrong but not knowing what or if they should come to him.

This form wasn't good at communication, but he could offer that much direction. He shook his head firmly at them.

The humans were doing a great deal of talking. Arjenie, too—she was angry at the man who still held her arm. The woman—she had an especially interesting smell—had hold of both boys, one by the shoulder, the other by the hand. She told the man to let go of his niece, who was an adult and able to make her own decisions, adding under her breath that Arjenie had better know what she was talking about.

A horse screamed. It was a stallion's battle cry, and it came from the barn. Where the door was open slightly. It had been closed earlier.

Benedict shot off the roof of the car, sailing over the head of the woman and hitting the ground at a dead run.

Someone followed him. Someone about one-twentieth his size and with no concept of the value of silence. Havoc barked furiously as she raced after him, either believing she had him on the run or delighted by the chance to pursue whatever he was chasing.

There was no point in stealth with the terrier ferociously announcing her approach, but the noise might mask the sound of Benedict's feet. He might yet surprise whoever or whatever had infuriated the stallion. He angled for the open door, charging inside.

What he smelled brought him up short.

When Muffin screamed, Uncle Clay's hand relaxed in surprise. That was all Arjenie needed to twist away—just as Benedict sailed off the roof of the car in one of those stunning leaps lupi were capable of. He hit the ground running flat out, which meant very fast indeed.

Havoc took off after him. And Arjenie took off after them both. She wasn't fast. She wasn't graceful. She had to be mindful of her ankle, which could turn under her if she wasn't careful. She wasn't much of a fighter, either, but she'd seen Benedict signal Josh and Adam to stay where they were. There was no way she was letting him go after whatever-it-was without backup.

Benedict vanished inside the barn well before she reached the halfway point. Muffin trumpeted again, sounding frantic—but having a huge wolf race into his domain would do that. It didn't necessarily mean he was being attacked and hurt.

Arjenie heard feet pounding behind her and stole a quick glance. Uncle Hershey and Uncle Clay. Good. They'd be better backup than she would. She kept going, anyway. Her uncles passed her about the time Havoc zipped into the barn, still barking.

The barn was 130 yards from the house. That was just over the length of a football field—American football, that is. In European terms, it was approximately one-and-a-third times the length of a soccer field—facts that Arjenie knew and had shared with her family years ago and was thinking about now because facts soothed her and she was afraid. Afraid for Benedict, for herself, for her uncles, and for silly little Havoc.

Though it was probably foolish to fear for Benedict, who was the best fighter in the clans. That was not her uninformed opinion but what she'd been told by any number of people in the clans—lupi, who ought to know. She'd seen him fight, and he was like one of those anime heroes, doing things that did not look real even when you saw him do them.

But teeth don't work against every menace, and *something* had pushed him into the Change. Which is why she pulled on her Gift as she reached the barn.

It wasn't true invisibility, but it worked almost the same as long as there weren't any cameras to fool. Or anyone nearby with really good shields against mind magic. Or Benedict, for that matter—he could always see her, even when she was hidden to everyone else. She eased inside the partly open door.

And stopped, her breath huffing out, and dropped the pull on her Gift. "What are you *doing*?"

Muffin was pacing and blowing, very agitated. Just outside his stall, at the far end of the broad center aisle, Benedict sat on his haunches, looking bored. Her uncles were about halfway down the aisle. Uncle Hershey stood with his legs wide, one hand out as if he was about to call fire. Which he so would not do in a barn. And Uncle Clay—her beloved uncle Clay—had his .45 in his hand and was pointing it at Benedict.

"You put that away right now!" She headed for him.

"Arjenie, stay back."

Uncle Clay spoke with such crisp assurance that her feet actually checked for a second, out of habit. Clay didn't give orders often, but when he did, all the kids obeyed.

But she was not a kid. "I most certainly will not. You pulled a *gun* on Benedict!" She was so mad she wanted to spit. Spitting mad. She had never really understood that phrase before. "How could you do that? Is that the kind of tolerance for those who are different that you taught me? Do you intend to shoot him if he moves? Do you realize he could knock that stupid gun out of your hand in a flash if he weren't too polite or maybe worried you'd accidentally shoot Muffin or something? You're only fifteen feet away. That is no distance at all for him." She reached the two idiots and started to go between them, because she wasn't so blindingly angry she'd try to knock the gun out of her uncle's hand. She wanted to, but she'd settle for blocking his shot.

Uncle Hershey grabbed her.

Rage just boiled up. She swung around and slapped him.

Sheer astonishment made him drop his hand.

She stared back at him in equal astonishment. She had never even thought about striking anyone in her family—well, except for her cousin Mike who was much too fond of practical jokes, but not in years. And not her uncles. Not ever.

And a beautiful, rumbly deep voice spoke behind her. "Arjenie, your uncles' response was inconvenient but reasonable."

She turned and scowled at Benedict, who'd Changed back to human in record time just so he could take her uncles' side. He was entirely naked, his clothes being back by the car. And he was entirely beautiful without clothes—broad and brawny and muscular—but she was not going to let that distract her. "Drawing a gun on my lover and their own guest is not *reasonable*."

"They don't know me. They saw me turn into a wolf and take off for their barn. They don't know why I did those things."

"Maybe we overreacted," Clay said. Arjenie glanced at him. He was putting his gun back into the belt holster she hadn't realized he was wearing because his jacket had hidden it.

"No," Benedict said. "You acted in advance of information, but sometimes that's necessary. You couldn't smell the intruder, as I did."

"Someone was here, then?" Arjenie asked. "Someone who made you Change and scared Muffin?"

"Muffin?" Benedict's mouth crooked up. "That fire-breather is named Muffin?"

"Seri named him. She was in her cute phase, and—never mind that. Did you see who it was?"

Benedict shook his head slowly. "I smelled him, though. It was Coyote."

Hershey snorted. "We don't have coyotes around here."

"Not a coyote. Coyote."

In the silence that fell, Arjenie could almost smell the disbelief rolling off her uncles, it was so thick.

Wait a minute. It was way too silent. "Where's Havoc?"

Chapter Three

The Delacroix family had a great kitchen. It was large, as farm kitchens often are, a big rectangle of a room with a long trestle table made of very old cherry wood at one end surrounded by mismatched chairs and one short bench. The cabinets were cherry, too, but not as old as the table; the stove was old, the refrigerator new, and there were lots of south-facing windows. It smelled wonderful. Meat simmered on the stove and four freshly baked loaves of bread were cooling on the counter.

Benedict was looking forward to the meal those smells portended, but that was still a couple hours away, so he'd eaten three pieces of jerky as soon as he was reunited with his clothes. It didn't pay to let himself get too hungry, and the Change burned a lot of calories.

He sat at the long trestle table drinking coffee and listening. Large as it was, the kitchen was crowded. Everyone but the twins was back.

Nate and his two oldest children, both teenagers, had returned from a ride while Benedict was still in the barn, pulling on the clothes Arjenie brought him. The others, save for the twins, had been hunting for a Yule tree. That bunch had arrived while Benedict was introducing his guards to Robin and Clay.

Josh and Adam were outside, of course. They might be sleeping in the house, but their duty was the exterior. They needed to familiarize themselves with the grounds. Benedict had donned his earbud so they could report as needed, though he wasn't keeping an open phone line.

The twins were still gone. They were either looking for holly or for trouble, depending on who was talking.

Havoc was still gone, too.

Benedict had offered to find the little dog—it would be easy to follow the dog's scent in his other form—or to send one of his men, but after thanking him, Robin had explained that she'd laid a mild compulsion on the terrier so he'd stay on Delacroix land. She thought he'd be okay.

Benedict did, too. Coyote liked dogs. He wasn't fond of wolves, but he liked dogs.

The kids had been sent to the rec room in the basement under the care of the two oldest, who were teens. That left twelve adults, counting himself, most of whom had something to say. Or thought they did.

The tendency to talk even if you had nothing to contribute was not an essentially human trait, from what Benedict had seen. Lupi did it, too. So did gnomes. Give most species speech, and they wanted to use it.

It was easy to pick out the Delacroix brothers from those married into or otherwise connected to the clan. They were uncannily alike—not in features but in build. To a man they were broad-shouldered, muscular, and between six foot and six two. Their hair varied from dark brown to black, and they all had blue eyes.

They shared a less visible trait, too. They were all Gifted. This was highly unusual. While the ability to work magic was often passed down, it seldom bred completely true.

Clay Delacroix was the oldest. He had the only beard, the most gray, a crooked nose, and thick, muscular arms and legs. Ambrose had a deep tan and wore his hair long, clubbed back at the moment. Nate—Ambrose's fraternal twin—looked more like a sergeant than a doctor, with his buzz-cut hair and the scar bisecting his jaw. Hershey could have passed for a lumberjack, right down to the flannel shirt, but was in fact a technical writer. The youngest, Stephen, was the leanest, with a narrow face, black hair untouched by gray, and very pale blue eyes. Benedict wasn't entirely clear on what he did. Some kind of artist.

Two of the Delacroix brothers sat at the table with Benedict—Nate and Stephen. Sheila and her brother sat there, too. The rest were standing around, except for Arjenie, who was pacing.

". . . as if you'd throw fire in a barn. And at a living being." She flung those words at Hershey, who looked sheepish and muttered, "She's really mad."

"I didn't think Arjenie even had a temper," Sheila said. "I've never seen her lose it before."

"People kept grabbing her," Benedict explained. "She doesn't like that."

Stephen slanted him a quizzical look. "Maybe that isn't the only reason."

"And you," Arjenie said, stopping to glare at Clay. "Never mind if it was *reasonable* to draw on Benedict or not. Why did you even have a gun? You don't wear a gun. You never wear a gun."

Clay exchanged a look with Robin, then sighed. "Nate had a disturbing dream."

Arjenie frowned at Nate, who was sitting beside Benedict. "What kind of dream?"

"One with lots of blood." The man shrugged. "Not that I expect it to be literally true, but it's one of the strongest sendings I've received. The overwhelming sense was that trouble was coming. Danger."

Benedict turned to him. "Precog?"

Nate nodded. "Not a strong Gift, so my hunches aren't always reliable. But when I do have a prescient dream, it's likely to be accurate. Not in terms of the dream's contents—my unconscious seems to make those up to fit the feeling, so I don't know that blood will literally be involved. But the feeling is reliable."

Arjenie crossed her arms. "And you all assumed that trouble coming meant Benedict?"

Ambrose protested, "Not all of us. I didn't know anything about

Nate's dream, much less that Big Brother"—he cocked an eyebrow at Clay—"was packing heat."

"Arjenie," Benedict said, "it's all right. I *am* dangerous."

She shook her head. "Not to them."

Robin sighed. "Ambrose, we didn't tell anyone about Nate's dream because we hoped to avoid scaring everyone. Arjenie, I understand that you're upset, but you aren't thinking. Clay carried the gun because of Nate's dream, not because of Benedict. We didn't expect trouble from any particular direction. We simply wanted to be ready."

Ready? And yet they'd allowed members of the family to ride or wander all over their acreage. Benedict shook his head. Either Robin wasn't being honest about where they thought the threat lay, or these people did not understand security at all.

Robin's revelation set off a new round of talk. Some wanted to know the details of Ambrose's dream. Others remembered other dreams he'd had and how they hadn't played out the way anyone expected but had fit events perfectly . . . in hindsight.

That's how precognition usually worked, from what Benedict understood. He did know one precog who was phenomenally accurate. His hunches were more reliable than many people's observed facts, and when he did—rarely—have a prescient dream, it was both literal and accurate. But most precogs weren't like that. On the whole, the Gift seemed more trouble and confusion than help.

Robin didn't contribute to the speculation, he noticed. She went to the refrigerator and started pulling out things—carrots, onions, celery. She asked Nate to get her a jar of tomatoes from the pantry, and would Clay taste the broth from the stewing meat to see if a bit more thyme was needed?

Nate went for the tomatoes. Clay gave Robin a knowing smile, a kiss, and told her to "give me that knife, woman, and don't mess with my soup." Within minutes, and with only the tiniest of nudges, Carmen and Clay were cutting up vegetables, Nate was showing Carmen's brother—Benedict couldn't remember his name—something in the living room, and Gary had headed to the basement to check on the kids. Hershey began rolling out a pie crust he'd taken from the refrigerator while Sheila and Ambrose peeled and sliced apples.

The chatter didn't stop, but it was more general now. Robin collected Arjenie with a glance. The two women came to the table.

Stephen smiled up at Robin. "I think all the chores are taken. You'll have to be direct."

"Directly speaking, then—go away."

Stephen chuckled and rose. "Good luck," he told Benedict, and wandered over to snatch a piece of carrot.

Benedict had already concluded that Robin was the one in charge here, though in that oddly indirect way humans seemed to like. Or maybe they didn't notice. Though Stephen had noticed, and Benedict suspected Clay knew exactly what his wife was doing. He wasn't sure about the others.

Arjenie sat beside Benedict and squeezed his hand. "I'm pretty sure Aunt Robin intends to interrogate you."

"I wouldn't put it that way," Robin said, sliding into a chair across from him. "But we do need to talk. We need to figure out what happened, why it happened, and how it might relate to the danger Ambrose sensed."

"I was forced into the Change. My subjective impression is that this was intentional—that I was shoved. Normally, that would be impossible for any being save my Rho to do." He considered that a moment. "Possibly my Lu Nuncio could force the Change on me, but he's never tried, so I can't say for sure."

"But you're certain it wasn't your Rho who did this."

"Quite certain." There was no mistaking the feel of the mantle enforcing the Rho's will. Robin, of course, didn't know about mantles. No human did, save for their own female children, who were clan; the Rhejes, of course; and those Chosen by the Lady. He looked at Arjenie—*his* Chosen—a bright bloom of happiness opening inside him.

"Well, that's reassuring."

Benedict looked back at Robin. "That my Rho didn't force the Change?"

She smiled. Robin Delacroix was a round sort of woman—round cheeks in a heart-shaped face, rounded body tucked neatly into jeans and a soft pink sweater. Her nose was just shy of pug, her eyes brown and warm. She was the shortest person in the room. "I was referring to the wonderfully gooey look on your face when you look at Arjenie."

Gooey? No one had ever called him . . . gooey.

"But that's not what we need to discuss. Not right now, anyway. Why did you think the intruder in the barn was Coyote? By which," she added, "we've been assuming you meant *the* Coyote of Native legend and lore. The Trickster."

"That Coyote, yes. I smelled him."

"How would you know what he smells like?"

He was silent a moment. "It is traditional among my mother's people not to speak of certain experiences."

"Are you talking about a spirit quest?" Her eyes widened. "Do you mean that Coyote is your spirit guide?"

"No!" What an appalling thought. "No, but . . . it is possible, on a spirit quest, to meet more than one Power."

"This spirit quest must have taken place many years ago."

"Yes."

"I know your sense of smell is much more acute than mine. However, I can't help thinking that to recognize a particular scent, after so many years, would be difficult. Rather like me recognizing a particular shade of purple that I saw once, in my youth."

"What if you had never seen the color purple in your life, and then you did? Only once, however. Many years pass, and then one day you saw purple again. Would recognize it?"

Her eyebrows lifted. "This scent is that distinctive?"

"Scents are distinctive in ways that vision doesn't approach. Coyote's scent . . ." Like a coyote, of course, the very essence of coyote, which included the meaty musk of a predator . . . but also sage and sand and wind, sun-baked earth and beetles, and the thin, clear singing of stars through air cold enough to make your eyes water . . . "There is nothing like it."

Arjenie nodded. "So you think Coyote pushed you into the Change—"

"I didn't say that. Coyote is around, yes. He was in the barn. I don't know if he's the one who pushed me into Change." Benedict shrugged. "It's the sort of thing he would do, though. Stir things up. Laugh about it."

Robin was frowning. "You think he's here physically."

"I smelled him. Your stallion did, too."

"The tribes native to this area don't include him in their lore."

"Coyote isn't always Coyote. Probably they knew him in some other guise."

"I should have said that their lore doesn't include a Coyote analogue. No trickster figures. I know some of the Native lore," she added. "When Adam and Sarah Delacroix came here in 1814, they were careful to learn what they could and pass it on. Remnant powers, even if they're no longer worshipped, can react unpredictably to Wiccan rites."

He shrugged. "Could be that too many people died to pass down the relevant stories." When Europeans showed up on this side of the ocean, they brought their diseases with them—smallpox, whooping cough, typhus, cholera. The experts argued about just how many died of the new diseases, but even conservative estimates put it well above the one-third kill rate of Europe's Black Death. "And Coyote isn't a remnant power, if I understand the way you mean that."

"A power indigenous to the land that has faded over the centuries."

"That's what I thought. Coyote hasn't faded."

Arjenie spoke up. "Coyote range—I mean little-c coyote—has increased greatly since the eighteen hundreds. They exist in all forty-nine continental states now, including some urban areas. Maybe that's why Coyote hasn't faded."

"Maybe." He had to pause and smile at her. Arjenie collected facts the way some people collect stamps or coins or *Star Wars* figures. She loved them, shared them, sucked them up like a vacuum cleaner. "Or maybe his little brothers have prospered because he's here." He looked back at Robin. "You don't believe it was Coyote."

"I'm sorry. No."

Arjenie shoved her chair back suddenly and stood. "We should take a walk."

Her aunt frowned at her. "Arjenie—"

"He needs to know. We can all three take a walk, or it can be just me and Benedict."

"You will not speak of it to him." The words were quietly spoken, but for the first time, Robin's authority was unsheathed. She meant it.

Arjenie didn't say a word. Just looked at her aunt.

"Gods help me," Robin muttered, standing. "You weren't this stupidly lovesick as a teenager."

Chapter Four

The problem with arguing with someone who raised you was that the other side had all the ammo. Arjenie considered her aunt's comment unworthy of her, a cheap shot, but if she pointed that out, they'd still be arguing, only about the wrong thing.

Stupidly lovesick. That stung.

Everything kept going wrong. She'd wanted so much for everyone to see Benedict like he really was, to appreciate him and stop worrying about her. And he'd been so anxious, determined to do everything he could to get them to like him, or at least accept him, and then the whatever-it-was forced him to Change and Uncle Clay pulled a gun on him, and she was so mad at Clay, and now she was mad at her aunt, too, and she hated that.

So Arjenie maintained a dignified silence as the three of them put on jackets and went out the back door. Not without a lot of questioning looks—and a few spoken questions—from the rest of the family, but she let her aunt handle those.

The sun was well on its way down. Shadows were long and crisp and the air had a bite. Not yet freezing, she judged, but headed that way, and the breeze had grown up. It was wind now, and a frisky one, suggesting a front was blowing in. Maybe they would end up with the snow the forecast called for. Not that a sixty percent chance meant it was a sure thing, but snow on Yule would be wonderful and . . . and it was stupid to be worrying about snow when she had more important things to settle. Only she'd had this picture of snow outside and the family inside, all warm and together and . . .

Benedict took her hand. She sighed at herself and smiled at him.

"We'll head toward the barn," Robin announced as she shut the door behind her. "No, wait. Will Josh and Adam be able to hear us?"

"Josh is on the roof of the barn. He'd certainly hear. Adam is patrolling."

Her mouth tightened unhappily. "I want to be flexible, but the idea of having people patrolling my land, peering down at me from the roof of the barn, is . . . uncomfortable. When you said you needed to bring guards along, this wasn't what I expected."

Arjenie decided to field that one. "I told you why the guards are needed. You know what happened in October. You know it's not over."

"That won't happen here."

"Maybe you're right. Benedict needs to know why you're sure of that."

Aunt Robin grimaced and started walking—heading away from the barn on the winding stone path that led to Uncle Clay's workshop and forge.

Arjenie remembered when they'd laid that path. Uncle Clay had done most of the moving of rocks, but she'd helped dig and she'd put the smaller stones in place. Seri and Sammy had been too little to do anything, but Tony had helped scoop out gravel for the under-layment, using a trowel instead of a shovel. He'd really wanted a shovel, though.

She smiled, but it faded quickly. She hated being mad at her aunt and uncle. Or not so much mad now—she never held on to anger for long—but its departure left this whole ache of sad behind.

After several paces her aunt said, "Benedict, Arjenie tells me your people are meticulous about honoring your promises. I'll need your word that you won't repeat what I tell you to anyone."

"I can't give you my word on that. First, I can't promise to withhold information from my Rho. I could promise not to offer the information to him unsolicited unless in my judgment revealing it might avert a serious threat. Second, the promise as stated would restrict me from discussing what you tell me with anyone, including yourself and Arjenie."

Robin's eyebrows climbed. She glanced at Arjenie. "Meticulous, you said. I didn't grasp how literally you meant that."

"Lupi are careful with how they word a promise because they consider it truly binding." She sounded stiff. She couldn't help it. "Not binding in a magical sense, but personally."

Benedict spoke. "If I may suggest an alternate wording . . . I will promise to hold whatever secret you share with me as closely as I hold clan secrets."

"The way I understand it," Arjenie said, "that means that torture couldn't drag it out of him, but in certain dire situations where speaking of it might save people, he might do that. Or he might not. It would depend on the situation."

"You want me to trust his judgment."

"Yes," she said. "I do. And I think you might trust me, too."

Robin gave her a look freighted with all sorts of things. Disappointment was part of the mix. Arjenie knew why. She knew what her aunt had hoped.

"Very well," Robin said after a moment. "Do I have your word, Benedict, as stated? You'll hold what I tell you as closely as you hold clan secrets?"

He answered without hesitation. "Yes."

"This land, Delacroix land, is protected and has been for generations."

"I'm familiar with wards. Wards wouldn't stop a Humans Firster from crossing onto your land and shooting one of us."

"I'm not talking about wards. The land itself is tied to me, as High Priestess. It tells me about all who are on it. If anyone or anything crosses onto my land, I know. If he comes with violent intent—as a Humans Firster would—I will know and take action."

Benedict was silent a moment. "You would also know if a small dog left your land, then."

That surprised a chuckle out of her. "True. Havoc's on his way back. He'll be here any minute."

"Good."

"I would also know if a Native Power showed up in my barn."

"Would you?" He gave her a sidelong look. "Coyote is called Trickster for a reason."

"Hiding his nature being a form of trickery, you mean?" Robin considered that. Sighed. "I don't know. It shouldn't be possible, but . . . I don't know."

"You've got a lot of confidence in your ability to read what the land tells you. It sounds like what sidhe lords do. Their power is tied to their land."

"Several hundred years ago, a Wiccan priestess did a great favor for a wandering sidhe lord. In recompense, she was taught how to link to the land. That teaching came with a price: she had to accept a binding such that she could pass it on to only one person, her successor. Both binding and teaching came to me from Clay's mother, Belle, when she decided to step down as High Priestess after Samuel died."

Benedict studied her face, his own expression intent. "You will pass this land-tie on to someone eventually."

"I . . . yes, of course."

"Had you planned to pass it to Arjenie?"

Arjenie's breath sucked in. Benedict was being far too clever today.

"I had hoped to," Robin said steadily. "She tells me that won't be possible now."

Benedict turned that intent look on Arjenie. "What had you hoped?" he asked very softly. "Was this something you wanted?"

It would be easier to tell him no, she'd never wanted to be High Priestess and custodian of the Delacroix land. But you didn't build a healthy relationship by lying. "Sometimes I did. Sometimes I didn't. I wasn't at all settled about it, and some of my uncertainty was because I hoped to find a life partner. If whoever I loved couldn't settle happily on this land, then I couldn't, either."

He studied her face a moment longer. "This is something you thought about before you and I met."

She nodded.

The corners of his mouth turned up. He touched her cheek lightly, then turned to Robin. "You have reason to be disappointed that I'm Arjenie's life partner."

"She was my choice for my successor, and she tells me you can't move here, that you have to live at your clanhome. So yes, in that sense I'm disappointed. But the most important elements about her choice of life mate have little to do with me and everything to do with you and her."

He nodded. "I can't tell you that I'm the best man for her, and there's little point in my speaking about what I'd do for her. Words prove nothing. You'll have to judge by my actions. I have some questions about the land-tie."

The abrupt change of subject made Aunt Robin blink. "There's very little I can tell you and, of that little, even less I'm willing to divulge."

"You literally can't reveal the technique, but you can speak of its existence. You don't, because you don't want word getting out that you have an ability some would be desperate to possess."

"That's right."

"You say you would know if someone stepped onto your land, and you would act. I'd like to know what type of action you're speaking of."

"I won't tell you that, but it would depend on the nature of the intrusion."

"What about when you're asleep? Is this knowing . . ." Benedict stopped. His head turned, his nostrils flaring slightly.

"It's Sammy and Seri," Robin said. "At last." She gave him a sidelong smile. "Havoc is with them, so you can stop worrying."

Aunt Robin always referred to Sammy and Seri by name, not as "the twins." She said they had enough trouble differentiating themselves without her group-naming them. Arjenie turned to look. Sure enough, Seri was opening the gate in the fence that separated yard from woods. Havoc trotted through the gate next to Sammy, who held a pair of burlap bags.

"I'd prefer to wait until they're inside to continue our discussion,"

Robin said. "They know about the land-tie, but they have opinions. About everything. I'm not in the mood to hear their opinions about my revealing it to you. That's purely my decision."

Did she mean the twins had opinions about Benedict already? Before they even met him? Probably. Arjenie had talked to Seri a few times since she met Benedict and moved to California, and her young cousin been typically nosy but hadn't seemed especially upset or worried. Sammy, now . . . he hadn't been curious enough, had he? Bright and cheery and full of his own news, not asking many questions. Which struck her as odd now.

"Arjenie tells me the stone used in Clay's workshop was quarried at the same place that supplied the stone for the White House," Benedict said conversationally.

Aunt Robin took up the topic gladly, talking about other local buildings built from sandstone as the twins approached—Sammy at his usual amble, Seri hurrying ahead with Havoc. ". . . used a mix of lime, rice glue, casein, and lead to seal the stone back then, which is why those buildings were—Seri, good grief."

Seri had wrapped her arms around Arjenie in a hug—and boosted her right off the ground. "It's so good to see you!"

Arjenie's cousin was a full head shorter than her and nowhere near strong enough to pick her up this way—except that her Gift gave her a boost. Telekinesis. "Okay, Wonder Woman, you've been practicing. Now put me down."

Seri did that but kept her hands on Arjenie's arms. "You look fantastic."

"So do you." Arjenie grinned and flicked a strand of Seri's very short hair—a new look for her, but Seri liked to change things around. So far she'd changed her major twice. "Got that unisex thing going, I see. It's cute on you."

"Unisex!" she cried, indignant.

"Now pretend you have some manners so I can introduce you. Benedict, this brat is my cousin Seri. Seri, this is Benedict."

Benedict had bent to offer Havoc his hand to sniff. Either the little terrier had forgotten their earlier encounter, or she'd decided all that dominance stuff was resolved. He straightened and held out his hand. "Good to meet you."

Seri let go of Arjenie and smiled to give Benedict the benefit of her dimples as she took his hand. "You're a big one, aren't you?"

"Big enough. I hear you like to ski."

"I love to ski, and I'm good at it. Much better than my twin."

Sammy arrived with a snort of amusement. "She likes to fall down. Good at it, too."

"And who broke a leg winter before last?"

Sammy turned to Benedict. "I'm the better skier, but like I said, she falls really well. Much better at falling than me. She's had so much practice. I'm Samuel, but everyone calls me Sammy."

He didn't hold out a hand, but then, his hands were full with those sacks.

"Good to meet you," Benedict said. "You've been collecting holly."

"For wreaths. Seri got this notion that she just had to make a couple wreaths, and nothing would do for that but fresh holly, so we've been tramping around the woods for hours. Not that the wreaths won't look great, but—"

"They know about Uncle Nate's dream," Arjenie told him.

"Oh. Well, in addition to looking gorgeous, they'll offer some protection when we add the elderberries and a whiff of magic."

"Hazel," Seri said firmly, and bent to pick up Havoc, who was panting tiredly.

Sammy shook his head. "Not hazel. I keep telling you—"

"Why reinvent the wheel when—"

"Persimmon seeds worked in the—"

"Which was a totally different—"

"But without the lemongrass. I know."

"Feverfew?"

"Not unless the North is—"

"I don't think so. West and Air."

"Air? Air? Are you nuts? See you inside," Sammy added to them, and the twins moved off with Seri stroking Havoc, arguing in the abbreviated way that made sense only to them.

Benedict watched them leave, his head cocked. "Are they telepathic?"

"Not in the usual sense," Robin said. "I wonder what they're up to."

"Ah." Arjenie nodded. "I wondered about the feverfew. Feverfew does not make sense for protective wreaths."

"Plus they were off the land for about an hour earlier."

"You didn't ask them about it."

"They'd tell me they were gathering holly. Which they undoubtedly did, and if I asked what else they were doing, they'd tell me what they saw on their walk, where they stopped to look at an ant bed or something. Everything that actually occurred except the thing they don't want me to know about." She looked at Benedict. "They don't lie to me, but they are ingenious about avoiding the truth at times."

His eyebrows lifted. "You think they called Coyote here?"

She shook her head. "They're up to something, but not that. They know better. Magically speaking, you can mix traditions in a spell if you're careful, experienced, and knowledgeable. But invocation is spiritual magic. Spiritual magic is accessed through faith, through a particular religious or spiritual practice. Basically, they're too Wiccan to try contacting Native Powers."

"You're sure of this."

Arjenie exchanged a look with her aunt. "They know better," Robin repeated.

"Feedback loop," Arjenie said.

A small V appeared between Aunt Robin's eyebrows. She looked at the house, where the back door was just shutting behind the twins. "Feedback loop," she said slowly, "is family shorthand for what happens when Sammy and Seri stop arguing."

Arjenie could tell Benedict needed more explanation. "When one of the twins gets an idea in his or her head and gets the other one to buy into it, a self-contained reality sets up shop in their heads. It is very hard to penetrate all that certainty. Sometimes," she added, wanting to be fair, "they're even right. Like with Amos Brown."

Robin sighed. "Being right one time in five just makes them harder to convince the other four times."

Arjenie thought about the summer of the aliens, the "gate" that blew up a small utility shed, and the time the twins decided everyone was wrong and telekinesis really could be used to fly. "They're older now," she said, trying to convince herself.

"Even Seri and Sammy couldn't suddenly believe that invoking a Native Power would work out well for them," Aunt Robin said slowly, "but an invitation . . ." After a moment she shook her head. "The use of invitation is so basic, so fundamental to Wicca. It's hard to believe they'd suddenly decide they could use it for other Powers."

"There's a difference between invitation and invocation?" Benedict asked.

Robin nodded. "A large difference, actually. An invocation is like tugging on a Power's sleeve—or even summoning one, if it's a minor power and you have enough power yourself. An invitation is more like an e-mail. If you address it right, it goes where you intended, and the Power can answer it, ignore it, or act on it."

"Wiccan rites usually offer invitations," Arjenie added. "We invite the Powers of the North, South, East, and West to bring their protection to a circle, for example. We don't compel."

Benedict's eyebrows went up. "Your spells depend on the whim of these Powers?"

"Rites and spells are different. Most spells don't have a spiritual component. In Wicca, the rites do." Wanting to give him a more complete picture, she added, "Non-Wiccan practitioners like Cullen will tell you that North, South, East and West are fundamental energies, not Powers. That's because these energies aren't animate, not personalities or beings, so the spiritual component isn't necessary. And they're right on one level. You can cast a circle and practice magic without being Wiccan or of any other faith. But we believe that the spiritual component both enhances our magic and grounds us in the larger reality."

He thought that over a moment. "Could someone offer an invitation without including the spiritual component?"

"I don't see how. Unless they somehow convinced themselves they were working with a type of energy and not addressing a Power, but no one who knows anything about it could . . ." Arjenie stopped. Because once in a while the twins convinced themselves that down was in fact up.

For a moment no one said anything. "I need," Robin said, "to talk to Sammy and Seri. Now."

Chapter Five

Benedict managed to get in a couple more questions as they headed back to the house. He needed to know how best to integrate what his guards did with what Robin knew and could do with her land-tie.

She did not give him much information. Of course, she considered herself in charge of security here and he was still largely unknown to her. Not that she came out and said so, but the assumption was implicit in what she did and didn't say.

Pity she didn't know what she was doing.

Knowledge bias was unavoidable in security work, of course. Generals were always fighting the last war. You couldn't help focusing your resources—which were always limited—on the threats you knew and understood. Take Homeland Security. They knew how to protect against shoe bombs and certain liquid explosives, but as the "underwear bomber" had proved, they didn't know how to guard against all explosives. And they completely ignored the possibility of a magical attack on a plane in flight. It had never happened, so how likely could it be?

Robin was in a similar position. Her family and her coven had been safe here for a long time. She knew how to protect them from familiar threats—suspicious neighbors, sensation seekers, the occasional fervent antimagic activist. She did not know how to protect against attack or infiltration by a determined enemy who possessed excellent technical, magical, and monetary resources. It had never happened, so how likely could it be?

Plus, Robin hadn't had the land-tie, and the responsibility that went with it, for long. The woman Arjenie called Nana—Belle Delacroix—had held it until last year, when she decided to turn over responsibility for the land and the coven to her son's wife so she could travel with Andrew, her remaining husband. Her other husband, Samuel, had died a little over two years ago.

Benedict's Chosen had not been raised conventionally.

". . . won't wake up if an animal wanders onto the land, no," Robin was saying, "but if a human does, I will."

She'd already said that cars created an interruption in the energy of the land, one that would wake her even if she wasn't on alert. But cars weren't the only way people moved around. "What about a human on horseback?"

"I can tell the difference between a horse that's being ridden and one that's wandering loose."

"In your sleep?"

Robin's mouth opened. Then closed in a frown. She was still frowning as she reached for the back door. "We'll talk more later."

In the short time they'd been outside, the temperature had dipped from crisp to chilly as day slid into twilight. The bright, warm kitchen was inviting. Benedict smiled as he stepped inside—taking the rear, because threats were less likely to come from the house.

The silence was his first clue. Then the smell—anger plus other emotions he couldn't sort out in this form. There were a lot of tense bodies in that warm, welcoming kitchen.

"What?" Arjenie said, frowning as she stopped and looked around.

"Clay?" Robin said.

"We need a family meeting."

"Wait a minute," Seri began.

"It's not always best to drag everything into the open," Sammy said.

"And at Yule—"

"Hurt feelings."

"Sit," Robin said. "And be quiet until it's your turn."

Carmen's brother's name was Ben, which disconcerted Benedict when he heard it again. How had he forgotten a variant on his own name? Pure distraction, he supposed. That other Ben was very politely asked to relieve Gary of kid duty so Gary could participate. Partners counted the same as spouses in the Delacroix clan—as family.

Benedict wondered if he was considered Arjenie's partner. He offered to go chop wood, but Arjenie told him he was family and an adult so he would certainly take part. No one argued, though Sammy looked uneasy and Seri tossed her head. But then the meeting was probably about him. Made sense for him to be there.

There was enough room for all of them at the big cherry table, though they were a bit crowded. Benedict had just enough time to check in with Adam and Josh before Gary joined them.

Robin sat at one end of the table, Clay at the other. A fat pinecone sat on the table in front of Robin. Gary seated himself on Benedict's right, Clay gave Robin a nod, and the two of them held out their hands. Arjenie took Benedict's hand on one side; after a second of observation he understood what was required and held out his other hand to Gary. Once everyone was clasping hands, Robin spoke. "We seek wisdom and clarity, and ask for the patience needed to reach these goals, and for the memory of who we are as individuals and as a family to guide us. Blessed be."

Most of the others echoed "blessed be," though there were a couple "amens" mixed in. Arjenie and Gary both squeezed Benedict's hands before releasing them.

"All right," Robin said, and set a pinecone on the table. "Clay, you asked for this meeting. I have something to bring up, too, but it may be connected to your issue. I'd like you to go first." She passed the pinecone down the table.

When it reached Clay, he held it in one hand as he began. "Seri and Sammy have a concern about Arjenie's relationship with Benedict. I don't care for the way they've expressed this concern, but it needs airing."

"I—" Seri started, then visibly controlled herself. "Excuse me."

Clay smiled and handed her the pinecone.

"Thank you." She sat up very straight. "I didn't want to do this in a family meeting because I thought it would hurt Arjenie. But here we are, so"—she turned to Robin—"I'd like to open this up."

Robin thought, then said, "Ten minutes open discussion."

Seri moved the pinecone to the center of the table. "Here's the deal. Arjenie didn't come home for my and Sammy's birthday."

"I explained that!" Arjenie protested. "And I hated to miss it, but I called. I sent presents."

"Yes, and I love the sweater, but this isn't about presents. You didn't come, and I . . . well, I'm sorry, but I didn't believe your explanation."

Sammy snorted. "Too busy at work. Yeah, that's believable."

Pink flags flew on Arjenie's cheeks. "Since my work involves helping the people who stopped other people from destroying the country, maybe it should be believable."

"Our birthdays were *after* those horrible Humans First rallies."

"And you thought that meant the problem was solved?"

"It's not like that's the only thing," Seri said.

Sammy picked up that thought and ran with it. "You moved across the country. Pfft. Just like that. You haven't been home since you took that mysterious trip to San Diego—"

"Which you have never explained—"

"Except that Dya was involved somehow, but she left before we got to see her. You stayed at the lupi clanhome and you won't tell anyone why—"

"Even though you didn't know any lupi before you went there—"

"But you stayed at their clanhome and met Benedict, and while you were there a mountain sort of collapsed—"

"When its node imploded, and I know you were involved, but you won't talk about it, and you say Benedict can't move here, but—"

"You won't explain why. You told Mom that you two are plighted—"

"But he's lupi, and everyone knows they aren't monogamous—"

"And you plighted after you'd known him a few days! No time at all for that kind of—"

"Life-changing decision, and no one in the family had even talked to him, so—"

"We think Benedict's controlling you somehow." Sammy finished with a scowl, which he aimed at Benedict.

There was silence for a moment. Carmen broke it hesitantly. "Arjenie deals with top secret information, with sensitive information . . . I don't think we can lump in her silence about the collapse of that mountain with her silence on other subjects."

"And yet," Stephen said, his narrow face thoughtful, "they're connected. Not directly, but there's a connection."

"Stephen," Arjenie said reproachfully. "You, too?"

He spread his hands. "I'm not jumping on the twins' bandwagon. Just saying that you're keeping a lot of secrets, and those secrets are connected somehow."

Stephen Delacroix had a weak but well-trained patterning Gift, according to Arjenie. He must have picked up on the pattern that connected Arjenie to all those event and their common denominator: him. "If I understand correctly," Benedict said, "open discussion means I can speak."

Robin nodded. "Yes, of course."

"Arjenie is a member of my clan now. She knows clan secrets that do connect obliquely to—"

"What?"

"She's in your clan?"

"Are you saying you turned her into a lupus?"

"Don't be an idiot. You can't get turned into—"

"Does that mean you're married? And you didn't tell us? I can't believe you didn't—"

"Lupi don't get married! Everyone knows that."

"So what's he doing here if he isn't Arjenie's plighted partner?"

"Enough." That was Clay, not yelling but putting enough volume and certainty in his voice to cut through the exclamations and comments coming from everyone. "I think," he said dryly as he claimed the pinecone, "we'd best go to directed discussion. Robin?"

She nodded, and Clay continued. "First I'll clarify that, yes, Arjenie plighted herself to Benedict, and he to her, so his place at our table is a given. Robin and I were aware she'd been welcomed into Nokolai clan. Arjenie had planned to announce that to everyone else herself, but I understand why Benedict felt he needed to tell you now. I believe the clans are pretty secretive, so she's constrained from discussing some of that with us."

"I don't like it," Sammy muttered—maybe too low for the humans to hear, but Benedict did.

"So the issue we are discussing," Clay said, "is not whether Arjenie has secrets. She does. The question is whether or not she has been, ah, unduly influenced by Benedict."

"There's a line," Hershey said gruffly, "between personal and family. You bring someone into the family, fine, that's family business. What's between you and him, though, that's not family business. Think we're crossing the line."

Clay nodded. "I'm thinking that myself."

Seri's face set stubbornly. "Which is exactly what I thought you'd say, which is why I didn't ask for a family meeting in the first place. But you're wrong. If she's been given some sort of lupi emotional jujitsu, we need to do something about it."

"Oh?" Robin focused on her daughter. "And what would you suggest? Possibly inviting a Native Power onto our land?"

Dead silence.

"Seri?" Robin prompted. "Sammy?"

It was Sammy who answered, his voice far too bland. "I haven't been in contact with any Powers, Native or otherwise, since the equinox."

"No? And have you been in touch with any energies that *I* would consider a Native Power, even if you don't?"

Sammy gave himself away with a quick glance at his twin.

Robin looked around. "Did anyone tell these two what happened while they were gathering holly?"

Sammy sent Benedict a dark look. "Benedict claims he was forced to turn into a wolf and that Coyote showed up and scared Muffin."

"And you don't believe him. Why?"

Another glance between the twins. Seri sighed and answered. "Because it wasn't Coyote we invited. Not that it was really an invitation—you'd call it that, but we altered the ritual so we'd be drawing on the underlying reality of the kind of protective energy we wanted, not a named persona representing that energy."

"Who," Robin said, "or what did you invite?"

"It wasn't an invitation. It was—"

"Seri."

"Raven."

Benedict sighed and rubbed his forehead.

"Benedict," Robin said, "you have something to say, I think."

"Yeah. You two got the wrong trickster. Protective energy? Raven?" He shook his head. "Raven's a lot of things, sometimes helpful, sometimes not, but at heart, he's a trickster, not a guardian."

Sammy managed to look both wary and vaguely superior at the same time. "Raven is a symbol, not an entity."

"He's both. And symbol or entity, he's not a protective figure. And you didn't get him. You got Coyote. I see three questions here. First, what were you really trying to do? Second, why involve a Native Power instead of the ones you call on in Wicca? Third, why did Coyote decide to show up?"

Arjenie spoke suddenly. "I bet I can answer the first one. Look at what happened. Something forced you to Change. I bet the twins cast some sort of 'reveal' spell—a variation on a truth spell that was supposed to force you to reveal what you really are. Only because they involved Coyote—"

"Raven," Seri insisted hotly.

"You may have been thinking Raven, but when you tinkered with the invitation, trying to make it not an invitation but something that fit your skewed notion of reality—"

"Skewed? Skewed? Let me tell you, we have been practicing this sort of thing with smaller spells for some time, and results clearly demonstrate—"

"You have, have you?" Robin said softly. "And where have you done this practicing?"

The glance the twins exchanged was easily read by nontwins this time—something along the lines of *Oh, shit.*

Robin waited. When neither of them spoke, she said, "This is now a coven matter. The family meeting is adjourned."

"But Mom—"

"Clay?" Robin stood.

He shook his head, but it wasn't a disagreeing shake. More like resigned and unhappy. Benedict wondered what coven rules the twins had broken and what the penalty might be. "She's right and you know that. We'll have to talk with you two privately."

Robin's face had gone still, as if she were listening to something. "But not right away," she said slowly. "We have a visitor, or will very shortly. I believe it's the sheriff."

Chapter Six

Sheriff Porter was a tall, ropy man somewhere between fifty and sixty with a luxuriant mustache and a prominent brow ridge overhanging deep-set eyes. Cop eyes, Benedict thought. Like Lily's. Porter turned down an offer of coffee and asked to speak with Clay and Robin privately.

The house was crowded enough to make privacy difficult to find, so they'd gone out onto the front porch. Everyone else had migrated from the kitchen to the living room; Benedict sat beside Arjenie on the loveseat. He'd considered finding an excuse to linger near the front wall where he'd be able to hear what the sheriff said but decided that might be seen as intrusive.

Arjenie was quiet. He wondered what that family meeting had meant to her. Earlier she'd been angry, but he didn't think she was angry now. Hurt, maybe, but Arjenie was even worse at brooding than she was at holding a grudge. This seemed to be one of her thinking silences.

"I bet he's got a case," Ambrose said. "Don't you think?"

"Of course." That was Nate. "We've helped out sometimes," he added directly to Benedict. "The coven, that is. Or now and then one of us is able to lend a hand on our own. Depends on what kind of help the sheriff needs."

Benedict nodded. The Delacroix family had been here for generations, so they'd had time to build trust both in the community and with the sheriff. Some law enforcement officers refused any sort of magical assistance, but others were more open-minded. And the only magically derived evidence the courts accepted came from certain Wiccan spells. "Arjenie tells me that Robin is a Finder. I imagine she gets called on often."

"Often enough," Gary said. "Plus there were those creatures blown in by the power winds at the Turning. A lot of us were involved then, rounding them up, but of course we couldn't send them back where they belonged."

"What did you do with them?" Benedict asked.

"The pixies left on their own. No one knows how, but they ske-daddled. The gremlins . . . well, not much you can do about gremlins except kill them, but fortunately we just had to find and hold them. The disposal was handled by the FBI's Magical Crimes Division. The most dangerous one was that snake."

"Oh man, yeah." Nate shook his head. "Biggest damn snake I've ever seen. At least twice the size of an anaconda, and it could hyp-notize its prey, just like they say dragons do. It ate someone, though we didn't know that until they cut it open."

"Your coven found and killed it?"

"Trapped it. We avoid killing if possible, especially if there's some uncertainty about the sentience of the predator. The snake died anyway, though, about three days later. Robin thinks it came from a high-magic realm and there just wasn't enough here to sus-tain it."

Seri grinned. "Or else it ate something that didn't agree with it."

"Seri," Hershey said reproachfully.

She shrugged. "Come on, Uncle Hershey, you know what John Randall was like. Beat that poor wife of his, even if she never would press charges. Too scared, most likely."

"No one deserves a death like that. Swallowed alive."

"So it was ugly. So was he."

Stephen shook his head, his mouth twisting wryly. "You and Sammy didn't see the body. It's easier to joke about that sort of thing if you don't see the object of your humor half digested."

"You didn't see it, either," Seri protested. "You weren't here during the Turning."

"True. I saw other things, however."

That sparked Benedict's curiosity. Stephen was a wanderer, according to Arjenie. The rest of the Delacroix brothers had settled near their homestead. Hershey and his partner were practically neighbors; Nate and Ambrose were about fifty miles away. Arjenie had moved farther than most, but D.C. was still only two hours from here. Stephen, however, kept a post office box in his old home town but had no permanent address. He traveled all over the country. Why?

"Benedict," Arjenie said quietly.

He turned to look at her. She had beautiful eyes. Ocean eyes, not blue or green or gray but partaking of all those and varying according to the lighting. Or maybe they reflected her surroundings and her self the way water reflects the mood of the sky . . .

At the moment, they were the color of the sea beneath a cloudy sky. He put a hand on her thigh. "Yes?"

"I'm going to tell them. Not all of them," she said softly, "but Aunt Robin and Uncle Clay. They need to know, and they'll keep our secret, just like you're keeping theirs."

Shit. She was talking about the mate bond. "We don't speak of that to out-clan. Ever."

Her chin came up. "And my family doesn't talk about the land-tie to those who aren't coven. Ever."

He frowned, trying to put into words down why speaking of the mate bond would be wrong when it hadn't been wrong for Robin to tell him about the land-tie. Which, admittedly, did seem the same, on the surface . . .

Arjenie patted his hand. "Don't worry. It's not your decision or responsibility. If Isen wants to yell at me later, he can."

The front door opened. Clay stood in the doorway. Something about him reminded Benedict of his father and Rho. Isen often stood just like that, his wide stance matching his wide shoulders. He sent a glance around the room. "Robin and I will be going with Sheriff

Porter. We're requesting volunteers, enough for a small circle. Arjenie, Seri, Sammy—we'd like you to participate, an' you so will."

Ambrose frowned. "You want the twins instead of me and Nate or Stephen?"

"Trouble's coming," Stephen said softly. "If Robin's going to be off the land for a while, and Clay with her, we need people here who can act, if necessary."

Ambrose accepted that with a nod. "You'll have to link us to the wards, Clay."

"Of course." Clay looked at Benedict. "Robin explained to Sheriff Porter about your heritage and abilities. If you're willing, you may be able to help, too."

That was convenient, since there was no way he was letting Arjenie go without him. He stood. "My men—"

But Clay was shaking his head. "The sheriff is willing to take a chance by including you, but he doesn't want to be, ah, surrounded by wolves who might not see things his way. They'll need to stay here."

Benedict considered signaling Josh that he and Adam were to follow discreetly, but decided to comply with the sheriff's restriction. They might be needed here. He didn't know what, if anything, Robin could do defensively when she wasn't on her land, and he and Arjenie would be with law enforcement officers. Not the backup he'd choose, maybe, but they had some training and they'd be armed. "All right. Will I need to Change?"

"No, you're fine."

"He means into a wolf," Arjenie said.

"Oh, ah, I don't know. Yes, probably. We thought you might be able to track by smell."

"My other form will be better for that. I should eat something."

"Ack." Arjenie popped up. "I'm a bad mate. I should've made sure you had something to eat earlier. Uncle Clay, can I dig in the refrigerator for whatever's defrosted?" She looked at Benedict. "I'm thinking that you eat faster when you're four-footed, so—raw?"

"Good thinking."

"There's not time for a meal," Clay said.

"We'll take some meat along," Benedict explained as Arjenie hurried to the kitchen. "I can eat after I Change. Like she said, I eat fast as a wolf." He decided they needed more information. "I've Changed twice already. The Change makes me hungry. A hungry wolf wants to hunt. My control is excellent, so you needn't worry that I'd be a danger to you, but hunger would be a distraction for me."

Clay looked at him a moment, then nodded and raised his voice. "Arjenie? *Not* the turkey."

Arjenie had always felt uncomfortable around Sheriff Porter. It was nothing he'd said or done or not done. It wasn't intuition or distrust or anything like that. It was memory.

Twenty-three years ago, he'd been a deputy. His was the first face she remembered seeing after the accident. She'd been told that she was conscious earlier, that she'd responded to the people who stopped after a drunk drove his pickup into them, but she didn't remember any of that. She remembered Ab Porter's face, those deep-set eyes dark and steady as he told her to hold still, hold on, that the ambulance would be there soon and they'd get her fixed up.

He'd been right about that, though it took three major surgeries, a couple of patch-ups, and a whole lot of rehab. And, of course, she was never fully fixed. They hadn't known as much about growth plate injuries back then as they did now. Her left leg would always be a bit shorter than her right, her ankle a bit weak.

Twenty-three years ago, Deputy Porter had climbed into the backseat with her, using his body to block her view of the front of the car. He'd stayed there until the paramedics arrived, in a position she realized later must have been hideously uncomfortable, given how smashed up the car was. He hadn't wanted her to see what two tons of truck had done to her mother.

Ab Porter was a kind man, a good man, and she was grateful to him. But she was not quite comfortable with him, so she would rather have ridden with Uncle Clay in the pickup. But when he said the twins would ride with him he used his "don't argue" voice, which meant he intended to have a talk with them. Arjenie ended up in the back of the sheriff's car with her aunt.

Benedict rode up front. That was her suggestion, and he'd given her a hard look when she made it because he didn't like anyone knowing about his vulnerabilities. Not that he was terribly claustrophobic, but neither she nor her aunt was bothered by that sort of thing, so why should he be uncomfortable? The back of the sheriff's car locked automatically. He'd feel like he was in a cage.

Anyway, she'd just said she wanted to talk to her aunt, so she hadn't given him away.

"I haven't met a lupus before," Porter said as he pulled away from the house, "much less worked with one. I need to know what to expect."

"First, you should know I'm armed. I have a concealed carry permit from your state. Do you want to see it?"

The sheriff did want to, so they sat there a moment with the dome light on—it was getting too dark to see well—while he inspected it. "What are you carrying?"

"Smith and Wesson .357 chambered with .357 Magnum JHPs."

In deference to her family, Benedict had left his weapon in their room with his jacket. But when he'd said, "I'll get my jacket," and gone to their room, she'd been pretty sure he'd come back wearing more than his new leather jacket. He did not, she noted, mention the knives. He was wearing at least two of them—one in his boot, the other in a belt sheath. Virginia law concerning knives was rather murky, but she suspected neither knife was strictly legal.

"That's a lot of stopping power," Porter said, starting the car.

"If something needs to be shot, I want it to stay down."

Porter grunted. "Resist the urge to use it. I need you for your nose, not your weapon. Robin says you'll be as good as a bloodhound."

"I did not say bloodhound," Robin corrected mildly. "I suspect bloodhounds can outsmell a wolf."

"Robin's correct," Benedict said. "Bloodhounds have extraordinary noses, and their ears and wrinkled skin trap the scent to help them track. But wolf noses are good—somewhere between ten thousand and a couple hundred thousand times as good as a human's, depending on which expert you listen to."

Porter nodded. "And you'll be able to understand us when you're a wolf? You'll still think like a man?"

"I don't think exactly the same way when I'm wolf as I do when I'm man, but I don't think like a wild wolf, either. I'll understand you just fine. I'll know who you are, that you're the sheriff, and what that means—law, the courts, the whole complex system. But that kind of complexity isn't interesting to a wolf. I have to make an effort to call up some things. Do you know how to find the circumference of a circle?"

"Ah—something to do with pi. Pi r squared . . . no, just Pi r. Pi times the radius."

"You had to stop and think about it. That's what it's like when I'm wolf. I know the same things, but some of them aren't at the top of my mind."

"Huh. Will the need to keep your teeth to yourself be at the top of your mind?"

Benedict chuckled. "Good way to put it. Yes, it will. Some things are . . . if not instinctive, then automatic. Ingrained."

"It's like asking an engineer or math teacher about pi," Arjenie put in. "It would be right there at the top for them, because they work with it a lot and it *is* interesting to them. The clans train their youngsters really well so that—" No, wait, she couldn't finish that sentence the way she'd intended. "So that they don't eat anyone" would not create the right impression.

"So that we understand the difference between people and prey," Benedict finished for her. "I will no more overlook that difference as a wolf than I would as a man. Nor will I mistake normal human actions for a threat, the way a wild wolf would, or become excited by certain scents."

Fear, he meant. Wolves could get excited by that smell, but to Benedict it would be information, nothing more.

Benedict paused, then added, "You will find it works better to ask me to do things rather than telling me what to do."

This time it was Porter who chuckled. "You're no different from most men, then. People generally prefer being asked. I'll try to keep in mind that you're not one of my deputies."

That made Arjenie grin. Benedict would certainly not look like a deputy.

"That will help. You want me to track someone or something."

"Something," Porter said. "Or that's what we think right now. Some boys—teenagers—found a body down by Moss Creek this afternoon. A man."

"Oh, no," Arjenie said. "Do you know who?"

"Assuming the ID in his wallet is accurate, it was Orson Peters. Robin here didn't think you'd know him."

She thought a moment, shook her head, then realized he couldn't see her. "I don't think so."

"He's an ex-con, so I've kept an eye on him. Did odd jobs mostly but he kept his nose clean, aside from some trapping I tried not to notice. He lived alone in a little shack not far from where the body was found."

Benedict spoke. "If you've kept an eye on Peters but couldn't ID him without his wallet, I'm guessing the body was in bad shape."

Porter nodded. "Looks like he was mauled by something with claws and teeth, then partly eaten."

"Which parts?" Benedict asked.

"Why the hell does that—"

"Humor me."

The sheriff shrugged. "The guts, from what I could tell. Things were pretty much of a mess, though, so don't hold me to that."

Yuck. Arjenie looked at her aunt in disbelief. She and Uncle Clay wanted the twins to be part of a circle investigating that kind of ugly? Even if the body had been removed by now—and she was hoping hard it had been—Arjenie would not have brought Sammy and Seri into this. They'd turned twenty a month ago. In some ways they were wise beyond their years, but in others they were naive, even immature. "Uh . . . has the body been removed?"

Porter gave her a look that said he knew some of what she'd been thinking. "Yes."

"You've got an animal attack," Benedict said, "but you haven't asked me where I've been today."

"Unless Arjenie wants to contradict what her aunt and uncle told me, you've been with her this morning, and with the whole family since you arrived around two. But Peters wasn't killed today. It's yesterday and the day before I'm interested in."

But not worried about, Arjenie thought, or he would have made sure Benedict was sitting back here, safely locked up, when he asked that question. Why wasn't he worried?

"I was in D.C. We flew in on the nineteenth, arrived at eight forty that night. Stayed at her apartment, which we packed up. Arjenie and my men can speak for my whereabouts the whole time."

Porter's eyebrows lifted. "Your men?"

"Josh Krugman and Adam Thorne. Bodyguards."

"Interesting life you lead if you need bodyguards. I'll want to talk to them, but later. Your story matches what Robin told me."

"And that's enough for you?"

"She also said that you make a very big wolf. A big black wolf."

Benedict nodded.

"We found a tuft of fur near the body, got caught on some branches. That fur's kind of an orangey brown, which doesn't prove anything . . . but we also have some tracks."

"Not wolf tracks, I take it."

"Not anything like a wolf's tracks. One of my deputies hunts. I've done some hunting myself, but not like Matt. Lots of experience with all kinds of game. He was pretty sure about those tracks, but I had his uncle come have a look, too. K. J.'s a pro—he's hunted pretty much everything you can hunt in North America, including bear. Made a couple trips to Alaska for that."

"K. J. Miller?" Aunt Robin sounded dismayed.

"I guess you don't much care for him," Porter said, "but he knows his tracks and scat."

"K. J. Miller is a misogynist," Arjenie explained to Benedict. "He thinks the world came to an end when women got the vote, and the rest of us just haven't noticed. He and Aunt Robin have butted heads a few times."

"The tracks," Benedict said. He was a tad impatient. "What about them?"

"Bear. One honking huge bear. Has to be a grizzly—black bears don't get that big."

Arjenie frowned. "There aren't any grizzlies here. Nowhere near here. We must be . . ." She thought a moment. "Yellowstone and Grand Teton. Those would be the closest places where grizzlies have been seen, and they're at least two thousand miles away."

"That's a problem, isn't it?"

Chapter Seven

A grizzly could be a problem, all right, regardless of how it got here. Benedict considered what he knew about them. Not enough, he concluded, but enough to be sure he'd rather not tackle one without a half-dozen clanmates in wolf form to help . . . or the .30-06 he had back home. Or, hell, if he was wishing, might as well wish for his M16. That one would stop small to midsize demons, so it ought to work against a grizzly.

Didn't do him much good now. "Arjenie. What can you tell me about grizzlies that might be pertinent?"

"The grizzly is a subspecies of brown bear—*Ursus arctos horribilis*. Adult males usually weigh between four hundred and eight hundred pounds. They're mostly solitary, though they tolerate each other in some circumstances, such as when they're fishing for salmon. They're called grizzlies because of the grizzled look of their coats, which is the reason for their other name—silvertip bear. I'm thinking that orangey brown fur doesn't sound like a grizzly. Other brown bears have more varied coats."

Arjenie's vacuum-cleaner memory came in handy at times. "What other types of brown bear are there?"

"On this continent, the other subspecies would be the coastal brown bear, which includes the Kodiak bear. They get even bigger than grizzlies, topping out at over a thousand pounds. I don't remember exactly how much over a thousand." She sounded apologetic for this failing. "But coastal brown bears live along the Alaskan coast and on some of the islands up there. They don't go walkabout and end up in Virginia."

"That's one of the reasons I wanted Robin and Clay in on this," Sheriff Porter said. "Maybe it's a bear that got loose from a zoo. We're checking on that, but so far no one says they've misplaced a grizzly. So maybe it's not a normal bear. Or maybe it's something else that shouldn't be here."

"I can tell you if it's a bear," Benedict said. "Not sure I'll know if it's a grizzly. Never smelled one." But he could talk to someone who had. "I need to contact a couple people."

"Who?" Porter gave him a sharp look as he slowed for a turn down a dirt lane. About a half mile ahead, Benedict saw headlights. Stationary, so maybe that was one of the deputies' cars.

"My men, first, to let them know."

"Put your phone up. I don't want word getting out."

"Understood. They won't be talking to anyone. I'm going to see if I can find someone who knows something about fighting grizzlies. I've never fought one." He was hoping he wouldn't fight one now, either—not up close and personal—but he wanted as much information as possible. He didn't think any Nokolai had had that experience, but he knew who had. Etorri's territory was in Canada. A few years ago, two Etorri had been badly mauled and a third one killed by a grizzly. Benedict didn't know how to reach those men directly, but he knew who could put him in touch with them.

"I told you to put the phone up."

"You've forgotten what I said about asking." Benedict had already sent a text to his men. Thinking it might be more diplomatic, being less obvious, he texted his brother instead of calling: *Call me. Urgent.* Rule would talk to the Etorri Lu Nuncio or Rho, who would have one of the surviving Etorri call him.

"It's too damn late, isn't it?"

"Yeah. But they won't be gossiping, so there isn't a problem." Benedict put his phone up. "Has this deputy of yours hunted grizzlies?"

"No. His uncle has."

"I'll want to talk to him."

"Mr. Turner." Porter was angry. Benedict could hear the tension in his jaw when he spoke. "You seem to be under the impression you're in charge here. You aren't."

Turner was his father's surname, not his, but Benedict let that pass. "I'm in charge of what I do. I'm not in charge of you or your men—or your deputy's uncle, for that matter. I'm not challenging your authority," he added, thinking he needed to put it bluntly. Humans had different rules. He wasn't used to operating under those rules and might be sending signals he didn't intend to.

"But you don't consider yourself under my authority."

"No." How could he be? Two people had the right to give Benedict an order—his Rho and his Lu Nuncio. No one else. Though he would probably obey if his Rhej told him to do something, that was a matter of service, not authority.

Arjenie spoke from the back seat. "Sheriff, when you say 'authority,' Benedict hears 'submit.' There's a whole language of submission for lupi, so it gets complicated, but I don't think he *can* submit to you. It might violate his duty to his Rho. He will, however, cooperate with you."

Well, he could accord the sheriff the leadership of the hunt . . . but he didn't think a human would understand what that meant. Besides, he didn't know if the man was good enough to take lead. "Allies," Benedict said suddenly. "That term means the same to you it does to me." At least he thought it did. "We're allies in this matter, but I'm in your territory, so I'll defer to your wishes as much as possible."

"Defer to my wishes." Porter shook his head and slowed.

They'd nearly reached those headlights, which did, as Benedict had suspected, belong to another sheriff's department car. A deputy stood beside it holding a rifle pointed at the ground. Good choice of weapon. He was talking to a man in civilian clothes—fifty or so, stringy hair, dark beard, also holding a rifle. There was a second vehicle parked on the shoulder—an old truck. "Is that your hunter?" he asked. "The misogynist?"

"That's him. You can talk to him later, I suppose." Porter sighed. "Robin, what have you gotten me into?"

So Benedict's inclusion was Robin's idea? Satisfaction flickered, deep down. Arjenie's aunt must trust him more than he'd thought. "I'll be useful," he assured the sheriff. "You'll be glad you brought me in."

The body had been found near the portion of Moss Creek that ran through Foggy Draw. That surprised Arjenie—she hadn't thought anyone lived near the draw. It was rough country. Also a lot closer to Delacroix land that it would seem from the time it took to get there. They'd had to go roundabout, to the far end of the draw where there was a bridge, then back again.

The deputy's car marked the place where they had to turn off the county road onto a pair of ruts that didn't really deserve the designation of road. Robin was telling Arjenie what they'd do as they headed down that tree-lined track. "First we'll cast for traces of magic. We want to know if this is a normal bear or something else. Once we know that, I'll try a Find, using that bit of fur they found as a focus. I may need to draw on the circle, depending on how close the creature is."

Arjenie nodded. One reason Wicca had survived when magic grew so thin after the Purge was the way Wiccan circles could pool their power so the high priest or priestess could use it. "You'll scry for magic first?"

"Yes. I'll do it in circle so we'll be ready to move to the defining spell if I find any traces of magic."

Though a circle always helped, it wasn't necessary to scry for magic. But the defining spell did take a circle, and the courts would only accept findings from a defining spell. It revealed the presence and type of magic to the entire circle, not just the principle caster, and having multiple witnesses testify to the same findings was supposed to eliminate individual bias or error. "If you're needed to Find the creature, I can handle the defining spell."

"If I'm not in the circle, the numbers are off."

"Benedict could participate."

Her eyebrows rose. "He can take part in a Wiccan circle?"

"I don't see why not. He can't cast spells, but he's got plenty of power."

Porter spoke. "This is as far as we go in the car."

The dirt tracks ended in a make-do sort of turnaround where cars had come often enough to keep grass and weeds down. Directly ahead a dark wall of trees and foliage marked the edge of the draw; their headlights picked out a bright yellow strip of crime scene tape tied between a small tree and a bush. Arjenie figured that marked the path they'd take down into the draw.

They parked next to another sheriff's department car. The deputy belonging to this one was female and stood outside her vehicle, holding a rifle. "Keep your weapon in the holster," Porter told Benedict, then clicked something that unlocked the back doors. Arjenie climbed out, the backpack she'd borrowed from Sammy in one hand.

Clay and the twins were right behind them in the weathered Ford truck Robin used in her veterinary practice. He stopped the truck a few yards back of the sheriff's car. There wasn't much room.

"All quiet?" Porter asked his deputy. The woman nodded and said she hadn't seen or heard anything but a raccoon.

The wind was stronger than ever, making Arjenie glad she'd brought her heavy jacket. Night had firmly fallen while they were on the way here, and while she had pretty good night vision, the sky was seriously overcast. She couldn't see well at all.

A few feet away, Benedict had his head up, looking around. Or maybe smelling around. Clay and the twins climbed out of the truck with a dual slamming of doors.

Arjenie had a flashlight in her backpack, but she couldn't resist showing off a little. "Shazzam," she whispered—and a ball of light sprang into being a couple feet above her head.

The word was a trigger, not the spell itself—which she'd learned from Cynna, who'd gotten it from Cullen, who picked it up when the two of them were in Edge. It was an almost purely spoken spell—those were rare—but everyone who wasn't a sorcerer like Cullen had to add one physical component: a drop of their own blood to link it to them. Once cast, though, the spell could be held in abeyance for days. Arjenie usually recast the spell once a week so she'd have it ready if she needed it.

"Nice!" Uncle Clay said, hands on hips as he studied the mage light.

"What the hell?" The sheriff was dumfounded.

"Arjenie! Is that mage light?" Seri's question sounded more like an accusation. "You know how to make mage light and you didn't—"

"Can't be mage light," her twin informed her. "No one knows how to make mage light. The secret to it has been lost since the Purge. It's a trick—but a pretty cool one."

Arjenie chuckled, enjoying herself. "Guess what? The secret isn't lost anymore."

Aunt Robin came closer, studying the ball of light appraisingly. "Excellent. Can you make it brighter or dimmer?"

She had told her aunt and uncle about the spell, intending to teach it to them over the holiday, so they weren't as delightfully flummoxed as the twins. "Dimmer is easy, but you can't make a single ball of mage light any brighter than this. You have to add more mage lights, and that takes a lot more focus. This one"—with a thought, she made it bob—"I can carry without paying it any attention, and the power drain is really small, but if I add more I have to focus, and I lose power faster. I carried three once, but I was very distracted. Cullen—I told you about him—has carried six and was still able to hold a conversation."

"I'd like to meet him sometime."

"When you come out to visit, you will."

"That's the damnedest thing I've seen in a long time," Porter said, "but we aren't here to enjoy this, uh, mage light thing of Arjenie's. Robin, you said you'd need to set your circle near where the body was found. That's down in the draw. We've swept the immediate area, but don't—Turner. Where are you going?"

Benedict had started for the truck. "Hitchhiker."

He didn't get a step farther before Havoc launched herself up out of the truck's bed, landed with her mouth in gear, and raced to Robin, her tail waving madly.

"How in the world—!" Robin snatched up the little terrier, who wriggled and tried to lick her face. "I could have sworn she was in the house. I guess she snuck out."

Seri grinned. "And hitched a ride in the back of the truck. That's a new trick, isn't it?"

"And not one I want to encourage. Into the cab with you, young lady." Robin carried the terrier back to the truck, where she opened one door, put the window down a few inches, and locked Havoc safely inside. "Sorry for the interruption," she said to Porter.

"Glad you caught her. Like I was saying, stick to the path and don't wander once you're down there. I've got two deputies keeping an eye on things."

"Might be best if I go ahead and Change," Benedict said.

Sammy had wandered over to the crime scene tape. He had a flashlight and aimed it down that path, which seemed to drop off pretty steeply. "Looks rough," he said. "Arjenie, did you bring your cane?"

"I won't need it."

Porter frowned. "I didn't think about that. You've got a bit of a hitch in your gallop. Should be okay once you get down, but the path's not easy."

"She'll let us know if she needs help," Benedict said absently. His attention seemed to be on Havoc, a small frown between his eyebrows.

"Arjenie?" Sammy hooted. "Drag her up a mountain and she won't admit she needs help, even when she's tumbling off of it."

That brought Benedict's focus to her obnoxious cousin. "You're wrong. She's stubborn, not stupid. She wouldn't jeopardize the rest of us or the mission through misplaced pride." Now he looked at her. "I'm going to Change before we head down. Come with me and take charge of my clothes?"

Silly heart. It had speeded up. Arjenie beamed at him, feeling all fond and warm. He trusted her to know her limits—to push them sometimes, sure, but at the right time and place. Which this wasn't. Her family, wonderful as they were, never seemed to think she might know more than they did about what her body could and couldn't do.

"Sure," she said. "Wouldn't want that nice jacket to lie around in the dirt."

"You need to go somewhere to change into a wolf?" Porter asked.

"I prefer privacy," Benedict said.

Which wasn't exactly a lie, Arjenie thought as she followed him to the far side of the pickup. But she suspected it was the knives he wanted to keep private, not the sight of him Changing. Just like it was his weapons he really wanted her to take charge of, though she'd keep his clothes for him, too. That's why she'd brought a backpack.

That, and it was a handy way to carry three pounds of hamburger.

"Turn down your light," Benedict told her as he shucked off his jacket. He paused. "Please. It interferes with my night vision."

She grinned and dimmed the mage light to firefly level. Benedict was getting better, but he was used to telling instead of asking. She unzipped the backpack and took out the hamburger, which she unwrapped and set on the ground. "Sheriff Porter has the same problem you do. He defaults to orders, not requests. I thought you wanted to ask that deputy some questions? The one who knows something about bears, I mean."

"I changed my mind." He slipped out of his jacket and held it out. She folded it, frowning. "Why?"

"Got a feeling. Partly it's a smell . . . faint, nothing I can identify, not in this form. But my back-brain doesn't like it." He unbuckled his belt. "You can get the knives after I've Changed, but I want you to wear my gun."

Arjenie made a face as she stuffed the jacket in the backpack. Until a couple months ago, she'd never shot a gun. Benedict had changed that, and she agreed that with a war on, however secret it might be, she needed to be able to shoot. The problem—and this was annoyingly girly of her—was that she flinched. Not every time, but sometimes when she squeezed the trigger, she'd flinch and the shot would be off. She'd stopped squeezing her eyes shut when she squeezed the trigger, but so far the flinch still happened about one-fourth of the time, which made her unreliable.

On the upside, when she didn't flinch she was a decent shot. "I'm wishing I'd let you talk me into bringing my SIG ," she said, accepting his holstered weapon. Benedict's .357 was too large for her hand, but she did know how to shoot it. "I flinch less when I use it."

He touched her cheek. "Is that almost the same as saying I was right?"

She grinned. "Almost. Benedict . . ." In the darkness she could feel the heat from his body. He was so warm. So powerful and *alive*.

"Yeah?"

"I remembered something else about grizzlies. They have a bite force of twelve hundred pounds per inch."

"I'll keep that in mind."

"A wolf's bite force is only four hundred pounds per inch. That's not really an 'only,' but compared to a grizzly—"

"I'll be very careful." He cupped her face in both hands. "You will be, too."

"I can make it not see me or smell me." Smell being especially important, since grizzlies were thought by some experts to have the best nose of all the mammals. Arjenie wasn't entirely persuaded by the methodology used, but there was no doubt a grizzly's sense of smell was extremely acute. "You can't. Plus you'll be trying to protect everyone." Because that was what he did. He couldn't help himself.

"I'll have help with that. The sheriff's made sure his people have rifles. My weapon has good stopping power for a handgun, but with a bear, a rifle is better. That reminds me. If you do end up shooting, empty the clip."

With that romantic utterance, he dipped his head and kissed her.

His taste flowed into her in a sweet rush—musk and man and wild, that pheromic hint of otherness her tongue surely wasn't clever enough to detect. Yet it did, or she did, or something. He kissed her with the controlled intensity he brought to every task, with a calm focus that announced there was nothing in the world more important than her mouth. Nothing more important than her.

When he lifted his head, she smiled, feeling twice as settled as she had a moment ago. He really was calm. That wasn't an act to reassure her. Meeting her family might have scared him, but a grizzly bear—that, he knew what to do about.

She rested one hand on his chest. The other still gripped the holstered .357, she was glad to notice. It wasn't a good idea to drop a loaded gun. "I sometimes wonder if, years ago, you determined the exact amount of fear that would keep you on your toes without being a distraction, and that's how much you allow yourself to feel."

"Fear can be useful," he agreed. "You want me to fasten the holster for you?"

"No, I'll get it." She'd worn a belt today, which was lucky, because she usually didn't, so she undid it and pulled it out of the belt loops. While she did that, he Changed.

In the darkness she couldn't see the Change, but even if she'd been staring straight at Benedict in bright daylight she wouldn't have seen much. She'd talked to several of the women at Nokolai Clanhome, asking what they saw when lupi Changed. Their answers were notable for how little they agreed and included things like "a swirling darkness," and "They sort of fold up and unfold at the same time," and "They flicker in and out." A few said they didn't see anything— one moment there was a man, the next a wolf. Or vice versa. Whatever happened in between, they either didn't see it or didn't remember what they'd seen.

The sheer variety of answers supported Arjenie's theory that the human brain wasn't set up to process what happened during the Change, so it made things up. Sadly, cameras weren't set up to process it, either. Digital or film, static or video, all they recorded was a spot of visual static.

Whatever the process, Arjenie knew it involved a great deal of pain, but the pain never lingered beyond the transformation. The faster a lupus could Change, the better, and some places made the

Change easier than others. She wished she could ask the enormous wolf now gulping down three pounds of raw hamburger how this spot measured up—compared, maybe, to Changing on Delacroix land—but she had to stick to yes-or-no questions when Benedict was wolf.

He'd finished eating by the time she gathered his clothes and shoes—and not two, but three knives, and where had he hidden that wickedly slim blade?—and got them stashed in the backpack. Then they went back to the others.

"Took a while," Porter said. He was staring at the wolf beside her.

"Did it?" Arjenie looked around. "Where's—oh, there he is." Sammy was on the ground, folding himself into slow, careful knots. Yoga was great for focus, and Arjenie always thought she should do it more often but never followed through. But Sammy had taken to yoga like a seal to water—as if he'd found his second element.

Benedict had trotted over to the crime scene tape that marked the entrance to the path. He sniffed around at the grass there, then looked over his shoulder at her. "Do you smell bear?" she asked.

He shook his head but kept looking at her expectantly.

"You want to go first?"

He nodded.

"He really does understand," Porter said.

The sheriff had a funny expression on his face—not exactly scared but not exactly not-scared, either. Amazement was part of it. "He told you he would."

"It's different, seeing it." He seemed to shrug off his reaction, turning brisk. "Okay. I've got two deputies waiting by the creek, and while you were busy I checked with them. Nothing happening down there. Let's go. Arjenie, you will let us know if you need help."

She agreed that she would and they set off.

Chapter Eight

Benedict ducked under the crime scene tape and started down.

As he had told the sheriff, some kinds of thinking didn't come easily for him when he was wolf. But this puzzle would need both sides of him, so he made the effort to hold on to words and concepts he knew mattered. It helped that this Change, unlike the one earlier, had been intentional.

He did not like relying on humans for backup. They were scent-blind all the time and literally blind on a dark night. Which this was. The moon might be nearly full, but most of her light was trapped by the low-hanging clouds. But you worked with what you had, and so far the only scents he was picking up on the path were human, with faint traces of other animals—raccoon, rabbit, mice, fox. The wind was from the southeast and steady, blocked somewhat by the brush and trees, but what reached him brought no warnings.

It was an easy descent on four feet. The two-legged ones following him were slow, but he was in no hurry. Their slowness was good for Arjenie, who was in the middle of the pack. The sheriff had arranged it that way, which earned the man some points with Benedict. Clay Delacroix brought up the rear.

Being human, the ones behind him needed flashlights, mage light, and words to make their way down the side of the draw. Most of their speech was to the point—*Watch out for that branch* or *There's a big step down here.* Twice Porter asked Arjenie how she was doing, which must have annoyed her. She'd said she'd let them know if she needed help. Was the man unable to take her at her word because she was female, or did he treat everyone with a physical impairment like a child?

The path leveled as abruptly as it had begun. Ahead was flat, gravelly ground tufted with grass—a cul-de-sac, he saw as he stepped forward. Rocky outcroppings that had refused to erode at the same rate as their brethren flanked either side of the flat, sandy area where the body had been found, spinning the creek in a wide curve around them. The water of that creek was smooth, dark, and almost silent.

The two men standing near that water were silent, too. And armed. And wearing uniforms. One of them aimed a flashlight at him, blinding him—but not totally. He saw it when the other man raised his rifle.

"Dammit, Rick," the first man said, "don't shoot him. That's the lupus the sheriff told us was coming."

If he knew that, why was he still shining that damn light in Benedict's eyes?

"Yeah, but—"

Benedict decided they weren't going to shoot and moved out of that annoying flashlight beam. And stopped, his lip lifting in a snarl and his hackles lifting—not at the men. At the stink—faint but unmistakable. He lifted his nose to be sure of the direction, then approached the bad-smelling place.

Blood, yes. But that was the least important of what he smelled.

"What's he doing?"

"How the hell do I know?"

"Turner." Porter, who'd been behind him on the path, was still misnaming him. "What have you—hell, I can't ask him that, can I? Lower your damn rifle, Rick. I told you what to expect."

"Is that where the body was found?" Robin asked. "I imagine he smells the blood."

Porter shook his head. "Rick, Jimmy—it would be nice if someone kept an eye out for that bear. Fan out and face out."

Seri said, "If he starts licking the grass, I'm going to hurl."

"Shut up, Seri." That was Arjenie, coming closer as she continued, "Benedict, do you smell bear?"

He took one last, deep sniff and lifted his head. What he needed to tell them could not fit into a yes-and-no set of questions. Sometimes this form was limited, but . . . he trotted down toward the creek. The ground was damp here and bare of grass. Good. He looked over his shoulder at Arjenie and waited.

She hurried to him. "You want me to see something?"

He nodded once, then used his paw, holding it at an angle so one claw only dragged through the damp dirt. It was awkward and would win no penmanship awards, but it worked. She her mage light lower so she could follow as he scratched out: D-E-A-T-H M-A . . .

"Death magic?" Arjenie exclaimed. "Is that what you smell?"

He nodded and kept writing: B-E-A . . .

"Death magic *and* bear?"

This time when he nodded he sat to let her know that was the full message.

"What in the world does that mean?" Clay had moved closer. "Can he really smell death magic?"

"I'm told it has a distinctive and highly unpleasant smell," Arjenie said. "Nothing we can detect, of course, and I don't know if magically null animals smell it. But lupi definitely can."

"If there's enough death magic present, I'll be able to detect it with the scrying spell," Robin said. "If not, we'll need the defining spell." She looked at Benedict. "Would you say there's a lot of death magic there?"

He shook his head. If the scent hadn't been so distinctive—and so distinctly unpleasant—the reek of bear and blood would have covered it up.

"What could death magic possibly have to do with a bear?" Porter asked.

Arjenie answered. "I guess we'll have to figure that out, but I can think of all sorts of possibilities. Maybe someone laid a compulsion on a bear using death magic. Or it might not be a real bear but some kind of phantasm summoned through death magic. Or someone used a bear somehow in a death magic ritual, then had him eat the body. Or it's something we've never heard of that involves death magic and a bear—maybe something Native American? Because—"

"Pretty fanciful." Aunt Robin gave her A Look.

Arjenie interpreted that to mean she wasn't to mention that the twins had been experimenting with calling on Native Powers. She could see the reasoning. Whatever they'd done, it hadn't involved death magic, and mentioning it now would probably mean lots of long explanations. Better to get on with what they came here for. "We can't eliminate the fanciful without more data."

"True." Uncle Clay was brisk. "Sheriff, it does look like we'll be needed. We'll get our circle set, but if there's death magic involved, you'll want to call in the FBI."

"I'm aware of that."

Robin had placed her tote on the ground and knelt there to unpack it. Spell stuff, Benedict assumed. His nose identified sage and rue and lilac. She had a small brazier, too. "Let's get started."

Arjenie moved near her aunt to help. Seri and Sammy—who'd been whispering to each other, perhaps forgetting what good ears he had—came to join them.

Those two were guilty of something. Most of their whispers had been twin-speak and he lacked a translator, but he was pretty sure they'd been assuring each other that what they'd done couldn't possibly have caused this.

He checked on the two deputies. They'd fanned out and faced out, like Porter told them. That was something, but the man should have sent one of them up onto that southern outcrop of granite. Good vantage point. Good place for something to launch an attack, too.

But he couldn't correct the sheriff's failings without speech, and at least those rocks were upwind. His nose should tell him if anything used them to approach their group. Better get on with what he came here for.

Clay came toward him. "We'll check that bit of fur the sheriff has, but I'd like some dirt from the place where you smelled death magic, too. Can you show me where to get it?"

Clay would get blood as well as dirt. The ground was saturated with it. Would digging there disturb the scene? Benedict looked at the sheriff, but the man was asking Robin something, not paying attention to Benedict. Well, Porter had said they'd already searched for evidence. If he didn't want Clay digging, he could say so.

Benedict pointed out the edge of the worst-smelling spot to Clay, then put his nose to work another way—following the bear-plus-death-magic reek the creature had left on the ground.

Following a scent trail was not as simple as humans seemed to think. It was easy to tell the difference between fresh scent and that laid down hours ago, but the scent he needed to track was at least a day old, and the bear had been all over this ground. That one spot smelled more strongly than the rest told Benedict the bear had lingered there with its kill for some time.

Yet it hadn't eaten much. Benedict considered that as he moved around the edges of the open space, sniffing. Not only had the bear left much of its prey uneaten, it hadn't bothered to cache the body for later. He didn't know for sure if bears did that, but it was a common predator behavior. But this bear had gobbled up the treats—the liver and kidneys, maybe—and abandoned the rest.

Not a very hungry bear, was it?

He'd nearly finished his check of the perimeter when he found what was either one wide scent trail or two overlapping ones headed for the creek. A little more checking confirmed that it was the only scent trail out of here. Damn. He couldn't track through water. Maybe he could pick up the trail on the other side of—

The sharp crack of a rifle split the air.

Benedict ran.

Chapter Nine

Arjenie knelt beside her aunt, who sat on the ground, hands linked with Uncle Clay. The two of them were meditating while the twins and Arjenie handled the prep work. Sammy was drawing the physical circle in the dirt with his rowan rod; he'd leave a "door" open for Seri, who was dipping water from the creek. Arjenie's job was the kindling.

It was especially important to do all the prep with clear intent since they hadn't had time to cleanse themselves ritually, so she gave her entire attention to each twig as she laid it in the brazier. Her Gift was allied with Air, so the fact of her laying the kindling brought that element into the mix, plus she'd place a feather on top to—

A single crack of thunder shocked her ears.

A speeding chunk of night sideswiped her.

She tumbled over on her side in the dirt. By the time she pushed up onto hands and knees, her mind had sorted those events into meaning. Someone had fired a gun. Benedict had knocked her down. And vanished.

Not literally. He'd moved too fast for her to see where he went, but being Benedict, he would be racing toward the gunfire, having told her the only way he could to *get down* while he ran off to fight or rescue someone—which, in his mind, were the same thing.

That shot, her memory informed her, had come from up *there*. Up above the draw, where the cars were. Where a single female deputy guarded the path with a rifle.

Maybe she'd fired by mistake? At a deer or raccoon or something, Arjenie thought as she got to her feet, and not at half a ton of bear. Or maybe the shot had hit the bear or scared it off and Benedict wouldn't think he had to fight it even though—

"Civilians, *get down*," Sheriff Porter ordered. "Get down and stay down. Don't run. Rick—"

A woman's voice called out from the top of the draw. "It was a cow. A damn cow. Stupid beast ran straight at me. Sorry, Sheriff."

Arjenie heard something. She must have, though the sound didn't really register in the busy din of her brain. But that barely heard sound sent fear flooding through her, made her spin around—and cast up one hand, fingers spread, and concentrate with all her might.

A half-dozen balls of mage light sprang into being. The sudden brilliance gave her a great view of the monstrous bear charging them like a freight train.

And the black wolf leaping off the rocks above it to land on its back.

A gun went off. She wanted to hit whoever did that—couldn't they see that they might hit Benedict? But the wolf had already bounced off, as if he'd used the bear's back as a trampoline. Maybe he'd just wanted to get its attention.

If so, it had worked. The bear turned to face its attacker, baring those horribly big teeth, and rose up. And up. And up. *Kodiak*, she thought numbly. That had to be nine feet of bear, and the only one that big was the Kodiak, which absolutely could not be down here in Virginia and—

Another shot. Another, at a different timber, and she saw that one of the deputies was shooting his rifle and the sheriff had his handgun out and maybe she should drop the mage lights and get out Benedict's .357, but oh God, they'd just made the bear mad because it dropped to all fours again and charged.

She sent one of the mage lights winging straight at its face.

It wouldn't burn. Mage lights produced no heat at all, which wasn't possible according to physics but seemed to be true. But bears were supposed to have poor sight. Having a light shining right in it eyes should blind it or at least confuse it.

The bear skidded, batting at the light with one enormous paw—which of course did nothing. Mage lights had no physical substance.

The wolf raced in—and latched on to the bear's nose.

It swiped at the wolf with that huge paw. The wolf went sailing—and a wall of fire sprang up in front of her. No, around her, all the way around her and Aunt Robin and Sammy. "Uncle Clay, Seri's still out there! I can't see! Drop your fire!"

Uncle Clay's strong arm gathered her close. "Hold tight." He raised his voice. "It's a thin ring of fire—you can get through if you hurry! Don't worry about your clothes—I can douse fire as easily as I can start it. Don't run, don't attract the bear's notice—but if you can get here without it seeing you, you can come through the fire!"

"No, don't say that! The bear can hear you!"

"The bear?" That was Sammy, incredulous. "The bear doesn't speak—"

More shots rang out, a dizzying cascade of shots that hurt her ears. At first she thought her ears were ringing oddly, but after a couple seconds she knew that wasn't it. She really did hear Havoc's shrill, excited bark.

"Havoc!" Robin cried. "Clay—"

"No." He said that in a final voice—*no* as in *I will stop you. Do not think of leaving the safety of this ring of fire.*

If you could get in through the fire without getting hurt, you could get out that way, too. "I'm okay," she told her uncle. Was Havoc's bark fading, going away? "I—no, Sammy, don't!"

Even as her cousin turned an astonished face her way—he hadn't done anything—Clay turned to look at him, his arm loosening just enough for Arjenie to pull free, suck in a lungful of air, and fling herself through the fire.

She stopped a few feet outside it and stood, gasping and only slightly singed, in the trampled dirt and grass. At some point in all the chaos she'd lost focus, and all of the mage lights but the original were gone, but that first one still bobbed obediently over her head. Plus the fire gave out light as well as heat, so she saw pretty well.

Sheriff Porter knelt beside one of his deputies. Rick, that was his name. The man lay on the ground. She couldn't see how badly he was hurt—the sheriff's body blocked most of her view. But she knew it was Rick because his skin was pale and the other deputy was black, and besides, when she looked around she saw that deputy running toward them from the other side of the cul-de-sac.

It was what she didn't see that held her mute and still. No bear. No Benedict. And no Havoc.

Arjenie had learned that adventures tended to be ten percent frantic action and ninety percent waiting. The next hour and a half drew a big, red underline beneath the waiting part.

Rick had still been alive when the ambulance pulled away. He'd been lucky in one respect. The bear had only gotten in one good swipe before taking off . . . and Sammy's Gift was healing. He'd been unlucky in that the swipe had been to his gut. Those claws had ripped through flesh and muscle like it was toilet paper.

Gut wounds were bad. She knew way too many statistics about them. Sammy had kept Rick going, had started the healing—but he'd emptied himself doing it. He'd drawn from Uncle Clay, too. Uncle Clay didn't have half the spellcraft that Aunt Robin did—it wasn't a big interest of his—but he had what might be a secondary Gift, or at least an ability that had been passed down in his family. He could share power with another Delacroix without a circle.

He and Aunt Robin were still down in the draw with the swarm of officers. They couldn't make a proper circle with Sammy depleted, but Aunt Robin could scry for magic and try to find the bear.

Arjenie was up at the top of the draw, sitting in the sheriff's car. Seri and Sammy were up here, too, perched on the trunk of the deputy's car. They were playing one of those phone games where you can invite someone to play against you—not with their usual high-spirited rivalry but quietly. As if they needed to think of something else, anything else, other than what had happened.

Arjenie was using a phone, too. Not hers. Benedict's. His brother had called him on it and Arjenie had answered. "Surgery," she repeated. "Well, obviously Nettie can't call me right away. But I really, really need to talk to her as soon as possible."

"I'm leaving for the hospital now," Rule said.

"Who is she operating on? Is it someone I know?"

"Noah Stafford. He doesn't live at Clanhome, so you may not have met him. We don't know yet what happened, but he was in bad shape when they found him."

"Do you think it has something to do with the war?"

"Possibly. His chances are good, since he's lasted this long, but one of the injuries was to his jaw, so he won't be able to speak for a while." There was a pause, and what sounded like a car door slamming. "As soon as Nettie's out of surgery, I'll ask her to call you."

"That's a lousy time to be hit with bad news. Or anxious news, rather, because it isn't really bad. Benedict couldn't have been hurt too much or he wouldn't have taken off after the bear like he did." Nettie was Benedict's daughter. She was a shaman and a physician and she was fifty-four years old, which was why they didn't advertise the relationship outside the clan. People weren't supposed to know that lupi lived a lot longer than humans . . . if they didn't get eaten by a bear, that is. "It can be rough being so far away and worrying."

"She'll be puzzled, as I am. It's not like Benedict to take off in pursuit and leave you undefended."

"I'm ridiculously defended. If I were any more defended I couldn't get anything done at all. But I need to find him. He'll be expecting that."

"I think," Rule said dryly, "he'd expect you to sit tight in the safest place possible and wait for him."

"That's what he'd want. It's not what he'd expect." Movement glimpsed out of the corner of her eye caught her attention. "Oh, the sheriff's here with my aunt and uncle. I need to talk to them. And you probably need to get off the phone, anyway."

"I can talk and drive, but you go have your discussion. I'll let Isen know what's going on. Call or text me when the situation changes."

"I will." She disconnected and frowned out at nothing in particular. In the last hour and a half she'd given an official statement, done some thinking, called Benedict's men, called Uncle Hershey—she'd volunteered for that, since Aunt Robin and Uncle Clay were busy—and called a friend she worked with in Research. Foolishly, she'd left her computer back at the house, and while she could surf the net on her phone, she couldn't access some of the databases she needed with it. But Susan had promised to do some digging and get back to her.

She'd also called Cullen, who basically agreed with her theory. Or at least he agreed it was a possibility, but neither of them knew enough about that end of things, so she needed to talk to Nettie. And now she'd let Rule know, and he would let their Rho know and see that Nettie called Arjenie. The question lingering in her mind was whether she should call Ruben Brooks in his capacity as head of the FBI's Unit Twelve. That's who would investigate an incident involving death magic.

Not that the presence of death magic had been confirmed officially, of course, but Ruben didn't have to wait on that if he didn't want to. The Unit had wide latitude to investigate where it wanted.

It was also spread really thin these days. She'd wait and see if the sheriff had contacted the FBI himself, she decided. Sheriff Porter would take the federal intrusion better if it was his idea.

Having done what she could, she opened the car door and got out. More waiting, coming right up.

Several miles away, a wolf lay on his stomach in a shallow depression in the earth tucked between the roots of a large oak. A small short-haired dog curled up next to him, panting softly, her eyes closed. The wolf's head was up, his eyes alert. He was as still as stone.

His stomach growled.

The little dog's eyes popped open. He gave the wolf an accusing look. *You're supposed to have such great control.*

Benedict had had some experience with mental speech, having conversed with a dragon a few times. It was harder to do in this form. Words were always more work when he was wolf. *I'm hungry, yet I haven't eaten you. That's control.*

The little dog sneezed.

Benedict sighed. *You can't find him, can you?*

I haven't found him yet, the other corrected him testily. *That is not the same thing as can't.*

Benedict stood. *I'm going to hunt.*

Of course you are. Maybe once you've filled your belly we can get back to saving your woman's family and however many others he wants to kill.

Benedict looked at him coldly. *The little one whose body you're using needs fuel. She lacks my size and my coat, and she's exhausted. Without food, she'll be unable to keep going much longer. If the weather continues to grow worse, the cold and exertion could kill her.*

A pause, then: *You're right. I dislike that.*

Stay in the hollow I dug, out of the wind.

The mental voice was very dry. *I might have thought of that myself.*

Had he been in his other form, Benedict might have flushed. Embarrassing to be giving such a one advice. However annoying he might be, he was a Power . . . or some portion of one.

He started to turn away. Paused. *Could you check again . . .*

On your Arjenie? The terrier cocked her head. *She's fine. At least, her cousin isn't worried about her.*

Benedict turned and tried putting some weight on his right rear leg. It hurt like blazes, but the wound had closed and he could use it if he had to.

You're sure about what she'll do? the other asked.

Yes. There was no doubt in his mind about that. She wouldn't be sensible and safe. She'd come to him, and she'd bring help. Arjenie didn't know what they were up against, but she would have seen that bullets didn't stop the bear, so she'd bring his men with her, not the sheriff. He didn't know how long it would take her, or if her aunt and uncle would accompany her as well. He hoped not. They were in grave danger. But with or without them, she would come.

Once he'd checked the function of his leg he switched to a three-legged lope. Using the leg would slow the healing. Fortunately, he didn't have to go on a real hunt. They'd passed a farmhouse shortly before stopping to rest, and Benedict's nose had told him that family kept chickens. They had a dog, too, which was less than ideal. He didn't want to hurt the poor beast. But perhaps they'd have brought the dog inside, out of the weather.

He resented the delay, but it couldn't be helped. He resented much more being drafted into another's service . . . even if it was by Coyote. Maybe especially because it was Coyote.

He'd had a suspicion. Nothing he'd put words to, but he'd wondered about the little terrier's ability to hitch a ride without anyone noticing. He'd thought she smelled different, too, but the difference was so slight he couldn't be sure. Then she'd gotten out of that truck—and the window hadn't been rolled down far; she shouldn't have been able to wriggle out—and charged a Kodiak bear.

Even a Jack Russell wouldn't do that. So when he heard the mental voice commanding him to follow, he'd been startled as hell yet not all that surprised. He'd followed. He'd done so automatically, and now he wondered if Coyote had laced that command with a hint of compulsion. But maybe not. Coyote had used his secret name, the one given him on his vision quest over forty years ago, the one he'd never spoken aloud. The one that, truth be told, he'd all but forgotten about.

Yet when he heard it, he followed.

Benedict had been the first to lose the trail. No blame to him for that; he'd been slowed by having to run on three legs, which let the bear pull ahead. Not that little Havoc could have kept up if Benedict had been running full out, but he might have been able to hold the bear in one place until the terrier caught up. But the scent had ended at an asphalt road. Even a bloodhound couldn't follow one particular vehicle's scent.

Coyote had taken the lead then, using some arcane means of tracking he hadn't explained . . . until suddenly he'd lost his trail, too. Benedict had wanted to go back, rejoin the others. Make sure Arjenie was okay. Coyote had assured him she was, which was when Benedict learned that the Power currently sharing space with a Jack Russell terrier had a link with Sammy. Coyote couldn't mindspeak the boy. He was only able to mindspeak Benedict because of that long-ago spirit quest. But when Sammy had called on Coyote, he'd formed a tie that Coyote could use for a limited sort of eavesdropping.

Not that Sammy had meant to call Coyote or that his reason for calling him had anything to do with why he'd chosen to show up. But the link was there. Sammy couldn't "hear" Coyote, but Coyote could eavesdrop on the boy.

At the farmhouse, Benedict's luck was in. The dog wasn't inside as he'd hoped, but it was a Lab. She submitted instantly, cringing until he licked her muzzle. After that, they were great buddies. The chickens made plenty of noise to make up for their guardian's silence, but he expected that, and the coop was easy to get into. He killed two—as many as he could carry readily in his mouth—and got out fast.

He loped back on three legs. Havoc or Coyote was right where he'd left her. Or him. Them. He deposited one hen on the ground and ate the other. The feathers were a nuisance, but fresh-killed chicken was delicious.

Havoc/Coyote ate with enthusiasm. *I don't believe Havoc has had raw chicken before,* Coyote commented. *She likes it.*

Benedict made a mental note to apologize to Robin for exposing her dog to a taste treat she shouldn't indulge in. Robin and Clay didn't keep chickens, but some of their neighbors did.

The terrier was hungry enough to eat all of the breast and the sweetmeats. Benedict finished off the legs when she—he—they were done, then led the way to a tiny creek. He lapped thirstily, as did the little dog beside him.

How's your leg? Coyote asked.

Not bleeding. Not healed. Benedict took a moment to focus his thoughts. *It's time you answered some questions.*

I told you why I'm here.

You told me what we hunt. You didn't explain why you're here instead of Raven. Why you're riding around in Havoc instead of a body of your own. You haven't even told me why you need me along.

The terrier cocked her head. *I'm sure you'll prove useful somehow. You did bring me dinner . . . no, no, don't raise your hackles at me.* Sly amusement coated the next words like oil on water: *You've never forgiven me for whatever I did when you came calling in the other world, have you?*

You've probably misdirected so many questers you can't be expected to remember all your tricks.

Silence, then, softly: *Not so many. Not anymore. The new people don't know us, and our people have forgotten so much . . . Even those few who still attempt a spirit quest seldom make it into the other world where we can guide them.*

For the first time, there were echoes and ghosts in that voice . . . shades and shadows and years upon years. For the first time, Benedict felt . . . a Presence. Not just power, but Presence.

Coyote shook off the mood physically with a brisk shake of the little terrier's body. *Ah well, times change. As for your other questions— Raven was busy, and this is more my sort of job, anyway. I'm with Havoc because she offered to host me, and it's devilishly hard to affect anything in your world without a body.*

You had a body when you were in the barn scaring the stallion.

Do you have any idea how much power it takes to manifest physically? Especially when a bungling neophyte does the calling. Only a small part of me was able to slip through, not enough to maintain a body. Fortunately, little Havoc here was happy to share.

The terrier wiggled again as if she'd been stroked.

Maybe she had. Who knew what Coyote—even a small part of him—could do? *You didn't tell me why you want me along.*

I didn't, did I? Some things I like to make up as I go along. It's time we were going.

Going where?

I found him again.

Temper rolled in like a thunderhead. *And you're just now mentioning this?*

I just now found him. I believe he must have gone into a town. So many other presences so close together could have masked his.

You could have told me that earlier.

I didn't know it would work that way. His dethru—

Dethru? Benedict asked.

Like a spirit guide, only more intrusive. That one hasn't been in this world for a very long time, so I had no experience of looking for him in a town. Now, I don't know about you, but I'm able to think and move at the same time. The little Jack Russell started trotting, tail up, head high, eager for adventure. *Give it a try. I'm sure you'll get the hang of it with a little practice.*

Benedict growled . . . and followed.

Chapter Ten

Everyone was very sympathetic to Arjenie about Benedict. It set her teeth on edge. "He did not just run off," she said again—this time to Uncle Clay. "He ran after the bear."

"I know, sugar." He patted her hand. "I don't think he was hurt too badly."

She was sitting between her aunt and uncle in Robin's pickup, headed back to the house. The twins were being dropped off by one of the deputies. Arjenie had arranged things this way because she had things to tell them that Seri and Sammy didn't need to hear.

"He'll come back to himself and find his way to us," Robin added in a reassuring voice.

"He hasn't lost himself. Being wolf doesn't make him not himself."

"But he thinks differently as a wolf. He told us that."

"Thinking differently is still thinking. He didn't just mindlessly chase the bear. He had a reason." Something about the way Clay looked at Robin and she looked back made her exclaim, "You are being so soothing! What is it you aren't saying?"

"Well—just that lupi sometimes go wolf, don't they?"

"Go . . . are you talking about that stupid *Howl* movie? They most certainly don't, not that way!"

"But they can lose themselves in the wolf."

"That's called being beast-lost, and it's rare, and only happens if a lupus spends way too much time as a wolf, or in other highly unusual circumstances. It has *not* happened to Benedict."

"You're sure of that."

"I'm positive."

Another glance exchanged around her. "The sheriff's had some training about this sort of thing, and he thinks Benedict has gone wolf."

"And you think Sheriff Porter, who never even met a lupus before tonight, knows more about them than I do? When I've been living with them for two months and am now part of Nokolai clan?"

Uncle Clay winced. "That's something I'd like explained."

"Later." She waved it away. "If Sheriff Porter has decided Benedict's beast-lost, does he think he's dangerous? Is he going to have people hunting the bear, or hunting Benedict?"

Uncle Clay's frown kept digging deeper into his face. "The bear will be his first priority, but . . . maybe we should call Porter." That seemed to be directed at Robin.

"I'll call him," Arjenie said, and bent to dig out her phone.

"No, let me." Robin had her phone out already. She gave Arjenie an apologetic smile. "He'll listen to me better. He still thinks of you as the young girl he met so tragically all those years ago."

He wasn't the only one who didn't seem to notice that Arjenie had grown up. It was distressing. She was thirty-two. Her aunt and uncle had treated her like a responsible adult for years. What was it about her falling in love that made them think she was thirteen?

Maybe because it happened so suddenly. And with someone they'd never met. Someone who turned into a wolf at times, brought her into his clan, caused her to move across the country all of a sudden . . . She sighed. This was why she had to tell them about the mate bond. They'd probably still worry, but they'd be worrying based on fact, not imagination.

Robin had connected with the sheriff and was using her Voice of Authority—the one that combined CEO with Wiccan High Priestess. It worked on almost everyone.

"You're planning something," Uncle Clay said suddenly.

"Well, it's up to me to figure out what Benedict expects me to do, isn't it? Then do it."

"Arjenie." Her uncle spoke firmly. "The only thing he could possibly expect of you is that you'll go home and wait for him."

"No, he knows me better than that. Never mind. There's something I need to tell you, and something we should discuss. I'm going to hit the second one first. I think we're dealing with a skinwalker."

Dead silence. Finally Clay said, "You ought to be joking, but you aren't."

"Hear me out. I don't know how many of those bullets actually hit the bear, but some of them must have. The sheriff and both his deputies kept firing. Did you see that they had any effect on it at all?"

"No," Robin said, "but that doesn't mean the bullets didn't hit. That was one huge heaping of bear. And even if you're right about that, a magically defended bear does not equal a skinwalker."

"There's more that does suggest it, however. First, we know that Coyote's here. He had to have a reason to show up, and it wasn't to protect me from Benedict, despite whatever Sammy and Seri had in mind. So there's a connection to Native Powers."

"Maybe it was Coyote, maybe not. I agree that there may be some connection between this bear and one or more Native Powers, but none of that adds up to skinwalker."

"Plus there's the way that cow just happened to show up and draw everyone's attention, giving the skinwalker a chance to attack. That was planned."

"That's a possibility, I guess. But so is coincidence."

"I think the cow was directed there, but you're right, it's possible the bear just took advantage of the distraction the cow provided. Either way, there was conscious planning behind that attack—which was deliberate and seemed to be directed at us. The bear didn't charge the deputies shooting at it. It came at us."

"The bear didn't know who was shooting at it!"

"It came at us, not the deputies," Arjenie repeated. "Now, bears will guard their kills, but the body was gone, so that's not what happened. A mother bear will attack to protect her cubs, but there weren't any cubs. That just wasn't normal bear behavior."

Robin was silent longer this time. "It might be rabid."

"It shouldn't be here at all," Arjenie retorted. "Someone imported a Kodiak bear—or the hide from one, which they used to turn themselves into a bear."

"Skinwalkers are myth. Legend. Nothing more."

"Dragons were myth and legend until they returned last year."

"Dragons were also theoretically possible. Skinwalkers aren't. For heaven's sake, Arjenie! You know enough about how magic works to know that skinwalkers aren't possible. The stories about them . . . well, some anthropologists believe there may have been early contact between the Native populations and lupi. That could easily have started the skinwalker stories."

She was not making a dent in what looked more and more like Wiccan bias on her aunt's part. If it wasn't possible in Wicca, it wasn't possible at all. She twisted to look her aunt in the eye. "Earth, Air, Fire, Water . . . and the fifth element is spirit."

For a moment Robin was confused. Then her eyes narrowed thoughtfully. "You're claiming that skinwalking uses spirit to accomplish what magic alone couldn't do. But spirit uplifts. Enlarges. It doesn't turn someone into a bloodthirsty killer—which all the skinwalker stories say happens to someone who takes an animal form that way."

"Spirit in Wicca uplifts and enlarges because we call on the Lord, the Lady, and the Source. There are other spiritual practices. Other powers and beings to call on. That bear was tainted by death magic, Aunt Robin. What is death magic but a perverted spiritual practice?"

Robin could not agree that death magic had anything to do with spirit. It was a blind spot Arjenie hadn't realized her aunt possessed. In her mind, *spirit* meant "good." Evil practices and energies, therefore, could not be spiritual, so the fifth element could not be used to create a skinwalker.

Religiously, "spirit equals good" was probably a perfectly fine doctrine. Magically, though, it was limiting. In the normal way of things, that limitation wouldn't matter, but it mattered a great deal now. If there was a skinwalker and he had attacked her family the way Arjenie thought, her aunt and uncle and everyone were in great danger.

They argued about it for another four or five miles. Finally Arjenie said, "I'm expecting a call from a shaman I know. She's trained in Navajo ways, and she's extremely accomplished. She'll be able to tell me if I'm off base about this."

"Well." Robin took a deep breath, as if settling herself down. "My ego might like it better if you'd take my word for it, but my ego isn't always the best guide. If you'll listen to this shaman, I'll be satisfied."

Arjenie wasn't at all sure that was true, if it turned out Nettie disagreed with Robin. But she let it drop. "What can you tell me about K. J. Miller? Do you think he might have some Native blood? Have you ever wondered if he might be Gifted?"

"K. J.?" Robin was incredulous. "Don't tell me you think he's your skinwalker."

"Not many people would have access to the skin of a Kodiak bear. He's hunted bear in Alaska."

Robin waved it away. "The man's deranged and downright nasty at times, but that's a long way from being a homicidal maniac."

"K. J.'s got some ancestor or another who was Apache," Clay said suddenly. "I don't remember how far back, but a great-granddaddy or something like that."

Robin gave her husband an accusing look. "Do not encourage her."

Clay returned her glance mildly. "I think we should listen to her. Not accept it as fact straight out, but listen."

"I've been listening."

"You've been arguing."

This silence was even heavier than the others had been. It made Arjenie's stomach knot.

About the time the quiet got too thick to breathe, Clay said, "I don't know half of what either of you do about magical theory, but it seems like we should hear what that shaman has to say before we makes up our minds."

Robin's breath huffed out. "Before I make up my mind, you mean."

But there was a thread of humor in her voice. "All right. Maybe I'm being a bit dogmatic."

Arjenie managed not to say, *You think?* Mostly because she loved her aunt dearly, but partly because they'd have gone off in another wrong direction then and they were nearly home and she still had to tell them the other thing. "I have something else to tell you that has nothing to do with Native Powers and magical theory. Well, possibly with spirit," she conceded. "At least I have the idea that it partakes of all five elements, but that's not my reason for telling you."

"I didn't follow that at all," Clay said.

"You have to agree to hold this as secret as you do the land-tie."

Robin gave her a sharp glance. "This is about Benedict."

When her aunt wasn't being close-minded, she was very bright. "Yes. It's a big lupi secret. Do you agree?"

They did, so she told them about the mate bond. How it was a gift from the lupi's Lady, who *might* be an avatar of the feminine half of Deity, but the lupi didn't think of her that way, so maybe not, and besides, the Lady didn't want worship. How the bond was a physical tie that let her know where Benedict was and vice versa; that it made them physically highly compatible; that it could only be severed by death. Also that a lupus would be utterly faithful to his bonded mate and that the bond placed limits on how far apart they could be.

". . . so I couldn't come visit when you asked," she finished, "because Benedict couldn't get away then. He wasn't being all Svengali and controlling, and I wasn't being all weak and dependent. We just can't put that much distance between us."

"This is . . . a lot to take in," Robin said. "You think this Lady the lupi believe in placed this bond on you? Not Benedict?"

"That part is certain. The Lady is real," she added. "Not a belief system or a creation myth. I haven't heard her, but I know those who have, and they are entirely reliable. She's an Old One."

Robin chewed that over a moment. "That's a rather large concept to digest. That you know people who have talked with an Old One, I mean."

Actually, she knew people who had fought an Old One. Not

face-to-face, maybe, but they'd fought her and continued to do so. In her own way, Arjenie was, too.

Uncle Clay turned into their lane. "I'm bothered by one thing."

"Only one?" She smiled at him. "That's less than I expected."

"This mate bond . . . I could have sworn you and Benedict were in love."

"Oh, I didn't tell it right! We are. The bond makes us lovers, but it doesn't make us love each other. We did that part on our own."

"Ah." His face creased in a smile that made his beard look much happier. "That's all right, then."

"You know where he is right now," Aunt Robin said suddenly. "Can you tell what's happening to him?"

"No, I only get a sort of directional sense and a really rough idea of how far away he is." She pointed. "He's thataway, more than five miles but less than twenty."

Her aunt's face took on a severe cast, one that went well with the Voice of Authority she used next. "Arjenie, you aren't planning to go looking for him, are you?"

Arjenie's eyes widened in surprise. She had to ask? "Of course I am."

Chapter Eleven

The wind had died. The temperature had dropped. Fat white flakes drifted down, reflecting light as they pirouetted toward earth. Benedict limped up yet another hill and snarled at the air.

His leg had gone from painful to searing every time something pulled on the damaged muscle. He moved it as little as possible, but why couldn't the damn bear have gotten his foreleg instead?

A foolish thought. The bear had meant to kill him. He'd twisted in midair and taken the blow on his haunch, which was vastly better than the gut wound he would otherwise have gotten. Pain was making him stupid as well as cross.

It didn't help that he didn't know where he was. He'd gotten spoiled. He could see that now. Back home he could have oriented himself easily anywhere within a couple hundred miles of Clanhome. Here . . . well, he'd looked over a couple maps before they came, but that, it turned out, wasn't enough. Had he stayed two-footed it might have been, but wolves don't orient themselves spatially the same way men do. At some point, he'd gotten lost.

We're about five miles from the south border of the Delacroix land, Coyote told him cheerily.

I wasn't thinking at you.

Then don't think so loudly.

Benedict glanced at the little dog trotting tirelessly beside him.

How could fifteen pounds of terrier keep going for mile after mile? *How are Havoc's pads holding up?*

They'll do. I may not have enough power to maintain my own body, but I try to be a good guest.

Did that mean Coyote was extending some kind of magical assistance to the little dog? Benedict hoped so.

The terrier stopped. Cocked her head. And something very like a sigh, coated with sadness, washed over Benedict. *I was afraid of that.*

What?

I'll tell you as we go. We have to hurry now.

There was a great deal of commotion when they got home. Arjenie expected that. She expected her aunt and uncle to try to talk her out of going to find Benedict, too, and so they did.

She did not expect to find the twins on her side.

"We'll go with you," Sammy said.

She looked up from lacing up one of the custom-made hiking boots she'd recently added to her wardrobe. "You will?"

"Of course we will," Seri said.

"You most certainly will not," Robin said crisply, then frowned as her phone tolled. Her ringtone sounded like cathedral bells. She pulled it from her purse and her frown deepened. "Don't anyone go anywhere until I take care of this."

"I'll go with you, too," Uncle Stephen said quietly.

Arjenie beamed at him. Uncle Stephen would be excellent backup.

Clay turned to his brother, frowning. "I don't appreciate—"

"She's going to go, Clay. Whether anyone goes with her or not, she'll go. Best if one of us is with her, don't you think?"

"It's not as if I'm going alone." Arjenie pulled on the other boot. "Remember Josh and Adam?" Who were in the kitchen now. She'd briefed them when she called, including instructions to eat plenty of dinner first. "They're going with me. Or perhaps I'm going with them, because the big reason for me to go is so I can bring Benedict's men to him. He'll need them."

Stephen's eyebrow cocked up. "You think you can find him, then? I don't recall that your finding spell was anything special."

"I won't actually use a finding spell. It's something else, and I can't tell you what, but I can certainly find him." Now she'd better get herself a sandwich or something. Unlike most Gifted, her magic was drawn in part from her physical body. Use much of it and she got terribly hungry. Use too much, and she passed out.

She'd used a pretty good wallop of it when she set all those mage lights blazing. She stood up. "Those who are going with me need to dress for a hike. Most of it will be cross-country, probably several miles."

"Arjenie." Seri was exasperated. "You aren't up for miles of hiking across rough country."

"I've been working out with Benedict—or rather, he's been training me. He's very good. I've gone for all-day hikes up and down the mountains out there without turning my ankle." Well, only one hike had lasted all day, and they'd taken several breaks, but that wasn't the point. "That country is a lot rougher than this."

"I suppose." Seri looked dubious. "I'll get my—"

"Clay." Some note in Robin's voice had everyone turning toward her.

She put up her phone. "That was Sheriff Porter. We're needed. A little girl has gone missing. Snatched, they think. They need me to find her."

In the end, Stephen went with Robin instead of Arjenie. So did Clay and Ambrose and Nate and Gary, whose Earth Gift was pretty weak, but he'd balance the circle. Hershey was staying here with Sheila and Carmen to protect the children. He was a powerful Fire Gifted, stronger even than Uncle Clay. And Carmen knew how to shoot.

It should be enough. It had to be enough, because Sammy and Seri were determined to go with Arjenie. She only hoped that Benedict was on the trail of the skinwalker still, because that meant the evil creature was several miles from the Delacroix home.

They did drive part of the way, taking the rutted old road Clay's grandfather had used to carry hay to the horses he'd raised back in the thirties. It took them to the edge of Delacroix land.

"Okay," she said when they got out. "Here's how this will work. I'm in charge of strategy, but Josh here—you're senior, right, Josh?— Josh is field commander. Tactics, in other words."

Josh was about five seven, burly, with dark hair and eyes and the sweetest smile. He offered it to her now. "Does that mean you'll do what I say?"

"If it doesn't interfere with strategy—which right now is to get to Benedict."

"All right. Adam, we'll be moving slow enough for you to take roving point. Change, please."

Good thing she'd brought the backpack again. Adam's clothes went in it, along with one of his two guns, a shoulder holster, phone, and shoes. The other gun went to Josh, who used Adam's ankle holster to carry it. "Two guns?" Arjenie said, eyebrows raised at the silvery wolf who wagged his tail at her.

"Adam likes to be prepared," Josh said.

"I told you that bullets didn't seem to do much damage to the bear. Maybe not any damage."

Josh nodded. "You think it's a skinwalker."

"A skinwalker!" Sammy looked shocked.

"We didn't hear that part," Seri said. "In all the commotion when you got home, we didn't have a chance to ask questions."

Sammy nodded. "And we have a lot of questions."

So for the first mile or so, Arjenie told them, in detail, why she thought the bear was a skinwalker. To be fair, she outlined her aunt's objections to this theory, ending with her suspicions about who the skinwalker might be.

"K. J. Miller?" Seri wrinkled her nose. "He's a complete asshole, but I don't think—"

"I don't know, Seri," Sammy said darkly. "Remember the cat?"

"Not the same thing at all. And if he had that kind of heavy-duty magic, why didn't he stop the Drews when they—"

"Because he didn't have it then. That was last year, doofus."

"He already had the bearskin."

"Wait a minute," Arjenie said. "You know for a fact that he has a bearskin?"

Seri nodded. "It's enormous. We, uh . . ."

"Snuck into his house one time." Sammy gave his sister a frown, as if she'd objected out loud. "We're going to have to come clean. About all of it. This is too serious."

"Not your fault!"

"Maybe it is." He plodded on several feet in silence, and his expression reminded her of Benedict when they first met—dark and closed and brooding. Finally he looked at Josh, who was walking a few steps behind them. "Could you . . . you're a nice guy and all that, Josh, but I need to . . ."

Josh looked at Arjenie, eyebrows raised.

"If you think it's safe to drop back a bit," she told him, "I'm good with that. We're not close to Benedict yet." Josh would have to drop back a long way to avoid hearing whatever Sammy wanted to confess, but she chose not to mention that. Josh wouldn't repeat anything he heard.

As soon as Josh was out of human hearing range, Sammy spoke without looking at Arjenie. "I've been experimenting. Not just with the spell that was supposed to use Raven energy but for the last couple years. Seri knows. She's helped me sometimes, but it's my deal. It's on me if . . . if something I did opened things up and let the wrong Power into our world."

Oh, by the Light, Lord, and Lady. Cautiously she said, "I don't think I'm the one you need to talk to about this."

"You're the one I *am* talking to."

That was hard to argue with.

"And you won't bullshit me," he added. "You'll tell me straight out."

"I can't tell you anything yet. I don't know what you've been doing."

For the next mile or so, he told her.

It was, she had to admit, intriguing. He'd put a lot of thought into his experiments. Unfortunately, he'd been trying to prove the wrong thing—that the Powers were nonsentient energies—but he'd gone about it brilliantly and had achieved a couple interesting if irrelevant discoveries along the way.

At last she said, "I'm afraid I still don't know. It's possible that your experiments did weaken whatever barrier lies between here and what Native Americans call the other world or the spirit world. I don't think so, but I don't know enough to say for sure. This is outside my experience and knowledge."

"That friend of yours—the shaman you mentioned. Would she know? Would she talk to me?"

"She'd talk to you, and she might know. She's really good. She doesn't use spells at all—not the way we do, anyway. It's all spirit. Well, except for her Gift. She's a healer, too, like you."

"She is?" A little light seeped back into his face. He looked so terribly young and hurt and hopeful. "And she'd be straight with me? She wouldn't sugarcoat things?"

"I doubt Nettie has ever sugarcoated anything in her life. What I don't understand is why you did it. For two years, sneaking around to conduct your experiments—which were brilliant, but stupid, too. Why didn't you just tell your mom and dad what you wanted to do? Aunt Robin can be a bit close-minded," she admitted, "but you could have talked her around eventually. And with her backing, what you did would have been safe."

Sammy exchanged one of those twin looks with Seri, who'd been unnaturally silent the whole time. She said softly, "You said it already. We have to come clean about all of it."

He heaved a sigh. "I don't think I want to be Wiccan. No," he said, his voice strengthening. "I don't think I *am* Wiccan. I've been . . . I thought the yoga would work, that it would be enough, but it wasn't. The experiments . . . I've been trying to find out what I am. What my path is."

Oh my. Oh, but it all made sense now. Sammy was mostly a gentle soul—it was usually Seri who led the twins into trouble—mischievous, yes, but without a shred of meanness. He worried about others' feelings and would go out of his way to avoid hurting anyone . . . especially his mother.

Who would not understand. She'd try. Aunt Robin really did believe that all religions were valid paths to the Source. But deep down she thought Wicca was the *best* path . . . and the Delacroix had been Wiccan for centuries.

Arjenie stopped and reached for her cousin and hugged him hard. "You are very foolish," she told him, her eyes teary, "but you have been between a rock and a hard place, haven't you?"

"You're not upset?"

"That you aren't Wiccan anymore?" She blinked the dampness back and smiled. "Some of the people I love best in this world aren't Wiccan. Like Benedict. He—"

Her phone picked that moment to interrupt. She huffed out a breath but released Sammy to take the phone from her jacket pocket. When she saw who it was, she was glad she had. "Nettie! I hope the surgery went okay?"

"It went long." She sounded exhausted. "I kept having to put him back in sleep. But yes, it went well. Rule tells me you think you have a skinwalker."

"Other people tell me that isn't possible."

"Oh, it's possible," she said grimly. "Unlikely, but possible. Tell me what you know."

Arjenie resumed walking as she went through it all again, including a bit about how Sammy had been experimenting with blending Wiccan and Native spiritual elements.

"That's not good. Magically, Wicca is based on sidhe magic, and—"

"No, it isn't."

"I'm sorry, but it is. Your distant ancestors learned spellcraft from the sidhe back when they came here more often, so while your magic has evolved, it is derived from sidhe spellcraft, which is not native to our realm. Native Powers are just that—native to our realm. They do not care for the sidhe or for sidhe magic. While many pagan practices can be incorporated into Wiccan spells, the Native Powers cannot."

Arjenie swallowed. "Do you think Sammy woke something up? Or weakened the whatever that lies between our world and theirs?"

"They're of our world, Arjenie. They . . . never mind. This isn't the time. It's possible Sammy had something to do with your skin-walker. It's more likely, I think, that the Turning did. The power winds blew in many an odd creature. They could have woken one who'd been asleep. You say your cousin called Coyote? And he came?"

"Yes, though Sammy thought he was calling Raven. Or the essence of Raven—I told you how he had that wrong. You think there is a skinwalker?"

"Yes. A skinwalker can't be killed with weapons when he's wearing his skin. It has to be hand to hand—or claw to claw, since you've got lupi to go against it."

"It's a bear! At least a thousand pounds of bear! Three wolves can't go against a Kodiak bear."

"You've got Coyote, too. Not that he can act directly, but . . ." She fell silent a moment, then muttered, "If Cullen was there he could see it. But he couldn't sneak up, so . . ."

"I don't understand."

"Talking to myself. Bad habit. Benedict and the others will need help. A skinwalker has one real weakness: the clasp that fastens his skin. Remove it and he's back to human. You'll need to sneak up on the bear and cut off the clasp."

Arjenie's heart gave one hard jolt and her mouth went dry. She was not terribly brave. "I . . . okay."

"The problem is, you can't see the clasp when he's wearing the skin. I could make it visible, but I'm not there. Let me talk to your cousin."

"Now?"

"I can't teach you the chant. It would have no power in your mouth. He says he's not Wiccan, and Coyote answered his call, so he must be right."

"Sammy," she said, holding out her phone, "Nettie Two Horses wants to talk to you."

Hesitantly, as if she'd offered him a snake, he took the phone. "This is Sammy."

Seri moved closer. "What's going on?"

"Nettie thinks it's a skinwalker. She's going to teach Sammy a chant to . . ." Arjenie kept moving but stopped talking. Paying attention to another sense.

"What?"

"Benedict's moving awfully fast all of a sudden. And it seems like . . ." She walked several feet and checked again. "He's headed for Delacroix land. We need to cut left, through the woods, and I think . . . I don't know why, but I think we need to hurry."

The house was a tidy frame cottage. Flowers had bloomed in its gardens last summer; those beds were trimmed and mulched now. There was a swing set out back. A bicycle and a tricycle waited for their owners on the front porch.

Inside, Sheriff Porter stood by the window in a small living room crowded with people—four Delacroix men and one woman who was Delacroix by marriage. Another woman, one with soft brown hair and terrified eyes, said frantically, "Nothing? You can't get anything?"

"I'm sorry," Robin repeated, feeling helpless. "It feels like something is blocking me. That's never happened before, so I don't know if . . ." Foulness washed through her. Her eyes went blind as the land spoke to her in its own language, one far removed from words. "Clay," she whispered.

He was already there, slipping an arm around her waist. "What is it?"

"It's on our land. It crossed onto our land. Arjenie was right. And it . . ." She swallowed. "I'm blocked. I can't touch it. And it has the little girl."

They must have walked five miles—two and a half out, two and a half back, though at an angle. They wouldn't be entering Delacroix land at the same place they'd left it, but coming in closer to the house. She hoped she'd triangulated correctly. The mate sense was certain, but the terrain made them veer this way and that.

Sammy had finally given her back her phone. He was murmuring to himself, repeating words she didn't know. Navajo wasn't one of her languages. "Nettie Two Horses wants me to go see her," he'd told Arjenie quietly when he ended the call. "When this is all over, she wants me to go to her. Do you think . . . could she mean to teach me?"

The hope in his face was so raw. "Did she say so?"

He'd shaken his head. "Only that I was a young idiot, and I was to come to her."

That sounded like Nettie. "Then you'd better come to California with me."

Five miles wasn't so much, Arjenie told herself. She had no business being tired already. At least all the walking kept her warm, except for her face, which was freezing. Had she already acclimatized to San Diego, or was it really as far below freezing as it felt? The snow kept drifting down. . . .

Her phone vibrated against her hip. It had occurred to her when Sammy gave it back to her that she didn't want it singing Christmas carols if they happened to be near the bear, so she'd set it to vibrate. She took it out. "It's Aunt Robin. Hello?"

Four minutes later she returned the phone to her pocket. "Sammy, what kind of shape are you in?"

"What?" He turned a puzzled face her way.

"Can you run four or five miles?"

"I suppose. But you can't. You're doing great, but running—"

"I know." Not in the snowy dark. Sometimes dignity had to be set aside. "Josh? Time for Plan B."

Benedict lay on his stomach. Over three hundred yards away, and so well out of sight if not hearing, a man chanted in a voice so low he picked up only the sound of it, not the words. Snow still drifted down slowly, some of it caught by the branches of the oak he lay beneath.

His haunch and leg throbbed along with his heartbeat. His breath frosted the air.

The little terrier huddled against him. *Settle down.*

He hadn't moved, hadn't so much as twitched.

You're twitching plenty inside.

I won't let him kill that child.

The terrier huffed out a breath. Benedict could see it in the cold air. *She sleeps. She isn't hurt. I've promised to let you know in time to commit suicide by bear if he finishes his preparations before they get here.*

We're too far away.

If we go any closer, he'll detect us, revert to bear, kill you and Havoc, then finish his chant and kill the girl. He's not finished. Wait.

He knew how to wait. He hated it, but he knew how to do it.

Havoc/Coyote shivered and tried to get closer.

Can't you use some of your magic to keep poor Havoc warm?

It takes a lot of power to watch him without him noticing me.

How close to the end of the chant is he?

I told you, the chant isn't a set length.

First the skinwalker would chant and dance to ready his mind, Coyote had said. Then he would chant and dance to gather power. *Has he started gathering power?*

A pause. *Yes. How close is she now?*

Benedict checked his mate sense for the dozenth time since they began this hellish vigil. *Four or five miles.*

She's not very fast.

He growled.

All right, all right. I know her old injury won't let her run over rough ground covered by snow in the dark, but . . . what?

She's coming faster now. Benedict paused, checked again. It made no sense, but . . . *A lot faster.*

Chapter Twelve

Twenty minutes later, Benedict decided the waiting was over. *She's almost here. I'm going to her.*

In your other form. You need to tell her about him.

I don't intend to hop to her. And if he Changed here, he'd be reduced to hopping. The wound on his right haunch would translate to his upper thigh. *I'll Change when I see her.* It was a lot of Changes in one day—a day when he'd covered twenty miles or so after being wounded. But that couldn't be helped. *You . . . Havoc won't be too cold?*

The little terrier snorted. *I'm going with you. Moving will warm us.*

The two-hundred-pound black wolf and the fifteen-pound, mostly white terrier set off together, one of them on three legs, the other's four legs working hard to keep up.

A single low hill separated them. Benedict crested it and saw Arjenie, Josh, Sammy . . . some distance away, Seri struggled to keep up, and while he didn't see Adam, the wind carried his scent. And in spite of everything, he grinned in the way wolves and dogs do.

His mate had found a way to move quickly. She rode piggyback on Josh—who could have left the human Sammy behind, even with his burden. Arjenie didn't weight much. That he hadn't meant . . . what?

Benedict headed down the hill to her.

"Benedict," she whispered as he drew close. "Oh, it's so good to . . . Your leg! You're hurt. I knew you were, but—how bad is it? Oh, you can't answer. Josh, put me down, I need to get down—"

Benedict stopped. Let the moon's song reach through him, uniting with earth . . . and wrenching into one solid, shrieking pain.

His fourth Change of the day took longer than the first three. Most of the pain vanished as soon as he stood on two feet once more, except the wound. Which had opened up slightly when it shifted from haunch to hip and thigh.

A hundred and twenty pounds of warm woman wrapped herself around him. "You must be so cold. I've got Adam's jacket—he's roving in wolf form—his pants and shirt, too, if you want those. Your poor leg."

He breathed her in for one second, then leaned back to look down at her. It was a lot colder in this form than the other. "No time. I won't stay in this form long. You and Josh and Adam need to know what we're up against."

She nodded seriously. "A skinwalker."

He grunted in surprise. "You . . . How could you know?"

"I figured it out. And I talked to Nettie, and she agreed and told me what to—is that Havoc?" Delight lifted her voice.

"Partly. You talked to Nettie?"

"She would know, wouldn't she? About skinwalkers and how to deal with one. And she did, which is why she taught Sammy the chant. He's not Wiccan anymore, so he can use it, but I am, so I can't. And what do you mean, that's only partly Havoc?"

"The rest is Coyote. He's riding inside her. Long story. We've found the skinwalker."

"Oh, thank the Light! Benedict, did you see him? He stole a little girl."

This time his jaw dropped. "How could you possibly know about her?"

"Aunt Robin was trying to Find the child. She felt it when the skinwalker crossed onto her land and she felt the little girl. She called me. Have you seen her? The little girl? Is she all right?"

"She's asleep. Or so I'm told." He looked at the little dog—who wasn't on the cold ground anymore but was being held and petted by

Sammy. Well, Havoc deserved it, whether or not Coyote did. "Did your aunt understand what the skinwalker intends to do?"

She shook her head, her eyes large and worried.

"The Power the skinwalker serves has been asleep a long time, but he's known to Coyote as one who hates the sidhe, and that hatred extends to those touched by sidhe magic—to Wiccans in general and your aunt in particular. He means to sacrifice the child in your sacred grove—the one consecrated to the Lord and Lady, where your coven meets. Where the token of your aunt's land-tie is buried. He'll create death magic there, blaspheming the land, and it will spread through the land-tie to your aunt, and through her to the whole coven."

"Sweet merciful heaven," she whispered. "Well. That stiffens my spine."

He frowned. "What do you mean?"

"I have a plan. Well, the basic idea came from Nettie, but I fine-tuned it."

A chuckle sounded in Benedict's mind. *And now you know why I wanted you.*

Benedict repeated himself this time silently. *What do you mean?*

Why, to bring her here, of course. And your men, who may be needed. And that foolish, bungling young neophyte with them.

Solstice Eve. Members of her aunt's coven would be getting ready for the circle to be held tomorrow night, the song and the music and the ritual. Just ahead of Arjenie, in the clearing consecrated to the Lord and the Lady, the clearing that faced the sacred grove, someone was getting ready for a very different ceremony.

She could see him. He'd lit a small fire, and she could see him moving in front of its dancing flame, bending and straightening rhythmically in his own dance as he chanted. The scent of the herbs he'd cast on that fire hung in the still air. She couldn't identify all of them, but she knew he'd used sage.

Sage was for cleansing. For purifying. It was as horrifying for her to find it used in such a rite as it would be for a Catholic to witness the desecrated cross at a Black Mass.

The skinwalker was a tall man, though nowhere near as big as the bear whose hide he wore. It trailed on the ground behind him, muffling the shape of his body in the dim light, making him look half man, half creature even now, when he wasn't transformed.

According to Coyote, via Benedict, the skinwalker could turn back into a bear with a single focused thought while he wore the skin, but he couldn't perform the death magic ritual in that form. They'd adjusted her plan accordingly.

A small blanket-wrapped bundle lay on the cold ground near the fire, unmoving.

Arjenie watched from within the cover of the trees, a couple yards away from the skinwalker's ward. She knew exactly where it was. When she used her Gift, wards spoke to her, telling her where they were and sometimes what kind. This was a simple warding, set only to tell its caster if someone crossed it. Simple, but powerful. A mouse couldn't walk over it without alerting the skinwalker.

She could, though. She was pretty sure of that. She wasn't at full strength, but her Gift was good at fooling wards. It had only failed her in that way once, and that had been an elf lord's warding. Compared to that ward, this one would be a snap.

It was what happened after she crossed that ward that had her hands shaking so much it was hard to pull the blade out of the small pocketknife she'd brought.

The snow had stopped. A little over an inch of it tossed back what light reached the ground, making the night brighter than it had been. The clouds had thinned, too, enough that Arjenie could see a big, glowy spot where the moon rode, as if the lupi's Lady was trying to reach them with her light.

Full moon. Wolf moon. Full moons arrived every 29.5 days, not a nice, even thirty, and twelve lunar months added up to about 354 days, which was eleven days short of the solar year. Which was where blue moons came from. Blue moons were the extra full moon that occurred every two or three years owing to this nonsynchronization of the lunar and solar calendars.

None of which had anything to do with what she did tonight, but her silly mind conjured and clung to facts the way other people might clutch a talisman or a teddy bear.

Her phone vibrated against her hip. That was the signal. She took a deep breath, pulled hard on her Gift, and stepped out firmly. She was quite sick with fear.

He didn't see her, even when she stepped out from under the trees. He didn't hear her, even when she stepped on a stick beneath the snow and it snapped, sounding horribly loud to her own ears. He wouldn't. She knew that, even if her scared-spitless heart pounded as if it were trying to run away without her. Her Gift kept him from noticing the sight, sound, or scent of her.

It only failed with one sense. Touch.

He was ten yards away now, weaving his slow dance around the fire and the sleeping child, his voice rising and falling in atonal ululations that didn't sound like words to her. He was naked beneath the bearskin.

If it hadn't been a child sleeping beneath that blanket—only one blanket, and with it so cold!—Benedict might have balked, tried to stop her, sent himself and his men charging half a ton of bear. But combat put the little girl more at risk, so he'd agreed.

Whatever fear she felt now, his was worse. It was always worse to wait, to hold back and watch the one you loved walk into danger.

Five yards. The man lifted his knees high as he bent down. His legs were hairy. Arjenie's mouth was so dry she thought she'd never be able to swallow again.

Benedict couldn't even be close. Apparently the Power the skin-walker served could sense presences even without the wards, if those presences carried more than a whiff of magic. Which all the lupi did, of course, as did Havoc, given whom she was hosting.

One of them, however, had barely a whiff of magic to him. One of them had emptied himself keeping the deputy alive. Arjenie's backup was her guilt-ridden, mischief-making, half-adult, half-kid cousin, who knew no more about fighting than she did. Maybe less. But Sammy wasn't Wiccan anymore, and Coyote had added something to the chant Nettie had taught him. Maybe it would be enough.

Maybe, she told herself as her feet carried her ever closer, it wouldn't be needed. As long as she didn't touch the skinwalker . . . or maybe even if she did. He might feel the touch without noticing her. She'd played that game when she was little, sneaking up on people while using her Gift, then touching them. Some of them saw her the moment she touched them. Some of them didn't, and the look on their faces when they felt that ghostly hand had struck her as hilarious.

Well, she had been little, and lacking in empathy.

She was close enough to touch him now. Only he wouldn't hold still. He moved slowly—now bending, arms spread, now straightening with his back arched and his head flung back. But he kept moving, and she followed him around in his circle, trying to find an opening.

She couldn't see much of his face. The bear's pelt he wore was shaped into a crude hood that hid everything his beard didn't. But surely this was K. J. Miller. The build was right, and the beard, which was almost as dark as the fur he wore—black in the dim light, except where the fire struck orangey red highlights. That gorgeous fur dragged in the dirt behind him in spite of being bunched up at his wait with a rope belt.

She didn't have to worry about the belt. The hide didn't have to fall away from him entirely. It just had to stop being fastened by that clasp . . . which was silver, about three inches long, with a narrow metal rectangle with leather ties at each end that were threaded through holes punched in the pelt.

She just had to cut one of those ties. Just one. Even if she touched him. Even if he felt it and saw her, if she cut the clasp away he couldn't change to a bear.

He could probably still kill her, even as a human.

Never mind that. He'd stopped, arching his back, raising his hands high—

Arjenie darted in, knife out. And tripped over the sleeping child.

She hit the ground rolling. That was automatic, part of the training Benedict had given her, and wouldn't he be glad to see it had taken so well? Except for the tripping part, but she'd held on to the knife and she hadn't sprained her stupid ankle, so she stopped rolling and gathered herself, getting her feet under her . . . and looked up. And up. At nine feet of truly pissed-off bear, reared up on two legs, snarling, and looking around. Sniffing the air.

He didn't see her. Relief blew through her like a whirlwind, making her shake. She'd tripped, but she'd barely touched him and he didn't see her, only now he was a bear, and this was going to be so much harder.

Someone stepped into the clearing at the far end, coming from the sacred grove. Sammy. He was dirty and pale, his jacket torn—when had that happened?—and looked so terribly ordinary in his black watch cap and jeans. He chanted softly.

The bear did see him. It dropped to all fours and charged.

Arjenie ran after it. As if she could do anything, anything at all, to stop that flesh and blood locomotive running twice as fast as she could, and Sammy just stood there, chalk pale but still chanting . . .

The bear slowed. Stopped. Wrinkled its nose, shook its head. And advanced slowly, clearly puzzled.

It had worked! Oh, praise the Lord and the Lady, or maybe Coyote, who'd taught Sammy the trick. Bears don't rely on vision nearly as much as they do their incredible sense of smell.

At this moment, Sammy smelled exactly like a female bear. In heat.

The bear was deeply confused. As for the man he'd been a moment ago . . . none of them knew how much man remained. A skinwalker didn't hold on to as much of himself when he changed forms as lupi did. With every change, Nettie had said, more of the man was lost—and what remained was often mad. They had no way of knowing how many times K. J. Miller had used his bear form, how much of him was looking out of the bear's eyes now, able to reason that just because this odd-looking animal smelled like a possible mate didn't mean he was one.

Sammy kept chanting, but his pitch changed. A different chant now. Arjenie kept running. She had to do this quickly. The others would be coming, and once the wolves arrived there would be fighting. The child could be hurt or killed. The lupi, Benedict—any of them could die.

The bear circled Sammy slowly.

Where was the clasp? All she saw was bear. Huge, enormous, furry bear. Was Sammy doing the chant wrong? How could she—

Something glowed at the bear's throat like an LED light. That was it. That must be it.

The bear stopped. It growled low in its throat, angry that it couldn't figure out this odd bear/not-bear standing so still in front of it. This time Arjenie didn't hesitate. She threw herself onto her knees in front of the bear and reached up with both hands, reached into the thick fur and at the bear's neck, breathed in its foul breath as its jaws parted in shock at her touch, found the clasp with her left hand as it looked down at her and saw her and such teeth, such big teeth it had as it lowered that great head at her. And she slashed the leather tie.

Oily black smoke, incredibly foul, boiled down into her face, into her lungs, making her eyes burn. She coughed, blinked her streaming eyes, and looked up at a naked madman.

He crouched over her, his hair long and stringy, eyes wild with rage, snarling as if he was still a bear, his hands reaching for her.

A wolf howled from a very short distance away.

He jerked, looking over his shoulder.

Two wolves shot into the clearing—one silvery, one grizzled gray and tan, both of them sleek and dangerous and so beautiful they almost took her breath away.

They were also ohmygod fast.

The madman who had been K. J. Miller howled in rage, a sound that didn't belong in a human throat. He must have known he wasn't a bear anymore, though must have retained some of the man because he yanked off the belt, let his bearskin fall, and took off running. Running away.

That wouldn't work.

"Arjenie," Sammy said urgently, kneeling beside her. "Arjenie, are you okay? He didn't get you anywhere?"

"Yes. I mean no, he didn't get me, and yes . . ." A third wolf raced into the clearing, moving slower than the first two—who whooshed past Arjenie and Sammy like cars on the highway. The third wolf was slower because he ran on only three legs. He was black and huge, and her eyes teared up with joy at the sight of him.

A small white shape shot out of the trees behind the black wolf. Barking shrilly and running after him.

"Yes," Arjenie told her cousin, grinning like a fool. "I am fine. I am perfectly, wonderfully okay now."

Chapter Thirteen

Arjenie was right, Benedict thought as he washed down the last bite of his coffeecake with a sip of coffee. Christmas morning at the Delacroix homestead was a riot of unrestrained greed. Not to mention chaos, noise, and tons of ripped wrapping paper.

That paper had mostly been gathered up now, and some of the legions had dispersed to other parts of the house, with a few venturing outside now that the sun was out.

Some, not all.

"Look, Uncle Benedict! Look!" Malik dodged a girl cousin, a bicycle, Havoc, and two adults on his headlong run to Benedict—who had somehow become an uncle to every child here in the past three days. "I figured it out! See, if you kill enough of the aliens, then blow up one of the wheel-shaped spaceships, you get a laser beam. You've gotta see what it does!"

Obediently Benedict looked. The boy's parents had given him a new iPod. Benedict had learned about that ahead of time and had gotten him a gift certificate to download the game of his choice. His choice seemed to involve a great deal of shooting and killing of aliens.

It was fun. Benedict had racked up a decent score when a voice said, "Scoot over, bud. You're in my spot."

Malik look up at Arjenie. "But we're playing *Space Wars*."

"You're still in my spot."

He heaved a great sigh but got up. "We'll play more later," he assured Benedict, who handed him back his iPod.

"How's the leg?" Arjenie asked softly.

"Not bad." Hershey had loaned him a pair of crutches he'd used a couple years ago, after being tossed off a horse. Benedict had used them for two days but the healing was far enough along now for him to dispense with them.

The footstool Sheila had brought him wasn't necessary, but he appreciated it. Having his feet propped up let him look at the hand-made leather moccasins he was wearing—one of Arjenie's gifts. She'd also given him two shirts, a book on archaic weapons, a beautiful custom scabbard for his machete with a smaller, matching one for his favorite knife, and a fistful of candy, toys, and novelties in his stocking.

Everyone who was in the Delacroix house on Christmas morning got a stocking. That was one of the rules. Even people who were supposed to be outside guarding the house, which had thrown Josh and Adam into confusion. There were other rules, like everyone had to have at least one item for everyone else's stocking, and you had to sneak to slip in your contribution. Arjenie had a big advantage on the sneaking part.

Arjenie must have noticed what he was looking at. "You like the moccasins."

"They're great. I can't believe how well they fit." Though he knew why they fit so well. His old moccasins had vanished for two weeks, mysteriously reappearing shortly before they left. She must have given them to someone to copy.

She snorted. "I give you shoes, a couple shirts, a book, and a scabbard. You give me a house. This is not exactly equality in action."

He turned his head to look at her. She was glowing, her eyes so bright and happy it made his heart stutter. "You're forgetting the nightgown and earrings and the holster for your Sig."

"Well, I do win on the number of presents given, but a house?" She snuggled closer, so he put his arm around her. "What do I get next year? A jet plane?"

"I was thinking of a nice casserole dish. Or maybe a blender."

She chuckled. Her eyes were happy, but the lids were drooping. They'd been up late last night, fashioning their own, private celebration. Then, of course, they'd been up early this morning. No one could sleep through a tornado of hyperexcited kids on Christmas morning, and who would want to?

All of these kids, happy and healthy and safe. Everyone here—safe.

Benedict's arm tightened involuntarily around Arjenie as he thought of how nearly . . . but she hadn't been hurt. Not even a scratch. And K. J. Miller wouldn't put her family in danger again.

The authorities ruled it a heart attack. The man had been over fifty and had smoked for most of those years, so that was believable. It might even be true. Benedict didn't know what exactly Coyote had done, but he'd never forget the look of utter terror on Miller's face when *something* drifted up out of little Havoc and swept down over the skinwalker.

It had worked out. It had all worked out, even the presents he'd been so worried about.

He'd made a bowl for Robin, hand-turned from the stump of an old elm, then hand-finished using beeswax, because that way she could use it in her spellwork if she wanted. For Clay he'd found an antique blacksmith's hammer—nothing he would use, probably, but he might want to display it. Seri and Sammy got lift passes at a ski resort Arjenie said they liked. Pretty much everyone else got gift certificates, which was a cop-out, but he hadn't known any of them yet.

Next year, he thought, he'd do better.

But the house . . . that had kept him awake nights. Was it too pushy? Would Arjenie see it as him tying her down or assuming too much? But one reason she'd hated giving up her apartment was that she'd put a lot of effort into decorating it, making it hers. He'd hoped that planning a house together, making it theirs, would ease the sting.

It seemed to have worked, even though, properly speaking, he hadn't given it to her yet—just the appointment with the architect. He'd put the man's business card with the day and time of the appointment in the small box he'd made out of mahogany. A real pleasure to work with, mahogany.

Naturally, the card had required explaining. When he did, there had been a moment of complete silence in the room. Ambrose had broken it, saying with a shake of his head, "A custom-built house? Way to blow the curve for the rest of us, Benedict."

Everyone had laughed then, and the normal chaos of paper-ripping, exclaiming, and zooming-around kids had resumed.

Havoc came trotting up, propped his forepaws on Benedict's leg—the uninjured one, fortunately—and inserted his head beneath Benedict's hand. Benedict chuckled and gave the little dog a good ear rub. Ever since their adventure, she'd considered him pretty much hers to order around.

In other words, she'd accepted him. Like everyone else here. He didn't understand. Nothing had gone right, not from the moment he'd stepped onto Delacroix soil. He'd turned into a wolf, then gotten caught up in circumstances that never let him present himself as normal. As one of them.

But the kids all called him Uncle Benedict now, and the adults were as relaxed and teasing with him as they were with each other. Maybe he'd gotten the sympathy vote because of his wound. If so, he'd take it.

He looked at Arjenie, intending to ask her about the little charm her aunt had given her, the one that had them exchanging sly grins. And smiled. In the midst of all the noise and commotion—outside, kids were shrieking as they pelted each other with snow—she'd fallen asleep.

Havoc apparently though a nap was a good idea, because she hopped up into Benedict's lap, turned around twice the way dogs do, and settled down. He grinned and stroked her head. Life was good. Life was very good.

In the woods behind the Delacroix home, a man sat on the snowy ground, leaning against a tree trunk. He was lean, with a compact body, neither especially tall nor short. He had a blade of a nose, a small dimple in his chin, and the high, harsh cheekbones of one of the People. His hair was like his height, neither short nor long, but it was definitely shaggy.

On this bright winter morning three days past solstice, he wore only jeans, boots, and a western-style snap shirt. He looked utterly relaxed sitting there in the snow, though his eyes were unfocused.

At the moment, he wasn't using them. He'd borrowed some from a friend.

After another moment of stillness, merriment jumped into those dark eyes. He shook his head and laughed. Oh, such plans he'd had. He'd intended to walk up to the door, knock, and present himself in this body—a perfectly good body, and he'd missed it when that silly cub bungled his calling spell. He'd been looking forward to seeing their faces. Especially Benedict's.

Once inside, he would have informed them he was there to complete the task he'd been called for. That was nonsense, of course, but they would have believed him. He was always believable—what kind of trickster would he be if he couldn't manage that?—and he'd had the best of motives. Benedict *was* one of his people even if he was a part-time wolf, and Benedict had wanted so much to be accepted.

The plan had been to tell them he was acting as judge of Benedict's relationship with Arjenie, then steer his witnesses—all of them, really, but especially those twins!—into explaining to him why Benedict was right for Arjenie. Then he'd have them explain why she was right for him. It was all quite obvious, but people were amazingly able to overlook the obvious if you didn't give them a nudge.

Even him. He chuckled again and got to his feet. He wouldn't be needed here, after all. That family pulled together just fine. But it was a nice day for a walk, a lovely, sunny day, and as he headed for the road he enjoyed the play of muscles and the sunshine, glad to be back in his favorite body. Maybe he'd find someone else who needed a little help.

Whistling softly, Coyote set off on the road, ready—happy—to lend a little of his special brand of help.

An Inconvenient Mate

LORA LEIGH

So many dreams and so many years waiting in painful anticipation.
So many pieces of a heart broken, so many nights spent watching the
darkness, wondering where you were.
I was here, and I was searching, always knowing somewhere, you
waited.
So many times I fought back tears, felt incomplete and feared you
weren't there.
So many nights I howled into the darkness, incomplete and searching.
I would have lost hope, I would have lost faith, then your smile lit my
world.
Your lips touched mine.
For the first time in such a long, lonely life, I touched love.
You held my heart in your hands.
I felt its warmth, its power and its promise.
So many times I only dreamed you were there.
Then the dream came true . . .

Chapter One

So many dreams and so many years waiting in painful anticipation.

WINDOW ROCK, ARIZONA

She couldn't keep her eyes off him.

Isabelle Martinez watched the male across the bar as he lifted the frosted bottle of beer and drank. He placed the mouth of the bottle at his parted lips, tilted his head back and seemed to relish the cold bite of the liquid.

The strong column of his throat worked lazily before he lowered the bottle, allowing his gaze to sweep the room. As though he hadn't been watching every movement possible in the small bar before and while he'd taken that drink.

Shaggy blond hair fell to his broad shoulders while the formfitting black of the uniform he wore shifted over his muscles with each move.

Mission uniform, that was what they called it, she thought in fascination. The black material wasn't skintight, it was simply formfitting, and it set him apart as exactly what he was—a lethal weapon. A creature no man nor beast should be stupid enough to confront.

"I double-dare you," her sister whispered at her ear.

Chelsea simply had no idea what she was doing.

"Not going to work, Chel." Liza, her best friend, laughed from across the table. "She doesn't have the guts to go for it. I told you, Holden drained the courage right out of her."

The mention of Holden Mayhew had a dark, sickening feeling

slicing through her and sent an icy chill down her spine. His gaze slid past hers, then sliced back, his eyes locking with hers for a second that seemed to last a lifetime as he motioned the bartender almost absentmindedly.

Isabella licked her lips nervously, and his eyes were on the action like a cat on a mouse.

A coyote on a rabbit.

Predatory.

Narrowed and dark. Were his eyes black or a blue so dark that the distance made them appear black? From where she sat and the shadows cast from the distance between them they could have been any color from dark brown to blue. One thing was certain, they were intent and gleaming with interest as they met hers.

He held her gaze now, though, as he lifted the ice-filled glass the bartender set at his side and brought it to his lips.

His eyes, narrowed and focused, remained locked with hers, mesmerizing her, holding her as no other man ever had.

Oh sweet Lord.

She could feel her breathing escalate, lust clawing at her senses as his lips touched the rim of the glass and he sipped the liquid before returning the glass to the bar.

Whiskey?

Of course.

The bartender topped off the drink, no doubt hoping for one of the tips it was rumored Breeds were prone to give.

It was one of the finest brands, and her favorite.

"Couldn't you just eat him up," Chelsea murmured at her side. And she could. One slow, luscious lick at a time.

"Come on, Isa." Liza breathed out in awe. "It's not like you can get a disease from him. Or get pregnant. Remember, their wives have to actually take those pills to get pregnant."

Isabelle didn't bother glancing over at her friend.

The documentaries they had watched over the years on Breeds were very enlightening. That, combined with every article they could get their hands on as well as every gossip rag Chelsea dragged into the apartment. Those stories, along with her father and grandfather's stories of missing members of the Nation over the decades, filled her head.

She had never been as fascinated by other Breeds as she was with this one, though. And he was so obviously one of the baddest of the bad.

A Coyote Breed. The news story released days ago about the restructuring of the Breed communities had shown the Coyote Breeds' new uniforms and identification.

The white curved fang on the left shoulder of the lightweight mission jacket, the new designation patch of the Coyote Breeds, showed clearly through the dim light of the bar. He would be carrying a picture ID and, if he were with the Bureau of Breed Affairs, an official badge and ID.

But she would have known he was a Breed without the uniform or the identification. They were easily picked out in a crowd. They were the most perfectly engineered creatures on the face of the earth and reflected the most perfect genetics that scientists could envision putting together to create a rough male beauty that seemed almost painful to look at.

The perfect height, the perfect strength and health. Perfect teeth, savage features for the males, classic beauty for the females—just perfectly, exquisitely dangerous.

A hell of a combination for a woman who now feared strength and danger.

"She's not talking to us," Liza pointed out, the smile obvious in the tone of her voice.

"'Cause he's watching her," Chelsea gasped in sudden surprise. "Oh my God, watch him stare at her. He's, like, fascinated with her, Liza. Do you think she's finally found a man she won't say 'no' to?"

Isabelle dropped her gaze and closed her eyes for a quick moment, hoping to still the racing of her heart and the sudden knowledge that her friends, and possibly others, were watching now. That silent, hungry exchange shouldn't be shared. She didn't want others to see it. She didn't want it remarked upon, or gossiped about. It seemed too deep, too intimate to spoil it in such a way.

There were few places a Breed could go where he or she wasn't watched. Watched, judged, criticized and often feared. Just as their lovers, wives or even their friends were hated, reviled and insulted. She didn't care if she was judged, or how she was judged, but that look, it was too special to risk, even here in one of the few places Breeds had found any acceptance.

The people of the Navajo Nation accepted them, did what they could to protect them and stood behind them when political or social reform was needed to ensure their safety and their survival.

It was one of the few places they could also trace their roots. Too many of the missing sons and daughters of the Navajo Nation had been taken by the Genetics Council for Breed research, and many of those families were desperate to claim the last ties to what they had lost.

Drawn irresistibly back to him, Isabelle lifted her eyes once again to find the Breed's gaze supposedly drawn to her left of her. As though he were watching the entrance.

He seemed bored. Waiting with impatient patience, she thought, almost smiling at the contradiction. She knew he was watching her; she could feel his touch like a ghostly caress against her face. A sensation of warmth and sensual hunger washed through her.

His fingers gripped the glass again as he brought the drink to his lips and sipped. And though his gaze was to her side, she knew he could see exactly where she was and every move she made. Just as he no doubt knew she couldn't keep her eyes off him.

"You are such a wuss." Chelsea leaned close and whispered in her ear, her voice amused and challenging.

"Meaning?" Isabelle lifted her own drink, the same expensive whiskey the Breed had ordered.

"Meaning, go talk to him, dimwit," Chelsea hissed, suddenly somber. "Come on, Isa, this could be the answer to your prayers. Holden wouldn't dare come around you if he knew a Breed was interested in you. Not now and not later."

Holden. God, she didn't want to think about Holden.

She had fought to put that night behind her, to eradicate the fear from her life and from her nightmares. It was impossible, though. That night had become so imprinted on her brain that she couldn't seem to shake the memories.

And she sincerely doubted anything or anyone would change Holden's mind short of a bullet. Perhaps even death itself. He wouldn't allow anyone, man or Breed, to stand between him and anything or anyone he decided he wanted. And he had decided not only did he want Isabelle, but he would have her. Whether she wanted him or not.

A shudder raced up her spine at the thought.

At the same time, the Breed's gaze was suddenly locked with hers once again, unblinking, his dark eyes glittering dangerously. He watched her intently, his nostrils flared, his whole demeanor appearing on guard, as though he perceived some threat.

Isabelle could feel her mouth drying, nervous excitement and a hint of fear lacing the arousal she couldn't seem to help.

She wished she knew more about the Breeds. Knew more about their strengths, or even their weaknesses. Amazingly, facts were sketchy, though the rumors were incredibly numerous.

Could he really smell her arousal?

Could he smell fear?

Did she care?

She licked her lips again. She had always held back where men were concerned, always refused to make the first move. She was still a virgin, determined to wait for the one man who would make the waiting worth it. In this case, the Breed she couldn't resist. She had a feeling this Breed wouldn't make that first move, though. Not with her. There was something in the air between them that assured her he would never allow her to hide from the fact that he was what she wanted. She would be woman enough to give an invitation that neither he nor anyone watching could mistake. If she wanted him, she would have to be woman enough to prove it.

Was she woman enough?

A part of her was screaming, "Hell yes," while another part was screaming, "No way in hell."

While her head and her heart were arguing over whether or not she was brave enough, the woman took up the challenge and went for it. She stood from her chair.

"Umm, this isn't good, Chelsea, maybe we should leave," she heard Liza mutter, an edge of something that may have been fear sharpening her voice. She ignored the other girl's comment and instead began moving across the room.

She felt drawn by him.

Mesmerized by that dark gaze and becoming a person she didn't wholly recognize. The woman she had always fantasized about being. Independent. Free. A woman facing the most dangerous adventure of her life. One that could leave her either eternally whole, or forever heartbroken.

She had always told her father she would know the second she met the man she wanted to give her heart to. That knowing him would never be the problem.

Holding him would be another story.

And Isabelle knew that several of her friends had thought they could hold on to one of the rapturously, sexually experienced males science had created, only to end up with a broken heart.

Having a future with a Breed wouldn't be the easiest job a woman could take on. Or the easiest challenge. Falling in love with one could be termed the height of idiocy. In that second, Isabelle knew her heart was now on the line as well. If she hadn't already lost it. Not that she had ever believed in love at first sight before. She wasn't certain she believed in it now. But she knew a part of her would grieve for a lifetime when this Breed walked out of her life.

"Isabelle," Chelsea hissed behind her. "Sweetie, I think we better go."

Isabelle ignored her. Her sister didn't seem panicked, just worried. Worried was okay.

She felt as though she were gliding across the bar, held by his gaze, so fascinated, so intent on the man watching her that she could barely breathe.

She was instinct. She was living every fantasy she had ever had in that moment. Stepping to him, her gaze still captured, her senses narrowed to this one moment, Isabelle reach for the broad, masculine fingers that held the glass.

She didn't take the glass from him.

Using her fingers, she urged the glass to her lips and he complied easily. Tucking the edge of it at her lips, he lifted it slowly until the icy liquid was touching her tongue, burning across her senses as she took a slow, sensual drink of the fiery liquor.

As he pulled back, she licked her lips slowly, realizing he had placed the exact spot his own lips had touched to hers.

"You're living dangerously," he murmured as her heart raced out of control, barreled into her chest then broke off to rush through her senses and overwhelm them.

"Prove it."

Oh hell. No. She hadn't said that. She really hadn't.

Hadn't someone said something about never, ever daring a Breed, especially a Coyote?

His lips quirked, an edge of smile filling eyes such a dark, dark blue they were nearly black.

"I can prove it." Pure confidence filled his voice.

This time, she lifted the glass from his hand, brought it to her lips and finished the drink before handing it back to him.

His fingers covered hers as he took it, a flame leaping in his gaze as pure, sexual awareness seemed to fill the night.

"Confident, aren't you?" she whispered playfully as a tingle of excitement rushed through her system.

"Very," he agreed. "And I would so enjoy playing with you."

A game? She'd never played sensual, flirtatious games. She'd never dared a Breed, and she'd never, at any time, challenged man or Breed to seduce her.

"We're playing, then?" she asked softly.

"You could say I'm hunting," he murmured seductively. "The sweetest, softest little morsel I believe I've ever scented in my life. You could become an addiction."

Her heart tripped, speeded up and began racing in excitement.

"Do I get a head start?"

Eek. Where had that come from?

His head tilted to the side, his eyes squinting just a bit at the corners, as though he wanted to smile. "Do you plan to use it?"

"Of course." She was going to run clear to the other end of the state just to escape the memory of her daring.

What was that expression that came over his face? It almost softened. His eyes gleamed and seemed to fill with something she would have called fondness at any other time.

"Are you sure you want a head start?" His voice dropped, sexual, heated, it stroked over her senses with an intimacy she hadn't expected.

"It would be wise. Just to make certain I know what I'm doing, mind you." She had no idea what the hell she was doing, and that was a fact.

His hand rose, his fingertip tucking beneath the hair that had fallen over her shoulder to find her exposed collarbone as he leaned closer, his lips at her ear. "When I find you, I'm going to undress you, then spread you out and lick all the lush, sweet cream I can smell flowing from your pussy. When I've drowned my senses in the taste of you, I'm going to fuck you with my tongue, lick more of you, then listen to your screams as you come."

She was going to melt right there in the floor. Isabelle swore her knees nearly gave out on her as sensual weakness flooded them. She had to tighten her thighs against the sudden nip of sensation in her clit. The swollen, sensitive bud throbbed with need, pulsing with a need so strong she wasn't certain she could deny it.

"I'm going to bite your chest." She sighed, then winced at the lack of explicit description.

But that was what she wanted.

She wanted to bite his chest.

His hand was suddenly clamped on her hip, long, strong fingers curving over the denim of her jeans as she felt his body tense, his breathing becoming deeper and harder.

"Are you sure you want that head start?" His lips lowered to nip her ear.

Then he licked the edge of her ear, exciting the sensitive nerve endings beneath the flesh.

A shudder raced through her, blistering hot, nearly catapulting her straight out of her senses and into an unprecedented orgasm.

Her thighs tightened as she fought to hold it back. Or give in to it? She wasn't certain which.

"I don't know," she murmured. "Maybe you're not good enough at this game to catch me if I take it?" Hell no, she didn't want a head start, but this was *fun*. It was the most fun she had ever had, the kind of fun she had dreamed of having with a man.

And in a moment's hindsight, she realized she wanted him to chase her. She wanted this game more than she could have ever imagined wanting anything like it.

He tensed again, a little growl rumbling between them, at once exciting her even as it sent a flash of trepidation racing up her spine.

She could see the hunger in his gaze, feel it radiating from his big body. The strength of it confused her, as did the answering force that surged through her own body.

"When I catch you, I will fuck you," he promised her, his voice rumbling at her ear before he pulled back to stare into her eyes. "All night, all day. Possibly all week." Pulling away from him was practically impossible, and forcing herself to walk away took all the willpower she could muster. Because she didn't want to leave. She wanted to stay there with him, wanted to rub against him and feel the sensual heat and power that she sensed was so much a part of him. She forced herself to move though. Forced herself to draw her gaze away from him and turn back to the table she, Chelsea and Liza shared. They had moved though. They were waiting on her at the exit, which was even better. Leaving was the best option, it would give him a reason to try to find her. If she remained in the bar, it would be rather anti-climatic. And she certainly didn't want that.

Chapter Two

So many pieces of a heart broken, so many nights spent
watching the darkness, wondering where you were.

Some nightmares refused to go away, even amid the most sensual, most erotic event of her life, the deepest terror she had ever known insisted on intruding.

And she wouldn't have known, wouldn't have realized the monster that haunted her dreams was even there if Chelsea and Liza hadn't rushed her so quickly from the bar.

Holden Mayhew was in the bar, and he had witnessed her flagrant teasing of the Coyote Breed. The one who had given her a head start. A chance to be certain this was what she wanted.

And she wanted him with every fiber of her being.

So much that her body was incredibly sensitive, her nerve endings still pulsing with the need for touch. For his kiss. For every sensual promise he had made to her in the dimly lit bar.

His fingers stroking against her flesh, his lips, the nip of his teeth. The feel of his hard body against hers.

And she longed, ached, burned for him to take her.

Perhaps she should have refused the head start, but the anticipation of being chased, of being a sensual prey, had been more than she could deny herself.

Isabelle stared at one of the fragrant candles flickering around the room, eliminating the hotel smell and bringing a sense of calm to her ragged nerves. It did nothing to ease the pulse and throb of an arousal that was becoming almost overwhelming. As a matter of fact, the soft, sensual scent that infused the wax might have made it worse.

But even the anticipation of the Breed and the pleasure that could overtake her couldn't eliminate the fear rising inside her now.

Someone had called Holden and told him she was there. Someone who didn't care that she wanted nothing to do with him. Hell, he didn't care that she wanted nothing to do with him. He was there, and once again, he was stalking her.

The flicker of light from the candles her grandmother had made for her held her attention again. The gift from her grandmother just hours before her uncle had called her to the hotel had surprised Isabelle. The scents of them were even more surprising.

Lavender, sandalwood and a darker, elusive scent that reminded her of dark sexuality and the Breed she had walked away from earlier.

The candles themselves weren't surprising. Her grandmother was always creating distinctive scents with individuals and their emotions or troubles in mind. That underlying scent of sexuality *was* surprising, though. She just wished she could put her finger on exactly what it was.

"What are you going to do, Isabelle?" It was rare her sister called her by her full name, as everyone else did. Chelsea usually used the shortened version of Isa, despite the fact that Isabelle didn't care much for the nickname.

"How long was he there?" Isabelle whispered as she watched the door. She could sense the nervousness raging through the other two as Isabelle felt fear tugging at her.

"He came in just before you walked over to the Breed," Chelsea said quietly.

"I should have told you the instant I saw his brother Harlen on his cell phone," Chelsea sighed. "I should have done more than just suggest we leave."

Well, that answered the question of who could have called Holden. She distantly remembered Chelsea saying something about leaving, had recognized the concern in her sister's voice at the time, but she had ignored it. Nothing had mattered but the Breed and connecting with him. Nothing and no one else had mattered. Her fascination with him was something so unusual for her that she had thought the concern her sister had felt had been because of her actions, not the man who had entered minutes later.

"And he saw me?" she whispered.

"He didn't take his eyes off you until you left the bar with us," Chelsea told her, anger beginning to tighten her voice. "The bastard. You should tell Dad, Isabelle. You can't let him keep doing this."

"This" being the steady harassment and stalking of her. He refused to accept the fact that Isabelle hated him.

Pushing her fingers through the long strands of her hair, Isabelle rose from the chair she had thrown herself in moments earlier and paced to the other side of the room.

She didn't need this. She didn't want to face it. She had hoped she could escape the nightmare Holden Mayhew had begun in her life, but it seemed he was determined to make certain she never escaped it.

Or him.

For a moment the surge of terror and fury she had felt that night raced through her again. The feel of his hands, painful in their cruel insistence, holding her down. The sound of his voice as he sneered down at her, determined to take what she was unwilling to give him. The ease with which he had torn her clothes from her was humiliating. The knowledge that he had nearly carried through with his intent to molest her was as terrifying as it was enraging.

She couldn't forget the fact that he had almost raped her. He had almost taken from her the one thing she had wanted to save for the man she would one day give her heart to. The gift she knew she had been so ready to give to an unknown Breed tonight.

Her virginity.

He hadn't completed the rape, but the terror was now such a part of her that she was shocked she had escaped the memory of it for those few minutes she had dared the undarable. A Coyote Breed.

"I say go back downstairs and bring that big, badassed Breed back to your bed. They may not be forever material, but he looked damned interested, Isabelle. He might take care of this little problem for you too, if you asked him. Hell, from what I know about Breeds, all you would have to do is tell him about it. He would take care of it," Liza suggested, her gray eyes filled with anger.

Isabelle shook her head as she paced to the window. Silent, still, she stared out at the dark landscape that surrounded the back of the hotel, five stories down. In her reflection she could see the pale, drawn features of her own face, and she hated it.

God, she wished she had killed him when she had the chance. She wished she had simply pushed Liza aside and pulled the trigger. There was a chance she could have escaped jail. She had been bruised, bloody, naked. It would have been so easy to prove the attempted rape.

If she had been strong enough to pull the trigger. If she weren't so terrified her father would pull the trigger after the fact, then she would go ahead and file charges against him. There was no way he could get out of it. Chelsea and Liza both had been there, and they were all employees and kin to members of the Navajo Nation Council.

If she had filed charges, or had the courage to do it now, then she wouldn't be reliving the nightmare on the night she should be enjoying the daring, sensual game a Coyote Breed had begun with her.

How long had she waited to meet that one man who would make her willing to give herself at a moment's notice? The fact that he was a Breed hadn't really surprised her. She'd known for years that the men she had met before him didn't have whatever it was the sensual side of her was searching for. The feminine, female part that demanded so much more from a lover than those who had presented themselves so far.

It wasn't that she hadn't waited, watched, searched for the man who would awaken her sensuality.

She had traveled the world with her father on his quests for information about his missing sister. She had met heads of state, politicians, ambassadors, geeks and physical laborers in her short stint as her uncle's personal assistant just after he'd been voted in as chief of the Navajo Nation.

She had dated, she had kissed, she had let herself be wined and dined, and that elusive hunger she had known had to be waiting inside her had never shown itself. That restless, waiting impatience had always followed her, had always been a part of her, until tonight. Tonight, when her gaze met a Breed and she had dared to tease him. That restlessness had eased. For a few moments, it hadn't even existed.

And now, she was terrified of the consequences of reaching out for what she wanted.

Lifting her hand, she rubbed at the small spot on her ear that the Breed had nipped. She could feel the imprint of his teeth, a heated reminder of that gentle bite, a brand against her flesh.

She didn't even know his name.

She hadn't even paid attention to the gold ID designation tag on the left of his very broad chest.

Breeds didn't display their names as other military, law enforcement or agency operatives did. They carried a number, hiding their identity to the casual observer.

Not that the number would have done her much good if she was searching for his identity. The only way to learn who owned the designation number was to contact the Bureau of Breed Affairs and jump through hoops, kiss ass and hope Jonas Wyatt was in a good mood the day the request hit his desk, though she had heard Wyatt was never in that good a mood. There were rumors he would even deny senators, Breed contributors and law enforcement officials that information.

"Isabelle, you're not listening," Chelsea chided her as she kept her back to them. "Come on, that Breed looked capable of protecting an army. You wouldn't even have to sleep with him to convince him to do something about Holden."

The fact that her sister made such a suggestion was a testament of how worried she was over the situation Isabelle was in.

"I don't want a protector," she said softly, turning to the only two women who knew the fears that plagued her. "I don't want a man in my bed because of Holden, Chelsea. I want a lover. I want more than a shield. I don't want to be afraid of what's going to happen when Holden finds out, or if he sees us together. I want to enjoy it while I have it so I can hold on to the memories when it's over. This will be my first time, Chelsea, I wanted it to be special. Is that so much to ask?"

Because few things lasted forever. Her mother had taught her that when she had died in an accident the morning Isabelle turned seven, just hours before the birthday party she and Isabelle had planned so meticulously.

"I think Holden knows better than to confront a Breed. But that doesn't mean it would make the Breed any less than your lover, sweetie," Liza assured her. "Hell, Isabelle, it's just that I can't think of anyone who would confront a Breed over one of their lovers. I hear they're rabid about them. And they're even worse where their wives, or mates as they call them, are concerned."

More than one non-Breed male had learned the idiocy of challenging a Breed over the woman he was with, whether he was sleeping with her or not. Breed males were said to be so intensely protective of women and children that even abusive husbands and fathers had felt the brunt of their displeasure. When it came to lovers and wives, though, they were fiercely territorial where other men or Breeds were concerned.

But despite what Liza believed, if she went searching for him, if she ended the teasing game she had so wanted to play, then it would also change the fact that he wouldn't be in her bed just for the pleasure they would share. It would be for the protection she may need. And that would completely alter every memory she could hold of any time they spent together.

Which meant that, until she had dealt with the Holden situation, having the Breed in her bed might not be the wisest decision.

"It doesn't matter," Isabelle sighed roughly. "Just let it go. Whatever Uncle Ray needed us here for, we'll finish then go home. I should have known better than to tease a Breed anyway."

"And boy, did you tease him," Chelsea said in awe. "Oh my God, Isa. I've never seen you like that around a man. I thought the two of you were going to catch fire and burn the place down. You were hot as hell for each other."

Liza shook her head, a mocking smile curling her lips. "Think what you want to, my friend, but that Breed so will not let you get away. Before your uncle is finished with these meeting with the Breeds, you're going to be fucked six ways from Sunday and begging for mercy."

She would settle for once on Friday and the memories she could hold on to after it was over.

Isabelle rubbed at her ear again. She was still hot as hell for him, and growing hotter by the second. She wished she could have stayed in the bar. She wished she could have danced with him when the band returned. She wished she'd had the courage to give him her room number.

"Having him would be a very bad idea," she sighed. "I shouldn't have gone to him. Hell, I don't even know his name."

"His name is Malachi," Liza suddenly announced. "While you were sharing his drink, I asked the two Breeds at the next table who he was. The big dark one was more than happy to supply his name."

Isabelle's brows rose. That was unusual for enforcers. They rarely gave information unless they had no other choice.

"Yeah, the blue-eyed one was scowling and said something about damned Coyote hormones and the heat. Only God knows what that means, because it wasn't hot in there. The other one, though, the darker one, his name was Stygian. He was just amused, and I swear to God I think I heard him give a wolf growl when you took that glass from his friend and finished his drink. I rather doubt he's a feline," she said musingly, as though more than a little interested.

Chelsea and Liza were watching her as though they hadn't yet figured out what had possessed her.

She didn't know herself what had possessed her.

"I don't want to talk about this anymore," she groaned as she rubbed at her ear, wishing she could rub away the warmth that reminded her of his touch. "I still can't believe I did that."

"And as terrified as you are of Holden, I still can't believe you didn't see him come into the bar." Chelsea was shaking head in confusion.

Her sister was no more confused than Isabelle was herself. That simply wasn't like her. She didn't come on to strange men, and she sure as hell never dared a Breed of any species. They were simply too unknown, and their temperaments too uncertain. Virgins should know better, she told herself in exasperation. They were so sexually experienced it should be considered illegal. Hell, it probably was illegal. They were lethal in more ways than one, but they would be hell on a woman's heart.

She knew plenty of them, and she was friends with several Breed females, but they weren't best buds. Just as the male Breeds she knew had never been lovers.

This Coyote, though, she would have loved to give herself to. Over and over again.

And she would have loved continuing the game tonight. They had friends in the hotel; she could have found out where his room was. Perhaps slipped something beneath his door. Dared him to find her, then gotten herself another room.

She would have had so much fun, and if that playful glitter in his eyes was any indication, her Coyote would have played with her. He would have broken all the rules. He would have laughed at her indignation. But she would have had so much fun.

If it weren't for Holden and his unpredictable behavior.

"Look, Holden doesn't know we're staying here at the hotel. He's expecting us to be heading home," Liza pointed out. "Malachi and his friends certainly are in this hotel. I checked with my friend, Mary, at registration. Malachi Morgan, Rule Breaker and Stygian Black are here as a Breed delegation to meet with your uncle." She frowned, her gracefully arched dark blond brows lowering in concern. "Do you know what it's about?"

Isabelle shook her head rather than lying outright to her friends. As her uncle's assistant, she knew she had to be careful about divulging too much confidential information. And there were things Isabelle knew that even her sister was unaware of.

She knew why her father, uncle and grandfather thought they were there, though she wasn't aware of the details.

Her uncle, the chief of the Nation; her father, one of the Nation's legal representatives; and grandfather, the Nation's medicine man had been discussing a rogue Breed and the search for him that the Bureau of Breed Affairs was conducting.

Isabelle had heard her grandfather's fears that the Breeds weren't telling the whole truth regarding why the delegation from the Bureau of Breed Affairs was there.

They feared it had something to do with the kid the Breeds suspected the Navajo Nation Council and the Martinez family had been hiding for more than a decade.

Isabelle didn't know if her family knew where they were or not. She knew though, that someone in the Council was behind the disappearance of Breed children who needed to cease to exist for their own safety. It only made sense they would do the same for any human child that had been a part of Breed research. All she knew was that there had been a teenage boy and young girl who had been found by her father years ago who had disappeared from the house later. Six Navajo dressed in denim, their faces decorated with war paint, their dark eyes fierce and intent, had taken the three away, and Isabelle had never seen them again. She had never told Chelsea or Liza about them. A short time later, Isabelle had heard her father and uncle talking about another girl. One her father had brought in after the other two, but she hadn't been able to hear the details, and she hadn't seen the girl. She wouldn't have known about any of it if she hadn't been such a nosy, sneaky kid, as her older brother, Lincoln, liked to accuse her of.

It wasn't the first time the Navajo Nation and the Martinez family had interfered in the Genetics Council's plans, or any of their counterparts'. The Breeds were a part of the Nation and its people. They were the sons and daughters of many of their missing that were taken by the Council. Too many of them carried their genetics to ever turn any of them away. And Isabelle knew that the three kids they had hid all those years ago had been taken from either the Council or one of their counterparts. They were part of the research, and the Martinez family and the Navajo Nation would kill to protect them.

"The meeting is tomorrow," Isabelle told them both while maintaining the secrets the others were unaware of. "It begins at ten. I know Dad wants to refuse their request to search for this rogue Breed because he doesn't trust their reasons for it, while Gramps and Uncle Ray are hesitant to deny them."

"Maybe Ashley knows what's going on," Liza mused as she mentioned the Coyote female who was a regular visitor from the combined Wolf and Coyote Breed community of Haven, Colorado. "She's in town this week. She called last week to see if I wanted to go to the spa with her while she was here."

Blond as well, though artificially colored, enhanced and streaked, Liza was known to spend an excessive amount of time at the spa in town pampering her hair, nails and glowing, soft skin.

To a point, both Isabelle and Chelsea were regular customers at the spa, but Liza and Ashley spent far more time pampering themselves than either of them did.

"I'm not nearly as worried about this as I am my sister. What are you going to do about this, Isabelle?" Chelsea asked as both she and Liza stared back at her in concern. "If I know Holden, he won't just leave you alone. He's going to keep coming at you until he catches you off guard again. And when he does, he'll make certain he hurts you. We both know he will."

For some reason, Holden Mayhew had it in his head that she belonged to him. It had taken only a single date for Isabelle to realize he was a man that wouldn't take no for an answer. The second date, an attempt to reason with him, had proven her right.

"I don't know, Chelsea." Shoving her hands into the pockets of her jeans, she was drawn back to the window.

"You could tell Uncle Ray," she suggested.

It wasn't the first time her sister, or God forbid, her brother, Linc, had made that suggestion.

"Or your father," Liza pointed out with a hint of mockery.

They all knew if she told her father, then Terran Martinez would likely attempt to kill Holden himself. And that was something she didn't want to have to face. There was always the chance Holden would harm her father or catch her brother unaware and hurt him. Or the chance that her father or brother would kill Holden and be willing to face prison to do so. Protecting her and Chelsea was all they seemed to think about at times. As though the haunting specter of Morningstar Martinez's kidnapping and disappearance more than thirty years before somehow threatened Isabelle and Chelsea as well.

"I wish the two of you didn't know about it." Isabel sighed.

"That would be hard to accomplish," Chelsea drawled. "If we hadn't shown up, sis, that night would have had a far different ending for you."

She would have been raped.

It had been Chelsea who had bashed Holden over the head with a lamp and Liza who had pulled the rifle on him that her father had given her when she moved into the apartment with Isabelle and Chelsea.

Naked, reeling from the attack, Isabelle had jerked the gun from Liza, cocked it and would have killed him herself if Chelsea hadn't stepped between the gun and Holden. It had given him a chance to run out before she could put the rest of the female population out of any more misery that he could deliver.

She would have shot his balls off.

"A far different ending for him if you had just stayed out from in front of that gun," she stated though she didn't turn back to them. "I should have just killed him before you had a chance to step between us."

There were nights she wished she hadn't allowed her sister to stop her. Nights that she had lay frightened, listening to his truck as it rumbled up their street. Her bedroom was at the front of the house, the other two at the back. Her sister and Liza never knew about the nights Holden tormented her, and she didn't want them to know.

If he had just let it go. If he had just left her alone. But since that night he refused to give her any peace. He was stalking her, his determination to rape her becoming an obsession she knew she was going to have to deal with soon.

"You should tell your uncle at least," Liza told her as Isabelle watched her reflection in the window.

Her friend rose from her chair and collected her purse from the floor. Dressed in jeans as well and a stylish cami, the other woman drew the straps of her purse over her bare shoulder before saying, "I have to get to bed if I'm going to be up in time to be in the conference room in the morning. Think about it, Isabelle. That, or find a man, or a Breed, that Holden won't fuck with. Otherwise, you're going to end in far more trouble than Chelsea and I saved you from that night. It's pretty clear Holden's fucked up in the head, and men like that won't let you rest until one of you is dead."

That was Liza. She didn't hold much back. And though she might appear cool, or unfeeling, Isabelle knew differently. Her friend rarely let herself show emotion. She had lost her family when she was no more than a teenager and she often had nightmares over it.

"Yeah, I have to head to bed too." Chelsea sighed as she looked around the room. "But I'm staying right here unless tall, blond and Breedy shows up."

Stubborn determination tightened Chelsea's normally pouty lips as she stared back at her sister, silently daring her to try to make her leave.

Isabelle turned back to both women. "What would I do without the two of you?" Tears flooded her eyes though she forced them back rather than letting them fall.

Liza had been their best friend for years. Though Chelsea was younger, Isabelle had never denied her sister the chance to tag along with them, and because of that, she had become part of the bonds of friendship that tied them together. Their friendship was set in stone, and their concern for each other was always there.

"You would be miserable, lonely and probably living by yourself with a house full of cats instead of two crazy women," Liza grunted as she headed for the connecting door. "Now, get some sleep. I'll leave the door open. If you need me, just scream."

She moved to the connecting room as Isabelle turned to her sister. "You could just do the same." She all but laughed at her sister's mutinous expression. "You're not tall, blond and Breedy, so I'm not sharing my bed with you."

"And you'd share it with him?" Her sister rolled her eyes. "You might have been all hot and bothered with him, but you forget, Isabelle, I'm your sister. You're not going to give it up to him any more than you've given yourself to any other man. But you're right. I can just leave the door open." She moved to the connecting door on the opposite side of the room. "Get some sleep, sis. I'll see you in the morning."

In the morning.

Isabelle turned back to the window and stared out at the desert landscape once again. Lifting her hand, she laid it against the window and pressed her forehead into the glass.

How many times over the years had she done just this? Stared into the night and wondered why she was so restless, wondered what she was searching for? Whom she was searching for?

Moving her arms to cross them over her breasts, she rubbed at her upper arms and tried to chase the chill from her flesh.

She felt hot and cold, nervous and yet so weary she couldn't seem to hold her eyes open. But closing her eyes just brought to mind the sensual threat Malachi had made. That he would fuck her all night long. All day long. Possibly all week long.

Her vagina clenched at the memory of his voice, his gaze, the way his body seemed to wrap protectively around her. The thought of having him wrap himself around her like that after fucking her into exhaustion had her body aching for the sensation of it.

Yes, she wanted him in her bed. She wanted him between her thighs. But strangely, God, she didn't even know him, but she wanted him in her life. She wanted to share that part of herself that she had never shared before.

Her heart.

While she had stood within his embrace, she had felt warm, protected and secure. She had felt as though nothing or no one could touch her, could harm her. And that was a very dangerous feeling for her to have.

Because she knew better now.

She knew better, and the monster that haunted those fears refused to let her go.

• • •

"Her name is Isabelle Martinez. She's my cousin, you mangy, fucking Coyote," Rule growled as he stared at the information on the e-pad he held. "Twenty-five years old, the daughter of Terran Martinez and Ellen Johnson Martinez. Her mother, Ellen, is deceased. She's the personal assistant to the chief of the Navajo Nation, Ray Martinez, and she'll be present at the meeting in the morning."

Malachi heard the edge of concern and anger in Rule Breaker's voice. Didn't it just figure. His mate was this bastard's first cousin. Just his luck. He rubbed at the back of his neck, irritation tightening his muscles as he fought back the need to find her.

Now.

Son of a bitch.

"She's your cousin, yet, to my knowledge, you and Lawe have never declared your genetic ties with the Navajo Nation," Malachi pointed out. "If you had, then it would have popped up on the cross-reference I did on my way out here. What makes you think you can claim the tie whenever it suits you to do so, while keeping it a secret at any other time?"

He watched the commander coolly, wondering at the difficulty the other Breed intended to give him where Isabelle was concerned. Where his mate was concerned.

His entire body tightened at the thought, his eyes narrowing back at the commander. "She's mine," he stated, attempting to keep the confrontation out of his tone. "Don't get between us, Rule."

"I'm not the one you have to worry about and we don't have time for this anyway." Rule speared him with a hard look. "My point is that you're integral to this negotiation, Malachi. I can't afford to have your attention divided."

Malachi arched his brows. "Sorry to inconvenience you, commander. I'll be sure to delay it just for you."

Rule grunted at the sarcasm. "Inconvenience is exactly what it is. Can't you just stay the hell away from her for a while? Surely it's not painful yet? Hell, you didn't even kiss her yet. It can't be that bad."

Malachi stared back at him in disbelief, just as Stygian and Ashley were doing.

"Wow, that's raw, Rule," Ashley murmured as she lounged back in the chair she had plopped into earlier. "Do you think maybe we should schedule mating, like you schedule training sessions and stuff? That way, it wouldn't disturb your schedule near so much."

"I can only wish it were so easy," Rule grunted as though unaware she had just sliced at his attitude with the sharp edge of her tongue.

"Her room number," Malachi stated rather than objecting or challenging the other Breed.

Rule glared back at him. "If you go to her tonight, you know what's going to happen. Give me a break here, Coyote. At least wait until we've found the bastard slicing Council and research scientists to shreds. Just if you don't mind."

Malachi lifted his brow. "Evidently I do mind. Do I have to call downstairs and give my security clearance to get her room number? I will if you don't turn it over in the next three seconds."

He wasn't going to argue, growl or challenge. He didn't need the commander to get what he wanted. It would have simply been easier.

Rule watched him, his blue eyes icy, no doubt looking for a sign of weakness. Rule might be the commander on this mission, but he had no authority over any Breed when it came to mating heat.

The commander had changed over the past month too, Malachi thought. A change that had begun even before his twin had begun carrying the mating scent and drawing back from active status. Even though Lawe hadn't claimed his mate, he had still shown his awareness of her by taking himself out of active mission status.

Rule Breaker and Lawe Justice had always fought together, even in the labs they had been created and trained in. They had covered each other's backs, taken bullets for each other and made certain each was protected while ensuring each mission went off in synchronized perfection.

Had the commander changed because his other biological half was no longer there to cover him? It seemed rather hard to believe, especially considering the fact that at times they had fought separately over the past few years and performed with the same stone cold precision as they did together. Anything was possible, but Malachi didn't consider this one probable.

"Five forty-two," Rule growled. "She's just across the fucking hall from you. Now, will you at least consider my request that you wait twenty-four hours? Mating heat and negotiations with your mate's uncle doesn't go hand in hand, Malachi."

"The candle room." Ashley's tone echoed with interest now as she sat up in her chair, ignoring the rest of Rule's statement.

"Damn," Stygian growled. "I don't know what scent she was using when we came up the hall, but it was so damned sexy I think even I was aroused."

"The one she used later was just as good. I don't know where she got those candles, but the coya would seriously love the person who made them. They smelled like heaven last night. I swear, the scent of lavender had me sleeping like a baby," Ashley sighed.

And that was nothing less than the truth. The scent of those candles had taken out the stale, acrid scent of too many strangers tracking after one another in the hotel. It was a hotel scent, one all hotels carried and all Breeds found unpleasant. But the candles' scent later in the night had been relaxing, a soothing blend that had eased Malachi as well, just as the earlier one had been so evocative of sex and seduction that it had intensified his arousal. He should have known the scent was coming from his mate's room. He should have realized she hadn't run far.

"Hey Mal-baby, make sure you find out where she got them," Ashley pleaded prettily. "So I can get some for the coya."

Ashley's coya, who was Malachi's as well, was the much loved, in some cases revered, female alpha of the Coyote packs.

"We need all our senses alert for this meeting." Rule sighed, casting Malachi another hard glare. "Lawe will be arriving within days, and when he does, our mission here will begin in earnest. Mating her now will only endanger her."

Malachi felt something shift inside him. A dark edge of primal denial raising its head with a shift in the calm he normally kept himself centered with.

"She's already in danger." He knew it. Had sensed it. But it had only been after her friend had whispered something to her and her gaze suddenly raked the room with a flash of terror in the cobalt blue depths.

"You don't know that, Malachi." Despite his denial, Rule tensed further, his tone becoming darker.

"Something frightened her, sent a particular scent of fear rising from her," Malachi stated as he straightened from the wall he had been leaning against, angry tension making him restless. "A fear I've only scented after our women were raped in the labs."

The three Breeds he faced came to instant attention then.

A low growl rumbled in Stygian's throat. Ashley's gray eyes narrowed, her hand dropping to the knife sheathed to her thigh as she rose slowly to her feet, but it was Rule's reaction that, despite the genetic tie to Isabelle, still surprised him.

His lips flattened, nostrils flaring as he flexed his fingers against the arms of the fine leather chair he sat in. Rage flashed in his ice blue eyes, burning like a cold flame before Rule managed to quickly bank the emotion.

The battle for control was short, but obviously difficult. Turning his head slowly, the commander flashed Ashley a look as the corner of his lip lifted, flashing a wicked sharp canine as a rumbled snarl vibrated in his chest.

"I have the room two doors down from her," Ashley stated, her gaze savage as she gave Rule a sharp nod. "Emma is two doors the other way. Trust me, no one will harm her while she's in her room."

Malachi and Stygian were both across from her.

And Rule expected him to stay away from her?

His mate?

His mate who carried the scent of fear and of a woman's soul scarred in one of the worst ways possible?

Did he have the strength? Malachi knew there was no way he could stay away from her for more than a few hours. The hunger for her was throbbing, not just in his cock, but in his chest. The protective fury that had begun building the second he had seen that terror on her face was hardening inside him.

She belonged to him. Her life was now tied to his and vice versa. Her health, her happiness, her pleasure, was now his responsibility. And if Malachi knew one thing, it was how to fulfill his responsibilities.

"Her sister, Chelsea, is in the room connecting to hers, and her friend, Liza, in the one on the other side of her." Rule returned to the e-pad, pulling up information as he spoke before lifting his gaze to Ashley once more. "I want a report on her and her friends by morning, and I want to know by God what it is she fears."

"And the other information you wanted me to gather?" Ashley asked.

The information on four young women, two of which could possibly be the two women the Breeds had been searching so desperately for.

"It can wait," Rule decided. "It's waited for twelve years now, it can wait another day to begin the search. Lawe should be here within the next two nights and we expect our suspect to arrive tonight, if he's not already here. At the latest, he'll arrive either just ahead or behind Lawe and Diane. I rather doubt we're going to have time to complete our mission as well as his before he arrives."

Their mission was to receive acceptance by the Navajo Council chief and it's head advisor to conduct the search for a Breed that had been systematically killing scientists and researchers attached to the Genetics Council and to a pharmaceutical research company tied to Breed testing and research.

Ashley nodded firmly. "It shouldn't take more than a few hours to get the information on them. They're well known enough they shouldn't be able to hide much of their lives."

But Malachi was already ahead of her. He didn't play one-up by informing Rule he had this covered. Let the commander play first cousin, he would turn down no help in protecting his mate.

But neither would he ever depend upon others to protect her either.

"The meetings should end about noon tomorrow." Rule lifted his gaze to Malachi now. "Just in time for Lawe and Diane's arrival two days from now. Protect her, learn what danger stalks her. But mating her before Lawe arrives is out of the question, Malachi." The order in his tone was clear. "After that, I can ensure both your protection and have another team in to cover your duties. Until then, for all our sakes, for your mate's sake, we need to make the mission priority."

Malachi nodded sharply. He didn't argue. He wasn't one to stand and debate or rage, and he sure as hell wasn't above lying if the situation called for it. He was, after all, a Coyote Breed. They took the path of least resistance whenever possible. Fighting and raging when they could achieve their objectives in a more efficient manner didn't seem logical. And Malachi in particular had always felt it best to move around an obstacle rather than punching his way through it.

He ignored Rule's suspicious look. Rule wasn't a stupid man, and he'd known Malachi long enough to know that it wouldn't matter the order given where his mate was concerned, Malachi would do as he felt best.

The commander had this night, and this night only, and he had it only because Malachi had promised his mate a sensual little game. A game he was certain she had no idea of the rules. A game that neither of them would lose, because once he caught her, the pleasure would change both their lives.

And they would both win.

Chapter Three

I was here, and I was searching, always knowing somewhere, you waited.

Wait. Why in the hell had he given in to Rule's request and in to that
so-called "head start" his mate had played for?

Dumb ass. His alpha had always said Malachi's sense of fair play
was overrated. The next morning he was beginning to believe him.

The horniness was killing him.

All he could think about was the woman. His mate.

He was supposed to be thinking about his job, not fucking her
until they both collapsed in exhaustion.

He was giving her the game though.

A sensual little note beneath her door last night, written himself.
*"My bed was cold without you to share it. I found you love, are you cer-
tain you need more time. MM"*

Would it be enough to satisfy her? If not, there was always the
small gold charm he had arranged to have delivered to her. That of
a single curved tooth, to match the emblem on the side of his mission
suit as well as his enforcer uniform. A token of his knowledge of what
she was to him. His mate. Though he knew she wouldn't realize that
until he actually had her beneath him.

Pacing the room, his dick throbbing, his tongue swollen, Malachi
struggled to keep his attention on the live video feed from the conference room. The human participants were unaware of the eyes that
watched and were attempting to dissect every move and every word.

It was all he could do to keep his eyes off the woman, though.

Off his mate.

She was exquisite.

So exquisitely not perfect that she had every dream he had ever dreamed of what his mate would be paling in comparison.

Breed females were perfect in every way. They were created to be just that, perfect. To mesmerize men, to lower their enemies' guard and heighten their senses. They were created to ensure the males they focused their attention on became willing sexual slaves to their beauty and to their sexual prowess.

Isabelle Martinez was such a polar opposite to what was supposed to be his perfect match that he could only feel a surge of immeasurable pride.

He had spent the night immersed in learning all he could about the woman he knew was his mate. He should have been researching those Rule was meeting with, but he'd been unable to get past Isabelle. Or the fact that he had found his mate in this place, at this time. As Rule said, a very inconvenient mating.

His inconvenient little mate.

He grinned at the thought.

A touch so simple as the nip to her ear had cemented what he had known before she had even walked across the room. An exchange so minimal as to be nonexistent in the sharing of a drink, and the glands beneath his tongue had begun swelling with mating hormone almost immediately. The spicy taste in his mouth, the surge of lust that tightened his dick and had his body aching for her, was wearing on his self-control.

But he had known as his eyes met hers across the room, as he'd sensed a hunger that matched his own, rising inside her, what she would be to him.

Her promise to bite his chest had that particular part of his anatomy aching to feel her sharp little teeth.

And he wasn't joking. Once he got his hands on her, he was going to fuck her for a week. Night and day. He was going to keep his cock buried so tight and so deep inside her that even the thought of releasing her would have her crying out in denial.

He'd elected to watch the meeting via live feed rather than being at the meeting. There was no way he could have kept his hands off her. No way he would have lasted through the meeting. He would have dragged her out of there within minutes and not long afterwards, she would have been screaming his name in pleasure.

That wouldn't exactly inspire her family to give the Breeds the permission they needed to conduct a search on Navajo Nation property.

"She's pretty."

He'd heard Ashley enter the room, but she was at his side before he'd realized she had the time to get there.

"Thank you," he murmured, feeling that surge of pride again.

She was pretty. So very very fucking pretty.

The compliment might have seemed lacking, but Malachi found no fault with it. The last thing he wanted was perfection or true beauty.

Pretty, though, pretty was warm and compassionate. It was filled with mercy, and with gentleness. Just as his mate was filled with it.

Everything he'd learned about her assured him that his initial perception of her was right on the money.

"She has a loyal sister and a good friend in Liza as well," Ashley assured him. "Neither of them were needed after the meeting started. I just had lunch with them, and neither of them are willing to discuss that scent of fear she carries. They refuse to betray her."

"But they admit she has reason to fear?" he asked her.

Ashley shrugged.

Malachi caught the movement from the corner of his eyes before turning his full attention to her.

"Let's say, I know the reason is there," she told him as he glared down at her. "They're clamming up each time I mention it, but even I can sense it, just as Stygian admits to scenting it before she left the table the night before and moved across the room to you. It was just for a second, though. As though the thought of something had frightened her."

He turned back to the screen that displayed the conference in the

meeting room which was being held on the secured twenty-fifth floor
that their rooms were on as well.

Isabelle sat calmly at her uncle's side as Rule argued for permission
for the Bureau of Breed Affairs to conduct an official search on Navajo
land and asked for the cooperation of the Navajo Nation Council in
finding the rogue Breed that Rule stated they *suspected* was in the
area.

The truth was, they knew he was headed there, if he hadn't already
arrived. A bloodthirsty murderous Breed who had sliced a path of
death and horror through the few remaining research scientists who
had worked for the drug manufacturer Phillip Brandenmore before
his death.

"It's hard to promise cooperation, Commander Breaker, when we
have no idea who or what this Breed is that you search for, or his
genetic ties to the Nation. You've also shown no proof of his crimes
and are unwilling to give us full disclosure of why you believe he's
here. He must have a reason for being in our territory at this time.
Added to that, you have no way of identifying this rogue Breed. It's
like asking Russia to let you into their secret service files because a
murderer used a knife specific to the USSR." Ray Martinez watched
Rule closely, as though already suspecting the deception Rule was
practicing.

And how could they suspect it if they didn't something to hide?

"Just as it's difficult for us to make the request, because we don't
have the information you're requesting, Councilman Martinez. And
I assure you, the rogue we're after has had far more time to devise
ways of killing his intended victims and avoiding us, unless we find
a link back to him." Rule sighed as he stared across the table at the
chief of the Navajo Nation. "I'm not asking for more than I'm willing
to give, sirs. We'll keep you informed every step of the way, but we
need the freedom to conduct our investigation before he kills again.
And he has every intention of killing again."

"Who does he intend to kill? We have no Council scientists or
researchers here. We have no one in the Nation who could be a
target to such a man." Orin Martinez, the Navajo spirit advisor,

spoke up, his gaze a endless deep dark blue as he glanced toward the eye of the camera supposedly recording the meetings.

For the briefest moment, Malachi had a sense that this particular human was well aware of any strange electronics around him, before focusing his attention back to the Navajo leader.

Tall, broad, his graying black hair straight and long where it was tied back at his nape, Ray Martinez was a confident, powerful man for his age of sixty-five.

He was in his second four-year term as chief of the Navajo Nation, and through the six years he had guided the Nation so far, he had kept the promises he had made to solidify the Nation and ensure its prosperity.

The Nation was gaining a powerful presence in the White House as well with the Navajo senator elected into office during the last term. Jobs were coming into the counties the Navajo controlled and more native small businesses were being incorporated. Added to the lower rate of unemployment, and Ray Martinez had ensured his mark in the history books.

"And what freedom do you believe you'll need in this investigation?" Ray crossed his arms over the fine white shirt he wore and leaned back in the comfortable chair he'd taken at the head of the conference table.

Now, this was where Rule was likely to get into a hell of a lot of trouble if he wasn't careful.

Not that Rule was never not careful. He simply sometimes forgot that tact and politeness were essential when dealing with such men.

"We'll need access to your Nation files to ascertain the possibility that our rogue could have formed any alliances with any of your people based on their familial ties, DNA and genetic connections as well as possible political affiliations or agendas. We don't know what he looks like, but we have the genetic and DNA profile used in his creation as well a working knowledge of the groups he's infiltrated over the past year. Several of which I know your people have access to as well. Our need for confidentiality requires we keep the genetic typing confidential for the time being, but the moment we're able, I promise we'll ensure you have that information as well."

How did a man stand in front of his uncle and deceive so easily? Malachi wondered. Which was exactly what Rule was doing. Standing before this man as though they shared no blood and lying straight to his face.

"He's good," Ashley murmured as she crossed her arms loosely over her breasts as she crossed one knee over the other and watched. "We should have made popcorn for this one." Instead, she popped the gum she was chewing.

Ashley and her love for bubble gum were almost legendary.

"There are times he's too good," Malachi commented as his attention moved back to the mate he'd agreed to delay taking. He was drawn to her like a moth to a flame, unable to keep his eyes from her and willing to drown in the fires he knew would burn between them.

Waiting to take her was a bargain he had regretted the moment he'd made it. Unfortunately, he had seen the wisdom in Rule's request. Had he mated her, there would have been no way she would have made that meeting. And there would have been no way to convince her uncle that she wasn't ill if the mating began as heated and fierce as he knew it would.

Hell, it was already driving him damned crazy and all he had done was drink from the glass she had drank from and nipped her cute little ear. He'd wanted to mark her. The urge had been nearly overwhelming to go ahead and sink his teeth in the base of her neck, where it curved into her shoulder.

He would have licked the little wound, but the hormone that had began swelling in the glands beneath his tongue would have already begun taking the pain from the bite. It would have entered her system at the point of the bite and made the need to have each other impossible to deny.

It was already impossible to deny. If she were there in the room with him, he would have already had her stripped, fucked and knotted.

His cock throbbed in his jeans. Thick and heavy, the iron hard flesh demanded the presence of his mate, demanded that he take her, mark her, brand her as his, no matter the obstacles.

"Damn, get your mating hormones under control there, Mal," Ashley grimaced as she glanced back at him. "All that male lust and testosterone are about to poison me."

"You're not tied to that chair, Ash," he grouched right back at her. "You can leave anytime."

"Yeah, if I didn't want to watch Rule weave a little bit of his magic. I just don't want to drown in the smell of your raging hard-on while I'm doing it," she snorted, her gaze flicking over him again before she turned back to the monitors.

The raging hard-on was about to kill him. He swore his dick had never been so hard as it had been since Isabelle had guided his hand, the glass clasped between his fingers, to allow her to sip from his drink.

Her eyes had been sultry, filled with feminine heat and hunger. He had sworn he'd seen a woman dying to taste the pleasure he could bring her, in that look. A pleasure Malachi knew would send them both racing to complete oblivion.

He forced his attention back to the monitor, forced himself to attempt to decode the expressions of the Navajo Council members as Rule attempted to convince them to give him what he wanted without restraint.

It wasn't working well at the moment because these were men who had something to hide. Something they feared the Breeds learning.

The argument raged between Ray Martinez and Rule. The chief refused to listen, just as Rule refused to give up.

"Young man, you seem to have a problem accepting the word 'no.'" Ray stared back at Rule implacably as the Breed lowered his brows and met his gaze.

Why the three Martinez men hadn't yet figured out their DNA ran strong and deep in the commander, Malachi didn't know. The resemblance to the Martinez family was damned strong, but the pure stubbornness and refusal to accept denial was identical.

"There is no disrespect meant to you or to the people of the Navajo Nation, sir," Rule assured him as he stared back at him from where on the other end of the conference table. He appeared at ease, relaxed and confident while the Martinez males were becoming irritated and weren't bothering to hide it. "The situation is simply too delicate and of too much importance not to make you aware of every aspect of the consequences if this rogue isn't found."

Ray grunted at that. "You say you have a rogue, yet you have no name, no identification, nor do you have, according to you, any idea who this rogue is, or exactly where he could be hiding on Navajo land. All you have is a genetic profile, that you refuse to share with the Council, or without our own genetic experts. Yet you expect me to give you unprecedented entrance into the records of our people and their ancestors in your search? Am I missing anything?"

"That about sums it up, sir."

Malachi frowned at the screen, his attention held by the chief of the Navajo Nation and a subtle look of secretive knowledge that suddenly flashed between him and his father.

The look was so subtle he almost missed it. If he hadn't been watching for it, hadn't kept his gaze locked on him rather than Rule as he spoke, then he would have missed it.

Malachi sat down in the chair facing the three screens and began to watch them. Forcing himself to ignore his mate, which was one of the hardest things he had ever done, he concentrated instead on the three Martinez men. Ray and Terran Martinez, the two brothers, were careful not to look at each other at all. But Ray was unable to keep from glancing at his father, Orin, the Nation's medicine man and spiritual advisor. And the look they exchanged, despite the brevity of it, was filled with concern.

His hard-on was still there. The hunger for his mate was still there. But the training for exactly what he was doing was rising to the fore. He was a collaborative interrogator. At least, that was what they called him at the labs.

There were the interrogators, who questioned suspects and persons of interest. Then there were the interrogation collaborators, trained to watch the interrogation process and pick up lies, anomalies and clues.

Public relations meant more than just speaking to the public or preparing speeches to reduce the threat of propaganda against the Breeds, or to minimize it or better yet, spin their own version of lies. It was watching, gauging expressions and atmospheres and separating the lies from the truth. It was catching the small, subtle looks and shifts of muscles bunching beneath clothing designed to hide such reactions.

Malachi's specialty was public relations and propaganda warfare among Breeds. A vital area of warfare within the many Breed labs that had once existed. After all, someone had to know how to keep the packs and prides and various personalities at one another's throats rather than giving them the chance to collaborate and escape.

It had been his and his trainers' jobs to filter through the information that came in from many different sources within and outside the labs, and use it to sabotage escape or rescue attempts, as well as gathering intel concerning knowledge of the Breeds.

It was a gift he was created to have, and one he excelled at. That gift had also helped him and his trainers to plant the intel in the right places to ensure that groups that would be sympathetic to the Breeds would learn of them and stage their rescues.

Protected in Russia, far enough away from the mainstream of the other labs within the Genetics Council network, Malachi, two other Coyotes and their trainers had pushed along the rumors and intel that had helped investigative reporters learn of the Breeds. That information, begun even before Malachi's creation, had eventually led the right people to the right information and had ensured the world learned of the horrors they suffered.

Three generations had gone into quietly ensuring the survival of the Breeds. There had been no way to do this quickly. There had been no way of ensuring public opinion would sway to the side of the Breeds unless that information came with the truth of the horrors they had lived through.

"You are asking more than our people would be willing to give you. Genetic and DNA profiles are strictly confidential. Would you give out your enforcers' identifications so easily, Commander?"

"To you, I would." Rule nodded with an air of sincerity.

"Bullshit," Ashley muttered. "He'd gnaw off his own arm first."

Malachi grunted at the comment as he kept his attention on the monitors.

"It's the only way we have of identifying who this Breed could be searching for," Rule stated quietly. "Perhaps the only way of finding him. I believe he'll seek out those he considers 'relatives.' He may even enlist their help."

The chief shook his head "no," which was no more than Rule had expected, Malachi knew. The elaborate deception the Breeds were a part of in this meeting could backfire on them, if the information they had was wrong.

Malachi didn't believe it was, though. Gideon was searching for the Bengal male and two human girls, one of them being Christine Roberts. Her own mother had revealed that her daughter had mentioned a friend named Terran who was willing to help her. And only Terran Martinez would have given a damn at the time.

He had been in the area at the same time the Roberts girl had come up missing. Just as he was suspected to be aware when the bengal Judd and the human girl Fawn had been rescued.

Unfortunately, in the two days they had been in Window Rock, they had found nothing. Not even a hint that Gideon or the Bengal Breed Judd and the two young women who had escaped further research were in the area. He glanced from the chief and the spiritual advisor back to his mate, Isabelle.

She was watching the proceedings with a blank expression, neither eyes nor face showing emotion. Every time the Breed commander spoke, she made a note. She never looked at her uncle, her grandfather, Orin, or her father, Terran.

She was watching Commander Breaker closely with that bland expression. Each time he petitioned for allowances in the investigation and was turned down, she watched him *very* closely.

What was she looking for?

"She's as good as you are," Ashley commented as he kept his gaze on the screen. "She hasn't shown so much as a hint of emotion or knowledge. I wonder what her scent is at the moment."

"Hmmm." His mate.

Pride enveloped him. Whatever her position was with her uncle, she was obviously very very good at it.

Sitting next to Terran Martinez was Isabelle's friend Liza. As Terran's legal assistant she made certain the files he needed were always available, and she began doing it with an efficient ease.

She seemed no more than reasonably concerned about the subject, and unaware of whatever secrets the Martinez men were hiding.

"What are they hiding?" Ashley wondered aloud. "Shouldn't they know by now that we'll figure out they're lying, Malachi? I mean really, what's the point?"

Malachi didn't comment. He didn't take his attention from the meeting or those attending it. Ray Martinez would have been far better off to have simply omitted the genetic typing from the registry they kept, if they felt it would endanger them, and allowed the Breeds to go through the rest. That would have allayed suspicion. This way, they were only cementing it, despite their protestations of the people's right to genetic privacy.

Whatever it was, they were protesting in vain, Malachi knew. Rule Breaker and Lawe Justice hadn't achieved their ranks by giving up easily.

Keeping his mate out of harm's way would be easy enough, though. If she knew anything, she would have betrayed herself, as the chief and his advisor had earlier. She had her suspicions, that was obvious, but her reaction hadn't been enough that he felt the need to appraise Rule of it. There was no sense dragging her into the battles that were beginning to be formed.

She was safe. And tonight, she would be his. He would make damned sure she wasn't dragged into it any further than her suspicions had already placed her.

He had waited on her for far too long. He had dreamed of her far too many nights to risk losing her because of a matter the two parties should have been cooperating on.

He had ached too deeply for her. Always knowing she awaited him, always knowing she was out there somewhere, perhaps even as lost within the darkness as he was. Looking into the stars and wondering when the loneliness would end.

As he stood outside her room at dawn, inhaling the scent of the candles and finding her unique scent within it, he'd felt something in his chest tighten painfully. Because that scent of fear was still there. Whether it be nightmares or memories, there was something his mate feared. That fear was something he had to take out of her life. He simply would not allow it to be a part of her life any longer.

She was his now, just as he was hers.

And tonight, he would ensure that nothing, or no one, ever had the chance to destroy it.

Chapter Four

So many times I fought back tears, felt incomplete and
feared you weren't there.

Her uncle and her grandfather feared that the Breeds had finally
arrived to track down the three individuals they had been hiding for
more than a decade. Isabelle knew very little about the events that
summer. She had been only a child herself and still dealing with the
death of her mother and Chelsea's antics.

Isabelle had barely been thirteen. Her mother had been dead for
six years, but the loss of the gentle, loving woman she had been had
devastated Isabelle and Chelsea for years. In ways, they still hadn't
recovered from the loss.

Their father had dealt with it by disappearing more often, searching almost continually for the sister who had been lost when he'd
been a child himself.

He hadn't found the sister or proof of her death—what he'd found
instead had been a teenage boy and a young girl. Several months
later another young girl had shown up and then disappeared within
hours.

It had been so long ago that Isabelle couldn't even remember what
they had looked like. They had been at her home for only a matter
of hours in the deepest part of the night. Isabelle had only seen their
faces for moments. Pale, suspicious, resigned faces. As though they
had made their peace with the world and whatever fate awaited them.
The part of the night that had always found Isabelle awake and staring into the darkness had also been the time of night that others

prowled the darkness. Others who came for the children took them away and ensured they were never seen or heard from again.

She had stared into the darkness after leaving Malachi the night before until she had found herself nodding off to sleep by the wide windowsill.

The night had always called to her, even as a child. Pulling her from sleep, it seemed the darkness whispered on each breeze that slid past her home, and on those currents of air she swore she felt the haunting cries of the coyotes singing through the air.

Was Malachi the reason she had always felt an affinity to those wild, often hated creatures?

The People knew the coyote, though. They knew him for the prankster he was, for the deceiver, but they also knew him for the vital part of the night that he commanded.

He wasn't all bad. He was equal parts human and supernatural being with all the faults and fallacies that came with them. At least, in legend.

Her lips quirked as she left the meeting, leaving the players in the game being conducted to deal with one another on their own. She had done her part. She had watched Commander Rule Breaker each time he pushed for what he wanted and each time he was denied. And each time she had written the same opinion.

He had expected it.

He had known her uncle and her grandfather wouldn't relent in turning over the genetic identifications of each of the registered human and Breed members of the Navajo Nation.

Genetic typing had begun when the Breeds had first made themselves known thirteen, nearly fourteen years before. When the Navajo Council had realized the number of their missing daughters who had been kidnapped to aid in the creation of the species, they had immediately set out to ensure they could identify which of the emerging Breeds were their own.

The Navajo weren't the only Native Americans to have contributed, though. The members of the scattered tribes spread across the United States had sent in blood, genetic identification and all the details that went with it. Just in case. Just in case Breed blood could save a chief or a medicine man, a child or a warrior or a mother. Just in case a daughter returned and children born of her stolen eggs, or a child born of her body, came searching for her.

In case the daughter didn't return, and the grandchildren did.

Isabelle knew that was her grandfather's dream. That one day something of the daughter he had lost would return to the Nation seeking the blood ties the Martinez family and the Navajo Nation represented.

As Ashley had done, along with her sister, Emma.

They had come searching, and had found a family they hadn't known existed for them. Small though they were, and as hidden as Ashley and Emma could keep them, still, the ties were there.

And Isabelle was finding a tie of her own, she thought as she returned to her room to change clothes.

Malachi.

He hadn't been at the meeting, but that didn't mean she hadn't been thinking about it.

He was all she could really think about.

Her ear still tingled with the memory of the nip and that tiny lick to the slight wound.

The rest of her body was heated, had been heated and refused to cool down.

Even the quick, cool shower she forced herself to have didn't help. As she used the soft, suds-filled cloth between her thighs, she swore it was more frustrating than trying to masturbate.

Each time the silky suds and the soft pile of the cloth raked over her clitoris, it was like being pierced with a hunger so heated she could barely stand it. It made the shower quicker, though, for the fact that she didn't attempt to masturbate.

Rinsing her hair and body quickly, she stepped from the shower and hurriedly prepared for the evening.

She dressed in a loose, silky maxi dress, the casual outfit falling to the floor at her sandals and giving her a feeling of intense, sensual femininity.

The brush of the cool, slick material against her hardened nipples was almost an unbearable caress. The feel of her bra had chafed the tender points until removing it had been imperative.

The long length of her raven black hair fell below her shoulders in long, soft waves after she blow-dried it. Her blue eyes, almost a cobalt, looked brighter, more intense than she remembered them being before.

Her complexion looked clearer, her cheeks flushed, her lips looked almost kiss swollen. Leaning in closer to the mirror, Isabelle stared at her reflection with a slight frown. She didn't even need makeup as she usually did. How strange was that?

This was what arousal did to a woman? Anticipation?

She could handle this. Her gaze fell to the small charm she had placed on a gold chain and put around her neck.

A curved fang, the symbol of the Coyote Breeds that he had left for her. Lifting her hand, she brushed her fingers against the fang as the need for his touch raced through her system.

Transferring a few necessary items to a small leather purse that matched her sandals, Isabelle found pulled the small note Malachi had pushed beneath her door that morning. The roses were in her bedroom next to the bed. A smile touched her lips at the thought of the Breed. She hadn't expected him to find her so easy. Liza's friend in registration had swore no one had asked for the room number, but Isabelle knew they would have other ways of finding that information.

Shivering at the thought of him being able to find her so easily, and wondering if he would find her again this evening, Isabelle left her room once again and headed for the elevators at the center of the hotel wing.

She had promised Chelsea and Liza she would meet them at the bar before dinner for a drink. The same bar she had met Malachi in the night before. The same one in which she feared Holden might be watching for her. The one she prayed Malachi would be waiting for her.

But if Holden were there, her sister and Liza would have called long before now.

She had no intentions of staying with them for long. She intended instead to find that damned sexy Coyote if he wasn't waiting in the bar. If he didn't take her soon, she just might go up in flames waiting for him.

She swore she was going to eat him up from head to toe and every point in between when he got his hands on her. Once he was naked, she would paint his body with her tongue and taste every inch of his flesh. Then . . .

Her mouth watered.

Then, she would move between his thighs and lick every inch of his cock. She wanted to do everything to him that she had ever dreamed of doing to a lover. She wanted to take his cock into her mouth and suckle it hungrily. She wanted to taste the essence of him and feel his body tense with the need for release. She wanted him so desperately it was a true, physical hunger.

She would swirl her tongue over the head and feel it throb as she sucked it into her mouth.

Her thighs clenched, the feel of her juices once again dampening her panties and causing her to bite her lip. She really didn't want to have to change panties again. She swore she saturated them as she sat in that meeting thinking about him.

It had been all she could do to keep her mind on what was being said and keeping the notes her uncle asked her to keep. Her perceptions of Rule Breaker's answers and whether or not she thought he was lying at important points of the conversation. In her opinion, he was lying in most of them.

When she had first arrived at the meeting, she had been disappointed that Malachi wasn't there, but, if he had been—she clenched her thighs again as her clit throbbed with the need to be touched.

Perhaps she should go change panties again.

Frowning slightly as she heard the elevator bell ping its descent, she was ready to turn and head back to her room. She was swinging around on one foot, her intent clear.

Changing her panties, because thinking about giving tall, blond and Breedy a blow job had her seriously wet.

The elevator doors slid soundlessly open.

She saw him from the corner of her eye. She could almost swear she felt him.

Poised to run, almost in the turn, nearly pushing off, and instead, she swung back around, straightened and stepped into the elevator as though she had never, not even for a second, considered not doing so.

Turning, her back pressing against the side of the cubicle, she stared across the short distance into eyes that gleamed almost black, the color was so blue. In those eyes, she read his challenge. Was her head start over? Because he had clearly found her, and there was no doubt he was ready to reward her taking the elevator rather than running.

Reaching back, her fingers curled over the side rail, holding tight, holding back.

She heard someone curse, a low, furious sound. But it wasn't Malachi. His lips weren't moving. He was staring back at her, becoming as locked within the air of sensuality swirling around them as she was.

Her glaze flicked to his lips once more.

She wanted to kiss him. Just one kiss. Just a taste of that sensually full lower lip, a flick of her tongue against his.

Would she be satisfied with it?

Never. But it would ease the ache in her lips. Maybe.

The elevator felt as though it were moving in slow motion. She felt as though *she* were moving in slow motion.

She tried to keep her fingers locked around the side bar, tried to hold herself back.

There was no holding back from him.

Isabelle swore she could feel him urging her to him. His gaze was intense, a swirl of navy blue, an erotic storm brewing around them.

They weren't there alone, but they could have been. They may as well have been. As far as Isabelle was concerned, Rule Breaker and Stygian Black didn't even exist.

Her tongue slipped out, licking over her lips as the sudden vision of her going to her knees in front of him flashed across her mind.

Her gaze flicked to the front of the black mission-style pants he wore. They were formfitting, though not tight. Still, the bulge beneath them was unmistakable.

She swallowed tight. And it was large.

Her eyes came back to his. She forced them up, because she may wish she were there with him alone, but she knew she wasn't.

Someone cleared his throat as she inhaled slowly, fighting for control. The taller, darker Breed blew out a rough breath. Neither Malachi nor Isabelle glanced toward him.

Her eyes moved to his hands. He was gripping the rail behind him, across from her. His knuckles white from the force of his grip.

The elevator came to a stop, the doors slid opened and a couple started in, stared at the Breeds and backed out. The doors slid closed again.

"Back up," Malachi said. It was a rough, rasping sound as Stygian obviously pushed the right button. The elevator started up.

Malachi reached out then, pushed a button himself and Isabelle heard Rule growl his name. A real, male feline sound of irritation. The commander wasn't happy.

Isabelle and Malachi both ignored him. The elevator stopped again.

"Do you really want to stay?" Malachi asked the two men without looking at them as the doors slid open again and no one moved.

No one except Isabelle.

Releasing the rail, she stepped across the distance separating them. She felt as though she were being drawn to him, pulled to him by some unseen force. His gaze held hers, his lashes lowering to half mast.

She was only distantly aware of the other two exiting the elevator. All that mattered to her was that they were gone. She didn't have to hold herself back. She didn't have to force herself not to touch him, taste him, kiss him.

She wanted that kiss. The kiss she had dreamed of. A kiss she had been certain she would never feel.

Moving to him, her hands braced against his chest, she went on tiptoe, but without his help, if he hadn't lowered his head, it wouldn't have happened.

Her hands slid to his shoulders, one against his neck as she felt the warmth of his breath against her lips.

"I caught you," he whispered.

Her lips parted as his touched, moved with his words.

"Or I caught you."

Suddenly, it didn't matter who caught whom, or if there was a head start, time to think or even a need for thought. His lips covered hers as his arms slid around her, pulling her closer, lifting her to him.

The taste of ambrosia filled her senses. It had to be ambrosia. The elixir of the gods. It had to be something not quite natural, because the taste of his kiss went to her head like a drug. Like a pleasure she couldn't deny herself because she had waited far too long for it.

For Malachi.

His fingers cupped the back of her neck, tilting her head back as his lips slanted over hers, parted them, and pure heat swept through her senses. His tongue slipped past her lip, swept over hers and tempted her, teased her to catch it.

She nipped it.

He growled.

Strong fingers slid into her hair, gripped and held her head in place as he turned her, lifted her with his other arm and braced her against the side of the elevator.

His tongue swept past her lips again and stroked against hers.

And she nipped again.

Exhilaration surged through her. Adrenaline surged through her veins as his fingers moved from her hair, cupped her jaw and his kiss became firmer, more dominating, demanding.

He wasn't asking permission. There was nothing exploratory about the claiming, nothing introductory. He was taking her with his kiss, with his tongue, and she knew what he wanted.

What she was aching for.

Her lips closed around his tongue, sucked with delicate greed as it pumped between her lips and the most unique taste, subtle and hot, filled her senses.

She couldn't define it. She couldn't describe it.

She wanted more.

A growl filled the air, a moan whispering around it as the kiss suddenly became hotter, hungrier. The arousal that had been brewing inside her became a firestorm, racing through her, tightening inside her.

This was hers. He was hers.

She'd known it the moment her eyes met his in the bar the night before, and she knew it now with his lips covering hers, his tongue pumping in her mouth and his hands pulling at her dress.

"Hell! Malachi. Honey. You have a room. Use it!"

Isabelle blinked as he pulled back from her. Flushing, she gazed around his shoulder to the elevator entrance.

Ashley stood, leaning against the elevator frame, holding the doors back. Fingers tucked into the snug pockets of her jeans, her blond hair falling over one shoulder, her eyes wide as she stared back at them.

Then her gaze slipped down and her brows arched. "Nice sandals there, Belle, but I think they should be on the floor, not wrapped around Malachi's hips while you're in the elevator."

Around his hips?

Yep, they were around his hips.

He lowered her slowly. As her feet touched the floor, his arm went around her back and he all but picked her up and carried her from the cubicle.

"Nighty night," Ashley called out as Malachi slid the electronic key quickly through the lock on his room, then pulled her inside.

His room was across from hers.

It was only a distant thought and it sure as hell didn't matter. Because he was holding her again, pulling her to him, his lips moving over hers and spilling the taste of pure desire to her senses.

"I warned you." Isabelle had only a second to understand the words that rasped from his lips before he was pulling the dress from her. "You're mine now, Isabelle. Mine."

As he jerked it up her legs, she might have heard a seam split and she really didn't give a damn because she was all but naked in his arms and he was picking her up and bearing her across the room to the bed.

"You made promises," she whispered as he laid her back then straightened before her.

"I made promises," he agreed. "And I promise you, mate, I intend to follow through on every damned one of them. All day. All night. Possibly all fucking week."

Chapter Five

So many nights I howled into the darkness, incomplete
and searching.

Malachi stared down at the woman he knew he'd awaited all his life.
The hours he'd spent pulling up every scrap of information he could
find on her only confirmed the fact that nature had indeed given him
a mate that suited him perfectly.

A small smile shaped her pouty lips, the sensual curve beguiling
and filled with promise.

"Are you going to undress, Coyote Man?" she whispered, the husky
need in her voice causing the steel-hard length of his cock to throb
almost painfully.

Lowering his hands to the belt of his jeans, he would have unbuckled it, but Isabelle chose that moment to move. She lifted herself to
her knees, her smaller hands covering his then pushing them aside.

Watching her loosen his belt, her graceful fingers releasing the
latch then moving to the metal tabs of his mission pants, nearly broke
his control.

His fingers curled as he fought to hold back, to keep from touching
her. If he touched her, there was no way in hell he could hold back.
He'd take her. He'd have her and there would be no stopping it.

That wasn't what he wanted for her this first time.

Her first time.

His entire body clenched as she released his pants. Gripping the hem
of his black shirt, he stripped it off, tossing it aside as Isabelle pushed the
waist of his pants down and released the engorged length of his dick.

Male Coyotes weren't like felines, who were sexually endowed more along the lines of their human counterparts. Wolves and Coyotes were another story. The width was unusually thick, and when they orgasmed with their mates, two to three inches at the middle point of the shaft would thicken even more, locking them inside their mates.

"Oh. My. God," she whispered, her fingers trailing down the length, sending pulses of pure electric pleasure shooting straight to his balls.

"It's okay. I promise," he muttered roughly, pulling back only long enough to quickly unlace and pull off his boots and pants. Naked, the glands beneath his tongue swollen and aching as the mating hormone filled his mouth, Malachi found himself so desperate for her he could barely stand to breathe.

"I'll never take it." She sounded dazed as the scent of her trepidation filled the air with a subtle edge of innocence. But she came back to him, her fingers reaching for him once again, drawn to his hunger as he was to hers.

"All you have to do is want me," he promised. "That's all, Isabelle."

He wasn't going to explain it, he couldn't.

He knew what would happen.

His alpha, Del-Rey, had explained it to the pack just after his mating with the coya, Anya.

"Malachi." She swallowed tightly again, glancing up at him as her silken fingers trailed down it once again. "I want you more than I've ever wanted anything in my life." And that confused her. He could see her confusion, he could feel it.

He wanted nothing more than to ease it. Later. He would ease the confusion and her fears later. Right now, the feel of her touch was too incredible to pull away from.

He reached for her. He cupped the back of her head as her fingers curled around the shaft of his cock. Not all the way, of course, her hand was too small, but enough to hold her steady as her tongue licked experimentally around the crown of his dick.

God, he wanted to fuck her mouth. He wanted to watch those

pretty pouty lips enclose the head of his cock as he thrust shallowly in and out.

He exerted just the slightest amount of pressure.

"Take it, baby," he groaned. "Open your lips for me. I want to feel my dick in your mouth."

The hunger for it was about to make him mad. The need to feel her sucking the sensitive crest of his cock had his entire body tightening to the breaking point.

Her lips parted. Rubbing them over the engorged tip of his hardened flesh had his pulse rocketing, his heart rate slamming. His fingers buried in her hair, tightened and held her still. Her gaze lifted to his.

There was no fear there. There was excitement, an edge of confusion. There were emotions that filled his senses and he was also filled with the knowledge that he had waited for this his entire life. For this woman.

For her touch.

Then her lips enclosed the tip of his cock, and slowly, so very slowly slid down until the entire head was enclosed in suckling, wet heat.

A growl tore from his lips. He tried to hold it back. He wanted to hold it back. There were times that the presence of the animal was something he preferred to hide. When making love to pure, sweet innocence, hiding it was imperative.

But rather than feeling or scenting her fear, he smelled her excitement. Pure, sweet, sensual excitement that flared so hot, so brilliant he swore it was sinking into his pores.

The hormones spilled from his tongue as he swallowed, his gaze narrowed on her, his hands holding her head as he moved against her. Watching. Watching her lips stretch around his cock, tightening on him, stroking with her tongue, lashing against it and stimulating nerve endings that sent his senses racing.

She was pushing him to a brink he'd never known before. Each pull of her lips, each flutter of her tongue against the underside of his dick, had the glands in his tongue swelling further, tighter.

The hormone was flooding his system, intoxicating him. And he wanted her just as intoxicated. Just as bound to him as he was to her.

He pulled back, ignoring her attempts to hold him, to tighten her lips on the overly sensitive head of his cock.

Cupping her face in his hands, Malachi bent to her, his lips covering hers, his tongue pressing between them, pushing against hers, demanding, desperate.

Her lips tightened on his tongue, the hormone spilling into her, pumping from the glands as he took control of the kiss once again.

Licking, stroking, pleasure and hunger merged to spin them both into a furiously heated, blazing pleasure that gripped their senses and tore aside any trepidation, any confusion she may have felt. Any hesitancy he may have had.

As the imperative need to fill her with the mating heat eased, the need to satisfy the heat with pleasure filled every fiber of his being.

Laying her back, Malachi let his lips roam down her neck to the full curves of her breasts as she arched to him. His thumbs raked over the tips, watched them tighten and swell harder as a soft moan of pleasure left her kiss-swollen lips.

His mate.

She was lifting to him, arching against him, needing and hungry for his touch.

And he wanted nothing more than to give it to her.

Isabelle had known. She should have known. Where there was smoke, there was fire, her father had always said. The tabloids were filled with the stories of a mating addiction. A heat that human women couldn't resist. One that bound the Breed male to her. One that created an endless, sensual feast for the couple.

That knowledge was a distant thought, a realization she couldn't hold on to as Isabelle felt Malachi's lips surround the tight, puckered tip of her breast.

She stared down at him, dazed, the pleasure she had felt before, with no more than the briefest caress, rising, becoming deeper, becoming something more binding.

The feel of his hot, sucking mouth tugging at her nipple was almost a pleasure-pain. Heat bloomed in the tender tip, radiated outward and rushed to her pussy, where her clit throbbed with violent demand.

His tongue rubbed against the sensitive point, then with quick, hard little licks flicked over it, lashing at it as a surge of pleasure and excitement sent fingers of electric sensation through her, clenching her womb and spilling her juices between her thighs.

She was so wet. So hot. She could feel the slick proof of her need for him as it slickened her thighs and swelled the folds of her pussy in anticipation.

Moving from one breast to the other, his lips played in exacting detail at the tight little bud. He sucked and licked, flicked at it with his tongue, and with whatever addictive quality she had tasted in his kiss, he sensitized her nipples further.

She had felt the swollen glands beneath his tongue as she suckled at it for those few brief seconds. She had tasted his kiss, redolent of a fire in winter with the spice of a summer rainstorm thrown in it.

Her fingers tightened in his hair as he released the tip, only to spread his kisses down her torso as his hands stroked to her thighs and parted them slowly.

Against the outside of her leg, Isabelle could feel the thick, heavy width of his cock and almost felt the fear that wanted to rise inside her. But there was no place for inhibitions as his fingers trailed higher, slid through the slick essence of her hunger then brushed against the curls that hid the swollen flesh from him.

His lips moved to her hipbone, then to the other before kisses were scattered to the sensitive mound of her pussy. His fingers tucked against the slit as she arched closer to him, desperate now to feel his kiss, his touch, on every portion of her body.

"Malachi," she moaned, the dark, sexual tone of her voice almost shocking her.

His fingers eased down the narrow crease between the folds of her pussy to find the hidden entrance where her juices pooled with silken heat.

His finger rotated as he moved lower, lying between her thighs, his breath whispering over the swollen bud of her clit.

That tiny caress, like a heated breeze blowing over the too sensitive bundle of nerves. Isabelle found herself jerking in reaction, her hands slapping against the mattress to curl into the blankets beneath her.

His head lowered.

Isabelle watched, entranced, as his tongue peeked out and licked over the tiny pleasure point with devastating results.

"Oh God, Malachi," she cried out, her knees bending and lifting, her legs parting farther as he drew her clit into his mouth and began suckling with quiet, hungry greed.

She had never done this before. She had never lain so open, knees bent and thighs spread, and given any other man permission to touch her intimately.

The fingers rubbing gently at the entrance to her vagina began pushing inside her.

His lips and tongue were torturing her clit with pleasure, and as Malachi begin to push his fingers inside her, she felt herself unraveling.

Two large fingers pushed in, twisting lightly, scissoring and stretching her open. She felt them rasp against the tender inner nerve endings and send impulses of pure pleasure racing through her.

Every cell vibrated with the rush of sensation. Isabelle could feel the sensations coalescing, tightening, threatening to implode inside her as he began thrusting his fingers shallowly into the snug opening.

She could feel the pressure on the fragile shield of her virginity as his fingers began stretching it, weakening it.

"Malachi," she moaned again as one hand slid beneath her rear, arching her higher to his lips and to the finger penetrating her sex. "It's so good. It feels so good." She couldn't keep it in. She needed him too much. Needed every touch possible with every fiber of her being.

He sucked her clit deeper into his mouth, his tongue rubbing against it now as the thrusting fingers began to move inside her with more demand, sending lightning-fast forks of sensation to tear through her womb, her clit and her pussy.

"Fuck me!" She cried the words out, desperation laced with

demand, but she had no idea where they'd come from. "Oh God, Malachi, I need you. I swear I've needed you all my life."

A growl rumbled against her pussy.

Her pussy tightened on the invading fingers as they slid free of her, then Malachi's head was lowering, his hands lifting her closer . . .

His tongue pushed inside the dripping, juice-saturated entrance of her pussy.

Like an erotic fire, his tongue so hot, so wickedly hungry, Malachi began to lick and stroke, fucking her with rapid, hard movements as Isabelle felt her body tightening, felt it bordering on mindlessness. A sudden, soul-deep implosion sent a cry racing past her lips as her orgasm convulsed her womb and had her screaming out in delirious ecstasy.

Isabelle couldn't stop the shudders or the hard, racking spasming of her muscles as the sensations seemed to go on and on.

Malachi rose between her thighs then in a hard surge. As he moved over her, Isabelle felt the head of his cock tuck between the folds of her pussy. There, just pressed against her entrance, his cock throbbed and she felt a hard, hot pulse of what had to be pre-cum spurting inside her.

But pre-cum didn't spurt.

Her eyes opened. Staring back at him, Isabelle felt it again, then felt a tingling rush of sensation that began invading the delicate tissue.

She had been horny for him before. She had been on the verge of mindless masturbation the night before, even after she learned that no matter how she tried, she couldn't find release.

But now . . . this . . .

This wasn't simply arousal.

As another heated spurt shot inside the swollen opening, Isabelle felt new sensations beginning to bloom in the flesh it touched.

She would have melted to the floor if she hadn't already been lying down.

Pleasure increased a hundredfold, and as his erection began to fill her, to stretch the tender tissue to an almost unbearable tightness, Isabelle knew with utter certainty what the fluid was.

The heated spurts weren't pre-cum, at least not entirely. Whatever it was, it allowed even the tightest flesh to accept this incredible stretch and penetration, and to find the most incredible pleasure possible in his possession of her.

Isabelle held her breath as she felt his muscles bunch and gather. He paused for a second, his gaze locking with hers.

"Just watch me," he whispered, his tone rougher than ever before. "Just watch me, baby."

He would have never attempted this at any other time. Malachi had never taken a virgin. He had never touched a woman who wasn't well experienced and aware of what she was getting.

But his mate. Sweet, pretty Isabelle had no idea.

Moving over her, one hand gripping her hip, Malachi felt another hard spurt of the hormone-rich preseminal fluid as it filled her, no doubt triggered by the snugness of her pussy.

Rocking back, he let her juices ease his way, let himself become accustomed to her before he took her virginity. Before he taught her exactly how different Breed males were from their human cousins.

She was a virgin, he reminded himself as he pulled back again, his whole body on fire from holding back, from the slow stretching of the virgin shield inside her to accommodate a painless possession.

God, it wasn't going to happen.

A growl, a groan of pure frustrated hunger passed his lips as he felt his hips push forward with too much force, with uncontrolled haste.

The width of his cock pushed past the thin membrane and surged only a few inches inside her.

Tight, tight muscles clamped down on his dick, flexed and rippled over the head as his teeth clenched and he felt like howling. Because he knew there wasn't a chance in hell he could hold back now.

Isabelle arched with a cry as she felt both the tearing of her virginity and a pleasure that tore through her, wrapped around her senses and tightened around her body with incredible bliss.

Her sensitive inner tissue was clamped on the intruder penetrating it, the engorged head throbbing furiously as she felt another hard, heated spurt of the fluid erupting inside her.

Her muscles tightened further as the nerve endings came alive with excitement. Forcing her eyes open, she stared up at him now, watching the savage planes of his face as his expression twisted with remorse.

"So good." She had to force the words out as sensation wracked her inner flesh once again. "Oh God, Malachi, it's so good."

His hands tightened on her hips, his lips came down on hers, and as he drew back, Isabelle knew he had finally given in to the need tearing through them both.

His hips began to move. His tongue pumped into her mouth as his cock began pumping between her thighs, shafting the delicate inner tissue of her cunt as it began flexing, clenching, fighting to hold him inside her.

Wrapping her legs around his hips, Isabelle tilted her hips higher, angling her body to his as she fought to separate pleasure and pain, and failed.

It was like being lost in a maelstrom of exotic, erotic sensation. Thunder and lightning crashed and clashed inside her body. Fingers of rapid-fire sensation, hot and extreme, raced through her, wrapped around her clit, shuddered through her womb.

Every stroke inside the depths of her body sent her flying higher as the taste of winter fire and summer storm intoxicated her further. Made her hungrier. Made the intensity of the sensations something to crave rather than to fear.

But no addictive kiss would have been needed, she knew. Nothing outside the touch, the taste of the man was needed. Because he was what she had watched the night for, and she knew it.

Tearing his mouth from hers, he growled again as he buried his lips against the curve of her neck. His hips were moving faster, the race to release suddenly consuming them both, tightening through them.

Isabelle cried out his name, begged for it, demanded it. Her vagina was clenching convulsively, her womb tightening as her clit burned and throbbed with each rasp of his pelvis against it.

Each stroke fueled the sensual fires already burning out of control. Her nails dug into his shoulders as she felt his teeth raking against the sensitive flesh between neck and shoulder. The skin tingled at the feel of the canines against them, at the sensation of his tongue spreading that heated hunger over it. He fucked her with male greed and a sensual intent to pleasure her. As he pumped furiously inside her, the width should have been agonizing with each thrust, and it was—an agony of pleasure. The sensations were torturous, the rising ecstasy rioting through her until she felt her body begin to explode from the inside out.

It was like being immersed in a cloud of pure rapture. As though ecstasy itself had enfolded her, covering every inch and every cell, consuming her.

She screamed. She heard herself scream.

His teeth bit into her neck with a sharp burst of painful pleasure. Then, with a final thrust, she felt his release as it began overtaking him as well.

The first hard spurt of semen as his cock throbbed and seemed to swell further. Then more. More.

Her eyes opened as strangled cries of another release escaped her throat. That swelling, in the most sensitive part of her pussy, stretching the convulsively tight muscles and throbbing against nerve endings that otherwise would have never known stimulation.

The stretching seemed never-ending until he was locked inside her, so tight she knew neither of them could escape.

The blast of his semen jerked his body.

His tongue lashed at the wound at her neck.

And Isabelle knew, deep, deep inside, she knew, life would never even have the chance to be the same again.

Chapter Six

Isabelle lay against Malachi's chest, her hand rubbing over the broad planes, feeling the presence of the pelt-like hairs that grew there.

Breeds seemed to have no body hair, and in a sense, it was true. What they had instead was a superfine hair, almost invisible to the naked eye.

It didn't even feel like hair, but more like a finer, softer fur than his animal cousins possessed.

It was warm to the touch, heated by his body and his tough, muscular flesh. His chest was powerful, incredibly broad, and beneath her palm she could feel his heart beating in a slow, steady rhythm that comforted her, even when nothing should have been able to comfort her.

His arm was wrapped around her back as he held her to his chest, keeping her warm despite the chill that wanted to overtake her.

"Did I hurt you?" he asked, his lips moving against the top of her head as his fingers stroked her shoulder.

"You didn't hurt me." And he hadn't.

The pleasure had been so incredible that she was still reeling from it, still trying to find her bearings as her mind fought to make sense of it.

Once the thick, heavy swelling in his cock had receded, allowing him to pull free of her, Malachi had risen from the bed, collected a warm damp cloth from the bathroom and a dry towel and proceeded to clean her gently.

She had blushed furiously. Hell, she was blushing now just thinking about how he had cleaned her thoroughly, even separating the folds of her sex and running the cloth gently through the narrow slit.

"I was created to kill," he suddenly said. "We all were. We were Breeds. Not animal, not human. When the rescuers liberated us, when Alpha Lyons declared our presence to the world, we learned that though God hadn't created us, He had still gifted us."

Isabelle sat up and stared down at him somberly, watching the heavy sadness in his dark blue eyes as he stared up at her.

Lifting his hand, he brushed the backs of his fingers against the side of her cheek before lowering them to her hip and curling them over it. As though he needed some small connection to her, no matter how slight.

"How did He gift you?" she asked quietly.

"He gave us our mates." It was an answer she didn't expect. "As far as we've learned in the past thirteen years, there's only one mate for us. Created just for us. Emotionally, biologically, physically. We have a mate waiting for us somewhere in the world, we have only to find her."

A frown pulled at her brows. "That seems awful iffy," she said. "What if you don't find your mate?"

He shrugged at that. "Then I would imagine we exist within that same vacuum we were created in. Alone. Knowing we can't have children no matter how strong the desire most of us have for them. Only mates, it seems, can conceive. Only mates can ease the soul, help heal the wounds and battle the nightmares most of us endured to just survive in the labs. Now, we watch, we search, and though many of us deny it, we long for that mate, Isabelle. For that one thing in the world that was meant to be ours, that proves that though we were not born, we were at least adopted by a force greater than man."

Isabelle dropped her gaze to her hands as they lay in her lap, studying her linked fingers as she felt her chest tighten.

His voice resonated with such dark memories.

"Coyotes were created to kill their cousins," he continued. "The Felines and the Wolves, we were to be their jailors. Our genetics were carefully chosen to allow us to lie, to cheat, to torture and to know no remorse or guilt."

She lifted her gaze once again. His expression was hewn from marble, savage with its planes and angles, the high cheekbones, the sharp angle of his jaw. He could have been a warrior from ages past rather than a creation of technology and of evil.

"Are you trying to tell me something, Malachi?" she asked.

His lips quirked with an edge of amusement. "I've searched for you for what seems like eternity, Isabelle. The night your gaze touched mine in that bar, I swore I felt you in my soul. Did you feel it? Did you feel something move inside you that you couldn't explain? Something that, at first, you wanted only to run from?"

She licked her lips nervously. "Yes." She wasn't going to lie to him. "I wouldn't be here now if I hadn't."

"And if you had suspected then, what happened in this bed earlier, would you have still run to me, rather than away from me?"

"You think I found it distasteful?" she asked him curiously. "Malachi, I was begging, scratching and pleading. Those are not signs of distaste."

"Nor are they signs of acceptance," he pointed out.

She could only shake her head as she looked around the room and tried to get a bearing on what she was feeling.

"I understand what you felt," she finally said as she brought her gaze back to him. "I felt as though I had known you forever the second I met you. As though I could introduce you to my family and my world, and rather than becoming lost in the craziness, you would conquer it instead."

Something that had never happened before. Most of her interested male friends had run screaming the moment they were introduced to her family and saw the craziness.

"But?" His lips quirked again, that little hint of mocking amusement and arrogance making him appear so very sexy.

"I didn't say but." She sighed. "I don't know, Malachi. I didn't imagine this happening." She waved her hand to the bed, indicating the "mating" that had occurred. "I don't know what you want from me, or what I'm supposed to want from you. Breeds aren't said to have long-term relationships, so I really wasn't thinking past morning."

He grunted at that. "You lie, even to yourself," he told her. "I saw it in your eyes, Isabelle. When morning came, you wouldn't have wanted me to leave any more than I could have gotten up and left you."

Was he right? Hell, of course he was right. It wasn't as though she knew what to do with him now either, but Isabelle knew she had wanted a chance with him.

"Whether or not I'm lying isn't the point anyway," she told him. "This mating thing is the point, Malachi, and I'm not certain it's something I'm ready for."

But she could still taste his kiss, and she still longed for more of that vibrant spice and the hot taste of it. There was nothing that could have prepared her for this. Nothing or no one could have told her that this would happen, and she would believe it.

"I've always been a creature of the darkness, Isabelle," he sighed then. "Not a part of either world that I was created from. I've waited for you, knowing that part of you was out there, and longing for you with every fiber of my being. But I know that you haven't."

But she had. She watched the night regularly. She had searched for him. She had known he was out there but she'd had no way of knowing who he was, or where he was. And now, she had no clue how to handle the situation she was in.

"How does it work?" she finally asked. "Are the tabloid stories true?"

"In some part." He nodded sharply. "They're stories we've leaked to the press ourselves. A propaganda war, if you want to call it that. To accustom the public to the knowledge before they learn it's the truth. We'll only be able to hide it for a short while longer now. This is the only way we have of lessening the threat mating heat could mean to the couples as well as those who haven't yet found their mates."

"Because of the fear. Because man doesn't want to accept what's different from him. Even when he believes he created it." She looked down at her fingers again, only to find his covering them as she did so.

"Isabelle, this battle is one you're only just coming into. Don't begin looking for trouble this quickly, love, because I promise you, it will show up soon enough on its own." He drew her to him, dragging her over his chest, though she did very little to resist him.

She should resist him. She'd just experienced something that should have been quite traumatic. After all, by time he had finished releasing his pleasure inside her, he'd bitten her, knotted her, snarled, growled and declared "mine," as though saying it made it so.

The problem was that when he'd declared "mine," she had felt an answering demand inside her own heart.

"What are you doing to me, Malachi?" she whispered as he turned, sprawling her beneath him as he came over her in a surge of strength and latent power.

"I've been crazy since meeting you," he rasped as he pulled the sheet away from her naked body. "Completely insane, Isabelle."

A graceful brow arched as her eyes suddenly lit with an inner amusement. "I would guess you were already crazy, Malachi, because I haven't seen a whole lot to suggest otherwise."

Malachi lifted his brow. "Baby, you haven't had time to draw that opinion. Once you get to know me, you'll realize I'm actually hardcore certifiable. It's a Breed thing."

"Being certifiable?" she questioned. "After meeting Ashley, I'm beginning to think that rather than a Breed thing, it's more a Coyote thing. I just hope it's not too contagious."

She was teasing him. Had anyone bothered to tease him before, she wondered as he stared back at her with that reserved, cool expression.

She wouldn't let it bother her, she promised herself. If he intended to stick around, then he may as well learn. She, Chelsea and Liza were always joking with one another, sometimes playing pranks and always having fun. She wasn't about to give it up.

"You make me want to laugh," he groaned suddenly. "And if I drop my guard enough for that, what will I do if you decide to try to fight the mating?"

"So it can be reversed?" Already she was craving his kiss with a strength that had her mouth watering and her body tingling. Like someone needing their next drug fix, she needed his kiss.

She needed him.

"There's no reversal." Cupping the back of her head, he pulled her down for his kiss, needing it, needing her.

His tongue wasn't swollen, the mating taste was only barely present to his senses, but still, the need to kiss her, to bind her now with pleasure, was an overriding impulse.

Catching her lips with his, he rubbed against the soft, pouty curves and tasted the warmth of them. It was a kiss of natural heat, the same passion and hunger that had flared between them when their eyes connected in the bar.

His tongue slipped past her lips, mated with hers, rubbed at it, felt the silken softness and the measure of the woman as she accepted him with soft innocence.

It wasn't mating heat. It was just a man and a woman, that was all. Surrounded by warmth, by the attraction and the flaring emotion that happened only once in a lifetime. When one man and one woman fated to be together, came together.

That moment had happened in the bar when their eyes met. When their lives had merged and destiny had given them that one and only chance.

One chance. One moment out of time and Malachi refused to lose it.

She was his mate.

Letting her go wasn't an option.

Holding her, ensuring her safety, her protection and, God, loving her. Those were his only options.

Easing back, he stared into the soft depths of her cobalt eyes and whispered, "For the first time in such a long, lonely life, I touched love." Trailing his hand from the back of her head where he'd held her to him, he let his palm cup the fragile line of her jaw as his thumb brushed over her kiss-swollen lips. "You're my mate, Isabelle. Frightening you is the last thing I want to do, but Breeds, like the animals we're created from, heed our instincts, unlike man. Every instinct that makes up the creature I am knows what you are to me. Courting you isn't an option. Wooing you isn't in the equation because nature won't allow the humanity inside us to chance losing that one moment, that single chance we have to claim what is ours. Or to allow our mates the opportunity to fear or to doubt and to turn away. That's all mating heat is, baby. That's all nature meant for it to be. Everything else is optional, but staying together, learning our way and learning what true love, what soul mates, were meant to be isn't a choice any longer. It's now a part of everything we are. It's like death and taxes. Inescapable."

She swallowed tightly. "Breeds don't pay taxes."

Trust her to have to point out the one flaw in the ages-old saying.

His lips quirked in amusement. Nature was indeed the perfect matchmaker, because this woman would be more than a challenge. She would keep him on his toes. There wouldn't be a chance to be the lazy, shiftless Coyote that all of his Breed pretended to be.

"Breeds don't pay taxes," he agreed. "We have mates to keep us in line instead."

Her head settled on his chest, her cheek against his heart as Malachi let his hand smooth from her shoulder to the middle of her back.

"It's not going to be that easy, Malachi," she whispered. "You know it's not."

He knew it wouldn't be. "What is the old saying?" he asked softly. "Nothing worth having is easy? If it were easy, baby, would it be as important?"

He found a curl of hair that trailed over her shoulder and caught it between his thumb and finger. Rubbing it, experiencing the softness of it, he stared up at the ceiling as he inhaled slowly.

"No, it won't be easy." The scent he caught assured him of that. There was very little time left. "We need to get dressed, baby."

She levered up and stared down at him. He could smell the trepidation, the edge of nervousness rising inside her. "Why?"

"We're about to have company." Moving from the bed, Malachi gathered her clothing, handed it to her then collected his own.

Rule was leading the pack, so to speak. He could smell his commander's anger, just as he could smell the anger of the men with him.

"What's going on, Malachi?" Nervousness was edging into fear as she pulled her dress over her head and allowed the silken length to fall to her feet.

Hell, they hadn't had enough time, not enough to combat what he sensed was coming, he feared.

"Commander Breaker, your father, uncle and grandfather are coming up the hall," he told her. "The commander is trying to delay them. Breaker never moves that slow, which means they're not heading to a meeting. They're coming here."

He glanced at the bed, and on the sheets he saw the proof of the innocence he had taken not long before.

"Great," Isabelle muttered. "Just what I need. How did any of them even know where I was?"

Exactly. Neither Breaker nor Stygian would have informed the three men of Isabelle's whereabouts, and her sister and friend wouldn't have known. At least not for certain.

A hard knock at the door signaled the arrival of the group.

"How did you know they were coming?" she hissed as a startled flinch had her jerking toward the door.

"I could smell them," he sighed. "The commander is pissed and your family more so."

Striding to the door, he gripped the knob and opened it slowly, placing himself in the small opening he made.

"Can I help you, Commander?" he asked Rule, though his gaze met that of her father, Terran Martinez.

"The Martinez family is here to collect the girl," Rule stated coldly. "Produce her, Malachi."

The order grated on the independence and pride that Malachi knew he had a surfeit of. He pulled his gaze slowly from the father and met his commander's. "They can see her, but no one is collecting her."

"The hell we're not." Terran Martinez was clearly furious. "I'll be taking my daughter home, Coyote, whether you like it or not."

Hell, this wasn't the footing he'd wanted to begin his life with Isabelle on.

He could feel her moving toward him.

"I feel I should inform you, Commander Breaker, Isabelle Martinez will not be leaving this room. To allow anyone to force her to leave will be breaking Breed law."

He had no idea how much these men may or may not know about

mating heat. There were times the people of the Nation knew more than anyone wanted them to know. He was informing his commander subtly that Isabelle was now his mate, and therefore under every Breed's protection. Including Rule's.

"Mr. Martinez," Rule said softly. "As I told you, this meeting will be held with civility, and the only way Ms. Martinez will go anywhere is if it's her wish."

Isabelle stepped to her mate's side. "Dad?" Confusion and hurt laced her voice as Malachi allowed her only a sliver of room to face the men confronting him from the hall. "What's going on?"

"Get out here, Isabelle." Stone-faced and furious, Terran Martinez spoke in a tone that had Malachi's hackles immediately rising and a growl rumbling in his throat.

Isabelle laid her hand on his arm, a move that was immediately noticed by all five men as they stood in the hall.

"Perhaps it would be best if we discussed this in the room," Rule suggested calmly, if mockingly. "You never know when or where a damned journalist is hiding."

And he was right, Malachi knew he was right, but he was loath to have the fury of the Martinez family invading the scent of his mate's pleasure that filled the room.

"Malachi," Commander Breaker growled in a reminder that the walls didn't just have ears, but could have eyes as well.

Turning his head slowly, he looked at Isabelle. He could smell her confusion, her fear and her hurt. The three scents were an affront to the protective instincts that raged inside him for her.

"Malachi, it's my family," she said softly. "I won't turn them away."

She didn't say she couldn't turn them away, she said she wouldn't. Restraining a sigh, he stepped back and steeled himself. Because he had a very bad feeling that this first test of the world against the union he had dreamed of could very well steal the dream from his desperate, greedy grasp.

Chapter Seven

Then your smile lit my world.

Isabelle couldn't understand why her family was standing in the middle of Malachi's room, their too perceptive gazes raking over the barely made bed she and Malachi had just left.

"Dad?" She stared back at her father in confusion. "What's going on here?"

Terran Martinez was younger than his brother, Ray, the chief of the Navajo Nation. Both men strongly resembled Orin Martinez, though, their father and medicine man of the Nation.

Her father crossed his arms over his broad chest, the dark denim shirt he wore straining over his biceps. "What are you doing here?" he asked, his tone dark with the anger she could read in his eyes.

"Terran, I warn you." Her grandfather spoke up. "Don't allow your anger to cloud your judgment. You can see before you the truth of this situation. Don't shame her when no shame is needed."

"No one will be shaming her," Malachi informed them all, while Isabelle felt like just stalking out and leaving all of them to fight among themselves. All but Malachi. She would have to take him with her, of course.

"Do you know the man you're consorting with?" Terran snapped at her then, shocking her with the lash of anger in his voice. "Did you even take a moment to pull up what little research exists on him?"

"Why would I?" Cocking her hip and propping her hands on each side, she confronted her father now. "Nothing else we read about the

Breeds on the Internet has been the truth. Why would I believe whatever I read on one individual?"

And it was the truth. The propaganda that had been placed on the Internet had been proven false over and over again.

Her father's lips flattened in disapproval, as if he was disappointed that she hadn't done it anyway.

"He murdered his own," Terran snapped furiously. "Ask him which lab he was created in, daughter. Ask him if he wasn't there when your Aunt Morningstar was murdered."

Isabelle swung around to Malachi. But it wasn't he who responded.

"Malachi wasn't in those labs." It was Commander Breaker who spoke instead, his tone heavy, almost too soft to make out.

Her father had obviously heard him, though. "And how can you be so certain?" he demanded, disbelief clear in his expression. "You of all people should know how easily those records could be manipulated."

Rule's expression only darkened. "I know he wasn't there, Terran. Malachi was created in Russia, far away from the labs your sister was in."

The tension that began filling the room was strangling. Isabelle could feel Malachi all but holding his breath, holding in whatever he knew, or whatever he would say.

"And how the hell do you think you can be so sure of that?" Terran sneered. "And why would I believe you over someone I've known for most of his life?"

Who?

Isabelle stared at her father in surprise. Who could have told him anything and known what they were talking about?

"I was reported to have been created in that base because there was no one left alive but Breeds to deny it," Malachi stated softly. "But I wasn't there. And even if I had been, nothing could have changed the outcome of her fate, Mr. Martinez. Nothing could and no one could have saved her that night."

The disappearance and death of his sister had haunted her father, she knew. So much so that he made certain he knew where his daughters were, at least their general vicinity, every second of the day.

"Even the dirty Coyote that reported the escape attempt another

Breed was initiating to get her out of there?" Terran snapped back at him. "That Breed was you, Malachi Morgan. You were there, and you reported the attempt."

"And I told you he wasn't there," Rule injected again.

"And you're lying for him."

Isabelle was shocked to hear her father raise his voice, to lose the calm that was always such a constant and steady part of him.

"Dad, please, don't do this." Isabelle stepped forward, shock and pain filling her at the fury in her father's face. "I don't know what Malachi did in those labs, but whatever he did, it was to survive. And I don't believe he would have ever deliberately brought danger to an innocent."

It didn't matter that his gaze had swung to her, narrow-eyed and strong, as he stepped to her. She may not know the particulars of the circumstances or the story behind his escape or anyone else's. What she did know was the man who held her in his arms and the fact that he couldn't have, wouldn't have, participated in her aunt's death. Not in any way.

"Isabelle, if you've ever trusted me, come with me now." Her father turned to her, the eyes she had grown up staring into whenever she'd needed answers, whenever she was frightened or confused, and that gaze was demanding she obey him. That she follow him. That she turn her back on the man she had already begun accepting into her heart.

"I trust you with my life, Dad," she whispered painfully. "But I need you to trust me. Trust me to know the man I've fallen in love with."

That was all she asked of him. Just for now, for this moment, trust her and allow her to make her own decisions. She couldn't bear being controlled, being forced, without a choice. Neither Malachi nor Commander Breaker was doing that.

Malachi stood close behind her, not touching her, trying not to influence her. The commander had his back to her, but her father was glaring at her.

"Terran, watch what you say," her uncle Ray advised him as it became obvious that her father's anger was only growing.

She stared from her uncle to her grandfather then back to her father. They were obviously there only to ensure her father didn't make a mistake he couldn't take back.

"What does he intend to say, Uncle Ray?" she asked softly as she felt her throat tighten with tears. "What do you intend to do, Dad, when I tell you that I won't walk away from Malachi without proof that he's done something vile? A mistake I can forgive. Anything he was forced to do in those labs I would have to forgive. It would break my heart that he were forced to be something he wasn't. That he carried the nightmares of it. But I wouldn't turn my back on him."

"Even if he killed your aunt?" her father yelled back at her, causing her to flinch. "You would forgive him for it?"

She was going to cry. Isabelle could feel the tears coming. She could feel her chest tightening, her lips trembling with the need to spill her tears, her pain.

"Even if he were forced to do that," she whispered. "I've never lied to you, Dad. I won't start now. I'm not saying it wouldn't break me in half. That I wouldn't live every day of my life knowing the unbearable weight of it, but what happened in those labs I won't hold against him."

"Then I dis—"

"No!" her grandfather yelled behind him as another voice broke over him.

Her father had been only a single word from disowning her.

"I was in that lab." Commander Breaker stepped forward and spoke as Isabelle's eyes began to widen in horror of what her father was about to say.

Her father swung around to the Breed. "What did you say?"

"I was there," Breaker growled. "I was created there. I was trained there. And I knew your sister. I swear to you, Mr. Martinez, on the soul I hold as my dearest possession. I swear to you, Malachi wasn't there. And I know he wasn't there, because I was."

Her father seemed to shrink before her eyes. His shoulders slumped, horrified remorse filling his gaze as he turned to Isabelle. He stepped back slowly, shaking his head in disbelief as his gaze swung back to the commander.

"I don't believe you," he whispered. "And you have nothing that will prove it."

To that, the commander growled with primal, deepening anger. "I have blood."

"And what the hell will that prove?" Her father threw his hands up in a gesture of fury. "How will your blood prove anything?"

"It will prove I'm the son of Morningstar Martinez," he snapped back at him. "And as you know, those bastards never, ever separated the male Breeds from their birth mothers. They used them. Tested us for compassion and sympathy with them," he snarled with animalistic rage now. "My blood will prove it, Mr. Martinez, and then as far as your daughter should be concerned, you should get fucked. Because a man that would turn his back on a daughter is no man. He's even less than the godforsaken bastards that created the Breeds."

"Enough."

Isabelle watched her grandfather through her tears, his lined, weary expression making him appear a decade older than his actual age.

"It is time to speak of this without this most precious child present. The sins and the nightmares of the past are for those of us who have faced the monsters in the world. Not those who we fight to protect from them."

Her breathing hitched as her grandfather stood staring back at her with all the gentleness and love he had always given her.

Malachi's arm went around her. As though he couldn't bear the physical separation between them any longer.

Her grandfather nodded as though in approval of the move.

"Take care of the gift I give you my consent to accept," her grandfather stated then. "What you have been blessed with, no man can tear from your grasp. Be foolish enough to turn from her love, though, and I will see you as no more than the sniveling child who knows only to blame others for his misfortunes."

"Thank you, sir," Malachi stated softly. "And I know well the gift I've been given."

Her grandfather turned away. As he did, her uncle nodded to her gently before following. It was her father who hesitated.

"I love you, no matter your choices or what you do," he finally said roughly. "But no matter the man or the Breed, ones with honor would never stand by calmly while one more innocent and undeserving died in agony." He glanced to Malachi as he spoke.

"And I don't believe that, Dad," she whispered. "Sometimes, to protect others you love, you have no choice but to put on a brave face and hide your horror or your pain to ensure the protection of others. I watched the documentaries. I watched the Senate hearings that are retelevised year after year, and I heard the stories of the horrors they faced. Every Breed who survived those labs, made it out alive and swore vengeance against their creators and tormentors are worthy of every second chance they can be given. If needed." She glanced up at Malachi, certainty flowing through her as his gaze met hers. Turning back to her father, she stated, "Malachi doesn't need forgiveness. He wasn't there. If he had been, he would have told me before anyone else had a chance." She was certain of it.

With tears glittering in his eyes, her father raked his fingers through the military short gray and black hair as he turned away.

"Who told you Malachi was there, Dad?"

He paused. Keeping his back to her, he shook his head and Isabelle swore she could feel the weariness that slumped his shoulders.

"I have the right to know. It's my life they were attempting to destroy along with the negotiations between the Nation and the Breeds."

"I gave my word, Isabelle." He sighed, his voice husky. "I won't break it."

And he wouldn't. No matter the cost.

"The next time it happens, if you have to give your word to retain the secrecy of their identity, then don't bring the suspicions to me where Malachi's concerned," she informed him, her heart heavy. "Because I won't hear them. Whoever is attempting to destroy these negotiations would destroy me, Malachi and my family without a thought. I don't want to hear anything else they have to say."

She had made a choice and Isabelle knew it. In that moment she'd chosen Malachi over suspicion, rumor or hints of wrongdoing whether they were real or imagined.

She had chosen him over everyone else in her life.

She may not know every act he had committed or every experience he had ever known, but she knew the soul of the man she had given her heart to. And she knew that soul was one that deserved her love.

That soul was the mate to hers.

Chapter Eight

Your lips touched mine.

He couldn't bear to feel her pain.

As the room emptied and the door snicked closed quietly behind Rule, Malachi turned his mate to his chest and held her there.

For the first time in his life he didn't just sense the pain, or scent it. He could feel it with every fiber of his being. It wrapped around his heart, his soul, and squeezed with a merciless grip.

"What's going on?" she whispered against his chest as she felt his hands smoothing down the silken material of her dress to her hips and back to just below her shoulders. There, his fingers tangled in the long waves of her hair, twisting them around to pull her head back.

"I don't know what's going on, baby," he told her, keeping his voice low, the pain emanating from her still too strong for his comfort.

It made the animal inside him rage, desperate to take the pain away and replace it with something more. Something more intimate. Something that would resonate with pleasure rather than pain.

Lowering his head, he let his lips settle over hers. Gently. The glands beneath his tongue were swelling in response to the emotions rising inside him, just as they had since the moment he had laid eyes on her.

Flicking his tongue against her lips, parting them, he let his lips fuse with hers before parting them farther and finding her tongue with his.

As though the taste of the mating heat was as much an addiction for her as the taste of her kiss was becoming for him, she immediately drew the taste of him into her. For lush, impossibly ecstatic seconds her lips captured his tongue and drew the heat from it.

Pulling back from her, his lips slanted over hers, rubbed against them, parted them with his, and they shared the taste. Mating heat fused them together, but Malachi knew where the heat came from: from the hearts of two souls that had searched the night.

Pulling the dress from her, he could only groan in anticipation and rising hunger as she released his pants.

There were no boots to take off this time—he'd met his visitors in bare feet, just as she had. It took only seconds to strip the pants from his legs and lift her to him, but the bed wasn't an option. As he palmed her breasts and took her kiss again, his thumbs flicked at her pebble hard nipples, rasping over them as he backed her the few feet to the couch and felt the primal instincts that rose inside him crashing through his control.

She was his mate. The need to take her, to mark her, to indelibly imprint himself on her was tearing through his senses like wildfire.

Though she had stood beside him and defended the accusations brought against him earlier, still, there had been an instinctive hesitation. The need of the daughter to give in to the father, to obey and accept the protection she had known all her life.

That hesitancy had terrified him. For the briefest second Malachi had felt pure, gut-wrenching fear, certain he would have to fight for her and chance destroying them both in the effort.

That streak of pride and independence had held her to him, for the moment. Now, God help him, the animal inside him was tearing loose now and asserting its determination to tie her irrevocably to him.

"Malachi," she whispered on a desperate sigh, her nails biting into his bare shoulders as he backed her to the couch before allowing his lips to trail to the sensitive column of her neck.

The ripple of response raced up her spine, sending the scent of summer heat to fill his senses. The smell of her passion, her sweet, soft, feminine lust, was the most intoxicating scent. He could live on it. He could survive the rest of his life with no other scent in his head.

The growl that rumbled in his chest surprised him. It was more animalistic than normal. It came from deeper inside him, from the depths of his diaphragm to vibrate in his throat, and sent a shiver chasing up Isabelle's back.

That response heralded the heated scent of her pussy and signaled the rush of her slick juices as her body prepared for him.

His cock, already engorged and throbbing in hunger, pulsed with a demand he'd never known before. He could feel the mating fluid building in the shaft as his balls tightened in a pleasure-pain that had that damned growl rumbling again. It was uncontrollable. It was primal and heralded a rush of hunger that stripped him to the depths of his being and to the animal that resided there.

Isabelle could feel the need rising like a storm inside her and racing through her bloodstream like a drug determined to overtake her. It wasn't just determined. It was definitely overtaking her. Washing through her body with a wave of heat as Malachi's lips blazed a path of fire down her neck.

Once he reached the small, sensitive wound he'd made earlier, his tongue brushing across it, Isabelle swore she nearly climaxed. A rush of sensation tore through the mark as a hungry kiss was applied to it before his lips began nipping and kissing their way to her breasts.

Her nipples were tight, hard with excitement. As she arched to him, Isabelle felt the brush of the fine hairs of his chest against them, the rasping pleasure dragging a whimpering moan from her chest.

She couldn't get enough of him. Not enough of his kiss, his touch, or the incredible pleasure that seemed to invade every cell of her body.

"I can't wait." The sound of his voice was part animal, part human. An equal mix of who and what he was and from where he had come.

"No one asked you to wait," she cried out as his hand moved between her thighs, his fingers finding the moisture that lay on her thighs and following it to the swollen folds of her cunt.

Parting the saturated flesh, he found the clenched, sensitive entrance, rimmed it then, and with a dominant, exciting thrust, filled the snug channel with two powerful fingers.

Isabelle went to her tiptoes, her cry muffled against his chest as her flesh clenched involuntarily, becoming tighter and rippling around his fingers.

"Malachi." She cried out his name as his lips found the tight, hardened peak of a nipple. Arching closer to him, she cried out again as he began to suckle the tip with strong, heated draws of his mouth.

Whatever the incredible taste that flowed from the glands beneath his tongue, the presence of it on his tongue now increased the sensitivity of her nipple. It hardened further, becoming so tight and peaked that the pleasure-pain of it had her nails curling against the flesh of Malachi's shoulders.

Her hips moved, writhed as she worked her pussy on his fingers, her clit rasping against the pad of his hand as he curved it against her.

Her juices were flowing over his fingers, saturating them as she whimpered with the rising desperation to climax.

She was close. She could feel it building, burning in the pit of her womb, the release she was reaching for so desperately tightening through her.

"Not like this." The words rasped from his lips as he straightened, his fingers immediately pulling free of the heated clasp of her pussy.

"No. Malachi, please . . ."

He nipped her shoulder. As a gasp of pleasure tore from her lips, he pulled back once again before gripping her shoulders, turning her around quickly and pushing her to the couch.

"On your knees," he growled as he pushed her down.

Catching her weight on her elbows against the high, thick pad of the armrest, she felt him coming behind her, over her.

Covering her like a warm, sensual blanket, a sexual creature intent on possession, Malachi braced his hand next to her elbow as he positioned the width of his cock at the entrance to her sex.

Immediately the heavy spurt of sexual fluid erupted against her entrance, heating her further. The flesh there became more sensitive, clenching tightly even as it stretched easier beneath the penetrating width of his cock.

Another spurt of slickening fluid invaded her, increasing the sensitivity, the pleasure that whipped through her senses. She could barely breathe. The stretching impalement of his flesh inside hers was like a whirlwind of sensations so intense, so brilliant she could only writhe in response. She pressed back, feeling her vagina milking the heavy width, drawing it deeper inside her as he worked his hips against her with strong, shallow thrusts.

"You're mine." With his lips at her ear, he made the declaration in that rasping animalistic tone that only increased her arousal.

"You're . . . oh my God, Malachi." Her back arched as he thrust inside her deeper, harder, sending spasms of sensation to throb through her pussy and echo to the swollen bud of her clit.

She was panting for air, tiny cries spilling from her lips until she wailed in pleasure as he pushed to the hilt inside her with a final thrust and a last spurt of the preseminal fluid that seemed to help the ability of her sex to take the incredibly wide cock that filled her to overflowing.

"You're mine!" she cried out, making her declaration match his. "Just the same, Malachi."

She was sobbing with the pleasure and couldn't seem to stop it. Pinned as she was, her hips arched to him, her cheek against the side of the armrest, she felt the violently sensitive nerve endings come alive inside her as he began to move.

He fucked her with hard, heavy strokes. Burying himself full-length inside her, Malachi had no hesitation, no doubts while impaling her with animal-like force, one hand gripping a hip, the other sliding over her as he braced his elbow against hers.

His fingers clasped hers. In a gesture as old as time and as intimate as a kiss.

"There, baby, fuck me back," he groaned as she worked her hips back on the width of his cock. "Milk me inside. Let me feel that sweet pussy take me, Isabelle."

The explicit words spoken at her ear had her body jumping with pleasure. She couldn't remain unaffected, nor could she stop moving, even if she tried. Nothing mattered but the tightening spirals of sensation beginning to tug at the nerve endings in her pussy and throbbing in her clit.

Behind her, Malachi was thrusting rhythmically, with each penetration pushing into her to the hilt as she cried out, writhed and thrust back on the heavy stalk of flesh.

She was dying beneath the onslaught of pleasure. There was no way she could survive it, she told herself, even as she rushed headlong into the burning release awaiting her.

When it hit, it enveloped her in white hot flames. Shards of bliss began ripping through her senses, and when he buried himself one last time and that first spurt of release began jetting inside her, she felt the incredible presence of the additional thickening in his cock as it stretched her farther.

Locked inside her, his release spurting to the very mouth of her womb as each heavy throb of his cock extended her release, Isabelle felt all the world disintegrate. All but the part of existence that she and Malachi inhabited. That was all that existed, all that sustained them.

And within that world, within the fiery haze of pleasure, pain and swirling intensity, nothing mattered as much as the beat of his heart against her back, his teeth locked at the flesh between shoulder and neck, and the man as bound to her as she knew she was now bound to him.

Nothing mattered but the bonds that she knew would hold them together and the hunger that would never abate.

And when all was said and done, the most important part was being his mate.

Chapter Nine

For the first time in such a long, lonely life, I touched love.

No Breed or human had ever claimed that Nature in all her glory didn't like to amuse herself with the children she was in charge of overseeing.

They were her amusement as well as her responsibility and she took both seriously, Malachi thought as he held his mate against his chest the next morning.

A warm, comforting weight, her head pillowed over his heart, one small hand resting at his side as the soft weight of her breasts pressed against him.

Sleeping with a woman had never been a comfortable experience. In the early days of the Breed liberations it was common for Breeds to be betrayed by their lovers. Council soldiers found it much easier to take the Breeds when they were distracted by a lover in the midst of intercourse. To a lesser extent it wasn't uncommon for it to happen now.

Sleeping with Isabelle was another story. He'd slept the deepest sleep he'd ever known in his life as he held her in his arms. Not that he'd slept unaware. The animal part of him never seemed to relax its guard.

He was aware of every move outside the door, but on a much more different level than before. The only time his sleep had been disturbed had been if a presence had paused too close to the door for the animal's comfort. And that had only happened a few times.

Now, awake, he watched the sun rise outside the narrow slit of the windows and hesitated to leave the warm weight of his mate.

But, he had a meeting. Getting out of it wasn't an option.

He wanted to know who had called Isabelle's father and who had attempted to force her family to convince her to leave his embrace. To use something as traumatic as the loss of her aunt and the tragic event of her death against Isabelle's father.

The only way to learn the answer to that question was the meeting Rule had arranged with her family. Terran, Ray and Orin Martinez had come to his room, intent on saving Isabelle from the monster who had supposedly allowed her aunt to suffer a horrendous death.

Did Morningstar's family even know how she had died? That, like many of the mates of the captive Breeds, she had been mercilessly dissected while still living? No anesthesia, nothing to dull the inhuman cruelty of the lethally sharp scalpel, she had been laid open and each of the internal changes mating forced on her carefully notated.

There were few who had survived that particular research practice. And never had a female mate survived it, human or otherwise.

Placing a gentle kiss to the top of Isabelle's head, Malachi pushed himself from the warmth of her body and left the bed, his lips quirking at the discontent in her drowsy little moan.

She didn't like losing his warmth any more than he liked being forced to attend this meeting rather than remaining with her. But, the means the unknown messenger had used to hurt his mate was unacceptable. He needed to know who to punish for the pain that had resulted in his Isabelle fighting back tears.

"Where are you sneaking off to?" Drowsy amusement filled her voice as he glanced back at her.

Rolling to her back, Isabelle watched him with cobalt blue eyes and a decidedly appreciative gleam in her eyes.

"I have a meeting," he told her, finding it excessively hard to turn away from her and continue to the shower. "It shouldn't take long though."

"Oh yeah? How long?" She stretched invitingly beneath the sheet as he turned to her from the bathroom doorway.

The sight of lush feminine curves barely shrouded by the expensive sheets and pouty, kiss-swollen lips were a temptation no mortal man should be forced to ignore.

His cock was steel-hard and throbbing, his balls tight and desperate for release.

He may just have to choke the answers he needed out of her father to ensure he returned to her quickly.

If only it were that easy.

Tightening his jaw against the sensual demand that he return to her, Malachi forced himself through the bathroom doorway instead.

But, he caught that smile that tugged at her lips. The adorable, sensual little curve that assured him she had very fond memories of the night they had just spent in each other's arms.

And, not all of it had been sexual.

She had told him of her aunt's disappearance, before her birth, and the guilt her father had always felt that he hadn't been with her.

He'd not gone to school that day because he had wanted to go tracking. He and several of his friends had slipped off to track a lone wolf that had been plaguing several of the ranches. His sister had known he wasn't at school, she had thought he didn't feel well. But, he had always felt that if he had been with her, perhaps she wouldn't have been taken.

Terran could have assured him that nothing could have kept her from being taken. Once the Council chose a breeder, they were known to go to impossibly insane lengths to acquire her.

The genetic research that had gone into each Breed had been exacting. The research that went into both the DNA required from the female, as well as the genetic information from the animal breed, was exhaustive.

The Council's requirements for each were high, but for the breeder, they preferred those women born with what they called the earth based gifts.

Native American, Romanian, Irish and Scots, and any bloodline suspected to carry psychic gifts. For some reason, those genetics, when combined with the predators chosen, had created the strongest, most powerful Breeds.

Rule Breaker and Lawe Justice were two such examples. Though no one was entirely certain what the brothers' greatest strengths were. One thing was for sure though—there was no doubt that the genetics that went into each Breed hadn't just made them better fighters, but better manipulators and leaders as well.

As a commander, Rule excelled where he had been restless and therefore rather testy as an enforcer.

His brother on the other hand was a strategist unlike any Malachi had come up against, other than Jonas Wyatt.

Dressed and ready to face the family she was unaware had returned to the hotel, Malachi stepped back to the bedroom and watched her as she lay dozing in the bed.

She had cried when she had told him of her mother's death on her seventh birthday. Holding her had been all he could do to ease the pain she had felt that long ago summer.

She had related some of her adventures. Her trips to England and to Rome, to Greece and to Japan. He knew about her first puppy, the kitty that had run away when Isabelle was ten, the changes in her brother, Linclon, after he had returned from the army wounded several years ago and the trials and tribulations of her younger sister, Chelsea.

He knew Liza was her dearest friend, and he knew when she mentioned the fact that they lived together, there had been a hint of carefully hidden pain and fear.

Though Isabelle didn't want to return to the house, not once had she asked him to protect her nor had she revealed the reason for that fear.

If Terran Martinez and his family didn't have the answers he needed today, then he would confront both Chelsea and Liza. They were already wary of him, though clearly not frightened. He had a feeling both girls would be willing to talk, especially once he explained the hazards to every living human involved in the cover-up should someone strike out at his mate.

Dressing in a gray silk suit, white fine cotton shirt and blue and gray striped tie, Malachi slipped his feet into expensive leather shoes and returned to the bedroom.

Isabelle was still dozing. Her eyes were closed, her senses relaxed. Sleep almost had her again.

Moving to the bed, he kissed the top of her head gently before straightening and leaving the room.

The sooner he completed the meeting, the sooner he could return to his mate and learn more of the details of her life, the little quirks that made her unique and enjoy the sense of humor that never failed to draw a smile from his lips.

Leaving the room he checked the door quickly before stepping across the hall to the room that had once been Isabelle's and was now Ashley and Emma Truing's.

On each side, Isabelle's sister Chelsea and her friend Liza were still registered. The two girls had come to the room the night before after Isabelle had called them. They had been as outraged over the lies that had been told to Isabelle's father as Isabelle was.

Turning up the hall he moved quickly to the small meeting room the hotel had set up for the Breed visit. Rule had sent a text earlier that the Martinez family was on their way for the meeting. However, the chief had warned him that Terran had no intentions of revealing the identity of the individual who had called.

Perhaps he didn't. Perhaps he wouldn't. But Malachi would make damned certain he knew the risks to his daughter and the consequences should Isabelle be hurt because of his refusal to speak.

Sliding the key card into the lock, Malachi stepped into the room, then came to a slow, wary stop. The Martinez men weren't the only ones who were awaiting him.

Rule stood to the side of the room watching silently as Isabelle's friend Liza dried her tears and Chelsea hung her head, staring at the floor somberly.

There was more going on here than whatever information Terran was hiding.

"Mr. Morgan." Terran rose to his feet, his expression more heavily lined than it had been the evening before, his dark eyes filled with sorrow. "I hope you will pardon my transgressions yesterday. I beg your forgiveness as I will be pleading with my daughter for hers after this meeting."

Malachi lifted a brow curiously as he glanced over at Rule. The other Breed shrugged with a discomforted shift of his shoulders. The formal politeness of the apology and the pain that flowed from Terran was thick enough to cause Malachi's hackles to rise.

"Chelsea?" He looked over at the younger girl. "Is everything okay, little sister?"

Her shoulders jerked, her breathing hitched as a sob nearly escaped. Placing her hand over her lips as she lifted the other in a gesture to stop, she turned her back on him.

Malachi could smell the tears.

The evening before, he'd noticed both girls had acted oddly after Isabelle had told them what her family had done. Her father's anger seemed to have especially upset both girls.

"Everything's obviously not okay," Liza spoke up at that point, her red-rimmed eyes full of not just pain, but anger as she turned back to Malachi. "Isabelle is like a sister to me, Malachi. She's the best friend I have in this world. And when she told us last night what happened, I had a feeling I knew exactly who had done it, and I was right."

His gaze flicked to Terran. The other man looked grief-stricken, and filled with rage. He turned back to Liza.

"Are you going to tell me who it was?" he asked, his eyes narrowing on her.

Her lips trembled for a brief second before she steadied them, lifted her chin and said, "The man who attacked her in her own home and nearly raped her. If Chelsea and I hadn't come home when we did, he would have raped her in her own living room."

Tears spilled from the girl's eyes again, but she continued bravely. "My dad had given me a gun. I pulled it from the closet and hit him in the back of the head with it. It gave her time to get away from him. When she jerked it from me, Chelsea and I kept her from filling his ass with buckshot. We should have let her do it. But all I could imagine was him suing the three of us and getting away with it."

It had been known to happen. Which was neither here nor there. It didn't matter in the end. Once he had the identity of the man, the three women wouldn't have to worry about being sued, they would only have to worry about what color to wear to his funeral. Black for grief, though he doubted they would choose such a respectable, somber color for the event. Perhaps red, he thought, for the blood the son of a bitch was going to shed.

"Liza, I want that name."

"You'll kill him," Chelsea cried out as she swung around to face him. "Then Isabelle will be pissed with us. And God forbid you be arrested for it, because she would kill us. You don't know what she's like when she's pissed, Malachi."

"Obviously, courageous and daring," he stated with no small amount of pride. "But, I prefer she not have to be courageous and daring again with this particular individual, and there's no doubt he won't attempt it again." He glanced to Terran. "It's the same man that called you?"

"She's my daughter," Terran rasped. "I'll take vengeance."

"God save me from all this familial guilt and self- punishment," he snapped, growing more furious by the moment. "I'll have his name and I'll have it now. If I don't, I promise the two of you I'll take Isabelle as far as possible from this place and you'll be lucky if she can convince me to visit once every five years." He turned to her father. "And if that's the case, then you can forget knowing any grandchildren she'll have because my faith in your ability to tell us anything that could endanger that child would be nil. Now one of you had better fucking open your mouths." His voice rose with the last words, his anger beginning to slip past the calm he always forced upon himself.

Chelsea and Liza stared back at him in shock.

"Holden Mayhew." Terran gave him the name he wanted. "He's the manager . . ."

"Of the Tri-Bar Ranch bordering yours." Malachi nodded as his fists clenched, his body tightening with rage.

The man had fists like anvils. Not that he was any match for a Breed, but for a woman as delicate and fragile as Isabelle, it would have been like being mauled by a grizzly.

"I'll take care of it . . ." A piercing phone alarm began emanating from both Rule and Malachi's phones.

Malachi's eyes widened as he jerked it from his belt activated the display.

"He has her, Mal." Emma's face was already swelling while blood oozed from her nose and split lips. "Ashley's down . . . Ash . . ." The phone fell.

Malachi was racing for the door the second the words made sense and running the short distance down the hall. He was aware of Rule behind him, shouting orders and pulling in the team being kept on a lower floor. The Martinez family was running behind, the father on the phone now, shouting orders as well as they all raced to Malachi's room.

Stygian was slamming from the door further up the hall as Malachi made the turn down the wing where his, Ashley and Emma's rooms were and skidded to a halt at the opened door of his room.

Ashley was down. Valiant, primpy, girly Ashley with her artificially colored locks, her fake nails and girlish innocence. The pride of the coyote packs, and everyone's little sister.

Emma was beside her, weak, but still valiantly trying to stem the blood pouring from her sister's chest wound as she sobbed with heartbroken fear.

"Ash . . . Ash please . . . Please don't leave me, Ash . . ." she was crying, her voice weak, dazed and in shock as Malachi and Rule slid to their knees beside her.

"She won't wake up, Mal," Emma whispered, turning her face to him as Rule quickly began assessing the wound and Stygian raced to them with a med-kit.

What the phone display hadn't shown was the other side of Emma's head. Her hair was coated with blood, dripping with it as she stared back at him with eyes nearly black with shock.

"We have her, Emma." Gripping the coyote female's shoulders he quickly ran his gaze over her as the room began to fill with Breeds. "Where is Isabelle, Emma? Did you see where he took her?" He was screaming at her. Panic and terror were clawing at his guts with razor-sharp talons.

Emma shook her head, obviously trying to fight off the dizzying weakness of her wounds. "He smells like motor oil," she whispered haltingly. "Isa cried for Ashley, but he hit her because she knocked the gun out of his hand. It's under the bed. He hit me first, took out Ashley then grabbed Isabelle. Isa took your shirt." She lifted her gaze to him again. "She's only wearing your shirt."

"Let's move." Malachi was on his feet, his gaze slicing to the tracker Rule had brought with them.

Braden Arness was one of the best they had, and the woman at his side, his mate, a Navajo empath that could find a fucking needle in a haystack.

Braden grabbed Malachi's shoulders, but he was expecting it. He stood still, the animal inside him snarling for action as the Breed inhaled the scent just beneath his ear and again at his lower neck.

It was there that the mating scent was strongest during the first stages of the mating heat. It was from there that Braden would have the scent of Malachi's mate, as well as the scent the shirt would carry.

Releasing him, Braden turned but his mate, Megan, was already hurrying for the door. "I told you something wasn't right," she reminded her mate furiously as they headed from the door. "I knew the pain I felt was tied to this. God, Braden, I should have looked further."

"We'll find her," Braden promised. "It's okay, honey, we'll find her."

And Malachi could only pray the tracker was right, because God help him if he lost his mate. Still, the howl that tore from his throat and echoed through the corridors of the hotel was haunting, filled with rage and grief. A coyote's mate was in danger. God help the bastard responsible because now death was his only option.

Chapter Ten

You held my heart in your hands.
I felt its warmth, its power, and its promise.

"Holden, don't do this, please." Fear crawled up Isabelle's back as she fought the sickening pain caused by the grip he had on her wrists as he dragged her down the stairs with him.

She couldn't believe this was happening. She couldn't believe he would have lost his mind to the point that he thought he could shoot one of the few coyote Breed females, and kidnap her and get away with it.

"You're hurting me, Holden," she cried as the dagger-like sensations stabbed at her wrists at every point that his flesh touched hers.

"Do you really think I give a fuck, you stupid little whore?" he screamed furiously as he dragged her down another flight of stairs. "You and those fucking bitches up there have just about ruined everything. All you had to do was be your usual stuck-up bitch self and stayed there alone after that Breed left. That was all you had to do."

He gave another hard jerk at her wrists as though in retaliation for the perceived slight.

The harsh tug as she made that first, stumbling step to a landing caused Isabelle to lose her balance and twist her ankle. She went down hard, fighting to catch herself to lessen the chances of serious injury.

Holden refused to release her wrists as she went down. The lack of support and her inability to hold herself up had her falling down the next step, her hip colliding against the edge painfully.

"Fuck! Keep it up bitch and I'll leave you to bleed out like I did that whore Breed."

Isabelle screamed out in pain as he yanked at her wrists at the same time his fingers buried in her hair and used the thick length to jerk her up.

"He'll kill you!" she screamed out at him, the pain and the humiliation enraging her. "Malachi will kill you, Holden. You know he will. You stupid bastard, you just possibly killed one of the most loved Breed females in the world. There's no way they'll let you live."

She kicked at him, sobbing at the pain as he threw her against the wall before tossing her behind him once again.

"Fuck you, bitch," he sneered. "He's not going to kill anyone. He'll be too busy chasing after you and the rest of them will follow suit. And I'll be far far away."

"You can't run far enough." She resisted, pulling her weight back and fighting his hold every inch of the way. "You can't find a hole deep enough to hide in," she spat in his face. "You're a dead man walking."

Ashley wasn't dead. She had seen the other girl moving, watched her eyes open as Holden dragged her from Malachi's room to the stairwell in the next wing.

Emma would have contacted Malachi immediately. She wouldn't have waited. God, she had to be conscious enough to have contacted Malachi.

Where was he?

She stared behind her, looked up, fighting to catch a glimpse of him, to catch a glimpse of anyone that could report the abduction.

"You're going to make me a hell of a lot of money, bitch." He laughed at her attempt to break free, the pain shooting through her wrists making her weak.

Dazed from the confusing effect of his touch on her wrists, and the earlier blow to her head that he had used to keep her from escaping the room as Emma and Ashley rushed in, Isabelle found it more difficult to focus by the second.

"You won't get to spend a penny of it." She stumbled on the next landing again, crying out brokenly as her knee connected with the unyielding metal beneath her.

"Son of a bitch, what's your fucking problem!"

The blow to the side of her head was humiliating. Not really hard enough to be disabling, just enough to rattle her senses and draw another hoarse cry from her lips.

Holden laughed, though the sound was filled with mockery and fury.

"If you had just been smart enough not to fight me that night," he snapped. "All you had to do was lie there and take it like a good little girl and everything would have been fine, Isabelle. I'd have married your stupid little ass, given you a kid or two and life would have been good. I'd have you, your daddy's ranch, and the respect I deserve. But you had to go fuck a Breed, didn't you?"

"I would have died before I would have done anything but killed you," she screamed furiously as the pain became excruciating. "I should have killed you while I had the chance."

"But you didn't, did you Isabelle? You let that puke-faced little sister of yours stop you. That was your second mistake." He was up in her face, nose to nose, his rough features twisted into a monstrous mask of anger. "The first was denying me."

A heavy, merciless hand gripped her jaw, pushing her head against the wall as he seemed to be trying to push it through the cement.

"Why are you doing this?" Isabelle cried out as he released her jaw.

The next second an openhanded slap knocked her to the side. The grip he still maintained on her wrists was the only thing that kept her from tumbling down the steps as she lost her balance.

She was weak, the pain rushing through her was worse than it should have been. Far worse. But he wouldn't let go of her. He kept touching her, and for some reason just his touch was like a thousand blades cutting into her flesh.

"Hurts doesn't it?" he rasped as he began dragging her down the steps again. "They were right about that. It hurts bad enough you can't even fight me."

They, who the hell was "they"?

Isabelle shook her head as she fought to make sense of what he was saying.

"What did you do to me?" She could barely breathe, the pain was building so much.

"I didn't do it, stupid," he bit out in disgust. "You did it to yourself when you let that dirty coyote knot you. If I'd known you like fucking dogs, slut, I would have brought mine over for a visit."

Isabelle shook her head, let herself fall against the wall and dragged back on his hold again as she tried trip them both.

He laughed at her efforts.

"Maybe if you're a good girl the men waiting for you outside will let me fuck you before they start experimenting on you. Like I didn't know who the hell they were," he snorted. "Only Council scientists pay that kind of money for a Breed's fuck, and they only pay that much for a special kind of fuck." He threw a tight, cold smile over his shoulder. "A mate. Are you his mate, sugar?"

Malachi would kill him.

Holden wouldn't make it out of the hotel . . .

The thought was heralded by a howl that seemed to echo through the stairwell, sharp and piercing, filled with rage and the promise of retribution.

Malachi was pissed now.

Isabelle collapsed on the step as Holden paused. "I told you," she breathed out weakly. "He's not going to let you leave this hotel with me. Let me go, it will give you a head start. It's the only chance you have."

"Move your ass." He jerked at her wrists again, his hold tightening as he tried to move faster down the stairs while Isabelle fought to slow him down.

It seemed to go on forever, but she knew with every step and every level, she knew they were getting closer to the ground floor.

"How did you know?" she whispered painfully as the weight came down too heavy on her ankle and she nearly fell again. "How did anyone know that I was his mate?"

He rounded on her, pushing her back into the wall, his hand wrapped around her throat as he glared down at her. "I would have worshipped you," he sneered in her face. "I would have given you anything you wanted, but you fucked that Breed instead. Fucked him and let him knot you like a fucking animal."

"How did you know?" she asked again, fighting to center her thoughts. There was no way she was going to get out of this if she didn't find a way to fight past the mind-numbing pain that rolled through her in debilitating waves.

"Stupid," he muttered, his voice lowering to disgust again. "Mating heat has a scent. They still have some Breeds who know their place and they're always searching for that scent. Malachi Morgan just so happened to have gotten careless with his mate. And now, she's gone bye bye," he laughed as he dragged her back to her feet.

"I don't think so."

Isabelle looked over Holden's shoulder as he froze.

The voice was unfamiliar, lazy, almost amused.

Holden jerked around, his hand going to his belt for the weapon Isabelle had managed to knock out of his hand as he shot Ashley. He hadn't been able to retrieve it.

"Fuck," he muttered.

Laughter echoed through the stairwell as Isabelle stared down at the strange sight in bemusement.

He had to be a Breed. A tiger Breed of some sort if the two stripes extending parallel across his face were any indication.

"Did you lose your gun, little man?" the stranger drawled as he reach behind his back and drew his own out. "That's okay, I have mine."

Holden's jaw clenched. His fingers wrapped in her hair and as he began to turn to throw Isabelle down the stairs, a shot rang out.

Blood splattered.

Isabelle stood carefully still, her hands now free and pressed flat against the wall as she let her gaze travel to where Holden was sprawled out on the steps at her feet.

His blue eyes were sightless, lifeless as he stared up in blank horror. The side of his head looked as though it had been peeled back, exposing raw meat and the bare white covering of his skull.

He had never been handsome, Isabelle thought, but he looked better dead than alive.

"You okay?"

Her head jerked around.

Somehow, she must have slid down the wall because the stranger was hunkered in front of her as the sound of voices, loud and enraged could be heard above as the pounding of feet moved down the stairs.

Her eyes dropped to the weapon that dangled casually from his fingers as he rested his wrist on his bent knee.

"Are you going to kill me?" She lifted her gaze again and met the emerald brilliance of his. There was an almost feverish glow to them, as though he were ill and in pain.

"No, I'm not going to kill you," he said gently, the look in his gaze filled with sadness.

The voices were getting closer. She swore she could hear her name being screamed from above.

"Malachi's coming," she told him, though she wasn't certain if it were a warning.

"Yes, he's coming." He nodded, his gaze somber. "When he's come down from the adrenaline rush, tell him I said our debt is clear now. He saved my life, I saved his mate."

"You tell him."

"Isabelle!" Malachi was screaming her name.

As the stranger jumped back, Malachi vaulted over the side of the upper steps as Emma, Rule and Stygian raced down the steps.

He came to a crouch, a vicious snarl tearing past his throat as he faced the other man, his body braced protectively in front of her.

"Easy there, old boy," the stranger murmured as Malachi growled low in his throat. "Let's not go feral, hmm?"

"What the hell are you doing here, Gideon?" Malachi snarled furiously.

Gideon. Dark blond hair striped with the prettiest golden brown streaks. It wasn't colored, it was natural. Emerald green eyes glittered with pain and sadness, but his stance was relaxed, his weapon held down.

Malachi's gaze dropped to Holden's body then, sprawled to the side, half his head blown away.

Gideon chuckled. "He thought he was going to sell her to a team of Council soldiers that guessed she was your mate." Gideon shrugged. "They caught the scent of her last night as they passed your room. You should start using candles when in public, it hides your scent."

"I'll keep that in mind," Malachi snapped as he tried to figure out whose team Gideon was on. When he had disappeared just after leaving the group Malachi had been a part of, rumor had been that he was pure Council. But, he hadn't been seen again and until now, Malachi hadn't known if he was alive or dead.

"You do that," Gideon nodded. "Until then, pass a message along for me, would you?"

"What message?" Gideon always had a reason for everything he did and an agenda that only he understood.

"Tell Lawe Justice this one was for you alone, not Breeds as a whole or because I'm getting soft or weak. I owe you, even more than this could repay." He nodded to Isabelle.

Malachi had never felt that Gideon owed him shit, but he was more than willing to accept the debt now.

"What does Lawe have to do with this?" Malachi snapped.

"Because, Gideon's the Breed we're searching for, Malachi," Rule answered for him. "We didn't want you dragged in the middle, so we didn't inform you of that fact."

Gideon's eyes narrowed. "You didn't know they were searching for me?"

"I didn't know," Malachi agreed. "But it doesn't change anything, Gideon. I took a vow to the Bureau. I won't break it."

"And I don't expect you to." Gideon nodded. "But after this, Malachi, take your woman from this place. Take her and leave, otherwise, both of you will get drawn in the middle of this battle. And it's a battle I intend to win."

"Gideon." Malachi tried to stop him from running.

Before Malachi could do more than say his name, the other Breed was gone. Just that fast he vaulted over the side of the stairs, made the jump to six landings below, a feat even Malachi wouldn't have wanted to try, and he was gone.

That didn't mean Rule wasn't trying like hell to catch him.

He and Stygian were down the stairs and running hard and fast, but if Malachi knew the other Breed, and he did, then he wouldn't be caught. Not this time. Not until Gideon was ready.

With the danger to his mate disappearing Malachi twisted around quickly and caught her against his chest. He may have been confronting Gideon, but every sense he possessed had been locked on his mate.

There had been no scent of internal bleeding. She was in pain, but not the kind of pain that indicated broken bones. She had been mauled, frightened and hurt, but she was safe.

"Never again," he whispered at her ear as he held her as close to his chest as he dared. "Never again, Isabelle."

"Damned right. Next time, I'll have my own gun." Then she pushed back enough to stare up at him, her lips trembling as tears welled in her eyes and flowed to her cheeks. "Ashley?" she whispered.

Malachi reach up and touched her cheek. "We don't know yet. The helijet was lifting off from outside town as we headed out of the room." He nodded to Emma as she sat on the step silently, her expression hard and distant. "We'll know something soon though."

"He came in on us." She shook her head in confusion. "I don't know how he got the room key. Ashley and Emma were talking about the spa. We are laughing at Em because she won't get her hair highlighted, then he was just there. He had the door unlocked and he shot Ashley as she jumped for him."

She bit her lip, the memory of it obviously so painful that her tears were falling faster now.

"Come on." Lifting her in his arms he cradled her against his chest as Emma stood more slowly, her shoulders slumped, her expression tight with grief.

"She always said she would die young," Emma whispered roughly, the tears she couldn't shed rasping in her throat. "The little bitch. Now, she's going to make the coya cry and Del-Rey is going to get all arrogant and protective, and I . . ." She broke off as a sob escaped. "I won't know how to survive without Ashley," she whispered before turning to run back up the stairs.

Malachi followed more slowly.

Emma was young, and many of the things she had scented or sensed she had no idea what they meant. Malachi did. Ashley was alive, and she was fighting to stay that way, that was all they could ask for.

His arms tightened around his mate as she settled her head on his chest and wrapped her arms tight around his neck.

"Who is Gideon?" she asked, refusing to let herself believe that anything could possibly happen to take Ashley out of their world. She was too vital, too much a part of the lives of those she loved, and those who loved her.

"A part of the past," he answered her softly, and Isabelle had a feeling the past was where Gideon probably should have stayed.

"Then why is he here now?"

To that, Malachi grimaced. "To open old wounds," he said with an edge of regret. "That's the only reason he's here, Isabelle. That's the only reason any of us came here. To open old wounds."

She laid her head back on his chest as Emma opened the stairwell door to the floor their rooms were on.

"We'll stay in your room," he told her as the other girl headed for the door of the room Isabelle had stayed in her first night.

Carrying her in, he didn't lay her on the bed, he didn't sit her in a chair alone. As Emma closed the door behind them rather than joining them, Malachi sank into one of the chairs, holding her close, his face buried against her neck.

"I would have died without you," he suddenly whispered, the muscles of his arms contracting as he fought not to hold her too close. As he fought to not pull her into his skin, to drag her straight down to the depths of his soul.

"Don't say that." Holding on to him, Isabelle knew it was true, just as she knew she would give her life for him, she knew without him, her life would lose hope.

It had only been days since her eyes had met his across that bar.

Less than forty-eight hours, yet just as her grandfather had once warned her, when she found her true love she would know it in an instant, and she would face death to hold on to it.

She was holding on tight.

"Don't leave me," she needed him. She needed his touch, his kiss, but more than anything, she needed the knowledge that nothing, no one could reach out to nearly separate them again.

Rising to his feet and stepping to the bed Malachi laid her down gently before stretching out beside her and taking her in his arms in again.

Simply to hold her.

"Our doctors were already flying in for our tests, so they're likely already with Ashley," he told her as she lay as close to him as clothes would allow. "The mating heat was different with us than with others, and our scientists have been working desperately to figure out what causes it and how to ease it."

Isabelle shook her head. "I don't want to know." And she didn't. Staring up at him, feeling the warmth of him, allowing herself to believe that she was really here with him, that she was really in his arms rather than facing the fate Holden would have sent her to. "I don't want to know, Malachi. I waited for you. All these years I watched and I waited, knowing, somehow, that what we would have would be different. That it would be worth the lonely nights and the fears that I had missed you somewhere." She gave a brief shake of her head. "I don't want to lose that."

What had drawn them together, the mating heat, as they called it. Was it really so different, so unique from what it was with those who didn't have Breed genetics? Or was it merely an amplified form that took out the process of waiting, denying, or turning away out of fear as many people did? As technology seemed to advance, so did the fears and the roadblocks that stood against love.

"I don't want to lose a second of what we are, Malachi," she told him as his head lowered, as his lips touched hers. "Not even a second."

Epilogue

So many times I only dreamed you were there.
Then the dream came true...

The coyote pack alpha, Del-Rey Delgado, and his coya Anya stood still and silent in the hospital waiting room. Joining them were more than thirty coyote Breeds as they ensured a heavy, protective barrier was kept between the couple and the toddler the alpha carried. A blond-haired, brown-eyed version of him in miniature form.

The coya had finally dried her tears, but her face was pale, her eyes red-rimmed. Every Breed in the waiting room pulsed with rage and helpless fury. There was no one to strike out at. No one to kill for their coya's pain and for the unpardonable sin of daring to silence Ashley Truing's laughter, her quick smile, or the hope she represented for every coyote Breed living who dared to oppose the Council. She was their best and their brightest, in many ways. She always walked where angels feared to tread, swearing that she wanted to live life rather than fight it.

Del-Rey looked around the room to take stock of the number that had joined them so far. They were still arriving, flying in from all over the world to be there just in case they were needed.

Surprisingly, his second-in-command, Brim, was there as well. Standing alone and silent in the corner of the room, his arms crossed over his chest, a scowl settled in deep on his expression. He felt responsible, Del-Rey guessed. Brim always took more upon himself than he should, especially where the girls were concerned.

"When Ashley was two, she developed a fever the doctors couldn't seem to bring down," Anya whispered as she stood beside him. Sitting on the couch next to her, Emma stared at the floor. "Do you remember that fever, Emma?"

Emma nodded.

"She came out of it, didn't she? When everyone said she wouldn't. She's a fighter. Ashley wants to live, she wants to shop and do her nails and her hair. She loves it."

Emma's head jerked up. "No, she enjoys it," her voice rasped. "She loves you, and the alpha, and me and Sharone and Marcy and Kate. But she's convinced she'll die young and the world won't miss one insignificant Coyote Breed." Emma's shoulders shook with silent sobs once more as Anya turned to Del-Rey, a free arm wrapping around her to drag her against him.

The air of grief that hung over the waiting room was a silent testament to the love they all had for the too tiny, too fragile young woman who acted as though she were made of titanium rather than flesh and bone.

Looking over Anya's head to his brother, his second-in-command once again, Del-Rey watched as Brim lifted his head to stare at the ceiling, blinking quickly before lowering it to stare at the floor once again.

Ashley was everyone's kid sister, and Brim took that responsibility seriously. He teased, chided and often shook his head over the girl's antics, but it was invariably Brim that convinced Del-Rey to give Ashley her spa days when she was being punished for endangering herself, or to ease up on her and let her have a new pair of shoes when she forgot to complete some chore in the Citadel, the lone tower of a mountain overlooking Haven that the coyote Breeds controlled.

And now, it was Brim bearing the brunt of the guilt for allowing her to travel to Window Rock when she pleaded so prettily to visit friends there.

It wasn't as though she would be the lone Breed there. Felines and Wolf Breeds had established minor bases there at the invitation of the Navajo Nation once their genetic ties were revealed. It wasn't as safe as The Citadel, Haven or Sanctuary, but it was safer than other locations she could have requested to go to.

Brim had approved the trip, and now Ashley lay fighting for her life because of her friendship and attempts to protect the niece of the Navajo chief.

Shifting the weight of his son on his shoulder, Del-Rey handed him over to his guardian, Sharone, as a newcomer entered.

"Del-Rey." Dane Vanderale, heir to the Vanderale Legacy and the first known naturally conceived Breed hybrid stepped to him.

"Dane." They didn't shake hands, rather as the two men reach out, they gripped each others' forearms in camaraderie.

"Is there anything we can do?" The Johannesburg accent was thicker than normal, a clear sign that Dane was furious.

Del-Rey shook his head heavily. "The man that did this is dead. I can think of nothing else that could be done unless you're a miracle worker and you can wave your hand over that wound and fix it."

Dane gripped his shoulder. "How about a far lesser gift. My men tracked down the two soldiers who were there to take Malachi's mate. They hadn't reported the mating yet, and they'll be endangering no other mate."

The savage gleam that flashed in his green eyes assured Del-Rey that those soldiers weren't wasting valuable oxygen any longer either.

"Did you identify them?" Del-Rey asked.

Dane grimaced at the question, his voice lowering. "They were coyote, Del. Council held. They had never been a part of Citadel."

That was a small comfort at best.

Wiping his hands over his face he turned to his mate.

Anya was there, her arms going around his waist as he pulled her to his side.

In that moment, Doctors Katya Sobolov and Nikki Armani stepped into the waiting area. More than thirty Breeds turned to them, automatically shifting and parting to allow their alpha and his coya to meet them.

"Doctors." Del-Rey nodded grimly.

"She's still alive," Katya stated, her expression drawn and exhausted after the hours spent in surgery.

"But?" Del-Rey injected. He swore he could feel it coming.

Katya looked away from a moment, obviously battling her emotions as the scent of grief touched his senses and clenched his chest.

"But, the next twenty-four hours will be the most difficult for her," she said somberly. "For all her bravado and strength, Ashley is too delicate for such a severe wound. She lost a lot of blood, Del-Rey." Her voice became an emotional rasp. "The bullet was difficult to extract, and it did a lot of damage going in." Her breathing hitched.

"Katya, your emotions," Nikki reminded her coolly before turning to the wolf Breed alpha that had flown in with them. "Wolfe, Katya needs something hot and sweet to drink. She's tired."

Wolfe, with his mate, Hope, moved to the young doctor, leading her from the waiting room gently as Nikki turned to the coyotes.

"I've seen many of you survive worse wounds," she stated, her voice resonating with strength and hope. "I've seen much, much weaker women survive worse. Right now, her survival depends upon her and her will to live. And I know Ashley, trust me, she does not want her sisters spending the slush fund her alpha set aside for their nails and clothes."

There was a general round of husky chuckles until Brim pushed through the crowd and left the waiting area. The mood turned grim once again.

"I don't want to risk transferring her to Haven or the Citadel until tomorrow morning. At that time, I'll need a medi-jet loaded with this equipment and waiting on the hospital's flight pad." She handed Del-Rey her list. "Contact Haven and your people at the Citadel. There are some supplies that only the Citadel has that we'll need for transport."

Ashley wasn't just going to shake this off, that was the message the doctor was giving them.

Del-Rey took the list before handing it to the coyote administrator next to him. "Take care of it."

The Breed nodded briskly before moving off.

"Katya's emotions break after surgery," Nikki sighed. "She's pure hell in that operating room. As cool and precise as any surgeon I've ever laid my eyes on. But she breaks while she's cleaning up. I've never seen her break like this though."

"She grew up with Ashley," Del-Rey sighed. "Sometimes, it's hard to believe they're so close in age."

Nikki nodded in agreement. "I believe she's going to make it, Del-Rey," she told him softly. "She's a fighter and she's stubborn as hell. That's all she needs."

It was the only hope she could offer them.

Del-Rey turned to the coyotes gathered behind him. "We take her home in the morning," he announced. "Until then, any Breed that lashes out, becomes involved in a physical or verbal altercation with any human or other Breed, or in any way detracts from Ashley's protection or our ability to protect her, will answer to me. Is that clear?"

Coyote Breeds could often be more hotheaded than the other species who were taught patience and logic over physical recklessness.

"It's clear, Del." One of the team alphas nodded firmly. "And if anyone needs reminding, then team alphas will take care of it."

Pride surged through Del-Rey. This was a vast improvement on months past when he'd been forced to have several enforcers cool their heels in a human jail cell for starting a bar fight. The coyotes were growing, adapting, they were maturing, and the proof of it was in the face of every coyote Breed there.

"You have a hell of a pack, Del-Rey," Dane's voice echoed with the respect Del-Rey and his men had fought to attain. "If you need anything, anything at all." Dane's look became more intent, somber. "The Vanderales are here for you. Welcome to the family."

This time, it was a handshake, and one Del-Rey hadn't been expecting. Not that he showed it. Inclining his head with calm acceptance, his handshake was firm, confident.

Vanderale's acceptance was the final hurdle to ensuring the survival of his people. Vanderale Enterprises "gifted" Haven and Sanctuary with all their military toys and were essential contacts to many of the military security contracts that were lining the wolf and feline Breed coffers. Del-Rey was eager to join the family, to gain for his people what the wolf and feline Breeds were kind enough to share with the coyotes. They wanted their own.

Breathing in deeply he turned and let his gaze flicker to the far hall and the wing he knew they were keeping Ashley in. Brim was with her, and that was the best protection she could have, but Del-Rey ached to see the young woman he had come to call "sister."

Turning to where Malachi and his mate sat on one of the far couches, Del-Rey made his way to them. Sadly, the scent of heat was, for the moment, cool. Isabelle's bruising and injuries had been such that it didn't endanger her life, but it had endangered Malachi's ability to enjoy his mate until she healed. But the coyote seemed content to take care of her. Like all male Breed mates, his devotion to her was clearly apparent.

Breeds didn't throw away what human men took for granted. Their mates were everything to them, and Malachi was no different.

They rose to their feet.

"I'm sorry, Del-Rey," Isabelle whispered, the proof of the tears she had been shedding showing in her red-rimmed eyes. "None of us expected Holden to do something like this."

Del-Rey shook his head. "No fault lies at your feet," he swore to her. He glanced at Isabelle and the exhaustion and bruises on her face. "Take your mate to the hotel, Malachi, so she can rest. There's nothing more that can be done here. We'll head home first thing in the morning."

"I'll take you up on that, Alpha Delgado," Malachi stated. "And once we've arrived at the Citadel, we need to talk. There's far more interesting information here than any of us imagined."

Del-Rey's brow lifted. More information? And from the sounds of it, something that didn't want to wait.

"Tomorrow evening," Del-Rey promised them. "Until then, get some sleep."

As they moved away Del-Rey sat down on a nearby couch and watched as his men began filtering from the waiting room, moving to find their hotels, a meal or a drink. He only prayed they managed to stay out of trouble.

He added that prayer to another. The prayer that Ashley was soon her bright and vivacious self again. Because if anything happened to her, Del-Rey feared that the war between Breeds and the remaining Council would only heat up further. Ashley was well loved by all the packs and prides, considered a little sister, a sometimes irritant, and represented all their dreams of a future. Because Ashley laughed. She played. She pulled pranks. But even more, Ashley reminded them all of what they wanted their children to be.

Full of fun and full of life.

Losing her could very well tip the balance and change the silent war with the Council to one that the world would clearly see in the color of blood.

And that was something none of them could afford.

TWO DAYS LATER

Malachi let his lips coast over the bruising of his mate's face as she lay before him, naked, aroused. The past two days had been free of the mating heat, the injuries sustained to her body evidently severe enough that it had ameliorated the effects of the heat.

The glands beneath his tongue hadn't swelled, the hormone absent until he'd awakened minutes earlier. Now, they were fully swollen, his cock engorged and throbbing, hunger pounding through his system and carrying with it the heightened hunger that affected Breeds and their mates during mating heat.

He wasn't the only one affected. His mate was moving against him, her thighs clasping one of his, the wet heat of her pussy rubbing against it. The swollen bud of her clit was a heated little rasp against his thigh as her sharp little nails bit into his shoulders.

His lips roamed along her jaw then to her lips, teasing them both with the need for the taste of the passion burning between them.

"You're killing me," she whispered, arching to him, her hard little nipples burning into his chest as he brushed his lips over hers.

"I've missed you, mate."

The hormone hadn't tormented them, but his need for her had still been there, keeping him semi-aroused and all too aware of her naked body against him each night.

He brushed his lips against hers again, groaning as she nipped at them, daring him to take her kiss as she needed. Slanting his head he took a hungry taste of her, still holding back, returning for another as she moaned beneath him, her nails rasping down his back.

The pinprick of sensation was his undoing. Added to the hunger raging brutally between them Malachi parted his lips against hers, parting hers, his tongue forging inside as she took it with a hungry little feminine growl of her own.

Isabelle whimpered at the pleasure, twisting against him, the rasp of her nipples against his chest adding to the burning hunger attacking the rest of her body.

Clamping her lips around his tongue as it thrust in and out of her mouth, she fought for every taste of the mating hormone spilling from his tongue. That unique, subtle, addictive quality of the mating heat pushing the hunger pounding through her that much higher.

She needed him.

"Now," she cried out as he pulled back to steal of the roughened, hungry kisses to her lips only before he turned his head to taste her jaw, to rasp his teeth against her neck. "Don't wait, Malachi. I need you."

He needed her just as desperately.

Isabelle spread her thighs as he moved, eagerly clasping his hips with her knees as he settled between them, the heavy width of his cock pressing between the swollen folds of her pussy.

The first, hard spurt of the pre-seminal fluid heated the entrance, the muscles flexing, milking against the overly wide crest as it began to push inside her.

The second spurt preceded the first, shallow thrust that buried the crest inside the burning depths of her sex. Pulling back, pushing inside once again, another spurt eased the natural, clenching tightness of her muscles further inside.

Each spurt of fluid was followed by a deeper thrust, a sensual pleasure-pain that had her crying out, arching closer as she ached for more, ached to feel his plunging inside her, taking her with the hungry desperation burning through both of them.

Coming over her, the fingers of one hand clenched on her hip as he gave a heavy groan and surged in to the hilt. That first deep, exciting full thrust unlocked the control he'd been carefully keeping.

His lips buried in the curve of her neck as he began moving, thrusting powerfully inside her, taking her to the base of his cock with every dip of his hips as Isabelle opened her thighs wider to take him even deeper. Her knees gripped his hips, her hips angling higher, cries escaping her throat as she felt pleasure rising fast and hard. There was no holding it back. There was no stopping this first, hungry need burning through them.

It felt as though it had been forever since she'd taken him. A lifetime since he had been able to hold her as she needed. Her orgasm rose, pushing higher through her senses, flooding them both with the sensations racing through them.

His thrusts became harder, faster. Each stroke rasping and caressing nerve endings so violently sensitive there was no way she could have held back longer.

Their release rushed over them. Like a firestorm out of control and exploding to consume everything in its wake. Ecstasy was a blaze that filled her mind, her senses, exploding through every cell of her body as she felt the first hard spurt of his release and the heavy swelling that stretched her, burned her and sent the catastrophic surge of pure rapture tearing through her.

With his teeth locked at the base of her neck Malachi shuddered with each spurt of his own release. The pulse of semen was another caress, another explosion burning through her.

As it eased, they were left exhausted, their breathing harsh in the dim silence of the room as Isabelle heard her own, tiny whimpers escaping her throat at each renewed pulse of incredible sensation caused by the swelling that throbbed against once hidden nerve endings.

Could she live without this, without him?

She'd waited too long, watched the nights for too many years, and dreamed too deeply of having that something, that emotion so unknown that her restlessness had tormented her.

She didn't want to live without him now.

Drowsy, ready to slip back into sleep, Isabelle moaned in loss as she felt the swelling recede and heard Malachi's pleasured groan as he slipped from her and collapsed to the bed beside her.

He pulled her against him, the warmth of his body shielding her, wrapping around her as she sighed at the perfect ending to the hunger that had flared so bright and hot. His hand smoothed along her shoulder, pushing back the damp ends of her hair as he kissed her temple gently.

"Del-Rey called while you were sleeping," he said, his voice still darker, deeper from the release they had just shared.

"Ashley?" Fear suddenly intruded, her gaze lifting to his at the thought of the fight her friend had gone through to simply live.

They had already nearly lost her twice. The wolf and coyote Breed doctors had fought desperately to keep her with them. They had brought her back each time, then sat sobbing with the alpha females of the packs and prides as they crashed from the fear and desperation each battle had wrought.

"She woke a few hours ago," he told her. "She was asking for you." He held her still as she started to rise. "Dr. Sobolov asked that we wait till afternoon to come in and see her. She's still weak and tires easily. Her transfer back to the Citadel has been delayed again. Del-Rey doesn't want to risk a setback or any complications. He's waiting until she's well enough to travel without the machines helping her to live."

"She's going to be okay?" she whispered, desperate, the guilt of her friend's injuries flaying her with a harsh lash.

"She's going to be okay." The edge of relief in his voice reassured her now. "Her recovery won't happen overnight, and as we learned with the feline alpha's injuries when he took a bullet to the chest over a year ago, it can come with complications as they heal, but she is healing."

Tears filled her eyes and slipped down her face despite her battle to hold them back. Malachi wiped them away with the edge of his thumb before laying a kiss at the corner of her lips.

"It wasn't your fault, Isabelle," he whispered, not for the first time. "None of it was your fault."

"I should have told someone," she cried as a sob tore from her. "I should have killed him myself. Something. Anything to have kept this from happening."

Malachi shook his head. "Some things you can't stop, baby. Ashley was running fast and hard toward an unlikely end. This way, it was contained and we were close enough to ensure she got the quickest medical care possible. She's been so damned reckless over the past few months that her alpha has all but chained her to base whenever possible."

Isabelle's lips trembled. "She just wants to live, Malachi. She wants to experience so much, and she feels there's so little time."

"And she nearly cut that time incredibly short," he sighed. "Maybe she'll slow down now. Just a bit."

Tucking her head against his shoulder he thanked God again that his mate was safe in his arms. Holden Mayhew had nearly taken her. He had nearly lost her to the depraved research the Council still hungered for.

"What now?" Isabelle asked. "Where do we go from here?"

She didn't want to leave her family, or the Nation, he knew that. And he had no desire to take her from it.

"We already have a presence here, as well as a sub-base." He shrugged. "I know Jonas has been looking for someone to head it. I've put in a request for the job."

She sat up. Sudden, heated happiness filled his senses at the hope that brightened her eyes.

"We don't have to leave?"

"Only when necessary," he promised. "Only if the danger rises. But I have a feeling your family will ensure I have the help I need to protect you."

He knew they would. She was a treasure to them, just as her sister was, and Malachi had found his own acceptance with them. Family, her father had told him. He was now a part of them.

"I love you, Malachi," she whispered, bending to him, her hair falling around his face as she brushed her lips over his. "With all my being, I love you."

"And I love you, Isabelle," he swore. "You're my breath of life. Always."

"Always," she breathed against his lips. "I love the sound of always, Malachi."

Always.

The whispered promise of their hunger, their love and the dreams that had filled their lives.

It was always.